Praise for *Autumn Laing*

'Miller's prose is so si~~~ly wro~~~~ it almost disguises ~~ ~ophistica-
tion... Like D~~~~~ h~ ~s not Miller's o~ ~~ ~ entered his
breast and ~ ~~~~~ Th ~sult transforms ~ ~oman's ~ring
words ~ ~~ ~ ~g art.
      —*The Australian*

'A magisterial work, multi-award winning Miller's longest and most
compelling, and a triumphant culmination of a series of novels about
art and the artist's relationship to it... Miller has taken real life simply
as a backdrop for ideas, the more potent because of its known realities,
and animated it with his own vibrant and intensely realised characters.'
      —*Adelaide Advertiser*

'Miller has triumphantly made art from [Autumn's] life. Like *Lovesong*,
Journey to the Stone Country and *Landscape of Farewell*, three of Miller's
finest works, *Autumn Laing* explores a geography of emotion – an
intimate, treacherous, burning zone where redemption is gained
through slow and painful self-interrogation.'
      —*The Monthly*

'This interest in the roiling mess of our inner lives is a trademark of
Miller's fiction and part of its moral seriousness. Over and over his
characters are seized by urges, by disgust and love in ways that are
mysterious and astonishing to them... A greedy, brilliant and impulsive
young woman and a stroppy, witheringly honest old bird, Autumn
is, herself, an unmistakably Australian work of art.'
      —*Sunday Age*

'That Alex Miller in a seemingly effortless fashion is able to gouge out
the innermost recesses of the artistic soul in his latest novel, *Autumn
Laing*, speaks volumes about the command he has of his craft and the
insights that a lifetime of wrestling with his own creative impulses
has brought. Miller has invested this story of art and passion with his
own touch of genius and it is, without question, a triumph of a novel.'
      —*Canberra Times*

Praise for *Lovesong*

'Miller's latest, and with luck, not final work not only beguiles as a wry, tender tale but will also remind his admirers, and alert his new readers to, how dauntingly gifted he is at taking an image and shaping a story.'
— *The Irish Times*

'Miller reveals most clearly the delicacy of his understanding of human nature… a tactful and intelligent writer.'
— *The Guardian*

'Miller's strength as a novelist [is] his ability to tell a simple story which shines a light into dark corners… A strong and subtle novel.'
— *The Times Literary Supplement*

'An engrossing, thought-provoking tale.'
— *The Sunday Herald*, GLASGOW

'An unusually warm, human emotionally true novel that slips its way into your mind and fosters a deep empathy and care for its characters.'
— *The Eastern Daily Press*

'It takes a very good writer indeed to get away with a title such as *Lovesong*, and Alex Miller does it triumphantly. His story is at once exotic and homely, telling of the sweetness of love and the sometimes awful cost of it to those caught up in its toils.'
—JOHN BANVILLE

'Full of wisdom and compassion.'
—ANNE MICHAELS, ORANGE PRIZE-WINNING AUTHOR OF *Fugitive Pieces*

Praise for Alex Miller

'The reader can't help but offer up a prayerful thank you: Thank you, God, that human beings still have the audacity to write like this.'
—*The Washington Post*

'Miller belongs... with Günter Grass, Ismail Kadare and JM Coetzee... He is essential reading.'
—*The Australian*

'Alex Miller is one of our most profound and interesting writers.'
—*Australian Book Review*

'As one expects from the best fiction, the novel transforms the reader's own inner life. Twice winner of the Miles Franklin Award, it is only a matter of time before Miller wins a Nobel. No Australian has written at this pitch since Patrick White. Indeed, some critics are comparing him with Joseph Conrad.'
—*Daily News*, NEW ZEALAND

'Miller is a master storyteller.'
—*The Monthly*

'Miller's fiction has a mystifying power that is always far more than the sum of its parts... his footsteps – softly, deftly, steadily – take you places you may not have been, and their sound resonates for a long time.'
—*The Sydney Morning Herald*

Autumn Laing

ALEX MILLER

ALLEN&UNWIN

First published in Australia in 2011 by Allen & Unwin

First published in Great Britain in 2012 by Allen & Unwin

Allen & Unwin
c/o Atlantic Books
Ormond House
26–27 Boswell Street
London WC1N 3JZ
Phone: 020 7269 1610
Fax: 020 7430 0916
Email: UK@allenandunwin.com
Web: www.atlantic-books.co.uk

A CIP catalogue record for this book is available from the British Library.

ISBN 978 1 74237 883 1

Printed in Italy by Grafica Veneta SpA

10 9 8 7 6 5 4 3 2 1

*The most enchanting things in nature
and art are based on deception.*

VLADIMIR NABOKOV, *The Gift*

For Stephanie

and for our son Ross and our daughter Kate

and for Erin

PART

one

1

New Year's Day 1991

THEY ARE ALL DEAD, AND I AM OLD AND SKELETON-GAUNT. THIS is where it began fifty-three years ago. Here, where I'm standing in the shadows of the old coach house, the boards sprung and gaping, this stifling January afternoon. I was thirty-two. I've retreated from the sun and smoke. The smell of smouldering paper has followed me. Blue smoke in the sunblades cutting the interior dark into shapes—in imitation of the work of a certain painter we once admired. There are things concealed and covered up here. The abode of the dead I should call it. In the shade, where I belong. Don't laugh. It's an old anxiety with me, this impulse to probe the rubbish with the toe of my sandal, disturbing the litter in the hope (or dread) of turning something up. I'm no longer a woman. Oh, you'll understand all that soon enough. The buckle on my left sandal broke last night when I was dragging my mattress onto the veranda to catch the breeze. Instead of the breeze I caught my foot against the back step. I've no strength left in my legs. My *legs*! Back in my smooth skin days I seduced him with glimpses of the purity of my pearly thighs, watching him ache for my touch, my insides churning. There was no stopping us then.

I saw her on the street yesterday. And last night I was sleepless thinking about her. The air burning in my lungs at two this morning. I thought of going down to the river bank and lying on the grass under the silver wattles for a bit of relief. But I can't manage it any more. I haven't been to the river for it must be fifteen years. If I could reach the river bank I would lie there naked as I lay with him. My body white and still and cold in the moonlight now. On my back (ready for it, Pat would have said), my life and their lives seething in my brain. His and hers. I'm little more than a skeleton these days. No, it *is* funny. I won't have it any other way. You can laugh all you like. I've never begrudged anyone a laugh. God knows, we get few enough of them.

Until I saw Edith yesterday I was ready to become that white corpse on the river bank. It's true, I wanted it. I have the means for my end tucked away in the back of the drawer of my bedside table. But instead of dying last night I repaired my broken sandal with the length of purple silk ribbon which was around the box of cheap chocolates given me by that cheap woman who called here yesterday. If it was yesterday. And was it after I'd seen Edith or before I saw her? It doesn't matter. She—the woman with the chocolates, I mean, not Edith—parked her car by the front door then walked around the side, coming through the rhododendrons to the back door as if she was one of our old group. She surprised me with my nightdress up around my middle at three in the afternoon, doing my corns. I should get a big dog. Or a gun. She stood with one foot on the raised course of bricks at the edge of the fish pond (no fish) and smiled up at me, her cheap offering held towards me. Wearing immaculate white linen she was. Her fat features glistening with the heat. Her fat body made for rolling down the hill into the river. That's what I thought as I looked at her.

'Who are *you*?' I asked. I wish I could have menaced her but there was nothing to hand. I couldn't stand up at once but I did pull my nightdress down over my ghastly shanks. Why are they always bruised? The bitch had given me no chance to conceal myself, to gather my dignity and hauteur. The truth of my decay was in her face. The ugliness of me. Her black eyes eating it all up. Writing my end. That was her cunning, to catch my lowest truth in the first moment without having to struggle for it. To arrive at Autumn Laing without preliminaries. She has the ruthlessness of a scavenger, and the luck. I know them, the scavengers. They feed off our flesh before we're dead. What is privacy to them?

'I'm the one who's writing your biography,' she said. Cheerful as a bee. Breathless with self-esteem. Fat as a turd, Pat would have said.

'You're after something more than my story,' I told her. I can be fierce. 'I've nothing to say to you. Get out of here.'

She came up the step and helped me to my feet, offering her cheap offering. I'm a foot taller than she is but I couldn't shake her off. She clung. 'You're after one of his drawings if you can lay your eyes on a loose piece about the place.' She had the confidence to laugh at this insult. She was as steady as a bollard. The peculiar smell of her. The chocolate box pressing into my ribs.

The mess of paper and rubbish here. There must be dozens of his drawings. Hundreds of them. I used to think I'd organise it all one day. Employ a young helper. Restore this house to something like a state of good order. When I was young I prided myself on being a good housekeeper. I imagined our papers boxed and numbered, ready to be carted off to the archives of the National Library. Then they could cart off my cadaver to the cemetery. I saw the end, my own, as neat and orderly. I always said I'd go when I was ready. But I'm less certain of that now. I have my pills but a gust of panic could knock me flat at any time and render me incapable. That's the fear.

The scavenger bitch biographer stopped me in the hall, her hand to my arm. To draw my attention to the exquisite blue of the Sèvres tureen on the hallstand, she said, where the sunlight was catching it just at that moment. As if I wouldn't have noticed. It was a ploy to convince me she has an *eye*, to let me know she is cultivated. But she is without respect. Without insight. I'll bet she didn't notice the crack in the tureen. It was Pat himself reeled against the stand, drunk or in despair. I should have given it to her. Here! Take it! A going away and *staying* away present.

They are all gone. Every one of them. Except Edith, his first. The laughter (I almost wrote slaughter) and passion are spent. Seeing Edith in the street shocked me. To know she still lives left me helpless. I had to sit on the bench outside the chemist's shop. The chemist's girl came out and asked me if I was all right. 'I can give you a lift home, if you like, Mrs Laing.' I told her I was all right. They only want to help. It's not their fault they're stupid.

Lying sleepless in the sleep-out last night (if it really was only last night and not weeks or months ago. Or was I on the veranda?) waiting for the dawn, Edith's presence was before me like an imperishable icon. I'm not sure why I write that. Except that it's the truth. The way it *felt*. The persistence of her vision almost religious. An apparition fattened by my unshriven guilt. *Let me shrive me clean, and die,* Tennyson said. None of us willingly dies unclean. Religious or not, to seek confession and absolution is an essential moral imperative of the human conscience, isn't it? To absolve means to set free, and that is what we yearn for, freedom. Young or old, it's what we dream of and fight for. We never really know what we mean by it.

By the time the freeway (now there's un-freedom for you) was waking up I knew I wasn't going to enjoy an untroubled death after all. Problem-free, with a silly grin on my stiffened features when the bitch scavenger found me. Seeing Edith after all these years snatched the prospect of my own orderly death out of my hands. If Edith Black was not done with life then I was not done with it. The question that refused to let me sleep was whether I might yet recompense her with the truth. To embark on the confession that he and I resisted for so long. That *he* resisted. Most of all, the confession he resisted. It was his truth, after all, that he denied to us. And in denying it to us denied it to himself. I was humiliated and left with nothing. But the largest burden of our cruelty surely fell on Edith, abandoned and alone with her child. The form of Pat's cruelty was always in his denial of things that made him uncomfortable. Even in that great expansive art of his, encompassing our entire continent, a truth was denied, was kept to one side of the picture, in the silence. And it *was* great.

His art, I mean. There was none greater before him and there have been none greater since. Not in this country. My poor sad country. This vast pile of rubble, as someone has called it, that we think so very highly of (it is all we have to think highly of). My soul was in his vision before he ever knew his vision's force. I gave it to him. I opened him to it. His country and my own. I and he together made this country visible. To make my claim on his art and compose the testament of our truth. A testament without which his pictures must remain forever incomplete. Forever mute. Deaf and dumb to the posterity they inhabit. The posterity of Edith and her child. Without my witness, Pat's claim that his art represented an inner history of his country and his life is just another deceit in the veil of deceits with which he artfully concealed his truth. A sleight of hand he became so adept at he fooled himself with it in the end. Who can say under which cup Pat Donlon placed his truth?

Pat was never deep. He was intuitive, but he was not deep. It was I who was deep. I who was left on my own to struggle with the fearful knots and tangles of our vicious web, while he sailed on in clean air, free of self-doubt, painting his pictures as if they were his alone to paint. So instead of eating my three little yellow pills I shall write this. Then I shall eat them.

Did I say I was on my own these days? I still have Sheridan, of course (my sweet Sherry). He will be eighteen this year and in the life of cats is even older than I am in the life of humans. Barnaby was the last of our company of human friends. Poor silly old Barnaby in the end. His blackthorn shillelagh is leaning in the corner by the door where he left it. Now there is no one for me to bully. He gave in at the beginning of summer to his persisting irritation with life. How I resent that! It was so selfish of him. How could he? Didn't he think of me carrying my pot of tea out to the back veranda and having no one to gossip with but Sheridan? When there are no other humans, a cat, even loved as I love my darling Sherry, is not sufficient company. Barnaby taking his own life, as if (and I enjoy the repetition) it were his alone to take. The handful of it that remained to both of us. Going off in that sad little way with his head in a plastic bag, like something from the supermarket. An old man should have acquired more dignity. But what am I saying, Barnaby was never old. Nor dignified. His motto surely was, *You have the dignity, I'll have the fun.* Until his parents died and the station was sold he left us each year for a month or two to revisit his birthplace and his friend in the Central Highlands of Queensland. His home was a cattle station with the lovely name of Sofia, deep in the mountains they call the home of the rivers. 'I go to refresh my source,' he said. 'Don't worry, I'll write.' And he did. He was always urging us to visit him there. When I at last went there with him and Pat, the visit changed all our lives. But you will hear more of that later.

If you knew Barnaby Green, the beloved poet laureate of our circle, you knew even in his decay a youthful man. There was nothing Barnaby could do to temper that out-of-time youthfulness of his. Whenever he ventured a patrician gesture he became laughable, poor man. Those who did not know him and love him as I knew him and loved him thought him a snob. I would not have predicted his suicide. He surprised me. Dismayed me. Angered me. His suicide made me feel as if I had never really known him. I felt cheated. Betrayed. Yes, I felt that in killing himself Barnaby betrayed me. Had he kept himself from me after all? His inner self? Barnaby's suicide, almost as much as seeing Edith in the street the other day (or whenever it was) shook my certainties about myself. That is what has happened. These things are not easy to understand. And you no longer expect it at my age. To have your certainties contradicted by experience, I mean.

I might have been prepared for some gesture of that heroic kind from the others. Their deaths were not surprising but confirmed the lives they had lived. Barnaby's left me wondering. About myself. And then Edith appears. As if a last dream has waited its awful moment to come upon me and make its terrible demand.

Since seeing Edith my memory has become the cathedral of my torment. Well then, I shall consecrate its old stones to my truth. Am I being grandiose? Melodramatic? I am old-fashioned and am not going to try to be modern. *My* truth, did I say? It was his truth too. Not Barnaby's, Pat's. Did Barnaby even have a truth? A man of such powdery illusions, such primal gaiety? I doubt if the gravitas of truth ever stuck to Barnaby for long enough to become his own. Pat Donlon's truth, I mean. His. Let me be clear. It is Pat, our greatest artist, if it is art that renews our vision of ourselves and our country, of whom I wish to speak here. And of myself. The torture that accompanies grand visions. That, and the beauty and the awful price of illicit love. The torture of seeing what others have yet to see. The torture of knowing what has been kept hidden, unseen, in the silence and the dark of wilful denial. All that. The suffering and the transcendent bliss. All right, yes, I *am* being grandiose. I like the sound of it!

I was christened Gabrielle Louise Ballard. From the beginning I hated my name. I refused to answer to Gabrielle and was teased to tears by my brothers with *Gabby*. When my darling Uncle Mathew came to visit and found me alone in the garden weeping, he took me on his knees and caressed my burning cheeks with his lips and called me his sweet golden Autumn. That is not a moment I shall forget. It goes with me into my grave—like the golden amulet of an Egyptian princess. Autumn is the name I have been known by all my life. No friend ever called me anything else. Freddy reduced me to Aught, of course. But I loved Freddy and forgave him. Gave him, indeed, the liberty of his dreams with me. But with Freddy it was always a game. Life. Nothing more.

It is the first of January, 1991. My first New Year's Day alone. I was born in 1906. So I must be eighty-five. Is that right? Some people still have vigour at eighty-five. Barnaby had the facade of it. Close to, however, one saw the vacant sky behind his windows. But I have obeyed the biblical laws and become a disfigured crone. Still tall, I am stooped and cranky and thin as . . . Well, as thin as something. Think of something yourself. My scalp is dry, with reddened patches visible through the stray wisps of silver hair that remain attached. Colourless, really, rather than silver. This is my last chance to tell the truth. I must remember that. Which is why I wear a scarf. Because of my hair, I mean, not because it's nearly impossible to stick to the truth. Not like the Queen's scarves, but more a scarf of the kind once affected by America's beat poets and the pirates. Tight to the skull. I have a long skull. Even with my stoop, once dressed and in public my appearance is tall and haughty. Today my headscarf is a fine Kashmiri pashmina. The deep green of dreams. The sacred colour. It needs a wash but I don't object to the faint warm odour of it. A peasant woman would never wash her scarf. I've become accustomed to strong animal smells here alone with Sherry.

Suicide is for strong people. Suicide is not for the likes of Barnaby. Barnaby has spoiled suicide for me. It is so annoying. I tremble and have no strength. The tea tray jiggles in my hands as if it will leap out of my grasp and run away laughing into the garden, like one of my tormenting brothers risen from his grave to mock me again. Each of the seven lidless teapots on the shelf above the Rayburn represents a period and a particular friendship. I realised this the other day when I broke the lid of this one. Don't worry, I shan't bore you with a catalogue of all that. My two brothers shouting *Gabby* into my face until I wept with fury and pursued them helplessly around the garden at Elsinore. Elsinore! You see how I was schooled in grandiosity. They became grey-suited chairmen of their own great companies. Members of the Melbourne and Metropolitan Board of Works. Terrified of publicity. Terrified of taxation. Both dead. Their wives dead. Elsinore given to the state. The garden cut up to make room for the developer's blocks of yellow-brick flats. That vast cold house a rehabilitation centre for the hopeless of this new age that is not my age. Elsinore, my childhood home that was never homely. It should have been bulldozed instead of classified. I turned my back on it and on them when I met Arthur. When my father met Arthur he said to me, 'There's only one thing wrong with your Arthur, my dear.' I asked him what that might be. 'Arthur doesn't think enough of money,' my father said. I answered, 'And your trouble, Father, is that you think of nothing else.' He did not forgive me. We were not friends. Were we ever? I loathed them all. I was afraid of them. I still am. They damaged me. My fear of them made me hysterical. I felt trapped with them and the only thing I could do was to scream and break things and refuse to eat. Even though they are dead the trap they set for me then is still in me now. I still scream and break things and refuse to eat. Not as often, but I do it. I dread what their cold world of money worship might yet do to me in the vivid nightmares that have begun to haunt my feeble years. You would not believe the awful conviction in the nightmares of the aged. They are a fearful assault. There is no resisting them.

Darling Uncle Mathew, he is still the saviour of my childhood. There was a touch of the poet in him and they despised him for it. He was the only one of them to die poor. They refused to help him. I have wondered if Mathew might have been the result of my grandmother taking a lover. Not the milkman, but some man cultivated, wayward and of a generous spirit. If she did have an affair, her manner gave no hint of it, unless in the very firmness of her implicit denial. Sequestered, she was. As tight as a dried fish in her corsets. The dowager Queen Adelaide. Her lips withdrawn into her mask. Severe in her reproach of all things joyful. The mistress of Elsinore to her last day. The laughter of children gave her migraines and she would not tolerate it in her house. My father's mother. Grandma Ballard. Mother to the founder of our fortunes. And there were several fortunes. For a time the brothers Ballard (excepting Mathew) accounted for the largest fortune in Melbourne. I shall say no more. That lot will not be resurrected by me here. I will not be lured into an account of their hideousness. Truth does not require it of me.

I was eleven when Uncle Mathew kissed me within the canopy of the peppercorn tree in the garden at Elsinore. So gently did he put his lips to mine that a butterfly might have landed on me, the touch so exquisite my body bloomed for him with a pang I have not forgotten. That pale afternoon the beauty of consolation entered my life. For Mathew consoled me, as he consoled himself, not only with his kisses but with the secret that we are each born with a gift. I pressed my ear to his chest and listened to the strong rhythm of his heart. His voice was soft and unhurried, and when he spoke wide acres of time waited to be filled with imagination's charmed possibilities. His was a landscape beyond reality.

'Not everyone uses their gift,' he told me that day, his hand on my side, his fingers warm through my dress. 'Some,' he said, 'do not even realise they have received a gift. For them the gift remains mute, dormant until the end.' I knew he spoke of his mother and his brothers. I said, 'You mean until they die?' I wished to hear him say it. His fingers pressed my ribs and he held me close in his embrace. 'Yes, my darling, until they die.' A hardness in his voice at this. And I wished then for the deaths of all of them. The smell of Mathew's skin through his linen shirt was of herbs and blossoms and strange distant places. 'Others,' he said, 'do not wish to acknowledge the gift. They see the burden of it and are frightened by what it demands from them, that it will challenge them to perform above themselves or else see them fail. They disown their gift in favour of the coarse reality of money. They loathe the creative life of others and strive to stifle it at any cost. They are best at cruelty.' His mother's fierceness stood over us and he lowered his voice and whispered, 'In their most secret thoughts they believe in an untried quality within themselves that would prove equal in merit to the merits of the most gifted—*if only they were to try it.* That is their secret despair, not to have tried their worth.'

That is the way Mathew talked; lover, poet and philosopher. He was too kind and gentle for this world and failed to leave an impression on it. He spoke to me as if admitting me to secrets gathered from places I would never visit. I loved him and felt safe with him. And wasn't he comforted by my innocence and my belief in him? None of the others spoke to me in his way. If they spoke to me at all, it was to correct me or to offer me advice or to mock me. They did not know how to speak of love or poetry. The imagination was a locked door for them and they feared it. I locked my lips and my ears to them too. It was the country of Mathew I was determined to inhabit when I grew up.

When I was seventeen and home from school for the Christmas holidays I saw Uncle Mathew for the last time. And perhaps he knew it was to be our last time. For we sat in the garden again on the seat in the shelter of the peppercorn and when I asked him, 'What is my gift?' he kept his silence for a long time, looking at me tenderly, before he said with an undeclared sorrow that puzzled me, 'My darling Autumn, yours is the gift of recognition.' It was his melancholy he would have me understand, not that the world is hard and sad but that life is beautiful and must end. I asked him how he could be sure this was my gift. 'You are the only one among them,' he said, and there were tears in his eyes as he said it, 'who has not scorned me or accused me of failure, but has celebrated my struggle to make something of my poetry.' I took his hands in mine. 'But I love you, Uncle Mathew. Whatever you had done I would have loved you for it.'

A year later he found his death, alone and destitute, in the backyard of a pub in a dismal village in County Kilkenny, Ireland, where he had foolishly strayed in search of the roots of his poetic gift. I wish I had been there to comfort him. I denied him my lips that last time in the garden at Elsinore. I was too awkward with myself at seventeen to permit it. And afterwards I regretted denying him. I still do. I could have let him have everything and it might have given him hope.

But he was right. I was gifted to recognise the strengths of others, often before they saw their strengths themselves. I was the one who gathered them together and brought them into their own light and into the confidence of the admiration of their peers, without which many of them would have faltered and fallen by the wayside, like poor solitary Uncle Mathew himself. He had taught me that the country of the gifted is a dangerous place to be alone in. I vowed that I would always keep myself at the centre of a group of writers, artists and thinkers. And that is what I did, with Arthur at my side. Until it was all torn apart by envy, betrayal and despair.

When I saw Edith on the street it shocked me. It was her walk that was familiar. That same balanced containment which, when I first met her, made me think her prissy and lacking in seriousness. That soft young woman's walk in an old woman. A demon voice whispering in my ear, *Edith Black! See? There! That's her in the green hat walking away from you.* The only woman on the street wearing a hat. I felt as if I'd been shot. She stopped and turned around and looked straight at me. My hand went to my face. When she started back towards me I thought she had recognised me. I was unable to move. But she walked past me and went into the chemist's, where I'd just been to get my prescription filled for the life-saving drugs I take every day by the handful. As I watched Edith go into the chemist's I realised she could have been my oldest friend in the world today instead of my oldest enemy. Instead of taking her man from her I might have put my arm around her and given her a kiss. She was without guile. My throat thickened and I wept. Why did I weep? I don't know. I wept, that is all I know. And something changed for me. I have always been indifferent to the why of things. It is what happens to us that matters, not why it happens to us.

I kept diaries all my life. Notebooks. What the Germans call *Tagebücher*. Notes on my days. The incidents that filled them, or the voids that made them echo with my cries of anguish. That smell of burning in the summer air today is them. This blue smoke in the sunbeams here within the coach house. I must go and stir the ashes. Books burn badly. My despair. My hopes. My girlhood dreams. All that stuff. It goes stale quicker than cabbages. When I got home after seeing Edith I went out to the back veranda and poured a large whisky and drank it off in one go. Half a bottle of whisky later I was in the study collecting my notebooks from the shelves above my desk. They went back to the days before Mathew kissed me under the peppercorn. The earliest of them had pressed violets between its pages from the garden at Elsinore. I must have been seven. What started me keeping a diary when I was seven? There was another with the impression of my girlish lips from my first lipstick (stolen from my mother's clutchbag). Later notebooks with boys' love letters pasted into them. I gathered them all from the shelves and stuffed them into an empty wine carton. This afternoon I dragged the carton along the passage and out the side door to the forty-four-gallon drum that Stony incinerates our rose clippings in. I reached into the drum with the iron poker from the library and stirred them around, pieces flying up and making me squint. I watched the pages curl and catch, my antique past in the flickering sparks crawling along the edges of the old paper. So what? It was time to burn them. An added delight in watching them burn (knowing there is no return from fire) was that Biographers love nothing more than notebooks.

Arthur's 1934 Pontiac. I'm standing here looking at it. We drove down to Ocean Grove in it to see Pat and Edith. It's parked over there where he left it, God knows how many years ago. The key is still in the ignition. I suppose the battery is dead. My poor Arthur. A scavenger has stolen the Indian head from the bonnet. My beloved Arthur and I that summer afternoon in 1935, three years before we met Pat and Edith. Here, in this old coach house, is where it began for all of us. It stood as crookedly then as it stands now. Arrested in its fall. When Arthur and I saw this place we didn't need to say anything. It matched our dream. Old Farm. It had been for sale for years. A piece of land beyond the suburbs. An old weatherboard house and this dilapidated shed with the open side. A sixteen-acre paddock and the river winding along the bottom boundary. Fragrant eucalypt forest on the far side of the river. Everything we had dreamed of. All wonderfully neglected and in need of the love we had to give. It is a big shed with a mezzanine, its boards sprung from its frame and grey with age. Now there is the roar of the freeway and the suburbs hem me in. It used to be that if you stayed in one place long enough you eventually became a local. Now if you stay in one place long enough you become a stranger.

I'm a remnant from another time. I don't eat properly. I can't be bothered cooking. My breath is foul and I fart continuously. I'm accustomed to the smell. My stomach is a fermenting tip. I eat cabbages every day. I'm like a poor Chinese. There is a box of them—cabbages, not poor Chinese—behind the kitchen door. The house stinks of my farts and boiled cabbages. I don't care. I *do* care! No, I *do* care, but I can't summon the will to do anything about it. I was such a skilled housekeeper. Stony brings me cabbages. He's the last of the market gardeners. He has hands like a stone breaker. When we came here it was cherry orchards and fields of strawberries around us. Now there's just Stony's cabbage patch and the suburban houses. All far grander than my dear old Old Farm. I might yet burn it to the ground. When this is done. There is no return from fire. We are not Shadrach, Meshach or Abednego. Are we? With no smell of fire on us. I can't remember now why those three young men were put to the flames in the first place. To prove something, I suppose. Their heroic faith, was it? Or something purer? Another distraction from reality. The smell of fire is on me today. This dress will hold it. It is a smell that will see me out. The smell of fire and boiled cabbages. There are worse fates than destruction by fire. The ancients knew that. We have forgotten everything strong. It can't have been today that I put my notebooks in the drum, can it? They must be still smouldering from last night. Oh, I don't know and it doesn't matter. Chronology's not everything, is it?

Arthur and I came here that summer day in 1935 arm in arm, in each other's arms. We knew at once we had found our haven from our terrible families. We were pure then. Yes, we were. Pure in our spirits and our intentions. And he was innocent. His family almost as wealthy and quite as mean and twisted as my own. He had given in to the love knots of his mother and become a city lawyer. But enough of that. There, just there by the back wall beside the Pontiac, is where we made love that first joyful afternoon. Where the hot eye of the sun is burning this very moment. Hay was piled loosely then. Loose hay for us. We were golden and young and in love (though not violently. Arthur was my refuge). I had to instruct him. I may as well tell you now, this story does not have a happy ending. I have never had a child. Not of my own. It wasn't possible. There was a simple, unpleasant, gynaecological reason. If that is how you spell it. And speaking of spelling, have you noticed that prenatal needs only the displacement of one letter to become parental? It doesn't take much. Ever. For one thing to become another. Usually its opposite. Love become hate. Heaven become hell. Good become evil. Laughter become slaughter. One letter. That is all it takes. You know the rest. Word and wound.

He—Pat I mean, not my dear gentle Arthur—was my greatest work of acknowledgment. He was the one on whom I spent my gift without holding anything back. I knew him the moment I saw him—well, not quite the moment, but within the hour. He squinted in the fierce light of his ambition. He was not like Picasso. He did not have those famous *hungry* eyes. Pat had a deep eye. That is what I saw. No one else saw it. Pat Donlon, with his white-blue eye that he tried to conceal from us by squinting. Concealing from us the terrifying nakedness of his ambition. Even he was unsure of it. Until I opened him to it, he was unsure. So there! He was married to Edith when Arthur and I first met him. She was a beautiful girl, lovely and sad. A little afraid of him and what she had done. Afraid of his intensity. Afraid of what she had done in tying herself to this man's course. But she loved him. And she had courage. We both saw that. Oh yes, how she loved him. If God, who made us all (I suppose) and gave us our passions were to give me my life to live over I would be kind to Edith. I would put my arms around her and take care of her and make her feel safe and loved. What did I do? I took her man from her. I took Pat. It was easy. He was offered to me by fate, so I took him. I never considered Edith. My gift of recognition was called on by Pat in a way it would never be called on by anyone ever again. It was my fate to take him from her. So I took him. Arthur trembled with it, but withstood it. My poor dear lovely Arthur. Like heartless Nebuchadnezzar with his three young men, I put Arthur to the fiery test. He survived but he didn't come out unscathed. Burned to the bone, he was. White as ash. A great innocent gentle part of him destroyed. Not to be recovered. My Arthur. What I made him endure. How I still love him.

Edith was forgotten by us. So I will give her portrait the first place in this testament. Pat will have to come second to her for once. The portrait of a young woman, at the time of life when we need our portrait painted: when we are young and beautiful. Not when we smell of cabbages and smoke and our own farts. I shall do Edith the honour of remembering her youth. You may not like *him* (Pat) and I can't expect you to like me. But you cannot dislike Edith. She was the first to be sacrificed to the violence and the hunger of his ambition. An ambition of such rapture its severity frightened even him. As if it were an affliction that came at him when the weather changed or the moon was full. She and their child, Edith and the little baby. The first to be fed to the strange dark blessing, the furnace of his art. If that is what it was. Or am I getting too melodramatic again? That speechless art of his that hangs today in its silence on our gallery walls. His art become a kind of silence itself. A shroud. Something awful about it that I still cannot confront. Why did we do it? Who has it served? Edith is forgotten. She was like a child when Arthur and I first met her, still obedient to the hopes and sacred values of her parents and her lovely grandfather. A girl incapable of revolt or betrayal against those who had nurtured and tutored her. She was shocked by such things. Embarrassed by them. Confused by them. I can see the blush rise to her lovely cheeks now when I spoke in her presence of my hatred for my family. That was something she could not understand. My revolt against them shocked her sense of what was right.

I was his acolyte. What is that? Acolyte? These days one needs to explain such words. *An altar attendant of minor rank*, my dictionary says. Not just his accomplice, but something sacred in the ministry of it. That was me. I drew him out and encouraged him and shared the mad illusions that made an artist of him. And I paid a terrible price for it. He was creative in the conventional understanding of that notion. An artist. But you will have to ask, as I have had to ask, whether what we destroyed in the service of his creations was of greater value than what he and I produced. Was he, was I, just as cold, just as ruthless in the struggle to deliver his art, as my father and uncles (saving Mathew) were in their struggle to amass a great fortune? At any price. Always at any price to others. Never to themselves. They sacrificed nothing. It was always others who were made to pay. Was there not as great a coldness in the way Pat and I exercised our ambition as the coldness I so despised and feared in my family? The coldness I fled from? My heart aches with this question: was I not my father's daughter after all? Inescapably branded from the cradle with his will? There may be no answer to questions such as these. Or the answers may be obvious. Something to do with the simplest moral principles of our humanity. We will all have a different answer, I dare say, those of us who love art and find in it our consolation, and those of us who live contentedly without it. But in asking the question we would do well not to forget Edith Black and her child. To forget them, as they have been forgotten, written out of our record, written out of Pat's history, is to lie to ourselves about the nature of our culture. To forget Edith and her child is to lie to ourselves about the nature of our art and what it is we worship in it.

Here she is then, Edith Black. The best I can do for you. A realist portrait. Realism, that most difficult of styles, filled as it is with intricacy and contradiction.

2

Edith Black, 1938

IT WAS A FINE DAY. THE SUN WAS SHINING JUST FOR HER. THE SEA running a heavy swell after the previous night's storm. The sound of the sea in the room with her now. He had raced down the track to the main road on his bicycle earlier without telling her where he was going or when he would be back. She stood at this window then, where she is standing now, watching him go.

It is already midday. The postman has been and there is a letter sticking out of the box by the gate, a white triangle catching the sun, as if a white bird has alighted there. The letter will be from her mother. She will walk down and fetch it later. She has come out of the studio and rattled the stove into life and made a cup of tea, a drop of bluish milk from the neighbour's blue roan cow, and a half teaspoon of their precious sugar stirred into it. She stands at the window sipping her tea and looking out at the green hill, the cup held by its slim handle in her right hand, the saucer in her left. The cup and its saucer are delicate pieces of English bone china decorated with a crowded pattern of lilac blooms. One set of a pair on temporary loan from her mother. 'Lilac Time'. Like everything in this house, and the house itself, temporary and borrowed. And not her mother's best, but her second best, or perhaps even her third best. Expensive nevertheless. A measure of her mother's trust. 'Until you two can get a few nice things of your own together.'

She is pleased to see that the horse is still there. The green hill, where the horse stands, sweeps upward from the foot of the garden to form the soft curve of her near horizon, like the warm belly of the earth. She half closes her eyes, permitting this thought a little space. High above the paddock immature white clouds silently approach from the troubled sea across the cold blue of the sky, which, she notices suddenly, is exactly the white-blue of his eyes. Yes, white-blue. Like the eyes of his hero, the poet Rimbaud, whose verse he never tires of reciting. She hears it now, her own voice translating for him, *I had caught a glimpse of conversion to good and to happiness.* She gives a small, nervous laugh at the thought of him, at the thought of where he might have gone this morning. Some sense with him always of the terrible disasters that await us in life, his urgency, his mad desire to be bodily engaged with the future.

The upward sweep of the green paddock is decorated with yellow oxalis flowers. It is a counterpane sewn with morning stars. Her mother's handwork, for example. Finely embroidered silk thread. The Latin names of the flowers done in sylvan green around the border, so fine a magnifying glass is needed to see the individual stitches, and even then . . . There is nothing cruel or cynical in her mother's life. All painful memories have been put down, like old family dogs. Quiet, calm, sensible. That is how it is at home, in Brighton and on the farm. Wherever her mother presides, there everything is as it should be. No daisies in the lawn. The past unpicked and restitched. The work goes on. Their saving routine. Church on Sundays, with Dr Aiken presiding at Flood Street, his thin nose and sad intelligent eyes. A good man in the claim of his grateful parishioners. His apologetic frown a perpetual reminder that there is some terrible problem to be resolved before we can all move confidently to a full enjoyment of our lives. Saint Paul advised the Philippians to *Rejoice in the Lord always: and again I say, Rejoice.* But Dr Aiken hasn't rejoiced. He has puzzled in the Lord. What he has missed is something vital, the key to happiness eluding him. His life has been without a companion. He has not seemed to wish for a woman by him. The manse a cold redbrick darkened by moaning cypresses, the shelves of his study closely inhabited by puzzling tracts to do with something he does yearn for, the Ultimate Truth and the Christian God—staples of his divine preoccupations. No touches of the floral, either in teacups or counterpanes, to lighten his days. And such a handsome man, his manner gracious, his hands fine and well shaped, noticeable when he bows his violin, and other features of nature's approval gracing his gentle person. A match. But all for nothing, so it seems. His solitariness a puzzle to her mother. For the Presbyterian assembly does not bar its ministers from the sacrament of marriage. Even so . . .

No, the floral counterpane is surely more exotic than that, Edith decides firmly and sets her cup in its saucer in the dulled stone of the sink, the sink's crazed glaze the perfect hue of old bones, the fine lines possibly an antique script. Clink, the cup says sharply to its saucer and Edith looks down and steadies it, breathing a murmured apology. Once again she has been dragged back into memory and her old home and her mother. Her mother. The decorated hill is not a floral counterpane at all but is something Persian and is not of her mother's world. A Persian embroidery. The work of silent hours and days when a woman in her solitude dreams of distant events that never were but might have been, and bends her head to her needle in the soft lamplight and smiles at the tiny golden flowers. Pretending that her dreams are memories.

Standing at the window, her fingers still touching her mother's lilac-patterned teacup, the smell of the wood stove in the air, something of hot iron and smokiness, Edith thinks: How peaceful it is here. How lovely. How at home I might so easily know myself to be in this little house with him, if only . . . The horse is a mare. It is an old brood mare, the points of its hips prominent, gut-hung, its spine bowed with the bearing of many foals, its brown coat dry and wintry. *Equus caballus*. Edith has known the companionship of horses since her childhood on her father's farm. The old brown mare stands side on to the hill, her hollow flank towards Edith. She, the mare, looks as if she is expecting someone to come over the horizon; her ears pointed forward, the imagination of oats in her distended nostrils. Edith wonders where she has come from and what has prompted their frugal neighbour to offer her the generous pasturage of his paddock. The horse was there this morning, large and brown, turning its great head towards the house when Edith came out the back door to feed the hens and collect the eggs, a newcomer like themselves, curious, alert and a little apprehensive. After feeding the hens—there were no eggs—Edith fetched a thick slice of bread from the house.

Gently coaxed, the mare approached the fence and lipped the offering from her hand. The calm innocence of the mare's eye. It is a fact well known among horse people that the horse has the largest eyes of any land mammal. 'Will you be lonely in Mr Gerner's paddock with only the milker for company?' At the touch of her voice the mare lowered her long lashes and bent her head. The horse is highly sensitive around the areas of its nose, its eyes and its ears. Edith stroked its silky nose. 'Stallions once trembled before your beauty.'

The Southern Ocean lies beyond the horizon that is formed by the swelling rise of Mr Gerner's green paddock. The *Great Southern Ocean*, her grandfather, the painter Thomas Anderson, called it. Encircling the world. Its boundaries indeterminate. Taking her hand in his large knobbly one and leading her forefinger on a journey across the old atlas, *Alexander Keith Johnston, F.R.G.S., 1857, on Mercator's Projection.* A great book all the way from the family home on the bank of the Nith between the lofty hills and fertile holms of Dumfries, the largest private house in the county. The book. Yes. Shelved there once upon a time in his own grandfather's library, another Thomas Anderson in a line of them from the Border country, the book's elephant folio sheets giving off a smell of the other world on the other side when he laid it open on his broad oak desk, as she stood close beside him in his studio in the house where her own mother had been born, a dwelling elegant and Victorian, on the fashionable foreshore of Brighton.

To speak of the other side is to refer to death by another name. Even then she knew it. Her grandfather's jacket smelling of Erinmore tobacco. The grip of his hand making the first joint of her finger bend like a hockey stick on the heavy paper as they made their imaginary journey together, crossing the ocean (whose breathing and sighing is with her in the kitchen at this moment), so firmly guided by him then; 'We sail past the stormy tip of South America, then touch South Africa. A big tack between Crozet and Kerguelen islands. And here we are already!' Leaning together, his moustache tickling her cheek now, 'The bottom of Australia. I—think—I—can—just—see—us. Can you see us? Yes! There we are! See, the pair of us?' His free arm around her, cuddling, just the two of them in the quiet of their own story, among the smell of old books and turpentine. She misses him. It is already four years since his housekeeper, Mrs Dress, found him lying on his back beside the long kitchen table, his feet together, a familiar old man clad in pyjamas and slippers, his glasses and his pipe and tobacco pouch neatly arranged beside him, his striped cottons freshly laundered. But, oddly, without his plaid dressing-gown. Perhaps he thought the ancient garment unfit for the occasion? 'So there you are,' Mrs Dress said, stepping around him, and made herself a cup of tea before telephoning his daughter. He had evidently felt the approach of the moment. A wavering light at the periphery of his vision, was it? A mild anxiety and tightening across his chest? We shall never know. And had prepared himself so as to cause the least shock and trouble to those whom he cared for and whom he was about to leave on this side.

Edith wonders if she will always miss him. He had no time to say goodbye but was gone, suddenly, without a word. She had found her mother by the telephone, sitting on the big camphor wood chest in the hall, weeping. Will she always carry her loss as she goes on through her life, Edith wonders, becoming old herself one day, a grandmother, her grandfather a noble resident of her childhood memory, loved and missed? Will it always be like that? Or do our dead eventually leave us? He is her inspiration for this life that she has chosen, and she needs his approval for her work. Art. Her mother's father. But Edith does not call herself an artist. She is far too uncertain of herself for that; too deeply conditioned to the habit of womanly modesty to openly admit the secret ambition of her heart. He, her grandfather on her mother's side—whenever sides were taken—had been either happily ignorant of or indifferent to the innovative schools and styles of his time. The great artistic debates and feuds had left him untouched. His palette throughout his life a range of golden browns with their own inner light, achieved with a knowledge of the classic craft. He had seen no reason to snub the tradition that had given him his splendid livelihood. He was not a visionary. He did not see it as his business to challenge the authority of his masters. His subjects were leisurely pastoral scenes, farm buildings, crops and roads leading somewhere or other, a girl sometimes with a straw hat and ribbon going somewhere or other, a workman in a field with a horse, the sound of birdsong and maybe a butterfly or two. His was the reassurance of a kindly nature for the drawing rooms of the well-to-do city folk and great country families who were his patrons. He might have been making sturdy chairs for the ease of their minds and their backs. A reliable craftsman, they were pleased to revere him and to acclaim his genius in the works he made for them. Occasional portraits, too, of children or their fathers (when honours were bestowed), commissioned by the wives, were competently produced when required. He was a Melbourne man. Solid, reliable, of good Scottish stock. Sydney did not know him. Although almost never hung these days, a work or two of his can still be found in the inventory of the Scottish National Gallery in Edinburgh.

He wore a dove-grey fedora with a wide black silk band and a grey three-piece suit with a plain bow tie. His moustache was large and brown and prickly. He looked like a painting of himself. A tonal head and shoulders of him, the brim of his fedora shading his eyes, hung in the parlour of the Brighton house, done by the controversial Max Manner—who *did* call himself an artist—and tendered in lieu of rent when Mr Manner brought his family home from France, stony broke and with nowhere to live, bolstered nevertheless by the assurance of his own genius. All that before the steady years of Manner's prosperity and influence. Comfort and opulence in the grand house in Kew, where his two daughters, lissom Elise and chubby Simone, lived on in genteel poverty long after the great man himself had gone over to the other side. As the years went on without him the house grew seedy, green around the brows from leaking guttering and failed damp courses, the garden splendidly overgrown, the two devoted spinsters insisting on the grandeur of their father's achievement to their last days together on this wonderful earth. Simone, the younger of them, played the role of maid to the elder's haughty chatelaine; Elise receiving her visitors seated in the parlour, veiled in layers of pink and apricot chiffon, her lips bright red (a little askew), her purpled eyes challenging her visitor to exercise the fine manners and graces of an earlier time. Their father's early poverty was never referred to.

Each of the three large mirrors in the parlour was mounted on castors, concealed with tasselled strands like the feathered feet of Chinese hens, the mirrors' shoulders draped suggestively with red or green brocades, their great wide eyes angled to reflect depths and elaborations of space and light. Manner's works on the walls, or resting back on easels, were set amid the hues and tones of their own origins by his daughters. The great man's reflected pictures, Edith recalled, had seemed to exist beyond her reach in a space of pure imagining, a world in which reversed reality held up for contemplation a mysterious order. As one entered the room, to glimpse in a mirror as if through a doorway, the mothlike figure of Elise fingering one of John Field's elemental nocturnes at the keyboard of the great piano, the enormous black lid like the wing of Satan cloaked above her, was not to be in the presence of something real but something imaginary. It was to have no presence oneself, but to be the witness of another's dream. As a child Edith had been struck with wonder by the achievement of this visual elaboration at the house in Kew; the endless play, not on words but on light and shade, scenes within scenes, corners and suggestions, tonal variations receding forever deeper, the centre and substance elusive, the eye drawn on in search of a point of rest. Dizzying. She had believed then that the Manner sisters were in possession of an arcane truth about the world and art that she would never come to possess herself. And in a way she still believed it. And in an even deeper way it was probably true.

The authority of her childhood years remained with Edith, the lives of her grandfather, his friends and her parents and their friends binding her to a respect for their values which she could not easily desert in her own art. She was convinced she had been born into a worthy tradition. And like her family she believed, often against her youthful inclination to rebel, that she owed a debt to that inheritance and was honour bound to repay it. Society, Edith understood, would require from her something of worth in return for the advantages of her birth. Indeed, that something was owed she accepted as a founding principle of her caste.

All that splendid illusion lying in the future for those two Manner girls when they were twelve and nine and Edith's grandfather offered their father a place to camp while he got his finances together after their return from France. Hence the head and shoulders study, dutifully hung in the parlour of the Anderson family's Melbourne home in Brighton, in case the great Mr Max Manner or his daughters ever returned for a visit. But they never did. 'He obscured my eyes with that dark shadow of my hat brim,' Edith's grandfather complained. But Edith had always thought the picture the very likeness of him, imagining within the luminous shadow of his fedora's brim the familiar light of innocent pleasure in his eyes. She had never known her grandfather sombre or preoccupied but on one occasion. She found him one summer evening in the garden at Brighton, sitting alone on the bench within the bower of the old apple tree. He was weeping. She did not ask him why he wept, but leaned her child's weight against him and took his large hand in both her own, and waited there with him in the shared silence of his grief—which, she remembers with sudden acute clarity now, was chipped away at by an angry blackbird in the laurels. She never learned the cause of her grandfather's grief that day.

As a young man her grandfather had studied in London at the Slade school, learning the tedious perfection of anatomical drawing from Henry Tonks. Then later, in Paris, he won a greatly coveted place in the Atelier of Fernand Cormon, where he met the Australian artist John Peter Russell. The young Thomas Anderson and the young John Russell were both skilled boxers and soon became firm friends. Thomas had no enthusiasm, however, for the revolt against Fernand Cormon's formal academism mounted by his fiery fellow students—among them the dangerously unstable Van Gogh, who liked to make threats of violence and to nervously finger a black revolver that he kept in his overcoat pocket. Crusaders for the revolution of modernism. Well, there did seem to be some kind of ultimate truth in it at the time that might even have been worth dying for (though none did) but was certainly worth living for.

It was not modernism that excited Thomas's imagination. John Russell's stories of his home inspired in Thomas an enticing vision of an exotic Australia on the far side of the world. John was happy to give his friend Melbourne introductions. When Thomas arrived at Port Melbourne it was a blustery winter day of bright sunshine and harried clouds rushing across the bay from the Southern Ocean, as if something out there had panicked them into making a dash for the safety of land. Ten minutes after stepping out of the customs shed and nearly having his hat blown off the end of Station Pier, Thomas met the beautiful young Gwendoline Pocock. Miss Pocock was at the port with her mother and father seeing her eldest brother off to England, where he was to study something useful at Cambridge. Thomas gallantly held the train carriage door open for Gwendoline and her parents. Encouraged by the blush on her cheek and her murmured, 'Thank you,' he stepped into the carriage after them and sat himself down opposite her. And he smiled. And she smiled back. It was the old story. He always said it was a telepathic call from Gwen that brought him to Australia. And who can say it wasn't? They were married after a decent spell of being engaged, all with the blessing of Dr and Mrs Pocock, and were soon settled in the Brighton house where, apart from visits to his folk in Dumfries and to relatives of hers in Derbyshire (or wherever they were), they remained for the rest of their lives. Gwendoline bore two healthy children, a son then a daughter. The son, Ian Augustine, was killed on the Somme, and the daughter was Maud, Edith's own mother. Thomas, so it turned out, had been just the man for the brown tones of the Melbourne world of art. His brothers in art from Cormon's carried on staging their revolution without him.

Edith steps away from the sink and draws in her breath sharply, her hand going to her chest. It is as if something binds her. It is always as if something is binding her. The whisper of the breakers coming ashore from the Great Southern Ocean, the concussion of them, a tremor transferred from the ground into the timber floor, a tremor within her womb. Four years after his death her grandfather's pictures have been forgotten. They appear from time to time among the effects of deceased estates and fetch very little. The tremor in her belly, where the child whose existence Pat does not yet know of lies . . . Perhaps the old mare is not expecting someone to come over the hill, but is from the hinterland and is in a state of passionate wonder at the exalted voice of the sea? Edith is comforted by the presence of the horse. It is like having a new friend. The binding in her chest is a kind of desperation. About all of it. Everything. Unlike him, she is not at liberty but is responsible. She must get back to her work.

She rinses her mother's floral cup and saucer and dries both pieces, then she sets them beside the other pair on the shelf by the icebox and returns to the studio. She cannot imagine where he has gone or what he is doing. Should she paint into her picture some notation of the yellow oxalis flowers? It is an oil study of the house and the field, sketched initially from the rear, where the great broken cypresses are. Or are they pines, planted there by the founding Scots a hundred years ago? Great black pine trees wherever the Scots have been, like the dooming drone of their pipes and the clenched averted silence of their religion. She closes her eyes and sees her painting before her, perfectly conceived. She is in despair. Her mother wrenching up handfuls of oxalis from her perennial borders. And each spring the oxalis returning more luxuriant than the previous year. As if decimation inspires the weed. Does her mother believe a spring will eventually come when the oxalis will at last be vanquished by her Presbyterian endurance? Edith's grandfather called oxalis by the gentler name of wood sorrel, and calmly painted fields of it. 'See! It closes its bells when the sun goes behind a cloud.' Another hour has gone and she is hungry. She cannot bear to look at her picture. The thought of it disgusts her.

She lifts her hands and sweeps her hair back from her face. Gripping her hair in a tight hank behind her head and closing her eyes, she reties the green silk ribbon, securing the bow with a final tug. Her hair has lost its lustre since they came down here. The trouble is the chip heater is rusted and not working properly. So there is no hot water, except what she can heat in a saucepan on the wood stove. He has said he will fix the chip heater. But can he fix rust? She is beautiful and young and she is in love. She knows she should not be unhappy. The light is poor at her end of the room. Pat stomped into the house ahead of her and took the sunny end of the room the first day and said nothing about it. Like an infantry captain leading his platoon up a hill, he secured the advantage.

She is not prepared to fight for it. She can't compete. His vigour is as relentless as the oxalis. It's not a fair contest. Before they had even looked at the house properly, he was lugging the kitchen table into the back room and setting it by the window, where it faced the light of the northern sky. 'Stay there!' he ordered the table, and went out to fetch his baggage of paints and brushes. And within minutes he had started painting on the back of his first square of cardboard, flat on the table, saying nothing, working with a rapid unhesitating energy, as he always does. As if he is afraid to lose the image. As fugitive as the memory of a dream on waking, is it for him? Afraid that if he pauses to reflect, the certainty will escape him?

Getting it down onto the cardboard, that's what he does. So that it's out there and is what it is. A thing. A reality. You can't argue with that. It's *there*. And there is nothing for you to compare it to. You might hate it, but you can't argue with its existence or the claim he makes for it. Art. You might resent it. Fear it even. Or fear his certainty about it. You might even say it is *not* art. And then he will laugh with delight to have provoked you to enter the trap. For there is no doubt that its existence and his certainty of its existence deny the worth of everything you do yourself, your care, your skill, the devoted craft of your earnest calling. You may think all this, but you can't ignore the reality of the thing he makes. The thing he has made confronts you. It has been produced with the speed and assurance of a child sitting on the floor in a kindergarten.

He invites the scorn of the trained artist. But he is *not* a child. He is a man. She sees the empire of his ambition in his eyes. It is this that attracts her and makes her afraid of him. This seriousness. It is this that is authentic: his determination to find a way. 'Anyone can have talent,' he says, dismissing the talented, not pausing in the swoops and dabs of his big brush. Listening to him she is made to doubt the worth of everything she does and believes.

She abandons her own work now and goes to his bright end of the room and stands looking down at the last painting he did yesterday. It is lying on his table by the window—the table that became *his* table when he carried it in here. The smell of the boot polish reminds her of her grandfather lining up her and her brothers and sister on Saturday evening (to be ready for church in the morning), newspaper covering the kitchen table, the five of them polishing like mad, singing 'Ol' Man River' and marching round the table, a shoe on one hand, a brush in the other, polishing like mad, Grandfather in the lead, stomping their feet in time and shouting, *'Eggs! Eggs! Walking about on legs, in the store, in the store. There were eggs, eggs, walking about on legs in the quartermaster's store.'* Someone once told her boot polish was made of animals' blood. She had watched Pat working yesterday, his tongue stuck out of the corner of his mouth. His anxiety to get on with it. She has not possessed the courage or the will to dispute his possession of the sunny end of the room, or even to remark on it. Her own art is not to be favoured. Ever. Obedient to the rules, her art has already been dismissed. She knows it herself. She hates the fact that she works at her painting as if someone in authority is watching over her shoulder. She hates the feeling that she has to get it *right*. For whom? It's not for herself, it's for *them*. Her teachers. Her grandfather. The traditions. The craft. How to shed the habit of obedience? What to do if she does shed it? Where to look? There is to be no nurturing from *him*. He has not inherited the habit of obedience. He owes no one obedience. He is alone. His sudden departure without explanation at high speed on the bicycle this morning. He is able to do such things without a need to explain or to justify himself.

For her, work is a subtle, delicate, mysterious coming together of the right mood and the right moment. Work is the difficult making of *art*. Striving, that is the word that characterises what she does. She has had to *settle in* to this house before she could begin, to feel herself to be in place. But not him. He was off. He had made five of his pictures by midnight the first night on his pieces of cardboard. She went to bed. After he had finished painting he sat in the kitchen reading and smoking cigarettes and drinking beer, and writing poetry in his notebook. He does everything at once. Writing, painting, drinking and smoking. He does not know if he is a writer or a painter. He does what he pleases. She was asleep by the time he came to bed and wanted to make love.

She looks at the work he has left on his table. It is a square of cardboard, two feet by two feet. It is the reverse of a bulk Rinso carton he asked the young woman at the corner shop to save for him. The young woman, who is already the mother of three children, looks at him with devotion. She will do anything he asks of her. Astonished by the confidence of his eye. Lying in bed beside her husband at night that girl will think of Pat. Edith knows it. He prepared the cardboard with dark tan Kiwi shoe polish, leaning over the table and burnishing it, his elbow going as if he was a devoted charlady polishing a family heirloom. In the centre of the cardboard is an abstract design. There is nothing to delight the eye, just a thick layer of light grey on top of a layer of dark reddish brown, the nameless thing roughly ovoid in form. Between the layers, separating them, a thin wavy line, the only note of uncertainty. She thinks of a chocolate layer cake her mother once dropped. Her mother called them into the kitchen to look and they all had hysterics.

Edith's suspicion is that Pat's work is not authentic but is an expression of his contempt for the *strivings* of his contemporaries. A week after she first met him at the Gallery School (before his contempt got the upper hand and they threw that over), the first time they made love in his room in town, the minute he had finished he reached for his makings and rolled a cigarette. When he had taken a drag on the cigarette he said—as if he had been thinking about this while he was making love to her and it was a matter of pride with him and he wanted her to know it about him at once—he said, 'I can't draw.' And he looked down at her and grinned, making something superior of this claim to the lack of the basic skill required of all artists. Making himself seem different. But he already seemed different to her without this claim. He made her puzzle about herself. Being with him was as exciting as being in a foreign country. He offered her the cigarette and watched her take a drag from it. 'You're a much better draftsman than I am,' he said, his hand caressing her belly, and he reached for the cigarette. 'You've absorbed their training. You're one of their best students.' He leaned over her then and thrust his index finger close to her eye, so that she flinched. 'It's *in* there now. You'll never be free of it. You'll never get it out. I'm not going to pollute my eye with their rubbish. We get one chance to make our own way.' Then he made that stupid boast. It was an unintelligent boast that made her doubt her belief in him. 'Mine is a higher calling,' he said. There was something almost sinister in his laughter at that moment of absurd boastfulness. She had objected, 'It's not intelligent to speak of a higher calling. It's the achievement that must be higher. *La main à plume vaut la main à charrue.* Remember? It was you who pointed it out to me. You said your dad being a tram conductor was just as important as my father being a farmer. But you didn't call Dad a farmer, which he would have been happy with. You called him a pastoralist. And Rimbaud's your god, not mine.' But it didn't suit him to remember having said any of this. She heard in his laughter that night how solitary he believed himself to be with his art. How completely alone with it he was. And she realised there was something ruthless in him that would never include her. She might suspect his work of being inauthentic, a showy gesture against conformity, but she does not doubt that his ambition and his need for art and for poetry and literature are real. He is greedy for it all. He knows he has been deprived and longs to catch up and overtake everyone who received it as a birthright. There are moments when his greed and his hunger make him ugly to her.

Standing there looking at his brownish squashed cake, Edith suddenly realises its tones belong to her grandfather's range of tones. She laughs. Not even Pat can escape from tones and colours. Pat's cowpat, however, is without that concealed source of illumination that gave her grandfather's pictures the mysterious suggestion that a story was lurking in them, if only its beginning could be grasped by the onlooker. In Pat's thing—it could not be called a picture of anything—there was neither a source of illumination nor any hint of story. It was a full stop. A refusal to be looked at with imagination. The onlooker was required to be silent and puzzled. To ask, 'What is this? What is meant by it?' And perhaps to feel inadequate for not being able to guess. For having no idea. To be struck dumb. To *feel* dumb. She has watched Pat enjoying the difficulty educated people have in finding something to say about his work. Gleeful at the effect he has on them. Knowing they fear to dismiss him. Knowing they fear him. She fears he will stop at nothing.

She hears a noise outside. It is a man's shout, or a laugh. She listens, then goes through into the kitchen and looks out the window. On the horizon of the green field their landlord, Mr Gerner, is sitting in his wheelchair. He is silhouetted against the white sky, two of his many dogs leashed at his side, as if he is a hunting god in his chariot. Pat stands to his right, also in silhouette against the sky, a rifle held to his shoulder. The horse is facing Pat from a few feet away. Everything is still. The mare collapses and rolls onto her side, her hind legs kicking out. Edith hears the crack of the twenty-two, like someone stepping on a twig in the forest. The old man urges himself forward in his chair, his great dogs rearing at their leashes. Pat leans and sets the rifle down on the grass and picks up an axe. He steps in close and stands over the horse, swinging the axe high above his head. Pat is a man who knows how to use an axe. The thump of the blade striking through flesh and bone. The old man leaning from his wheelchair, holding the leashes of his eager dogs. They are howling and rearing at their straps . . . She is out of the house, running up the hill, choking on the thick air. She has witnessed her father's manager butchering sheep on the farm and is not new to bloodshed and butchery, but the sight of this destruction tears at something in her.

On the summit of the hill she stands looking at the bloodied grass, the blue and green swath of steaming guts, the reek of it, the two great dogs snarling at her as if she has come to take their meat from them. The neighbour is shouting something at her, throwing down a bundle of hessian sacks at her feet. The sudden hot stench of the disembowelled horse in her throat . . . Now she is the small figure of a young woman clutching her stomach, stumbling down the embroidered hill towards the white cottage, the faintest wisp of blue smoke issuing from its red-brick chimney, paint peeling around its window frames, like crusts of scale around the eyes of a half-blind beast. The dark patch of turned earth, the spade abandoned upright in the soil, the hen run along the back fence by the shed overhung by the darkness of the broken pine trees. The heels of her black court shoes catch in the oxalis, her blue skirt flies up . . . She is a fugitive figure in her own composition.

3

Pat Donlon

HE SNATCHED THE LETTER OUT OF THE BOX ON HIS WAY THROUGH the gate. The gate was permanently sagged open, clutched at its base by tight fists of kikuyu grass. He had stamped the creamy envelope with a thumbprint of jellied blood. He looked at it. The letter now bore his seal. He wiped it against his trousers, the blood patch becoming a livid slash, defacing her mother's elegant handwriting. He stood looking at the smear across the perfectly ladylike hand of an educated woman, the expensive stationery with its printed address on the back, *Mrs Maud Black, Craigellachie, Bairnsdale, Victoria.* On the front, *Mrs E. Donlon, John's Cottage, North Track, Ocean Grove.* His wife. Mrs E. Donlon. It still made him smile to see it. Mrs E. Donlon was his mother.

The blood stain might have been the confident final flick of a Chinese master's brush as he lifted it from the paper. A smile of private triumph from the old poet painter. Was her mother's handwriting what they called copperplate? He didn't know and would not ask. It was another gap in his knowledge of them that could stay a gap. Some gaps didn't need filling. Whatever kind of handwriting they called it, he could see it revealed nothing personal but perfectly concealed his mother-in-law's character behind the blind regularity of its elegant curves. Better to have a gap you could see through than fill it in with knowing something useless. Maud Black had made it plain to him that she thought her daughter marrying out of her caste, and to a Catholic, would bring nothing but heartache and trouble on all of them.

The Blacks were tall people, the men broad with it. Big fellows. Thighs like bullocks. Country boys. Highland or Borderers in their origins, they had the weight and presence of farmers or fighters, a tight violence of ownership in them. Perhaps it was a remnant of the Viking. Just the men for throwing hammers and tossing cabers. Pat himself was of a slight build, like his mother, and might have been a dancer or nearly a jockey. He felt like an elf standing with Edith's father and brothers. A shifty little Irishman from the back streets of St Kilda, one of the Black boys was heard to say of him. A Pat, they said, dismissing him. Indeed he was, and did not wish to apologise for it. Wasn't marrying that Irish scallywag the very worst thing possible our Edith could have done? Why ever did the girl have to go and fall in love with that scrawny little bugger?

He knew Edith defended him. 'Pat is going to be Australia's greatest artist one day.' Her mother nearly choked on her apple crumble to hear this from her daughter. 'Oh, not the *world's* greatest then?' she said, and was intending to develop a sharper sarcasm but a piece of the crumble went down the

wrong way and prevented her from speaking. She took a gulp
of water, everyone at the table watching her sideways, and
cleared her airways before she was able to go on, getting just
a little beetrooty in the cheeks with the effort of fighting the
crumble. 'Even Max Manner never made such an arrogant
claim as that.' A thick wheeze still in her delivery. Dabbing at
her lips with her napkin. 'It's all right! I'm all right! Don't look
at me!' There was still something throttling her speech, as if
a persistent crumb in the airways might yet get the better of
her. 'And the good Lord alone knows,' she went on valiantly,
'Manners is a man with a very high and mighty opinion of
himself.' She needed to breathe, however, and had to pause and
blow her nose again. They waited in respectful silence for her.
'Your grandfather would have been ashamed to hear such a
thing from you. The *greatest*, indeed!' They ate in silence for
a while, subdued and sombre, looking down at their bowls of
apple crumble, knowing it was the disaster of Edith's man that
was choking the wife and mother of them and was not the fault
of the crumble at all. Edith ought to have been ashamed of
herself. But that girl was too stubborn for shame. What would
Grandpa Anderson have said if he'd been alive? His favourite
little peach hooking herself up with a Mick? And Edith's
brothers ever after greeting him with, 'And how's Australia's
greatest artist today?' Slapping their thighs and looming about
the place laughing.

Maud Black, Edith's mother and the author of the blood-
smeared letter in his hand, was not, in Pat's opinion, a generous
woman herself and was unlikely to ever come around to his way
of seeing the world. When he told her he was a sixth-generation
Australian on both sides of his family (the only family distinction

he could think of that might amend her displeasure), she closed her eyes and drew herself up and murmured something about the first Catholic priests to arrive in Australia being convicts. He told her he and his family didn't give a tap for religion. But like the crumble this seemed to go down the wrong way too. So he went silent and withdrew into himself and thought about something interesting that had nothing to do with his in-laws. Fuck them.

Still standing by the gate with the letter in his hand, he looked at the defaced handwriting on the envelope. He noticed the dried horse blood on the brown skin on the back of his hand had formed a lovely crackly look over the prominence of veins. He examined the effect with interest. He was wondering what might be done with it. He picked flakes of the blood off with the nail of his thumb, experiencing the same pleasurably private guilt he experienced whenever he picked his nose. He tried a flake of the blood on his tongue. Something metallic. For sure, he might have been defensive about his own handwriting once upon a time, for it *was* childish and awkward-looking. When he wrote he stuck the tip of his tongue out the corner of his mouth. It was for steadiness. Having his tongue under control helped him concentrate on the point where the nib was moving across the paper, releasing its lovely mysterious snail trail of dark ink. A trail that could, and indeed would, take on meanings of all kinds for him. There was, if you thought about it at all (which he was surprised to find no one but himself ever did), no limit to what the ink trail could manage in the way of uncovering and portraying likenesses and even thoughts. The ink, he observed with astonishment, had states of mind in it.

The day Miss Tasker issued the class with pens and nibs and inkwells Pat was smitten with the power that was handed to him and fell in love with the life of the ink trail. That day, his secret life of words and art began their mysterious dance, embraced so intimately the one with the other that he had never been able to decide since whether he was poet or painter. Copperplate, or whatever conformity of regularity it was Miss Tasker was required by the Victorian education department to impose on their hand, was the enemy. He refused it with a fierce intuition. Seeing the trap at once. To bring the ink trail under their control. That's what they were up to. Old Miss Tasker, with her yellow ruler and the smell of offal on her breath, her long grey hairs falling onto your paper when she leaned over you, had no success curing him of his protruding tongue or his wayward pen and she exhausted herself finally in the futile effort of opposing him. 'You are a gipsy!' she shrieked at him, her cheeks flaming, as if him being a gipsy excused her failure. She made him stand with his face to the map of the world, pushing his face into it (Mercator's projection), on which Australia was a big pregnant pink island. Now there was a shape for you! A bold outline to be laid down in his memory and never forgotten. His country. He was blessed with the entitlement of being native born. And she clouted him on the ear with the side of her ruler to bring home to him his failure. He mistook her fury for a most convincing act. 'There is no hope for you, Patrick Donlon!'

His mistake was understandable. Gipsy was the worst insult Miss Tasker knew. But for Pat, being called a gipsy did not carry the demeaning force of an insult, implying instead the exotic, a hidden promise of something uncommon that not everyone had. He took it as a distinction and from that day was confirmed in his sense of being different and superior. You might say that his teacher, this grey and harried old lady, had addressed not him, the boy wearing the dirty khaki shorts with the rent in the bum, but his demon, the invisible elemental presence within him. It was the first time anyone had spoken so personally to the genie of his imagination, and it made Pat realise something obvious he had always known but had never described to himself: he lived in two worlds, the private world of his imagination and the public world of breakfast and walking home from school with Gibbo and riding his bike and being clouted on the ear by Miss Tasker and longing to touch the back of Catherine Phillips' knees. Miss Tasker's fury was a revelation, and he came thereafter to think of her as his secret ally and to treat her with great respect and kindness, taking all her nastiness and her punishments and insults as part of a game between the two of them to keep the truth of their unusual alliance a secret from the rest of the class. He thought sometimes she overdid it a bit. His mother asked him why his right ear was always inflamed. He said it was nothing and wouldn't let her look.

His attachment to his teacher was a circumstance that bewildered the crabby old maid, and she remained convinced that it was Patrick Donlon's singular aim in life to make fun of her in front of his mates. The more exaggerated he was in his politeness, the more she saw his behaviour as cruel and satirical. When they were all gone home and everything was quiet and she was alone in the smelly classroom, on more than one occasion she put her head in her hands and wept, wishing she was young again and had the energy to defeat the boy.

That a boy with dirty feet and occasional head lice, who stuck his tongue out of his mouth while he struggled to copy the alphabet in large capitals from the board, should bow to her when he came into the classroom could be taken as nothing less than intentional insolence. And the class laughing their heads off and hissing with delight at the performance. So she used her ruler freely on him. But failed to rule him with it. Which eventually helped drive her to despair about herself and everything else. Her failure to turn up for work one day was never satisfactorily explained to the children. Her replacement was of no special interest to Pat. Miss Tasker had done her job well and would not be replaced in his special affections.

When Pat asked his mother if there was gipsy in him, she said he was born with a shock of black hair and that you could never tell what was in you if you were Irish, there having been in Ireland every kind of person and strange being you could ever imagine, including leprechauns and Spaniards and heaven knows what else in the way of witches and fairies and goblins and that kind of thing, and it all went back too far to ever know what bits of this or that might have got into you along the way. 'You could be a moon boy for all I know.' No one, she said, bending over the washtub and scrubbing the last of his father's shirt collars against the ripples of the board, breathing hard through her open mouth, no one knew who they really were if you went deeply enough into it. 'So have I got gipsy in me or not?' he wanted to know. 'You might have a bit of gipsy in you and you might not.' She would not commit herself beyond that. 'It's even money then?' he said, using a phrase he had often heard his dad use when talking with his mates about the gee-gees. 'I suppose so,' she conceded. It was good enough odds for him and he took the offer of it. 'And have you and Dad been to Ireland then?' he asked her. 'You should be at school,' she told him. '*Have* you?' he persisted. 'No, we haven't.'

He thought about this for a while, watching the rinsing and bending and breathing going on fiercely beside him. But he wasn't quite done yet. He wanted one further point of fact cleared up. 'If you and Dad have never been to Ireland, why do we call ourselves Irish?' She straightened and eased her back, the palm of her hand pressed to her kidneys. 'What else are we going to call ourselves, you ninny?' She flicked suds at him and bent and picked up the basket loaded with rinsed shirts and collars and pushed him out of the wash house, holding out the dripping basket ahead of her and threatening to wet him. 'If we're not Irish, what are we?' She laughed as she went out into the sunlight of the backyard, a shapely young woman still in those days and filled with wonder herself at the curiosity of her eldest. She ached with anxiety to think of him going into the world on his own one day and would have liked to keep him at the age of holding hands and looking up with belief in his innocent eyes asking her his lovely silly questions. Did he suppose they could call themselves English? As she pegged her husband's dripping shirts on the line, Edna Donlon said to the blackbird that was watching her from the overhang of the neighbour's plum tree, 'And isn't he going to be breaking hearts with those sky-blue eyes of his one day?'

He got his bike from the shed and rode down the street to Gibbo's place. There were two things that day he swore to do when he grew up: make the acquaintance of a fair-dinkum full-blood gipsy and see Ireland for himself. Had he been hoping to encounter ancestral affinities with this wish list, even then?

Wondering if meeting a gipsy would be like meeting a long-lost brother? And if being on the soil of Ireland would give him a queer feeling he didn't get from being in the country of his birth? Some expectation of this kind, of encountering a world more real than the one he was in? Beginning to ask, in other words, the grown-up question: who am I really? Where do I belong? The same question wearing different clothes. And what did he think of all that now that he was a grown man of twenty-two? Did it still matter to him?

He ran up the path and took both veranda steps in a stride and snatched open the flywire door. In the kitchen he nipped a corner of Gerner's ten-shilling note with thumb and forefinger and withdrew it from his trouser pocket. He put the precious note on the draining board beside the letter. Blood money. While he was butchering the horse for Oscar Gerner's dogs, his axe aloft, a big idea had come steaming into his mind, like a train arriving at the station, and he the only man alive waiting there for its arrival, a solitary figure on the platform knowing it was his destiny to step on board and take the journey. His train. In that poised instant, before burying the bright steel blade in the poor beast's groin, the flesh still quivering, Pat conceived his bold plan of escape. Audacious it was, and not one of their mates they'd left behind at the Gallery School would have been game to try it on.

The thought of it was making him hot with impatience. He would do it. There was nothing to stop him. He would carry it out. He turned on the tap over the sink and washed the blood off his hands. There was blood on his khaki shirt, too. His mother would have had the shirt off his back and soaking in cold water in the laundry tub by now. He cupped his hands

and leaned and drank, the water chill in his throat. A poet
warrior of the old Icelandic days, he was, Egil Skallagrimsson,
his axe beside him, taking his feud to the king himself, bending
to drink from a sacred spring that had been pouring out of its
magical crevice since before the gods retreated from the face
of the earth, knowing themselves cursed by the death of poetry
among men. Would he learn the ancient Greek and read their
great literature in the original? Was it possible? And French.
To hear Rimbaud as Rimbaud had heard himself. He envied
Edith the fluency of her French. In his mouth the words were
tortured out of shape, chipped, hard and separate, insisting on
being Australian. She made the flow of them all running
together sound as natural as thought. A song she had learned
in her infancy. How could he ever get to that? There was so
much to read. So much to learn. So much catching up to be
done. Surely he had started too late and would never be
convincing on their terms. Hadn't he always known that he
would have to do something else? His *own* thing. Something
they were not already expert at. Something they and their
teachers had never thought of. There was already one thing he
had done the others had not, and which stood him in advance
of their reading. For while they were poring over the novels of
D.H. Lawrence, he had been reading the Icelandic sagas.

Father Brennan had given him them. 'The man who has
not read the sagas remains uneducated in the literatures of his
race.' Which was the way Dan Brennan spoke. Grandly. As if
ordinary life itself were a heroic epic, and there was something
vast and nostalgic and lost to the world that would never be
recovered. A kind of melancholy dream, it was, for Father Dan
Brennan, that he might have shared with the poets themselves,

but never claimed to, out of modesty, a light of secret pleasure in his green eyes, some inner conviction of a greater humanity in it all than the inbred resolutions of the Vatican's official bleating. The only priest Pat's mother had ever had any time for. It's something, she used to say, to thank religion for, an educated priest. Pat still had the volume. If only there were a way of instant reading, holding a book tightly in your hands and closing your eyes and thinking yourself into it. But enough of this! He had to get on. Right at this minute he could have downed a cold beer. He dried his face and hands on the tea towel and tossed it onto the bench and called, 'Are you there, darling?' He picked up the letter and the ten-shilling note and walked down the dark passage and out into the wonderful light of the back room.

'I've got a plan,' he announced. Edith was at her easel but she wasn't working. Standing there troubling herself about something, pale and thoughtful in her white blouse and blue skirt, the light soft where she stood, half her lovely features cast in shadow. So neat and careful in her manner of work there was not a dab of paint anywhere to be seen on her clothes, not even on the wrists of her blouse. He felt himself smiling. His admiration for her was enormous, a rich pleasure and gratification in seeing her standing there that he could not talk about, not even to himself. He wasn't a talker. Or measure. Well, it was bigger than anything he could think of. His gratitude, wasn't it? His envy of himself almost. That this young woman should have chosen to love him. But she had. In another's life, a life that could never have been his own whichever way you looked at it, he would have liked to share with her something of the quality of the love she'd shared with her dead grandfather, the conservative old painter from Scotland. To have known something of that quiet richness between the two of them. He didn't have it. A calmness in it that was not in himself. There was a need for quietness, too, wasn't there? A paradox for him, this desire for quietness of the soul.

His existence was a torment of contradictions. A torrent of ambition and disgust. Tides in him that swirled and drove against each other. Powerful undertows that dragged him out into the deeps and sucked him down to solitary places where there was no bottom to his despair and his longing. The dance force in him was never still. Reeling and swaying to the speeding minutes of his days. It was all beautiful and terrible. He wanted to touch his lips to the soft bloom of her cheek and close his eyes and be gently with her. To still the agitation in his brain. He loved her. He supposed it was love. How are we to know? 'Vows are nothing,' he said to her the night of their marriage as they lay in each other's arms. He had still been feeling irritated by having to mouth those stupid matrimonial promises. The glum sweating oaf in the registry office nodding his big ugly head as if he thought he was getting the better of the two of them. 'It is how we feel, not what we vow,' he said to Edith as they lay in bed naked together that warm summer night, their new home a single room above a tobacconist's shop in Swanston Street.

She had turned to him and touched his cheek with her fingers. 'Feelings change, my darling. It is our vows that are forever.'

In what Edith said there was a contradictory view to his own and his mother's view, and it unsettled him to hear it from her. He was intending to keep quiet and let it pass. Then suddenly he was saying, with more heat and impatience than he'd intended, 'Vows are just an expression of the principles of the church and the state.' His mother would not have wanted him to let such a view go unchallenged. 'It's them getting us to conform to their stupid bloody rules. It's our feelings that are us. We'll make our own rules.' He lay beside her frowning into the silence until Edith leaned over and kissed him and put her hand on him and murmured in his ear, 'I want you again.'

And when the high moment of their passion was reached she cried out with a kind of despair in her voice, the breath catching in her throat, 'I love you, Pat! I love you!' Why was love so painful?

He stood in front of her now holding out the blood-smeared envelope. 'A letter from your mother,' he said. 'Old Gerner gave me ten shillings for doing the horse.' He waved the note at her then folded it and tucked it into the back pocket of his trousers. There was a button on that pocket, which he fastened. Edith reached and took the letter from him. He would have kissed her but she drew back from him. 'You've got something on your forehead,' she said, making a face.

He put his hand up to his forehead. 'It's only blood,' he said, scratching at the dried scab of it. 'I thought I'd got it all.' He stood looking at her picture, his head on one side. 'It's very good. Do you know that?' He put this to her with a certain seriousness, and not in his usual bantering way. 'Your grandpa would have been proud of you.'

She thanked him. His approval was a joy she had not been expecting at this moment, and she saw her picture with a sudden new confidence, as he might be seeing it, through the window of his eyes. And for that brief glimpse her doubts were banished and she too thought her work accomplished. She was grateful. 'Maybe I'm getting somewhere at last. Thank you,' she said again. 'It's nothing like anything you'd do.'

He shrugged and turned away, and walked over to his work table.

She wished she had let him kiss her, but she was not yet sure that she had forgiven him for the horse. Seeing that axe rising and falling she had felt a loss within herself, something more intimate than the loss of a farm animal. A portent. It was him, wasn't it? She did not know what it was, and was not able to attend to it. But it wasn't just the brutal death of the old brood mare. There was always brutality in the butchering of the animals. Something deeper had been signified, something had been touched for which she had no name. Wounded, she might have said. She knew Pat's generous mood was partly due to the ten shillings; but it was lovely all the same, whatever its cause, when he was feeling like this, *meaning* his compliments instead of giving them an edge of derision. And was he shocked himself by the killing of the old beast? Or had he dismissed it from his thoughts already? She didn't know him well enough to be sure. She thought of asking him but decided not to. He was standing there looking down at his work, the sun falling across his features, across his work table. She knew not everyone thought him as beautiful as she did.

She took the two one-pound notes from her mother's letter and put them in the pocket of her skirt. She turned so that the light from the window fell on the letter—the felled horse before her, falling . . . One day she would know what it was. *My very Dearest Girl, Our great news here is that the Reverend Golder Burns (how auspiciously named he is for your father!) has accepted a call to Scots. At last Melbourne is to have its own minister again after these years of uncertainty . . .* Her mother's austerely beautiful hand, every word inscribed as if the perfection of the script would endow it with lasting significance, the familiar broad and narrow strokes, the newness of the nib she had fitted to the holder before beginning. Keeping unused in its box on her desk the expensive fountain pen her husband had presented her with. The stately ritual it was for her mother, the writing of letters to loved ones, the attention, the care, the pleasure, the skill and the thought that went into it. She wrote letters to the members of her family the way her own grandmother had written them, responsible to her highest sense of the task, to her finest sense of her relations with the person she was writing to. Living at home Edith had taken such refinements for granted and had not appreciated how precious they were until she saw that in the life of Pat's home there had never been anything of that sort. Her mother's hand was as familiar to Edith as her own embroidered eiderdown on her childhood bed in the Brighton house, a warm and loving home. Reading her mother's letter, Edith could smell her old home. She could smell her mother.

He stood at his work table looking at his picture. 'Horse's blood,' he said aloud, talking to himself without knowing it. He was gripping the edges of the table with his outspread hands, leaning forward and looking down onto his picture. He might have been a general examining a map of the terrain over which his forces were to engage with those of the enemy. Puzzling after a strategy that would give him the advantage. How to deploy his strengths so that their disposition would leave no opportunity for the enemy to mount a successful defence.

Outrage, that would be their response when he showed this painting. Boot polish and cardboard. His materials alone would provoke them. They would conclude that his intention was to insult them and their standards. It would make them squeal and tremble like little pigs. They would not know which way to turn. They would see his work as an affront to the grand dignity of their sacred calling to teach their students how to draw after the manner of Leonardo. Not for art's sake, of course, but for the coveted travelling scholarship. What else? A recommendation to Sir Malcolm for the annual travelling scholarship. A privilege bestowed upon the Gallery School's anointed. A ticket to freedom from Australian provincialism for which every young artist and writer of Pat's acquaintance would be happy to pawn his soul. For a year or two, at any rate. He was smiling. He would title his picture *Homage à Rimbaud*. Partly to rub it in, but also because that's what this piece of work really was, a homage to the boy poet's visionary response to life. That's what everything was that he did these days. They would be affronted by the sight of it. His offensive against their conformity. The banality of their souls. His repudiation of them and their academy of ideas. They would snort and ask each other, Who the devil does he think he is, giving his bloody nonsense a French title? He lifted the painting from the table and set it with its face to the wall. An instinct in him revolted against submitting himself to their approval. He would find another way. His own way. And now he had a plan. To become one of their anointed, you had first to be on your knees to them. Well, he would never go to his knees for anyone. It would be they on their knees before he was done with them.

He picked up the roll of butcher's paper and undid the string. He laid the sheets flat on the table, their cheesy pallor and faint odour of raw meat reminding him of his mother's kitchen when she unpacked the shopping and he looked to see what she'd got for their dinner. He stood smoothing the sheets with the palms of his hands, feeling the slight undulations of the table top through them, the way a blind man might know his own work table by the intimacy of touch. Imagining himself to be the blind seer. That's what he was. Being the *voyant* of Rimbaud's youthful intoxications. Alone. Accountable to no one. Inside the fortress of himself. Where he would not be called upon to make common sense of his work. He was remembering riding down the Hume Highway on his bicycle when he was nineteen. Alone with the wind and the hum of his tyres. Sleeping by the roadside at night. It seemed to him now that he had ridden his bicycle the thousand miles to Sydney and back in a dream. His eyes closed. Seeing some other world. A beautiful solitary journey, it had been. And wasn't he that same man today? To be alone dreaming his dreams. He had forgotten Edith.

He was drawing quickly on the sheets of butcher's paper. Freely wielding the narrow brush. He loaded the brush from the bowl of rich black ink, carelessly flicking spots and drips of ink about the place. Flicking some of it on purpose. On himself. To join the spots of blood. Scattering his seed. A warrior. Perhaps it was naked figures he was drawing. Something like that. It was too early to know what he was doing. He didn't want to know. Wild sweeping lines of disrupted ink that had begun to suggest the outlines of human forms. Limbs and torsos confusingly disproportionate and summary. Perhaps tussling and in some kind of movement against each other. He couldn't draw for nuts. He worked quickly, without hesitation. He could feel it in his balls. The drawing. Tight and hard and thick with intention. An aggression in him. Without stepping back to consider what he did. Without correcting his line. On the battleground of his own choosing. Making it.

As he covered each sheet he slid it off the table to the floor and started on the next, not bothering about smearing the wet image of the discarded sheet. Did he think he could force a result? Did he imagine he could coerce the ink and the paper into revealing true art to his eye without troubling himself to search for some sort of order in what he did? Without taking care? Without paying his dues to the craft, like everyone else had to? Yes, he did. He was convinced of it. Fuck them and their painstaking fucking everlasting fucking drawing classes. Once that was established in your eye you would never rid yourself of it. You would belong to them and to their tradition for the rest of your days. Like the copperplate trap, he wasn't falling into this one either. Trying to be like Leonardo! Bloody fools.

Edith gave an excited yelp and held up her mother's letter. 'Guess what? Hilary Trafford at the *Argus* has invited me to submit some of my illustrations to her.' She was looking at Pat working at his table, his figure moving against the light from the north-facing window. A slim man, his shoulders almost as narrow as a woman's, and not tall, but perfectly made, his aura illuminated *contre jour*. How well Mr Sickert would have rendered him. She stepped across to him and shook the letter at him. 'Did you hear what I said, darling? Money!' Her voice had taken on something of the command of her mother's voice whenever her mother wished not only to be heard but to be listened to by the men of her household. 'Ten shillings for every illustration she takes. We'll have some money of our own.'

'You sound like your mother,' he said, not pausing in the work. 'I've got a better idea.' Sheet after sheet. Nothing to stop him. Travelling his wild ink trail. On the train. It was, he often observed to himself with a pleasurable detachment, as if some weirdo inside him believed the application of a consuming impatience to create would force paper and ink to yield their astonishing perfections to him. A weirdo. Yes. Himself. His other self. He wasn't going to ask him to stop or to slow up. Without the liberty of untutored energy that weirdo's life would not be worth living. Without his liberty, Pat knew he would drown in the sorrows of self-loathing. He had not been offered a choice. It had been born in him. To lay it down would be to lay himself down. Life was good only so long as the genie had his freedom. He had no idea what he could expect from his genie. And that was the way he wanted it to be. In the dark with the fear till the new light struck him. No guarantees. No commercial opportunities sidelining him.

Edith was shouting at him that he was being unbending and too filled with pride for his own good. 'There's a limit!' she shouted again, her voice rising, leaning to look into his face. 'We need the money!'

No doubt she was right and there was a limit. And wasn't he intent on finding that limit? And then going beyond it? Wasn't he already beyond it? Wasn't that just what he was doing? Liberating himself from her limits. Not just being unbending. Unbending wasn't it at all. Wasn't he repudiating the confines of a dead tradition by the shortest cut? He had not reasoned his way out of it. He chanted Rimbaud loudly over the sound of her angry voice. '*Where are we going? To battle? I am weak! The others advance. Tools, weapons . . . time! . . . Fire! Fire on me! Here! Or I surrender.—Cowards!—I'll kill myself! I'll throw myself . . .*' He couldn't remember the next line. But if Rimbaud could do it, then so could he. They were both men. Both human beings. Both young. So why not? Who was to stop him? He had the energy.

At the edge of his vision he was aware of Edith leaving the studio. The gentle loving part of him wanting to catch up with her and give her a cuddle and be nice to her and make things fine and glorious between them. But the weirdo wasn't having any of that. The berserker Egil Skallagrimsson swept his brush across the large sheet of paper in which meat was supposed to have been wrapped by Mr Creedy, or by his assistant, his big dark-complexioned daughter with the eyes of black glass. Jet, wasn't it, that he was thinking of? The black jewel of women's mourning. So was it *her* figure he was after here? The rounding of her ample thighs and arms, her weighty breasts? And here she was, found for a line, then lost again. A figure in the torment of lust. Elusive and not to be invoked by artifice or technique. She had smiled a smile of womanly welcome at him with those jet-black eyes of hers when he went into the shop. He had asked if she could please let him have some of her paper. Without a word, as if she had been expecting his request for years, as if it was her destiny to know his need, she turned her back and rolled up this generous bundle, her eyes catching at his in the mirror with the arch conspiracy of it, dimples in her elbows as well as in her cheeks, lifting her bare arm and tying the roll of paper with the twine her father used to tie the rolled roasts with, snapping it with an expert jerk of her chubby wrist, then turning back from the mirror and presenting him with the paper, her understanding of what she did swimming in the generous Gulf Stream of her gaze, her offering to the artist for the work he was to undertake. And would there be something else the artist might be wanting from her? Body and soul would it be that he wanted from her? Is that all then?

He had tied the paper on the back of his bike and ridden home with his booty. And as he rode he daydreamed that big motherly girl waiting in her father's shop all her life to render this service to him when he came by, knowing through some primitive instinct in the welcoming warmth of her bowels that he, the warrior artist and poet, would surely be coming one day, her destiny to become his accomplice. It was a nice little daydream that he played with as he pedalled hard up the hill, the chain creaking, the tyres spitting stones. He had no idea then what he would do with the daydream, but here it was. She was a fitting mistress for a warrior poet . . . Black ink staining the paper now instead of the carmine blood of the slaughtered sheep and cattle and the screaming pigs. She was his satanic apprentice. He didn't know her name. He would not ask it of her next time he went into the shop. He might have called her his muse for this enterprise, but muse was a notion he had rejected along with all the other old nonsense from the Gallery School masters. Satanic apprentice had more energy in it. More possibility. More concealment and uncertainty. More brutality. What, after all, did he mean by it? He knew, and he didn't know. He didn't want to know. He was not after understanding. He just wanted to enjoy the feel of it on him. In his sweat. In his balls. That was the way he liked it. Fuck their understandings. Perhaps over time the richness of its meanings would unfold to him: his satanic mistress. He liked the sound of it, carrying her generous body with it. That was enough. The glow of possibility in her black eyes. It was a story. A poem. Her plump fingers gripping his cock. That would do. Who gave a fuck what it meant? It was private. It didn't have to have a meaning. It was just for himself. It was a story that hadn't been told yet. They wouldn't be hearing about it. His own private truth in it. They wouldn't be getting the chance to tell him it wasn't any good and would have to be improved. He was done with them. They'd hear from him when he was ready for them to hear from him.

He had forgotten for a minute or two why he was doing this. His idea for getting away overseas. That was it. A folio of drawings of the butcher's daughter, then, to impress the great man. It was a liberating discovery to know whose body it was he was drawing. A confirmation to know who the subject of all this was. The particularity of it giving the enterprise a new force of its own, as if it was coming from outside himself. From some authentic and mysterious source. The weirdo in touch with the ocean of the unconscious. Was that it? He had been sure he was drawing someone or other and was very glad to discover it was her. The big girl in the butcher's shop. The need for such generous volumes of flesh was beginning to make sense to him. He would never have thought of it himself. She couldn't have been much more than seventeen and already had a young child of her own. Her maternally noble manner, that she was surely not aware of. Just as statues are not aware of the thoughts they kindle in poets who stand and gaze at them in the moonlight. A young woman conceived by the generous hands of the sculptor Aristide Maillol, and not simply the splendid daughter of Mr Creedy, the Ocean Grove butcher. A treasure waiting here for him. And him not knowing it till he had the idea of going in and asking for some paper. Our triumph must be our own secret. Triumph belongs to the interior life of the artist, not out in the street. Such things wither when exposed to the sceptical gaze of social realities. So it was for himself. All this, it was just for himself.

•

Later, after he had sobered up a bit and he and Edith had made up, he told her his plan. When they had eaten their sardines on toast and Edith had gone to sleep, murmuring an apology to him for a last fishy burp (she had complained during their lovemaking about the distraction of the rats in the ceiling cantering back and forth above their heads. He told her the rats were having a polo match up there and made her laugh), he got up and went out to the studio and sat at his work table, the Tilley lamp humming to itself beside him, casting its trembling light against the walls. He bent and picked up the last sheet of butcher's paper from the strewn collection of drawings on the floor, and underneath the generous buttocks of the butcher's daughter he wrote the poem of his day:

> The Chinese masters of the brush
> Wrote their poems with the blood of horses.
> To dwell secretly in the solitude
> Of my convictions,
> What a state! What an achievement!

To know there the triumph
Of the old Wen-jen masters
In the final flourish of my brush,
My triumph secret, my brush loaded
With the blood of horses.

He didn't read his poem but pushed it to one side and sat looking at nothing, dreaming of his audacious plan for the next day, the first day of the battle, the day his forces would engage in a frontal assault on the headquarters of the enemy. They would not be prepared for him. He was sure of that. He was wondrously tired and elated, a surge of oxygen in his blood and his brain—it was a state of meditative lust that required no immediate action from him. If he'd had a cigarette and a bottle of beer now he would have been in everyman's heaven.

4

March 1991

THAT'S WHERE I LEFT HIM, SITTING THERE SURROUNDED BY HIS drawings of the butcher's voluptuous daughter. It was Arthur's generosity that brought Pat Donlon into our lives the following day. Arthur's innocent announcement to me over the telephone from his office that evening that he was bringing someone home for a meal. 'I think he might interest you.'

I've been ill. I collapsed. I shan't bore you with it. It's more than two months since I've had the energy or the courage to come near this. Writing their portraits exhausted me. I had no idea it would be such an ordeal, all that recollecting and imagining. *He* exhausted me. He drew me into himself again. I developed a terrible headache writing him. I was nearly blinded by the time I put the last word to him: *heaven*. Writing him brought him back. I sat here night after night at the kitchen table, writing him and cursing him and weeping for him and for myself. He was *in* me again. It was the heaven and hell of *us* all over. He and I. I hadn't expected it, this terrible reanimation of memory. He drained me and I wonder if I'm going to have the strength to finish it. Writing her was so without conflict for me that I was off my guard when I began to work on him. But I soon discovered that dealing with my regrets had been a breeze compared to the exquisite agony of recalling the love and torment of my tortured life. While I wrote him Pat was with me day and night. I could get no rest from him. The truth, terrifying when you consider it, is that nothing is so forgotten it cannot be brought back to haunt us. In the deeps of memory it seems our past is never put to rest but lives on, preserved and catalogued according to a system unknown to us, every detail retrievable at an unbidden signal, ready to remind us that the comfortable autonomy of our consciousness is nothing but an ignorant illusion.

The night after I began writing Pat's portrait I was sitting on the toilet when I found myself suddenly remembering Anne Collins' telephone call. There she was with her coolly dignified tones—a delay in those days all the way from England, how many years ago is it?—telling me he had died the previous night with my name on his lips. He and I had been estranged for years at the time of his death. I was transported at once from the toilet seat and returned to that moment when I had stood in the bedroom here at Old Farm with the telephone in my hand, my gardening gloves held in my other hand, the French doors open to the lovely spring day and to my beloved garden, the smell of lemon blossom in the air, Anne Collins' voice in my ear. A bee had come in with me and while I listened to Anne I watched it probe in turn each of the blue and citron blooms of an arrangement of fragrant Cupani sweet pea that I had placed on my dressing-table earlier in the day. It was all there, perfectly preserved for this moment, each bloom of that flower arrangement, the individual items on my dressing-table, the lemon-scented air. In the retrieved memory each detail was charged with meaning. I sat on the toilet, my knickers round my ankles, transported, sobbing to see once again that honeybee at its eternal labour. I had not known there was so much memory and so much weeping left in me. What have I done to open this door? Will I yet regret the day I dared look into the black doorway of my past? Pass through that door and re-enter those times.

While I was writing him I ate buckets of codeine tablets but they scarcely touched my headache. It was more than a headache. After I put the last word to him I woke up under the table with Sherry lying on my face purring, my notebooks scattered around me. I was frozen to the bone. It was a Sunday. I managed to crawl to my bed, howling and moaning, then I rang Andrew.

Andrew, dear foolish man, came around at once and had a look at me. 'You're exhausted,' he said, confidently making his diagnosis and arranging himself on the edge of my bed, settling himself into his bedside manner. Being professional. His breath smelling of wine. I'd probably dragged him away from his dinner. He was trying to ignore the stench in this place. 'You must be more careful,' he said, drawing breath slowly as if he inhaled a deadly gas. Andrew is a boy. He's forty but he's a boy. It hasn't occurred to him yet that one day soon he's going to be eighty. Yes, soon.

He asked me what I'd been doing to get myself into such a state. Debilitated was his word for me. I obediently lifted my nightie for him and told him I'd been writing my memoir.

That's what I called it. A mild enough term for the scourging whip of memory. He raised a tawny eyebrow and repeated the word, 'Memoir.' Surprised, no doubt, to discover that memoir writing could be so ravaging. 'You've had an unusual life,' he said, leaning over me and tapping my ribs with the hard point of his index finger, so that a faint booming could be heard, as if I have an ocean cavern inside me. 'I'm sure everyone will be interested to read about you and your famous circle of friends.' That's how he put it. He advised me gravely to get someone in to help with it. Someone to whom I could dictate my thoughts and who would then go off and type them up and bring them back for me to check over. He has no idea. In Andrew's world there is a practical solution for every problem. But are there practical solutions for the torments of the soul? What a laugh. I laughed. 'An amanuensis, you mean?' I said. But he didn't know the word for what he was prescribing. I said, 'Is that the way you prescribe drugs too?'

He had no idea what I was talking about. He was listening to the wheezing of my lungs filling and emptying, not my voice. That cold thing shoved up my nightie, his hand on my bony shoulder. He is gentle and kind. I am an old woman and do not belong in the realities of Andrew's world, nor he in mine. We do not communicate directly with each other but perform a kind of verbal ritual of appeasement. Old people are not young people grown old but are another species. We are transformed as pupae metamorphose into the imago, unrecognisable from our former state. I was reborn into old age, physically unrecognisable from my youthful self, supplied with another skin and another set of intentions than those I possessed when I was young. God knew what he was doing when he invented death for us. Andrew has three young girls, all under ten years of age. Why should he listen to me? I don't expect him to. I am past being listened to by young men. I had my full share of being listened to. All I wanted from him was some strong painkillers. And a kilo or two of infallible sleep inducers. Bombs for my tormented head. Memory killers for the long nights I would have to endure.

After Andrew had been to see me, except to do my business and to give Sheridan his daily scoop of dry food, I didn't get out of my bed for a week. I survived without nutriment. A sip of water in the night. A solitary creature in the stench of its own den. That was me. Debilitated, alone and barely breathing. Terrified the nightmare of memory would find me in my vulnerable condition and return to torment me. You might have heard a cough if you had passed by. I never thought for a moment I was going to die. I knew by then that my death wasn't going to be that easy. My mother telephoned me six weeks before she died. We had not spoken for years. She addressed me as if she and I were close, and had been used to sharing our most intimate anxieties with each other, though of course this had never been the case.

'I've had an offer of death, darling,' she told me. I replied, 'It's probably the best offer you're going to get at your age, Mother.' She was then the age I am now. She did not respond to my lack of generosity. Perhaps she did not register it. 'Three angels dressed in long white gowns came for me,' she said. It was hardly original. 'One stood either side of me and took me by my hands, which I stretched out to them willingly. The other stood behind me and told me in the softest voice that I could fall back into her arms and I would be safe forever.

I almost let myself begin to float away with them, a blissful calm entering my soul like the effect of anaesthetic.'

There was a long silence and I realised how deeply serious my mother was. How moved she had been by her night vision, and how she had known I was the only member of the family to whom she could confide such a thing without being scoffed at. 'Then what happened?' I asked. I was interested to know. 'You are still here. What did you do?' I heard her breathing. She said, 'I resisted.' Her voice was small and filled with guilty regret, like the voice of a little girl who has done something that will displease her elders. 'Do you think I should have gone with them, darling?' she asked me timidly. I said, 'Yes, Mother, I think you probably should have.' She died slowly, suffering a terrifying six-week decline into blindness and insanity, before the angels had the grace to come for her again. I have the means to take my own life, but will I have the presence of mind to judge the moment? I fear a death such as my mother suffered.

Andrew sent a local nurse to care for me. I loathed having her in the house. She made herself cups of coffee and talked. Even on her first day she began to bully me. 'There's a funny smell in here,' she said, looking about the kitchen that morning, raising her snout and sniffing the air.

'I fart a lot,' I said.

She seemed to take my confession as a licence to tell me about her private life. She stood with her back to the stove, clutching her mug of Nescafé in both hands and gazing wide-eyed at nothing. She had brought the Nescafé herself. 'I've been obsessed with orgasms since I was eleven,' she said. 'I don't muck about. I'm not coy. When a bloke comes in I get all my gear off at once and we get on with it. There's no need to be coy about sex.'

'But surely,' I said, 'there is every need to be coy about sex.'

She stepped across to where I was sitting at the table and tugged roughly at the collar of my dressing-gown. 'It was tucked in at the back,' she said severely, reprimanding me, as if this was what she had been hired to do.

I informed her haughtily, 'The eyes are the organs of seduction.'

'Not any more, love.'

Could this be true? I looked at her. She was short and rounded and very pale and, in defiance of the traditions of nursing, was dressed entirely in black. 'But doesn't a big naked white body standing in front of them put your men off?'

'That smell's really quite awful,' she said. 'What do you eat to make your farts smell so bad?'

'Cabbages,' I said.

When I told her to leave she said Andrew had warned her that I would make difficulties and had told her not to take any nonsense from me. She stood over me to tell me this, her fat hands on her hips, her big round arms sticking out like elephant ears, her massive breasts fit to suffocate any bairn that got within sniffing distance of them. I wasn't used to being bullied, but I knew she knew I was too weak to resist her. I'm sorry to say I quailed rather and didn't try. My fear of her demoralised me and I began to think I would have a relapse and sink helplessly towards my mother's death while this lump glowered over me.

A week later I was sitting dejectedly at the round table out on the veranda, where I had been ordered to stay, a mug of cold Nescafé and a dirty saucer of dry toast in front of me (I had been forbidden cabbage), when a movement in the garden caught my eye. I looked up to see the bollard stepping daintily towards me across the dewy grass in her red patent-leather shoes. With a leap of the heart I knew the bollard would be a match for my orgasmic attendant.

She stepped up onto the veranda. 'Mrs Laing!' she said, joy in her eyes. 'It's me! I'm back!'

'Yes,' I said. 'So I see. And I am very glad to see you, Adeli'—her real name, and only an American could possess such a name, is Adeli Heartstone. I had wondered if it mightn't be a corruption of the warmer hearthstone, but I shall never know. I said to her (all at once no longer despised but now to be my anchoring bollard), 'Will you please go into the kitchen and tell the woman there to get out of my house?'

Adeli did not wait to take off her overcoat or to put down her things. Those two might have been sisters. I expected a fierce cat fight to erupt in the kitchen, but Adeli returned a minute or two later and laid her notebook and a small package on the table. She stood behind a chair and looked at me and smiled. 'It's chilly out here. Would you like me to help you into the kitchen, Mrs Laing?'

'Well?' I enquired sharply. 'Did you tell her to leave or not? What did she say?'

Adeli smiled a calm smile. 'She's gone. She won't be back.'

'What did you say to her?'

'I told her I was your daughter and that I would be looking after you from now on.' She looked down at me, her smile one of knowing celebration.

'I don't have a daughter,' I said.

'A long-lost daughter who has at last returned from America.' She laughed, a careful laugh, testing the firmness of the newly won ground upon which she stood. Not braying. She would bray later.

I looked at her. 'And that brute believed you?'

'Well, it might be true.'

'I never had a daughter. I never had a child of any kind.'

'Oh yes, I know that. But you might have.' She looked me in the eye, serious, setting forth on her journey. 'And I might have been that child.'

'Choose one of his drawings for yourself,' I said, struggling to get up, my legs stiff with the cold. 'If you can find one among the mess in the dining room. And give me a hand up.'

She took both my hands and helped me stand. 'I'll make us a hot chocolate,' she said, steadying me against her. Her overcoat, or perhaps it was her blouse, had been liberally doused with Chanel No 5. I would know that scent anywhere. It always makes me sneeze.

'I don't like hot chocolate,' I said. I was not about to hand myself from one bully to another.

'You'll like this one, Mrs Laing. It's special. A treat.' She held the flywire door for me.

I turned to her. 'That woman claimed to have six orgasms a day.'

She followed me into the kitchen and I sat at the table. I was enormously relieved to be rid of the orgasmic blob. Adeli took her coat off and measured milk into Arthur's copper pan. She paused with the milk carton half tipped and looked around at me. 'Not *every* day, surely?'

'Yes,' I said. 'I think every day.'

'Did you witness any proof?'

'Like a demonstration, you mean?'

We both laughed.

And that is how I acquired Adeli. Andrew having his way after all. Adeli wept tears of sincere sorrow when I told her I had burned my diaries and day books.

•

When Arthur called me from his office in the city that fateful day a lifetime ago to tell me he would be bringing someone home for dinner, I was in the garden here at Old Farm planting roses with Barnaby. My existence, if not innocent in those days, was blissful. I was ignorant of the storm approaching us from the Great Southern Ocean. Arthur was at his rooms in Collins Street, poor man. Still ravelled up in his mother's love knots. Slave knots, I called them. Her dream that her son would be a High Court judge before she died making his days miserable. I was no match for that woman's clutches and never loosened her hold on him. Death did that for me. She was one of the few women whose will defeated mine with a man when I was in my prime. It was not until her death that he mobilised the courage to abandon the law. Mothers have the womb of advantage over us with their sons.

I was ten years older than Pat. And taller. By a good inch. When I was at my full height. Which is not now, is it? We shrink. When I was wearing heels, passing shop windows on his arm I looked half a head taller than he. But Arthur was the seriously tall one. Two and a half inches taller than me. Beside Arthur, Pat was a shrimp. Arthur had stooped since third form at Scotch, at which time he shot up and was abashed by his alien body. A lost boy in the wretched body of a man. An expression for a youth that: shot up. That was Arthur Laing when I met him. Estranged from his father and from himself, a young man longing for invisibility. He held his stoop to the end of his life. It suited him when he was older. It made him look what we used to call distinguished. This can't be said of anyone now, with everyone wearing T-shirts and those terrible baggy shorts. No one looks distinguished any more. Or wishes to. We have become a nation of the undistinguished and indistinguishable. Which are not the same thing. Though no doubt they soon will be.

It's raining and cold. I've been writing here at the table in the kitchen. The Rayburn is going. I've managed to get the oven needle around to hot. A real woman would be making scones. Adeli is not here. I wonder if she will make scones if I ask her nicely? I love the smell of the Rayburn, hot iron and a fragrant haze of red-gum smoke in the kitchen. It reminds me of my pre-cabbage days when this house was filled with people and the aromas of my wonderful cooking. Yes, I was known to be a fine cook.

I miss cigarettes on indoor days like this. Sheridan is pretending to be asleep in his basket beside the wood box, one eye half open in case a mouse decides it's safe to skip across the floor. Sheridan is a long-haired ginger tom and is no longer quick enough for mice, but he likes to count them. Stony came earlier with a load of wood. Felled and split green two seasons ago with his grandfather's axe. I don't know where he goes to get his wood but I do know Stony does not believe in chainsaws. He is a refugee from the past. He might almost be a liberated serf from the forests of Yasnaya Polyana. He's Bulgarian, however, not Russian, from Chirpan, now a desolate Bulgarian town littered, I've been told, with abandoned Soviet factories. Stony is not his real name. We called him Stony because when we first knew him he rode a four-wheel bike designed and built by an eccentric English friend of his whose real name *was* Stony. A man from Norwich. A failed artist. That real Stony is dead. The bike had a trailer. Our (my) Stony's real name is Zahary Deliradev. A beautiful name that's wasted here as no one in Australia can be bothered to pronounce it. He lives alone and has little need of speech. He is a man without language. Arthur used to call him our silent witness. And maybe that is what he was, and still is. When he came round with the wood this morning I said, 'Good morning, Stony. Can you manage that on your own?' He grunted and got on with unloading his truck—a green Bedford from the fifties. His clothes smell of wood resins and earth mould and herbs that have been crushed against him. He is a true peasant. His perfect solitude in the midst of this teeming suburb is immensely impressive. To see him lifts my morale; so calm, so silent among the frenzy, independent, confident and alone in his old ways, he asks for no further authentication. As I watched him straining with a great armload of split red gum this morning I asked myself, Which of us two will go first?

After Adeli turfed out the so-called nurse it rained heavily for several days (it's raining now). I woke in the night to the rushing sound of the river breaking over the rock barrier. I got up and went out onto the back veranda. I love the sound of the river in spate and had not heard it for years. After a few minutes I realised I could smell the fragrance of the drenched ground cover in the remnant of bushland they have left to us on the far bank, cut through now by their elaborate bicycle track. Except for the occasional car swishing by on wet tyres the freeway was in its silent hour. The usual stench of diesel and petrol fumes dispersed, the old smells of this place risen again to greet me.

In the clarity of the night I breathed once again the innocent air of our youthful days here and was moved to give thanks. But to whom was I to direct my gratitude? I need hardly tell you this: I wept. That brief moment alone in the night with our dear old smells deserved a good cry, with lots of snuffling and hiccupping and sucking air and blowing my nose several times on the hem of my nightdress, remembering my darling Arthur holding me tightly against our vanishing years. That wretched dog next door must have heard my weeping and began to bark. Why must they all keep a dog? As if they are going to be called on to become nomads. We had cats. Cats make a home. Sheridan is the last of that tribe. He did not come out onto the veranda with me but stayed in his basket beside the stove.

My resolve to continue with this returned that night. When I came inside I fetched my abandoned exercise book and read through what I had written up to the point where I left Pat that evening, surrounded by his crude drawings of Mr Creedy's naked daughter. Those sheets of butcher's paper must still be stored somewhere about this place. But where? Some of them were destroyed. I was with him when Pat destroyed them. Others were stolen, filched by scavengers when he became famous. Others lost. I rescued some from Freddy one wintry afternoon. He was very drunk and was trying to light the fire in the library with them. But there were a lot of them and some of them must still be here. I should like to find the one he wrote the poem on. The last one. There is decades of stuff here. It's everywhere. I went into the dining room and switched on the light. The enormous mahogany table is piled with papers to a depth of more than two feet, the space underneath crammed with cartons of stuff. The mice have probably built their citadel in there. I couldn't bear to touch it and switched the light off and closed the door on it. I shall leave it to Adeli to tackle. It will be compensation for her loss of my diaries.

Before I get to Pat and the day he and I first met I should tell you that I haven't seen Edith again. I've watched for her. Adeli drove me down the street in her pale blue Toyota and waited, watching me through the windscreen while I sat outside Woolworths and watched for Edith. But like snakes, we never see people when we are alert for their presence. It's only when we cease to look for them that they're suddenly there in our path, their gaze on us, giving us a start—reminding us that we are helpless in the face of our fate. We will either meet a certain person or we will miss them by half an hour, or by minutes. Wasn't that the fate of Burke and Wills, to miss their rescue party by half an hour after months of struggling towards a rendezvous with them? This is all I mean by fate: the critical moment. The kind of seemingly random event that determines life and death and which remains in the collective mind of the nation forever after. The plane one was late for which crashed, all passengers and crew killed. That kind of thing. The fate of Burke and Wills. We all know what that is. Their tragedy. Which would have been a triumph if they'd arrived at the rendezvous half an hour earlier.

I should tell you, or you will never know it, this is all being handwritten by me at the kitchen table. The sun comes in here during the afternoons in autumn. It's a lovely room. Homely. It's where we all gathered and is much nicer than the dining room, which is gloomy and damp and smells of mice even more strongly than it smells of cabbages in here. Nothing good ever happened in the dining room. In the library, yes; lots of good things and lots of difficult things happened in the library. The library at Old Farm is a room of the sublime and the tragic. The library was for winter evenings and was the place where a few of us, three or four, sat and squatted around the open fire. I loved and feared library evenings. I seldom go in there these days. The library witnessed my hysterical outbursts more often even than our bedroom. The library, unlike the dining room, was a room in which we found our reality. There was no escape in the library.

I'm writing in school exercise books that Stony brings me when he brings the wood for the Rayburn. They are second-hand, kids' names and form numbers on them, most of the pages unused. He gets them from a school bin for recyclables. I write with a pen. A fine felt-tip. And no rewriting. You're getting this just as it comes out, like toothpaste from the tube. I'm with Christina Stead on this. Rewriting is erasure. Like repainting. The thing gets muddy. Pat never repainted. He never refined a line. All Pat's works are first drafts. Paintings, drawings (as you already know) and poems. Painting is simple, he said. The painter is simple. There was never any reconsideration with him. If it wasn't right the first time it was never going to be right. He wasn't striving like the rest of them to get to something fine and finished. He wasn't striving at all. Striving was not what Pat did. It was what everyone else did, including Edith. Pat was heeding his imagination without questioning the direction it offered him, following the prompts. That was his god. His line untutored. He loved that. And when I say he dashed things off I am not disparaging what he was doing. That is how he worked: dashing things off, to catch the fierce and true while it shone for him. To hold it on the page or on the piece of cardboard, or the square of masonite (his preferred backing after Sofia Station). Pat Donlon wasn't Alberto Giacometti, throttled by the need for the perfectly realised image. Constipated to the point of being unable to cross the road unless he could step on the same cracks he stepped on last time he crossed the road (or was it to avoid stepping on them?).

I introduced Pat to the work of Christina Stead by telling him she too never reworked her stuff. He loved that. He read her three books. Reread them avidly (*rereading* was permitted) until he was familiar with them, like someone who listens to Bach's Preludes and Fugues time and again because they hear in the music's deceptive simplicities everything they need to hear. For a while Pat neglected his beloved Rimbaud for Stead. He was even thinking at one time of doing a series from *The Man Who Loved Children*, but he never did. That's how Pat lived his life. If it shone for him he took it. And when it no longer shone for him he did not try to repair it or to develop it or to shine it up again but abandoned it and never looked back at it. Not till the very end. Then he made the mistake of looking back, just once. It was the same with his friendships and his lovers. When they ceased to shine for him they were discarded. Pat never nurtured anyone and he didn't expect nurture from anyone. Sentiments that were formed into a harsh poetry in which sentiment had no place. He made great art and strewed suffering and disillusion in his wake. In this he was like his heroes of the sagas. Cruel. There were those who never recovered from their encounter with him. And those who never understood him. And perhaps my deepest and most hidden motive in writing this is not to deal with my guilt about the wrong I did to Edith but to discover if I am one of the ones who never recovered from him. The permanently damaged. Am I?

Pat always said that the stuff we erase with our rewriting and repainting is more revealing of our truth than the stuff we overlay it with, our second and third thoughts. Our unconscious motive in rewriting and repainting, he claimed, is always to conceal ourselves. The unbidden truth that stares at us, ugly and blemished. So we erase and rework in the name of art, in the name of refinement and perfection. And we do this not to reveal the reality of the thing, but to distract ourselves from the problems of depicting its reality. Art is the expert lie, he said. It was one of Pat's favourite provocations at the table. He wasn't much of a talker but whenever the conversation began to bore him he would come out with something like that. Art distracts us from reality. That's what he said. People thought he was being provocative, but he meant it. He believed it.

From the moment I opened the first of these exercise books, here at the kitchen table, and put my fine black pen to paper and wrote *This is where it began fifty-three years ago*, I promised myself I would write those very things I felt most strongly prompted to leave out. Erase nothing, I said to myself. Dear

God in Heaven, let Edith live! Let me see her once again and look into her eyes and know she lives. Let me keep the illusion of my purpose. This is not my prayer. It is the prayer my mother would have said had she been in my position. Dear God in Heaven; this invocation so often prefacing her statements is on my lips now.

•

Pat made his way to my darling Arthur by a roundabout route the day after the horse slaughtering. It was only by chance that Arthur was still in his office and had not already set off for the station by the time Pat called on him. Usually he was out of there as soon as he could decently manage it. So their meeting, the meeting that changed all our lives, was the opposite of Burke and Wills missing their rendezvous with the support party. The amazing chance of it all. So I shall attempt to follow Pat's tracks that day from the cottage at Ocean Grove to Arthur's office in Collins Street. Only one thing, one small decision, one trivial incident, need have been a little different during those hours and we would not have met. Whither then our fates?

The meeting between the two men in my life to whom my soul will remain in thrall to my last breath—there can be no more important moment for me. I dread to approach it. But I need to approach it more than I need do anything else in this remnant of living that is left to me.

Sometimes I pray despite myself. Pray even though I don't believe in Him. To whom, then, do I address my prayers?

Your Honour, I ask no more than to find the courage to tell his story and mine truthfully and in my own words. For this, imagination will be required. It is not fiction and truth that oppose each other. Fiction is the landscape beyond reality and has its own truth, the truth of our intimate lives. The place of empathy.

5

Edith's announcement

PAT WAS STANDING AT THE KITCHEN WINDOW FOR THE LIGHT. HE was holding up Edith's silver-mounted hand mirror, tilting his chin to examine himself. The glitter of his unshaved jaw in the chilly morning. His pale eyes looking down his nose at himself, a touch of dismay in his expression. It's true, he was thinking, I'm not a serious-looking person. That other man inside him was rehearsing those insecurities of his that never left him free of doubt about the outcome of any project he set himself, hearing the doom of his dreams always in the voices of the bosses, hating himself for hating them for being born to what they were. The thought of appealing to one of Edith's mob for help was oppressing him. The anxiety he had of them since his childhood, and from which he never liberated himself as a grown man. But who frees himself from childhood's pains and dilemmas?

Regarding himself that morning in Edith's lovely little hand mirror, Pat was theatricalising the scene, Sir Malcolm's reception of him later that day, an imaginary conversation that went something along the following lines:

SECRETARY: There's a little Irish larrikin out here insisting on seeing you, sir.

SIR MALCOLM: Is that how you would describe him?

SECRETARY: He says he's an artist.

SIR MALCOLM: A bullshit artist, is it?

SECRETARY: More than likely, sir. He says he's been recommended to you by the director of the Gallery School.

SIR MALCOLM: Bernie Threshold? I'll be damned.

SECRETARY: So he says.

SIR MALCOLM: Well, you'd better send him in then. We can't go upsetting one of Bernie's little angels, can we?

Pat fingered his bristles and turned to look out the window, something catching his eye. It was the first of the sun lighting the highest point of Gerner's hill, an emerald gold where he'd spilled the guts of that poor old nag yesterday. There was every reason to be anxious. Getting to where the money was had always been the hardest thing for the Donlons. The most unnatural thing, he might more truly say. He and his mum and dad and the uncles and aunts. So far he'd stayed honest, and what good had it done him? The best-paying job he'd ever had was serving pies and sausage rolls to the late-night drunks at Bill Tetley's stall in Swanston Street. Keeping himself in tucker and saving the best hours of his days for painting and writing. He had seen men get so confused by the need for money they had robbed their mates. And in David O'Grady's case, his own mother. Poor bastard. There had been no need to step under a train because of the shame of that. A terrible mistake. David O'Grady. He had not been a bad man in himself. Not in his heart. Dreadful scenes of destitution and violent events along the way of keeping yourself sane and on some kind of track that would get you somewhere. He had gone to school with Dave. It had not been easy avoiding the traps. And then not bending your knee to the bastards.

'You don't *get* money,' his dad tearfully told his solemnly assembled family that Saturday afternoon after he'd done his wages on a certainty at the Caulfield track. 'You have to already have it.' And he was right. The way of the world, they called it. It was the kind of family gathering that stuck in your memory, that one. But his mother wasn't crying. Your thoughts take you back to those memories every time you're faced with a crisis to do with not having any money. And wasn't there a kind of fatalism in what his dad said that had an irresistible throb of the truth in it for them? Hadn't the Donlons always repelled money? Wasn't that the plain fact of what his dad meant? Wasn't it something in the family make-up? An ancestral lack of merit, or something like that? If there is ancestral nobility and merit then there is surely a lack of it too. His own lot. There hadn't been a single accomplished man or woman among them. Not one for all those six generations of trying their luck in Australia, the land of opportunity. A bunch of no-hopers. The Donlons and the Egans too, on his mother's side; the little Egans of Ballyragget. As far back as anyone could go. The ten bob from Oscar Gerner was a miserable little miracle and Pat was ashamed to think he had waved it triumphantly in Edith's face yesterday afternoon. His confidence fled now at the thought of himself doing that. Could he seriously hope to be the exception in his family? After umpteen generations of nothing much, could he really expect to shine among the gifted men of privilege of his own generation? Wasn't he just another good-for-nothing Donlon? For God's sake, waving a miserable ten-shilling note in his wife's face!

He looked at the mirror in his hand and turned it over, not wanting to catch sight of the self-loathing in his eyes. Her initials were engraved on the back, *ERB*, the capitals elegantly entwined within an oval cartouche of grapevines. The middle letter was the initial of her grandmother's maiden name—the Ritchies of Melrose—as if Edith were the daughter of a noble Scottish household and this was their coat of arms. A solemn assurance of her legitimate accession to worthiness, this mirror. He was in his underpants and singlet. He curled his toes, the lino chilly against his bare feet. Rain was coming down now and the light was gone, a shower invading from the ocean. A drift of low cloud wrapping the hill like a skull and killing the light. The rain a sudden engine on the tin roof. He had hoped it was going to be fine. Living here at the bottom edge of the continent was almost like being out in the Great Southern Ocean itself, squalls coming up from the emptiness out there, then gone again just as suddenly, leaving you wet and surprised in a tranquil field of sunlight if you were lucky. The mood of the weather here was not to be predicted. It was one of the delights of the place, the unpredictability of moods. As if you weren't expected to be settled and complacent if you lived at the bottom of the world, looking out at the vast ocean on which no man had ever made his dwelling place or left his mark. Oscar Gerner would be over there in his hovel with

his dogs, grinning out his kitchen window like something out
of Dickens, watching his grass grow. For Gerner, the landowner
and man of substance, and none of it earned but every bit of
it inherited from his immigrant grandfather, it was *raining*
money. His dad was right. You either had it or you didn't have
it. Gerner's pile under his mattress, no doubt, if a man could
coax a way past those dogs. The old bugger had only to sit
there in his wheelchair to be making pounds and shillings by
the hour with this lovely rain on his clover.

'Mary Mother of God,' Pat said. (It was the only blasphemy
his mother ever permitted herself.) 'There's nothing I hate so
much as having to leave the work to make money.' Every day
was a day for painting with him and any day lost to painting
was a day lost to himself. The thought of losing a day was
putting him in a bad mood.

If it had not been for their dire need of some cash, nothing
would have convinced him to set out on this desperate caper this
morning. He'd be down there in the village buying tobacco and
papers and a bottle of beer at the pub with the ten bob instead
of wasting the best part of it getting himself into Melbourne
and back. It was just the weather today for stoking the wood
stove and staying indoors, and giving himself up to painting and
reading, and maybe writing another poem—if one happened
to come his way, and he had the feeling it might have, if only
he'd had a moment to himself. He loved days like this, grey
and cold and isolating. He and Edith snugged away down here
cosily in this little cottage at the bottom of the world, getting
on with their work in the quiet of their own time. He was
going to have to wrap the roll of drawings in something or the

absorbent paper would disintegrate in the wet. He'd better get on with it, or the day would slip away and his resolve with it.

He held up her mirror and smirked at himself. There! It wasn't such a bad picture, was it? He could see the fine hairs up the fellow's nostrils. They flickered palely as he breathed in and out. Little golden hairs, they were, and surely rather nice for nose hairs. He had always kept a neat appearance and until today had almost never missed having a shave in the mornings. When he'd told her his plan last night over their sardines on toast and a cup of tea, Edith said, 'If you're going to stand in front of a man like Sir Malcolm and have any chance of convincing him you're worth his money then you're going to have to do something about your appearance.' She laughed at him. 'You look more like an accountant than a bohemian. Appearances are everything with these people. I know them. They're *my* people. If you look as if you're starving for your art you might have a show of convincing them you're the real thing.'

She didn't see how it was going to work, this absurd charade he was proposing, and she told him so. And mightn't it even be illegal? 'They don't part with their cash that easily. That's why they've got so much of it.'

He set her mirror down on the sink (where it became an oval of grey sky) and went out to the studio and collected the drawings from the floor. He shuffled them together into a neat pile on the table, standing a moment considering whether to put the drawing with the poem on top, where it would be the first to be seen. He put it under the others, where it belonged—under Mr Creedy's daughter's great swaggering bottom. If he'd been at all interested in depicting the realities of the girl's anatomy he might have asked her to pose naked for him. But it was something in himself he was after, not another picture of a girl's bare bum.

He felt uncomfortable with the idea of making himself up to look like your typical art student, unshaved and his clothes unpressed. It wasn't him. 'We might be poor,' his mother said to him time and again, slapping at the back of his jacket with the flat of her hand before he went out, 'but we'll keep that to ourselves.' The only times he ever saw his father unshaved was on Sunday mornings. His dad sat in the front room reading the newspaper by the light from the window, in his braces, his collar off and his boots not shined. But he never went into the street looking like that. Not even just to go next door for a yarn with Don Foley. Pat had always worn his hair short and neatly parted on the left side. Looking in the bathroom mirror over the sink at home, his head at an angle to concentrate, his tongue between his teeth, drawing the comb over his scalp from back to front to get the white line of demarcation clean and straight, like his dad's. When he thought about it, it seemed a funny thing to be doing, but he did it all the same, like everything else he did. Wanting to be the man his dad expected him to be. Even when he was little they didn't hold hands, he and his dad, but walked down the street side by side, going for a swim on Saturday at the sea baths with the other men from the tram depot. None of the others taking their boys with them. They had always been mates, he and his dad, from the beginning.

His hair was without a curl, fine and pale and sitting flat to his skull. Whenever he had let it get a bit long it looked lank and wispy, framing his features with an unflattering weakness, especially around his eyes, which he was inclined to squint. He was squinting now thinking about it. His were not the glorious locks of a wild bohemian. He knew that. Edith was right, he looked more like an accountant. His mother had slicked a wayward forelock with her spit for him, 'There!', before sending him off to school with a quick peck on his cheek, which he had begun to close his eyes to and flinch from when he was seven or eight years of age. 'Oh, you big man, you. Now get on with you!' The minute he was out of her sight he wiped the kiss from his cheek with the back of his hand, not because he didn't treasure his mother's affections, but because he was afraid his friends would detect the cool imprint of his mother's lips on his cheek if he didn't wipe away the feel of it—it had a lovely private smell to it, sniffing the back of his hand, like nothing else, faint and delicate and suggesting her love for him, like the elusive scent of a wildflower on the breeze one spring day. The smell of his mother's kiss was the smell of home and of love.

He carried the roll of drawings into the bedroom. Edith was sitting up reading her book, her green velour dressing-gown draped around the soft curve of her shoulders and her breasts, the green uplands of his beloved landscape. He smiled to see her. She was in her own quiet world of reading. He envied her the ability to be so content. He set the drawings down on the bed. 'Is your tea not right?'

She put her finger on her place and leaned and looked into her cup. 'I forgot it,' she said. 'It's lovely. Thank you, darling.' She picked up the cup and took a sip of the tea. 'I like it cold.'

He put on the old pair of paint-spattered trousers with the hole in the left knee and the frayed turn-ups. They smelled damply of the back of the cupboard. He was reminded of his early death. The trousers of a dead man. He had woken up with a headache and it hadn't quite left him. It wasn't much of a headache, but he worried about it. Surely it signified the onset of the disease that would carry him off before his next birthday? Rimbaud had quit writing his poetry when he was, what? Nineteen or twenty, wasn't it? The deep malady of the body that will defeat a young man. The first sign, this throbbing of a piston in an unvisited chamber of his being, driving the engine of his demise. His premature death . . . It worried Pat a great deal. The notion that he was sure to die young. He often thought about it but was too superstitious ever to write about it or to speak of it to Edith. To express his fear (he feared) would be to give it encouragement, proffering to the dread of it a foothold in his reality, from where it would flourish, the roots of its being drawing sustenance from the roots of his own strength and sapping him. Hollowing a great space beneath him. Undermining him.

There were times when he was so besieged, so alone and vulnerable with the thought of this great echoing vault of nothingness beneath his life's enterprise, that he completely seized up. In this state he could neither think nor do anything. A seizure of silent panic, it was. Gripping him. If he were ever to speak of these episodes to Edith he feared she would plead with him to submit to the discipline of the great tradition and be like all the others. Be like herself, following her beloved grandfather. She would ask him to retreat from his solitary enterprise and play it safe with the support of companions and fellow students. Everyone in the same boat. The comfort of it. But he would never do that. He *couldn't* do it. He didn't know why this was so. Secretly he was proud that it was so and knew that his isolation was necessary to him. Knew he would either succeed on his own or would fail on his own. But he would not withdraw from his isolation and join the others. It was how he was. He couldn't change and it was no good trying.

Often he was in such a hurry to get work done that the least interruption enraged him. He excused his rages. He understood the reason for them. There was so much he had to do. And there were days when his fear of premature death drained him. If he had a few bob he found someone to drink with. Something his father had warned him against. For there had been a run of the drink among the uncles of Wicklow, his father's five brothers. It was not his rages but his drinking that shamed Pat.

He buttoned the fly of the smelly trousers and tied them at the waist with a length of Gerner's pink baling twine then sat on the side of the bed and put his bare feet into the ancient pair of plimsolls. Their rubbery soles were colder than his feet and he gave a shiver. Both his little toes poked from holes in the sides of the plimsolls, the frayed edges of the material like lashes, his toes the eyes of crustaceans peeking nervously from their shells, knowing they were in for it any minute.

Edith leaned over the side of the bed and looked. 'Your feet will get wet in those things. Hadn't you better wear your boots? You'll catch a chill.'

Her concern for him was like his mother's concern for him. But it would not be a chill that would carry him off. He stood up for her inspection. 'So what do you think? Am I shabby enough for him?'

'You're putting on a shirt, aren't you?'

'I will. Do I look that daft in these?' He looked down at himself unhappily. To be dressed like this threatened to demoralise him. Disguising himself as a bohemian was surely as good as pretending to be one of *them*, wasn't it? Being poor might be a man's fate, but poverty was not to be mimicked, the disgrace not in poverty itself but in flaunting it in public, in becoming a whining beggar at the table of a rich man. 'What choice do I have?' he said, miserable suddenly with the prospect of the day ahead of him. 'Can you think of something else I can do? I'd drop this in a bloody flash. You know that.'

'Only what the others do,' she said. She laid her book face down on the bed cover and held out her arms to him. 'Come here! You're not going to do that.'

'Is it what you want me to do? Give in to them?'

'No, darling, it's not. I know you can't do that. You are my untutored genius. It's for that I love you most of all.'

He went to her and she took his hands and he leaned down and kissed her.

'Do you remember the first day we met at the Gallery School?' she said, looking up, her dark eyes shining with the memory. 'We'd all caught the tram down to the Swanston Family after the class. You were standing next to me in the doorway looking out at the crowd in the laneway? Do you remember?'

He did remember. He had promised himself at the school that day, If *she* goes to the pub with the others then I'll go too. And if she stays behind, I'll stay behind. Their eyes had already met, but not their bodies. Never with other girls, but suddenly with this girl he had been too shy to speak. And then at the pub she came and stood beside him in the doorway to the lane. It was a narrow doorway and her shoulder touched his. Without a word she took his hand in hers. Just like that. As if she trusted her decision. It was a while after that they kissed. In the park he asked for her name. And she told him, I'm Edith Black. And he knew it should mean something to him.

She reminded him now, 'You said, when we were in the park afterwards, it was a kind of warning to me and I knew it was a warning, I mean if I was thinking of going with you for good, as I was, you wanted to warn me not to expect anything. You said, and you were being very formal and there was a kind of anger in your tone as you said it. I was a little bit afraid of you. You said, You should know I'm never going to get a proper job and I'm never going to do the kind of art they teach at the Gallery School.'

'You remember that?' He was pleased.

'Whenever I go past the park in the tram I think of you saying it. It thrilled me. I knew you were different to the others. I knew I'd go with you. Wherever you wanted me to go.'

'It wasn't my good looks you fell for, then?' He laughed. He had forgotten to think about his headache and his fear of death. He sat on the side of the bed and took her hands in his lap. Her hands were soft and warm against the chill of his own hands, her fingers long and tapering. Her book lying face down on the blanket, the author's name on the cover in small black letters, Guy de Maupassant. The title in the same tone of red that reapers and binders were painted, *Une vie*. A life. A woman's life, he supposed it was. Perhaps it was a premonition of the storm gathering in his head, but after they had made love two nights ago he had felt terribly alone suddenly and was unable to sleep. He asked her to read to him. He did not ask her to translate, but lay with his head against her bare shoulder, smelling her skin and listening to her reading the French the way he listened to music, his thoughts released from anxiety and free to wander. And after a while the agitation in his mind was soothed and he began to feel sleepy.

He turned to her now and bent to kiss her gently on her lovely lips. He smiled into her eyes. She was tearing up as he expected her to. 'I didn't think I had a hope with you. Then you took my hand. I'm not likely to forget it.'

He loved her gentle refinement, her calm, the feeling of abundant time she carried with her, the quiet certainty of her spirit. 'We are opposites,' he said. 'You and I.'

'That is what I fear sometimes.'

'I wouldn't be doing this if you didn't believe in me.'

'I believe in you.'

'What is it?' He squeezed her hands. 'Is something up? There's nothing to be afraid of. I'll be home tonight and we can have a laugh about all this.'

In a voice of quiet tenderness, which was very nearly an admission of her greater fears for them, Edith told him her news. 'We're going to have a baby.'

6

July 1991

THERE WAS SNOW ON MOUNT DANDENONG TODAY. SUMMER IS JUST a memory. I hear my mother sigh and say, 'How the years do fly away!' I've begun to doubt it was Edith I saw. Is she alive or is she dead? It is a terrible anxiety out of which nightmares have begun to fashion themselves. Oh yes, the dire effects of imagination, our curse and our saving grace. There were half a dozen of us sitting round this kitchen table drinking wine and beer and smoking cigarettes and talking about art and life and flirting with each other one lovely summer afternoon, when someone—George Lane it was, the darkest and fiercest of the artists among us—said, 'We would be better off without imagination.' Poor George was drunk and had failed the previous evening to seduce beautiful teasing Alice Meadows, so he would most certainly have been better off without imagination that day.

Although Freddy was already drinking far too heavily at the time and was probably drunker than George, he was still a practising psychoanalyst and felt compelled to say at once, 'Our imagination is the way to ourselves, George.' Easy for him, you might say, not being a tormented artist like George. I saw the look George gave Freddy, the flicker of detestation in his black eyes. Freddy probably saw it too but he persisted. 'All mental illness, all human cruelty, is a failure to heed the prompts of the imagination, George.' I hear Freddy's voice now ringing out in this kitchen, and the sound of his laughter. Already the seeds of despair were in him, bathed by a constant stream of alcohol. Freddy loved vast generalisations of this kind, but on that occasion he was also turning the blade in George's sensitive liver. Freddy's pronouncements were often dismissed by more temperate people than himself as merely an excessive bravura of style. But I thought there was nearly always a kernel of wisdom embedded in these baroque gestures of his. Tragically, for he had a good mind, Freddy acquired no insight into the maladies of his own soul and became a hopeless alcoholic, impotent and unable to control the functioning of his bowels. He shot himself when he was forty-three. I kept his note for years. He had been off the grog for a year at the time of his suicide. *I live without my first love. Her name is Wine. It is no longer possible, darling Aught, to persist with this torment. By the time you receive this I shall be dead. I have borrowed Ray's little .22 and a bullet. The dear man believes I have a rat in the wainscot to dispose of.*

Could it have been her daughter I saw? Edith gave birth in 1939 and her daughter would be fifty-two today. Some people age quickly. Alice was such a one, our beautiful Alice, a rapid ager. She, poor girl, developed anorexia and looked sixty before she was forty. Perhaps she would not have become ill with that dreadful self-denying disease if she had encouraged George that day and had lain down for him with her dress up and abandoned herself to the pleasures and torments of sex. I sometimes wonder if we weren't a sick generation, the whole lot of us. Denying this and denying that, for no better reason than our own narrow prejudices about life and art—our beliefs, as we called them. Prejudices, in fact, which we mistook for passions and vision. Our view of life and art required a narrowing of everything to the single dimension of our own orthodoxies. No one got a look in with us if they weren't strictly of our persuasion. Now they're all dead does it matter to anyone what we believed?

I'll wait on the bench outside Woolies next time I get my drugs. If Edith went to my chemist once, she will go again. They give us discount membership cards these days to make sure we're loyal to them.

Adeli brings the smell of California with her and is at the forefront of all the latest fads. I put non-organic honey in her herbal tea the other day and watched her to see if she would notice. But she sipped and smiled and babbled on, heedless of what was going down her pristine throat. Her virginal, unsullied throat, I'll bet. She is not the frequently orgasming nurse. It was Adeli who brought the herbal tea. Not I. I drink Bushells tea for preference. Strong, black and without sweeteners. When she first told me her name, I said, 'Adelie penguin.' I suppose everyone thinks of the penguin when she tells them her name and would *like* to say so. It was bullying of me to actually say it. She offered to stay overnight. To keep me company, she said. She doesn't seem to notice the stench of this place or that I dislike people. I asked her the other day to go and fetch me a packet of cigarettes from the corner shop that is clinging to its final threads of subsistence half a mile from here. The Vietnamese woman who runs the shop looks eighty but is really only fifty. There's rapid ageing for you. It can be done, it seems, if the circumstances are favourable to it. She has five daughters. Her husband died last year. She keeps her shop open all night in competition with the 7-Eleven. She and her daughters gaze out of a darkness of deep fatigue. 'Get me some cigarettes,' I said to Adeli. 'I don't care what sort they are.' She went very still and silent and examined her podgy hands in her lap. Then, in a small voice—I might have asked her to fetch the shotgun and a box of shells—she said, 'Cigarettes, Mrs Laing?'

I said, 'You should take them up. You might lose some of that fat.' She persists in addressing me as Mrs Laing and I find I've grown to rather like it. She is not an Australian, after all, so does it matter?

Don't say I didn't warn you that you probably wouldn't like me. I don't like myself much.

'The spelling is different,' she said, and sipped her herbal tea. 'It is Adeli without an e.'

She bounds in through the flywire on to the veranda, bringing something or other that I'm supposed to like but which really it is she who likes. It was those cheap chocolates the first time (the purple ribbon is still holding my sandal together) then the South American hot chocolate. Now it is herbal tea or exotic Asian fruit from the Prahran Market. It was bright orange dragon fruits last week. I threw the ridiculous things onto the back lawn. The white cockatoos tore them into vivid shreds. When the cockatoos had done and had flown away screeching, it looked as if small animals had been dismembered on the lawn.

Adeli's summer linen has been exchanged long ago for cashmere twin sets, rose pink and apple blossom. They make her bust look a size fifty. She smiles and pulls out a chair and arranges herself at the table, undoes her buttons and puts her notebook and her pen (a woodgrain-finished fountain pen, for God's sake) on the table in front of her and crosses her fat thighs and folds her hands in her fat lap. Ready! I tell her nothing. She continues to disapprove of my cigarettes, closing her eyes and wrinkling up her nose whenever I light one. What am I supposed to do? Australia has become a nation of wowsers. I said to her, 'Tell me there is something better for me at my age than the pleasure of smoking.' Bullying fat Adeli entertains me. I can't help it. I almost like her but *I* don't have to be liked in return. I don't *need* to be liked, it is she who needs to be liked (as all Americans do). Anyway, she's an American. Naturalised naturally. But still American. Still twanging her California up her nose. She'll never get past that here. It isn't possible for an American to become an Australian, no matter how long they stay. We believe it to be our birthright as Australians to bully solitary Americans who venture into our midst. That big bright red overcoat and those red patent-leather shoes. Who does she think she's kidding? And purple stockings the other day. I've lived too long. But Adeli is not the only aesthetic scourge in my life. The woman next door jogs in her lycra while pushing their ugly baby in a three-wheeled thing and leading that vicious dog on a lead. She almost knocked me down the other afternoon. I was bending to fasten the front gate when she brushed past me as if I wasn't there. Loathing rises in my gorge at the sight of her silver and black body-hugging suit flashing along our road. I do not wish to admit that such creatures as she have come into existence in my country. My own species is endangered by them.

I have handed over the dining room to Adeli. She is in her seventh heaven. She's in there now, sorting things. I asked her to keep the door closed, then rattled the key after she'd gone in. The door flew open. 'Please don't lock me in, Mrs Laing!' I smiled and left her to it. I'm like a child sometimes. I was tempted to tiptoe back and turn the key in the lock. Fierce little visions sweep into my mind like evil fairies. The mummified corpse of Adeli among the Laing papers when the dining room is opened forty years from now. Absurd, but stinging me with a guilty delight I do nothing to resist. Time is nothing. The silent vengeance of the aged. If only I could be a winged goddess!

•

Something of great importance to me happened two nights ago. Stony brings me the cabbages from the remnant of his market garden. He doesn't park his Bedford at the front of the house as Adeli does but drives in by the double gates and parks next to the coach house, the old tradesman's entrance. He carries the box of cabbages in through the side garden and sets it down inside the kitchen door. If I am still in bed when he calls I hear him talking to Sherry, and Sherry answering him. I leave his money on the table under a glass ashtray.

It is all Stony grows these days, drumhead cabbages. Enormous things. Cannonballs. I can hardly lift one of them. He has grey horny hands with deep black cracks at the base of his thumbs ingrained with our river soil, like the feet of elephants. He is probably my age or even older and was market gardening with his father when Arthur and I first came here, at a time when this was the country, or the edge of the country. In those days Stony and his father sold us the varieties of vegetable we were not clever enough to grow for ourselves. Their neat little fields and glasshouses have gradually been squeezed into a tiny pocket surrounded by the new suburban mansions and their dogs and trampolines and tennis courts and swimming pools, the mansions all vaguely influenced by the holidays of their owners in Provence or Tuscany. This country influences no one any more. The old Australian Australia has gone. That remnant sense of the pioneer. It is all mock European now.

Stony is still a strong man. After his father died he never married or had a companion, except his cats. I never met his mother but it is his mother's genes that dominate his features. You have to know his father was Chinese before you see it in Stony. When he gets the mood on him Stony breaks his silence and talks to everything, whether there is anyone around to hear him or not. He talks to trees. To the earth. To his cabbages, especially to those that allow the grubs of cabbage whites to make colanders of their leaves. Boxes. Sherry. Furniture. Kettles that boil slowly or too fast. But he only sniffs at the comments of people.

Two nights ago I dreamed the answer to where Pat's nude drawings of Mr Creedy's daughter were. I didn't see the drawings in my dream but woke *knowing* where they were. I wasn't in bed but was sleeping here at the kitchen table in my dressing-gown, my head on my arms. I'd had to get up earlier for a pee and was too lazy to go back to bed. I've no idea what time it was. The Rayburn was going and the kitchen was cosy. Suddenly I sat up, wide awake.

I got up in a fever of excitement and went out to the coach house. (It was our poet laureate, Barnaby, who insisted we call it a coach house. Pat refused and always called it the shed. And of course he was right. It is an open-fronted shed with a loft from which hay bales were once tossed down to feed the horses.) The air was chill and fresh after the warm fug of the kitchen, and there was a great white moon standing high in the sky behind the branches of the red gum. The night reminded me of the time when Pat used to drop me notes. *Look at the moon!* It was our code for the lust that ruled our lives, our longing to be with each other. Arthur looking up from his book, his hurt gaze following me as I jumped up from the couch clutching Pat's note and went out of the library through the French doors into the garden to stand in the night and gaze at the moon and wait for him to find me.

Standing under the moon I threw my head back and moaned and ran my hands over my body. It was ridiculous and undignified, but we are animals and at such times know nothing of what is sensible or dignified. It was the full melodrama of youthful love. And I was over thirty then. Nowadays the only thing that gives my skin that feverish sensitivity is the prelude to a migraine or when I'm getting diarrhoea.

Our ladder, the one and only ladder we ever had, was made by Arthur from dowels and poles that he cut and fashioned himself with great care and love from young casuarinas along the river bank. It took him weeks and was painful to watch. I found the ladder at last the other night, embedded under an accumulation of rubbish behind the Pontiac. It was lucky there was such a bright moon or I would not have found it. By the time I'd freed the ladder and dragged it out into the open

I was shaking violently and had to sit on the running board of the Ponty hugging myself for half an hour before my body recovered. As I sat there I was remembering Arthur down at the river getting the poles, his shirt off, his skinny torso blazing white in the glare of the sun, wielding his axe so inexpertly I thought he must surely lop off one of his feet before he died of sunstroke. I went down to him and shouted at him angrily, 'Leave it! Let Pat do it when he comes.' But Arthur, poor man, was trying to compete with Pat.

Arthur was not a practical man. He was not one of those men who can pick up a bag of tools and go off whistling and build a house for his family with his own hands. Arthur loved books and artists and poets and musicians. He liked to sit and drink whisky and smoke his French cigarettes on the veranda with a friend or in the library and talk all day and all night if he were allowed, or lose himself for hours in a book, preferably a history of art or the life of an artist. There was no envy of the gifted in Arthur, except at that time his envy of Pat's easygoing ability to do anything practical. Arthur felt his manliness to be at risk and could not forgo the challenge. Freddy stood with me by the pond and we looked down the hill to where Arthur was working. Freddy lifted his glass and said, 'Behold the Christ fashioning his own cross.' We laughed and drank our wine, then linked our arms and turned and went inside and left Arthur to it. If he was fool enough to do it, then it was his own fault and no one else's if he got sunburned and cut his toes off. We would care for him while he recuperated.

If old age inclines us to a withering of the spirit of generosity, youth is surely more cruel. Had I the chance now I would go down the hill and help Arthur save his manhood. But perhaps he would not wish me to.

The ladder was a one-off for Arthur. Having done it successfully he believed he had proved something that would not need proving ever again. 'If I have to, I can do it. So there!' That was the moral of Arthur's ladder. When he finished making it he was absurdly proud of it, and was even rather smug. Which was not like him. Barnaby called it *The Ladder of Divine Ascent*. Freddy of course said it was the ladder of divine assent. If Arthur was present when it was being used, those who were using it had to admire it extravagantly. But it was often used when Arthur was not present. For the loft of the coach house was an ideal hidey-hole for lovers, hence Freddy's little pun. Lovers climbed up to the loft and pulled the ladder up behind them and were safe as the monks of Glendalough hiding from the Vikings in their stone towers.

Things were sometimes deposited in the loft, and as the years passed they were forgotten. Or the one who put them there eventually died or went overseas and never returned to retrieve them. The loft was a place where you might stash something you loved but to which painful memories were attached. A thing you wanted to keep, but to keep out of sight. Barnaby christened it the mezzanine, but no one else would come at that and it remained the loft for the rest of us. I had no memory of putting Pat's drawings up there, but when I woke from my dream I knew that's where they were. Had I put them up there myself? Or had someone else put them there? My memory was a blank on the matter, but I trusted the message of my dream: *Look at the moon!*

The dream, indeed, was of another landscape. A moonless darkening country, kin to Alice's Wonderland or a time lord's Tardis, defying perspectives and deepening into mysteriously luminous vistas that my unease cautioned me were filled with threats to my existence. When I woke I knew at once the sinister landscape of my dream had referred to the loft of the coach house. Then I realised the obvious. Why had I never thought of it before? Some things wait their moment, held in the anteroom of our consciousness, like messengers from a far kingdom, until they are called into our presence. Servants of our destiny, Freddy once called them, then laughed tragically and tossed back another generous tumbler of Arthur's favourite single malt, The Famous Grouse. Before his system's tolerance for alcohol collapsed Freddy could finish a bottle of whisky on his own in the library before lunch then emerge and drink a bottle of good shiraz with lunch and you would not have known from his manner that he had drunk anything at all. Freddy was in a kind of heaven with alcohol for years. We envied him and thought him blessed. The end came suddenly. It was a shock to all of us, for we had foolishly believed him to be immune. He was waiting for a tram in Swanston Street after lunching with a friend at the Athenaeum Club when his bowels let go.

I was trying to raise Arthur's ladder and lean it against the open front framing of the loft floor. But each time I got it halfway up my strength failed and the ladder began to slide away from me. It was all I could do to stop it crashing onto the Pontiac. The Ponty was Arthur's one great extravagance. He paid more for it than we paid for this place. Its paintwork had never received so much as a scratch. In 1934, when he bought the car, it was imported into Melbourne from the General

Motors plant in Detroit as a bare chassis and engine. In those days customers went to their local coach builder and had the bodies of their cars custom made. Old Mr King, the founder of the famous Melbourne firm of coach builders Martin and King, was a client of one of Arthur's senior partners and offered Arthur the services of his firm. The Ponty was not just any car, it was a unique motor tailored by Australia's finest coach builders to fulfil Arthur's dream. And it did. I could not bear the thought of being the one finally to damage its beautiful coachwork.

Many sacred and quite a few less-than-sacred moments of our years together were lodged in the smell of the Ponty's wood and leather. The weekend after Pat Donlon arrived in our lives, Arthur suggested we motor down to Ocean Grove and pay the pair of them a surprise visit. Arthur referred to them, rather insouciantly when you consider what was warming on the hob between Pat and myself, as the young people—as if our lives and theirs were to be innocence and gaiety in summer woodland glades. We packed the Ponty's boot with a heap of goodies: wine and beer and fresh bread and tins of this and that, and a whole ham. And several bottles of very good French champagne from Arthur's cellar.

Arthur drove up the gravelled lane to their little white cottage blaring his claxon and halloing, and I hung out the side window waving a bottle of champagne. But the joyous picnic we had anticipated failed. Edith was suffering from nausea and was in bed, and Pat was in a grim intractable mood. He resented what he called our charity, until the champagne loosened his wildness and he dinked me down to the sea on the crossbar of his bike. I took everything that day to be a sign from the gods that my fearful enterprise was blessed. When we arrived at the cottage I went into their bedroom and sat with Edith and took her hand in mine. My other hand lay on the sheet beside her, where I knew *he* must have lain, naked as the palm of my own hand, I assumed. I could not then imagine Pat wearing pyjamas. Even Edith's sickness, which conveniently removed her from our company, seemed to me to be a blessing. I had no sympathy for her but made the most of my opportunity to advance my cause with her husband. That is the truth of it. It might seem an odd way of putting it, *to advance my cause*. But that is what it was, a cause. It was never for me to be merely a George and Alice situation, in which seduction was to have been the end. That was not my aim at all. With Pat Donlon, seduction for me was always to be a beginning to something much larger and more encompassing. I knew it from the moment he walked into the house with Arthur. It would be more truthful of me to say—and it is truth to which I am committed—that I did not *know* it, but felt it stir within me, a demon aroused by Pat's glance from a long slumber.

After the fourth try to get the ladder up I was exhausted and decided to call it quits and wait for Stony to come in the morning and do it for me. I loathed my feebleness, however, and was consumed with anger and frustration at the thought of having to ask for help. I have always hated asking for help. I stood looking up at the loft *knowing* Pat's drawings were there, almost within my reach. A surge of defiance against my feebleness fired me with new resolve. It was that interior voice, which remains forever young and vigorous, berating me scornfully: *So Autumn Laing has become a quitter.*

We would see about that. I got a fresh grip on the ladder
with my claws, and grunting and cursing and staggering about,
I managed at last to touch the very top of it to the front beam
of the loft floor. I stepped back, my chest heaving, waiting to
see if it was going to move. It stayed. I took hold of the side
poles with both hands and set myself to begin the perilous
ascent. My heart was beating so hard I had difficulty getting
my breath. My left foot raised, I placed it on the first rung.
There! My bare foot was set on the rung and would not slip
off. Cautiously my right foot bucked up the courage and joined
its sister. There they stood, side by side, sedate and innocent,
the pair of them. I straightened my legs. We had risen from the
ground!

I stood gazing around from the eminence of my one-rung
elevation. It was surprising the difference this small achievement made to my view, I mean of the world and of my life
altogether: I was on my way up. It gave me a lift to know it.
Encouraged, I placed my left foot on the second rung and stood
poised like a trapezist teasing her audience, withholding the
climactic moment, my legs trembling and wobbling, gripping
Arthur's old casuarina side poles with all the puny strength
in my claws.

I am a woman of considerable courage and have proof of
it, but I panic. I know this too. It is a distressing fact. There
have been two or three occasions in my life when panic (not
hysteria, but panic), swift and unaccountable, has defeated my
courage and flung me sideways howling. I knew, as I stood there
ready to ascend, that when panic strikes, true panic, not the
flutter of fear in the belly, we cannot answer it either with our
will or our determination. I knew that in a state of panic the

body's physiology conspires with the mind to defeat the will. I prayed silently that I would not be overcome by this enemy.

I shan't give you a rung-by-rung account. Imagine me ascending, if you will, slowly by this means, my billowing dressing-gown lending me the sombre appearance of a monk in the moonlight, my wisps of silvery hair gliding about above my long skull, my bruised legs trembling, the soles of my feet tortured by Arthur's narrow dowels, stopping at each rung to gain breath, and closing my eyes to pray to Him in whom I do not believe. Imagine Mrs Autumn Laing at eighty-five climbing *The Ladder of Divine Ascent* in the moonlight of her last days, seeking absolution. Was that it? What I was after? Relief from my guilt? If it was, then I was to be disappointed.

My eyes at last topped the lip of the loft and I gazed, fascinated, into the sinister depths of its recesses, vertigo induced by the emptiness of moonlit space below me, reflux souring my gullet. Was I going to faint and fall to my death?

A vixen barked twice down at the river, and I steadied.

But how was I to get from the ladder onto the floor of the loft? I didn't have enough strength in my legs to get me back down the ladder. I was stuck where I was. Like the duke, neither up nor down. I couldn't stand there all night, or even for much longer. The last of my strength would soon drain from my shuddering legs and arms. I saw my white corpse spreadeagled in its flaring dressing-gown on the roof of Arthur's motor car, my ghastly thighs parted. I gazed fearfully into the luminous shadows of the loft before me—the darkening landscape of my dream indeed. The top of the ladder reached only one rung above the level of the floor. Hugging the ladder against my chest and mouthing Pat's sweet curses, I sneaked up two more rungs until I stood with my waist on a level with the loft floor. There was nothing more for me to hold onto. I was teetering dangerously. I could go no higher and could not balance for long where I was.

I thought it was blood running down my legs, then realised with relief that I had only peed myself. There was only one thing for it. A desperate thing it was. But I saw at once that I must do it without delay or fall to my death. I let out a Comanche howl and flung my top half forward onto the floor of the loft and dug my fingers into a crack between the boards at the full stretch of my arms.

My flailing feet sent the ladder screeching sideways. It fell with the drumbeat of doom onto the roof of the Pontiac. One way or another I suppose it was the night when the Ponty was going to be pounded. I lay stretched out on the boards of the loft, my head reeling, my heart crashing about wildly, the lower part of my legs and my feet sticking out above the moonlit emptiness. Indeed I may as well have landed on the moon for all the hope I had of ever getting myself down to the ground again. I thought of screaming for help but was afraid the lycra-clad woman would hear me—I would rather die than live owing my life to such a creature. Imagine, after doing me such a favour, if she were to ask me to babysit that awful child of hers?

I lay there shaking and trembling with the shock of it. Eventually I drew in my legs and curled myself into the classic foetal position of regression and self-pity. The poor little orphan girl missing her mummy. Or could it have been the consoling arms of my darling Uncle Mathew? These days dear Mathew would be condemned and hounded to his death not for being a poet but for interfering with his little niece. He was, and remains for me to this day, my beloved Uncle Mathew. Do we ever lose our faith in our first love?

I woke to the shrieking of cockatoos in the red gum that bowers the coach house. Stony was loudly berating the ladder for beating up the bodywork of the Pontiac. It was the pink grey light of early morning, a few minutes before sunrise. I was deeply chilled, my limbs stiff and bruised. I heard myself groan as I crawled to the edge of the loft and peered over. Stony's upturned gaze measured me, as if I were a plank of wood he might have a use for.

He addressed the ladder in his usual dry, detached and ironic tone, as if he himself were not implicated in the childish follies of humanity but stood at a distinguished remove from the rest of us. 'So what's our Mrs Laing think she's been doing with herself up there in the loft all night, then?' His tone did not express interest in an answer to this question. And when the ladder did not answer him he raised it effortlessly and set it firmly against the lip of the loft and climbed up. As he climbed he counted the rungs aloud, and might have been counting out change in one-dollar coins to a customer.

I was so glad to see him it took me a moment or two to register the sharpness of his derision.

'Eleven,' he announced to his world when he reached the top of the ladder. He stepped onto the floor of the loft as if he did it every morning. He did not look at me but stood with his back to the vertiginous fall, his hands on his hips, surveying the dim interior. His reason for climbing the ladder had, it seemed, not been to rescue me. There was a job to be done and he would do it. In my state of weird exhaustion, dream and reality playing with my exhausted mind, the cockatoos bansheeing hysterically a few feet from us, I wouldn't have been surprised if Stony had reached into the rubbish and pulled out Pat's roll of drawings; 'Out you come, you little buggers! They've been looking everywhere for you.'

We searched among the jumble of discarded things, disclosing the layers of the years. Most of it was junk—transistors, toasters, old blankets, yellowed pillows, a rat's nest or two. I wondered which of us had thought to store bundles of newspapers tied neatly with butcher's twine? His drawings were not there. I felt betrayed and was convinced someone had visited the loft and stolen them. Something else was there, however. Something I had never expected to see again. Stony handed me Edith's modest oil of their white cottage and the embroidered field, as if he knew this was what I had really been looking for—had I only known it myself. I had long ago forgotten that Edith insisted Arthur take the picture with him the day of our abortive picnic.

Propped there on the floor of the loft with my back supported by the bundles of newspapers, my purple shanks stuck out in front of me, I held Edith's picture across my legs and looked at it. I saw at once that for a young woman of twenty-one it represented an extraordinary level of skill. It is on the kitchen table in front of me now, a pile of books behind it, facing the veranda so that it catches the light. She solved her problem of the oxalis with simplicity and wit, the golden yellow of that wild weed an ironic reference to Monet's cardinal fields of immemorial poppies. Everything I see in this good light confirms my first impression that Edith's embroidered hill is a first-rate work. To have been guilty of stealing her husband and destroying her little family was crime enough, but it is clear to me now that I also destroyed her chance of establishing herself as one of the very few truly gifted Australian women artists of her time. And for this surely there can be no redemption. If her embroidered field is any guide, had she persisted with her art Edith Black may well have been the foremost among the women painters of her time.

I had never really looked at her painting before. Had I done so I would not have been capable of 'seeing' it. I was so one-eyed in my belief in the rightness—indeed, the righteous-ness—of modernism's cause that any artist who worked in the conservative tradition as Edith did was automatically excluded from my serious attention. The least suggestion in those days that I might be mistaken in my attitude earned my disdain and derision. It was war. A moral war. And like all wars of belief, especially those between siblings, it was cruel and unjust. Edith's painting had belonged for me in the camp of the enemy. Seeing her picture for the first time now I was reminded of the career of the great European, Georges Braque, his development during my own lifetime from a gifted young follower of Cézanne to a leader in the world of post-war art, and how all through that development Braque retained his deep attachment to and affection for the traditions of his craft. So why not Australia's Edith Black?

Why was I so implacable in those days? If only I'd had enough wisdom to be Edith's champion as well as Pat's, how different this story might have been.

Sitting there in the bleak morning light of the loft, the sharp edge of her picture's stretcher biting into my shrivelled thighs, I felt old and weak. The true enormity of the damage I had done to that woman was at last clear to me. How she must hate me still. How for her I must be the cruellest of enemies and the most unjust of women. Autumn Laing, the ogre shadowing her life. To this day, to hear my name spoken in her presence must be to feel a chill in her soul. So why did she not fight me for him? Why did she not fight me for herself? Why did she give in so easily? If only she had not accepted defeat so meekly but had fought for what was rightfully hers, I might yet find some justification for my own implacable attitude then. But her modest submission denies me even this. In this story I am cast as the dragon and Edith is the helpless maiden chained to the rock. So where was her Saint George? Might her champion yet appear on the stage, lance at the ready to dispose of the evil dragon?

Arthur was never fierce. Not in anything he ever did or said. He was never scornful of the work of others. All work for him was worthy trial. Arthur was much wiser then than I, and gentler. Nor was he afraid to recognise in Edith's painting of the embroidered field a splendidly soulful example of her own period and tradition. I remember now laughing at him and calling him a sook for his timidity. He smiled and did not resent my stupidity, or even point it out to me. I had quickly dismissed Edith and her picture from my mind and forgotten the exchange with Arthur. I never gave any of it another thought until this moment in the loft.

Stony stood over me, waiting, I supposed, for me to begin the perilous descent. I looked up at him. 'I believe it is in negotiating the descent from the summit,' I said, 'that most deaths occur among those who climb mountains.' I didn't expect a response from him and wasn't disappointed when I received none.

Edith didn't fight me because she had neither Pat's brutal confidence nor my arrogant certainties. She was overwhelmed by us. Edith didn't have the capacity to push herself forward and persist in her ways without the support of her loved ones. She was a modest young woman. But clearly she was also a young woman of great talent. Edith's sensitive spirit was broken by what Pat and I did to her. She loved Pat and believed in him. When he praised her painting that day after slaughtering the horse she was encouraged because she knew he had given her his honest opinion. But to go on believing in herself day after day she needed his belief to be reliably there for her all the time.

Pat needed no such support. He thrived on the most savage criticism of his work and was energised by mockery. The more his peers laughed at him the more certain he was that he was doing the right thing.

I see it's not raining. If Adeli turns up later I'll get her to drive me down the street. I'll sit on the bench outside Woolies and keep a lookout. My dread is I'll be keeping an appointment with a ghost. Is it in my fate ever to meet Edith again? It is the question that is in my mind when I wake at two in the morning and lie in my bed and stare at the bedroom ceiling until I can stand it no longer and I get up, light a cigarette and go out onto the back veranda to sit with the sounds of the past and watch the white mist rising along the dark line of the river, and wait for the vixen's bark. But no one wants to go to their death despising themselves, do they? And so I leave the veranda and come into the kitchen and rattle the Rayburn into life and I take up my pen and go on with the story. Without Him in whom I do not believe, to write our story is the only hope of redemption left to me.

7

The big picture

IT WAS STILL RAINING HEAVILY WHEN PAT TURNED OFF THE FOOT-
path and ducked in under the shelter of the awning. He had
been travelling for hours since leaving Ocean Grove that
morning, Edith sitting up in their warm bed with her cold cup
of tea and her book beside her. She blew him a last kiss as he
turned at the door, dressed in his raggedy get-up. And just as
the screen door banged behind him he thought he heard her
call to him, 'I love you, darling.' It sent a lonely pang through
him thinking of it now. He hadn't called back to her.

He was a man masquerading as someone he wasn't for
purely mercenary reasons and the lie of it was digging a hole in
his confidence. He stood under the shelter of the canopy and
looked up. A high green copper dome, it was, like a parachute
frozen in its graceful descent to earth, rainwater jetting from
its corners in imitation of a fountain. On occasions such as
this one, momentous occasions, when he was determined to
challenge his fate, Pat knew himself to be obedient to an impulse

that had its source in a deeper and more obdurate place than mere common sense. It was a kind of precious intuition, this irrational compulsion to act in a certain way no matter what, and had been there since he was a lad dreaming of going to Ireland one day and meeting a true gipsy. It was himself, that's how he thought of it. So despite feeling a bit of a fool for being dressed up the way he was, he wouldn't be turning back now.

It was a grand and imposing building. Where the money was, you could see that. He took off his hat and knocked the water from it against his leg. He'd had nothing to eat since the slice of toast for breakfast and his stomach was letting him know it. He was facing a pair of heavy bronze and glass doors. In the eight bevelled glass panels eight identical shabby men were reflected back at him, each of them clutching a bundle under his arm, the shoulders of his jacket dark with rain. It was the anonymous figure of an unfortunate stranger. A beggar off the street. One of the hopeless tribe he had passed a few minutes ago slouching against the wall in the undercroft of the railway station.

Supposing his dad's tram was passing at the moment he had been waiting to cross Swanston Street just now? The idea that his dad might have seen him looking like this sent a chill into Pat's empty stomach.

The bell on the town hall clock was striking the hour. He listened for the next stroke. He wasn't in a hurry to confront them. He was regretting not having had the courage to come as himself. It was two o'clock. Would the old bugger be back from his lunch yet? To have his appeal turned down by these people as his honest self would have been no disgrace at all, but to be refused by them unshaved and got up in this ridiculous outfit was going to be a humiliation. If his dad *had* seen him waiting to cross the street, his dad would tell his mother but would never mention it to him. And he would never be able to ask his dad if he had seen him or not. He wasn't worried about what his mother would think. She would dismiss the idea of it. 'Pat's in Ocean Grove with Edith, you ninny.' But his dad would brood on it, figuring from it something strange and troubling to himself. The brief sighting of his son from the driver's cabin of his tram an apparition, was it? The thing he most dreaded to see? His boy a derelict waiting at the kerb to cross the road? Had he made it up to frighten himself? It would be a deep puzzle for his dad to unknot in the solitude of his sleepless nights. No, his dad would not forget it, but would tease it this way and that until he was hopelessly ravelled up in the tangle of his own fears for his boy.

A man came out of the doors, shattering the reflections, and Pat stepped to one side to let him pass. His feet were cold and wet in the sodden plimsolls. These people were not going to believe him. If only Edith had been firmer with him. Why hadn't she made a serious attempt to talk him out of it? She gave in to him too easily. She wasn't timid exactly, that wasn't it, but she never insisted on having her own way. She never forced an issue in her own favour. He wished she would be more determined sometimes, instead of always letting him win. Was he too hard on her?

He took hold of the handle of the door and pulled it open. The pointed tip of the handle—an intricately cast bronze representation of the armhold of an ancient warrior's shield—snagged the buckle on the belt of Edith's old mackintosh, in which he had wrapped his drawings, and he was hauled back on his heels. He unhooked the buckle and stepped through the doorway.

He was in a vast echoing area of shiny marble surfaces under the soaring vault of a high-domed ceiling. An enormous painting in a black metallic frame was hanging on the back wall in the magnificent importance of its own specially mounted spotlights. The painting was at least fifteen feet high by ten feet wide. A young woman was sitting at a desk underneath it. She was watching him. But it was the painting, not the young woman, that had Pat's attention. It was obvious what it was. A grand masterwork by one of the great European moderns. But which great European modern? Pat's heart contracted. A confident arrangement of sweeping geometric forms in tones of carbon blue and sea grey. What seemed to be represented were gigantic human forms, naked and leaping about in some energetic activity, dancing or fucking or fighting. Or all three. The painting was brazenly self-assured. It had no doubt about itself. Pat had seen nothing like it before outside the pages of glossy art magazines. He felt it like a slap in the face from a man. Not from a woman. A slap from a woman would have thrilled him. This humiliated him. It embarrassed him. He had imagined himself to be daring to dream of something not yet dreamed by other artists. But even in his grandest dreams for his work there was nothing as forceful in its authority as this picture. It was a thing that believed in itself and in nothing else. It did not ask to be understood but proclaimed its own reality, standing in a place of its own, beyond the understanding of the onlooker, indeed contemptuous of the onlooker. It was a work of art. He understood that. That is what it was. The first grand work of art he had ever seen in real life.

For the first time in his grown-up life Pat was afraid of art. He was afraid of his lack of the extremes of energy and imagination that would be required from him if he were ever to conceive something as bold and successful as this picture. It made everything he had dreamed of doing seem trivial and of no consequence, and forced on him the admission that what he had hoped to achieve one day had already been far surpassed by the artist who had painted this picture. Beside this his own works were nothing more than the casual and inconsequential gestures of a feeble intention.

People were coming through the doors behind him and stepping around him. One of them brushed against him. He was embarrassed by the mediocrity of his own ambition. He would never be able to compete with this kind of thing. There was a deep panic rising in him; he would have to make a new beginning. He would have to abandon the abstract and find something else. But what? He couldn't join Edith in her gentle pursuit of the old traditions. He would rather do nothing than do that. He would rather die now and be done with it than do that. Was he an artist at all? he asked himself. Or was he a small man playing at being an artist? A charlatan? In fact, wasn't he that very worst thing, that most feared and despised thing of all, a self-important dilettante?

He reached into the side pocket of his jacket and took out the slim green packet of five cigarettes he had bought from the machine at the station. The thin paper of the packet was crumpled, the damp cylinders of the cigarettes on the point of disintegrating. He smoothed a cigarette and put it between his lips. His hand trembled as he held the unsteady flame of the match to the tip of the cigarette. He closed his eyes and drew the smoke into his lungs, trying to stem the panic.

He stood in the silence of the suddenly empty foyer dragging on his cigarette and asking himself with disbelief how he could have mistaken his puny ambition for something grand. The drawings under his arm shamed him. And that pathetic boot polish and cardboard thing he had left against the wall of the studio. The truth was, he had done nothing worth a second look. It had all been empty bravado and arrogance with him, pretending to be the young Rimbaud. The thought of creeping back shamefaced and defeated to the crowd at the Gallery School made him feel sick. After his contempt for the meekly obedient students, what a perfect destruction it would be for him if he were to turn up at their life classes now—lifeless classes, he had called them. The most arrogant and least able drawing student among them. Leonardo's arsehole, that's who he'd be. His mimicry of Rimbaud's youthful revolt was a joke. Before he was twenty-one Rimbaud had abandoned poetry and had never touched it again as long as he lived. So was that what he must do now? Abandon art? Get an ordinary job and live an ordinary life like his dad? Was that the truth of it? Was the dream over? Was he finished?

He walked across the foyer towards the back wall. He felt weak in the stomach. He was going to be a father in seven months' time. He would have to earn a living for the two of them. And there would be more kids to follow this one. Without greeting the young woman he went behind her desk and looked for a signature on the painting. He turned to her. 'It's not signed!' The sheer effrontery of the absent signature. The intolerable confirmation of the artist's disdain for his own fame and the onlooker's opinion. It was exactly the standard he had dreamed for himself, to be above critical opinion, to stand alone in a place beyond concern with public approbation. Just to be great. To be himself. Alone and out of their reach.

'Isn't it?' the young woman said.

He looked at her. 'So who's the artist?'

'I don't know, sir.'

'Why are you calling me sir?' He suspected her of derision.

She said coolly, 'I'm instructed to call everyone sir who comes in . . . sir.'

'Women too?'

'Are you an artist yourself, sir?'

'Do I look like an artist?'

'I've learned in this job you can't tell what people are by the way they look. Except lawyers.' She laughed, showing her teeth. 'Lawyers always look just like lawyers.'

He noticed the way her two front teeth overlapped, like small white pincers. He had an urge to reach into her mouth and prise her teeth apart with his fingers.

'But you're not a lawyer,' she said.

He turned back to the painting. 'So you don't know who did it.'

'I don't like it. I don't care who did it. It's Sir Malcolm's great prize. I can't imagine what he sees in it. I liked the picture he had here before. That one *was* signed. It was real art. It was of cows in a paddock. A wonderful artist. The sun was just coming up—or maybe it was going down, but I liked to think it was coming up. There was a lovely mist lying along the ground. I couldn't imagine how an artist could do that. It was so real and beautiful you could smell the freshness of the morning.

The smell of the grass and the cows.' She looked up at him. 'You know? The rays of the rising sun were shining through the mist among the gum trees.' She thought for a moment, turning and looking at the large abstract canvas but evidently seeing in her imagination the painting it had replaced. She made a rounding gesture with her hands. 'And mountains in the background, blue and distant and mysterious. It was lovely.' She looked at Pat looking at the picture. 'Which do you prefer in a landscape, sunrise or sunset?'

'I couldn't give a rat's arse about nature.'

'You can't be an artist then,' she said coolly, 'if you don't care about nature.'

'I didn't say I *was* an artist.'

'Why would anyone go to all the trouble of painting something like this?' She looked again at the picture on the wall behind her desk, her head on one side, her red lips pursed. 'What sort of pictures do you do yourself?'

'You've stopped calling me sir,' he said.

Their eyes met and she smiled.

'I'm Pat,' he said. She had nice eyes, grey with flickers of green. If you ignored her front teeth she wasn't too bad. A decent girl from a modest home. He could see that. His mother would have described her as *one of our own people*, and would have warned him not to give the girl the wrong impression about his intentions. Standing here chatting to this girl he was aware that his life was in crisis. It was as if he had just been told that someone dear to him had suddenly died. Someone he had always relied on for his confidence. For his sense of who he was. For his certainty of where he was headed. They were gone and so was his certainty. He would never see them again. He had been set adrift. There was no one he could tell. No one with whom he could share his sense of loss. No one to know his panic and his fear. He remembered then who it was this girl reminded him of. Catherine Phillips, a girl he had gone to school with. Catherine had the best legs in the class. They were lovely and shapely even when she was only eleven years of age. He could look at the backs of her knees all day and not get sick of them. He could see the enticing little dimples in them now. For years Catherine had sneered at his lustful stares and he had grinned back at her. Then one Saturday afternoon she and her friend were in the queue behind him and Gibbo at the Palais. Catherine was his first girl and for a week or two he was in love. Sometimes when he went home he saw her down the street pushing the pram with the baby in it, her older girl holding onto the pram handle. She always gave him a smile and asked how things were going for him. She was a lost woman.

'I'm Helen,' the girl on the desk said and looked around the empty foyer. She lowered her voice. 'If someone comes in you'd better call me Miss Carlyon. What are you looking like that for?'

'Don't you get sick of sitting here all day, Miss Helen Carlyon?'

'It's interesting. I like watching people. Did you just come in to look at this picture?'

'This picture has changed my life,' he said. He considered telling her everything. 'Do you want to come out for a drink?' He was going to be a father. It would be as if he and Catherine had got married after all and he had stayed in St Kilda and worked on the tramway. He could smell the grease of the pulley.

'Don't be silly. Are you serious?'

'About this picture? Yes. I came to see your boss.' He knew there was really no way of telling this girl his story.

'Which boss is that?'

'Sir Malcolm. How many bosses have you got?'

'You won't get in to see Sir Malcolm without an appointment. What's your surname?'

'Donlon.'

She turned to her desk and ran her slim forefinger down a sheet of pencilled names that lay on the desk in front of her.

'I'm not there,' he said. Her nails were rounded and pink. 'You've got nice hands. You look after them.'

'Thank you.' She looked at her hand holding the pencil. 'No, you're not. No Mr Donlon here.'

He leaned over her shoulder and tapped the sheet. 'Put me in.' Ash from his cigarette fell on the incline of the paper, disintegrating across the page, a tiny avalanche of silver. He wondered if he would really go through with it.

She blew on the ash gently, hurrying it, then brushed her hand across the polished surface of the desk.

'My name's not here,' Pat said. 'But *I'm* here. Okay? Write me in, Helen. I've come all the way from Ocean Grove. I'm going to ask him for money. What do you think he'll say?'

'Writing you in won't help.' She dusted with her fingers at the last of the ash. 'It's Miss Barquist you'll have to convince, not me. She's Sir Malcolm's keeper.' She laughed. 'He calls her his guardian angel. If you're not on Agatha Barquist's list you won't get past her.'

'I bet you I will,' he said.

'How much?'

'Five bob.'

'You're on.'

They shook hands on the bet.

'Tell Miss Agatha Archangel Barquist that Mr Threshold has given me a private recommendation to Sir Malcolm for one of his bursaries.' He was just taking it along now as far as it would go. He was not sure if he was kidding or serious. But what was he going to do if he didn't go through with it? Head for the nearest pub and spend the few bob left from old Gerner's ten-shilling note? Was that it? Do what his uncle would have done.

'Is that true? Has he really?'

He looked into her honest green-flecked eyes. 'Would I have come all the way from Ocean Grove on the off-chance of being admitted into the presence of the great Sir Malcolm McFarlane without having a personal recommendation? Do I look that silly?'

She thought about it. 'Yes,' she said. 'You do look pretty silly actually, Mr Patrick Donlon.'

He tapped the phone. 'Just mention the name of Mr Threshold to her,' he said. 'That'll do the trick. You may as well give me the five bob now. You've done your dough on this one, Miss Helen Carlyon who knows all about art.'

'Don't worry, I know who Mr Threshold is. I've met him. He's nice. He often comes in to see Sir Malcolm. They go to lunch together at Sir Malcolm's club.' She frowned. 'If I lie to Agatha it will spoil things between us. She trusts me. We're loyal colleagues.'

'Loyal colleagues,' he said. 'What's that supposed to mean? She's your boss, for God's sake. The bosses are only out for themselves.'

She looked up at him. 'She's not that kind of boss. She chose me from a dozen applicants. All of them qualified. I'm not going to lie to her. Anyway, she'd know I was lying. Agatha's not stupid, not like some people.'

'But you wouldn't *be* lying.'

'Wouldn't I?' She was disbelieving.

He looked around for an ashtray.

Without taking her eyes from him she pulled open the top drawer of her desk. A small circular brass ashtray lay sleeping quietly in the corner of the drawer, a collection of lipstick-stained cigarette butts snuggled inside it like a litter of pink piglets.

'Can I trust you?' she said.

He stubbed out his cigarette. 'Give us a go, Helen! I need this. You won't be lying to your mate. Honestly.' It looked as if he was going through with it. A worm of anxiety twisted in his empty stomach. Fuck him anyway. What could they do? They couldn't have him shot. He laughed. It was not a happy laugh.

She slid the drawer closed on the crumpled remains of his cigarette, a wisp of smoke making a quick escape, the throat-catching smell of the cheap tobacco. 'I don't believe you,' she said. She was uneasy with his attempt to charm her. 'Are those your own pictures?' She indicated the bundle under his arm.

He flourished his bundle, the belt buckle dangling free. 'My passport to Europe, Helen. My fate's in your hands now. You can turn it all around for me.'

'I don't know why I'm doing this,' she said. She picked up the phone and dialled a single digit.

He leaned over and whispered, 'You won't regret it.'

She drew away from him, cupping her hand over the phone and speaking too softly for him to catch what she was saying.

He put his mouth close to her free ear. 'Tell Miss Barquist I want to know who painted this picture.'

Helen hung up the phone. 'You can go up. It's the fourth floor. You won't get past Agatha. She'll tear a strip off you for trying to con me. And don't forget to pay your debt on your way out.' She pointed. 'The lifts are over there.'

'Thanks, Helen.' He bent and kissed her on the top of her head. Her hair smelled surprisingly of roses.

'You're too cheeky by half.' She reached up and touched her hair. 'Get on with you.' She was blushing.

As he straightened he caught a whiff of his warm rubbery plimsolls—or was it his body warmth bringing out the cupboard smells of his damp trousers? Would the fearsome Agatha Barquist be repelled? He was nervous. He turned away and lifted his hand in a gesture of helpless farewell, then walked across the foyer towards the lifts.

Helen Carlyon called after him, 'You're a sight, Pat Donlon. I bet you haven't even got five bob on you.'

He waved again, not looking around, a wordless sign of acknowledgment. He was still behaving like a free man. What would his dad think? He was going to be a father. Holding their baby in his arms at midnight and shushing it to sleep before he knew it. Helen was right. He *did* look a sight and had only three shillings and sevenpence in his pocket. He knew the amount exactly. He had counted his change after he bought the fags. As he walked across the empty foyer he felt the great painting at his back.

The feeling was with him now that he had nothing to lose. He could see Edith at the cottage in her shadowed end of the back room, painstaking in the sincerity of her pursuit of her art, the cottage and the green rise of the paddock to be rendered on her canvas in oil paint in a manner worthy of praise from her dead grandfather, a work true to the academic standards of her teachers. She would complete the work. She believed in it. He envied her having something to belong to but he could never be like her. He waited for the lift to descend, watching the arrow drifting steadily from 7 towards 0, as if time were speeding past. He felt indifferent to it all. Indifferent to his own fate. He turned and looked across the foyer towards Helen. She was speaking on the telephone.

Pat stepped into the lift and pressed the brass button with the red number 4 on it. The lift obediently shook itself and began its unsteady journey upward, murmuring some little ditty of its own. There was a lingering fragrance of someone's cigar, the smell putting him in mind of something he might have called a man's mature ease. A smell of quiet comfort and enjoyment, it was. Money. What he had come for. The smell of confidence in living. In front of him a photograph mounted behind glass was set inside a brass frame that evidently received the vigorous attentions of someone whose duty it was to shine it up every morning. The polished frame of the photograph was let into the panelling on the back wall of the lift. It showed the front of the building from a vantage point across the railway yards; the impressive descending parachute canopy at the doors was already a familiar feature to him, as if it belonged to the history of another self in a past life. With a contented sigh the lift arrived at its destination and stopped. It had no further responsibility. The rest of this was up to him. 'Thank you,' he said and hauled open the door.

He stepped into a glade of deep green, the carpet liberally spread with a self-patterning of ferns, something to invite the cushioned footfalls of the invited guest. For a moment he had forgotten his purpose in coming. The morning's headache was returning, the piston starting up again, thumping quietly in the back room of his brain. He saw his mother bending over his corpse, giving his marble forehead a kiss of last farewell. There were moments when he would not have minded dying.

The walls of the reception area were lined to the height of a man's head in panels of softly lustrous native cedar. The wood glowed in the warm light from several large glass bowls set into the elaborate plaster of the ceiling. Above the cedar panels, on the long wall facing the lifts, was a row of portraits of serious-looking men, all framed in gilt and rendered in the gloomy academic manner of Sir John Longstaff. Not a smile or a wink from any of them. The seven members of this earnest tribe might have been brothers, or a line of fathers and sons. The patrimony, wasn't it? Pat could not see them dancing with their girls or enjoying a beer with their mates. All the money in Melbourne was with the Scots. That was the trouble. There never had been enough left over for the likes of the Donlons and the Egans. It was all tied up here. With the likes of Edith's people. This was the citadel of her mob too. Her brothers would have felt at home here.

A short fat woman with neat grey hair tied in a bun and wearing a brown wool cardigan over a flowered dress was standing behind a desk set at an angle midway between the lifts and the far wall. The woman was resting her chubby fists on the desk, her enormous bosom squeezed between her upper arms, stretching the material of her flowered dress and threatening to burst out in a riotous blossoming of pink flesh—the jungle plant that blooms monstrously at midnight once every ten years. To be there when her breasts made their rare appearance! She was examining him over her spectacles, as if she had got up from her chair in readiness to greet him when the lift arrived. She was not the fierce guardian angel Helen had prepared him for.

'I've just this minute made Sir Malcolm his cup of tea,' the woman said, giving Pat a big smile, her cheeks pink and dimpling, a light sheen of perspiration on the tight skin of her forehead. 'Would you like a cup yourself, Mr Donlon?' Her accent was a soft Glaswegian. Homely, his mother would have called it. Bairns and hobs and wee things strung on the line to dry. 'Helen tells me you've come all the way from Ocean Grove in this terrible weather without a bite of lunch. You must be chilled to the bone.'

He stood before her. He felt like a schoolboy receiving the favoured attentions of the headmistress. 'Thank you,' he said. 'That would be lovely. Are you Miss Barquist?'

'I am,' she said. 'I hope Helen didn't frighten you with her stories about me. That girl has a wicked sense of humour. Please!' She pointed to the leather armchair beside him. 'Sit down, won't you?' She came around the desk. 'Do you have milk and sugar in your tea, Mr Donlon?'

He lowered himself into the armchair, cradling his bundle across his knees, the damp brim of his hat gripped between thumb and forefinger. 'Thank you,' he said again. 'Yes, please. That would be lovely.' He was conscious of the slightness of his own stature beside the heavy body of this woman. The Irishness of himself, he thought of it, and was remembering the picture of himself standing between Edith's giant brothers. Why did the Scots have to be so big in their bodies? Weren't we all related once? What happened?

She smiled down at him. 'Well, I'll just see to it then. The kettle's only boiled this minute. I could make you a piece of toast and honey to have with it? Would you like that?'

He looked up at her. 'I would. That would be great.' As she went by him Pat caught a whiff of the same rose perfume he'd smelled on Helen's hair. He imagined the elaborate friendship of these two women, sharing their scent and lipstick, braving the weather and going out for tea together at the teashop on the St Kilda pier on weekends, holding onto each other and laughing, the wind blowing their dresses against their legs, one short and fat and struggling to keep up, the other slender and slipping along like a little sailboat dipping and rising over the waves. Telling each other their gossip. He wondered he hadn't seen them. His head thumped gently. It wasn't too bad. A reminder that he was going to die. That was all. Nothing serious.

The lift woke with a quack of surprise. Pat started. He turned his head and watched it sink into the void of the building, grumbling to itself. A man was laughing in a nearby room. It was a big confident laugh of pleasure and goodwill. He eased himself deeper into the chair. He could smell himself, dampness and something warm and human. He was proud there was nothing rancid about his smell. Proud that it was a clean manly smell like his dad's smell. Whatever else they might be, they weren't a family of stale-smelling people. It was surely the laugh of the contented man whose cigar had perfumed the lift.

Miss Barquist came back and handed him a cup of tea. The teacup and its saucer were flower-patterned, like Edith's mother's cups and saucers. Two patterned shortbread biscuits rested on the saucer.

'I thought you might like a couple of these instead of the toast,' Miss Barquist said. 'They're Sir Malcolm's favourite. Dundee shortbread.'

The tea smelled like the kitchen at home. Did the biscuits come in a tartan tin like the one on the mantelpiece where his mother kept her housekeeping? He looked up. 'It's very kind of you,' he said. His stomach made an eager little gurgling sound, preparing itself for the hot drink and the biscuits.

Miss Barquist caught him looking at her as she was tugging her dress into shape against the struggle of her breasts to make their escape. She must be always at it. She sat down, putting her arms on the desk and clasping her fingers. 'Isn't our Helen a dear?' She spoke as if they were all old friends and knew everything about each other.

'Yes, she's very nice,' he said. He munched the first biscuit. While he sipped the hot tea and ate the crumbly biscuits Miss Barquist watched him from behind her desk. The warmth of the tea going down his throat and spreading into his chest and his stomach. He had a small fart coming. He smiled at her and held it in.

'So you like our Wyndham Lewis?' she said. 'Sir Malcolm will be delighted to hear your opinion of it. Most of his friends hate it and don't make any bones about telling him so. I don't like it much myself.'

Wyndham Lewis. So that's who it is. But it didn't matter now. He was no longer pointing in that direction. Was he pointing in any direction? The painting in the foyer was the blank wall where the dead end of his mistaken journey into abstraction had come to a halt.

Miss Barquist's features settled into a thoughtful alertness suddenly, as if a sombre thought had stalked across her view of things. The look in her eyes revealed to Pat a corner of the depths of fortitude that must enable Sir Malcolm to rely on this woman in all kinds of stressful weather. 'We'll go in when you've finished your tea,' she said. 'There's no hurry.'

But there was. He felt it in her now. An impatience to get on with it. He was hoping his nerves weren't going to get the better of him. Why couldn't Sir Malcolm be this woman? My God, life would be so much easier if they were all homely women with big tits instead of old men with heavy eyebrows and thick moustaches. 'So he *will* see me then?' he said. He knew he sounded like a boy. If only he were more measured and steady, more a man of the world in his style, a man certain of his direction. To be sure of his own worth, like the portraits in the foyer. How was it done? It was going to be hard to make any sort of real substance out of his claims for himself in this place. He could see that.

'Of course he'll see you, dear. Sir Malcolm loves meeting young artists.'

He set the cup and saucer on the edge of her desk and stood. 'Thank you,' he said. 'That was just what I needed.'

She struggled to her feet, lifting the load she carried with her everywhere. Fancy having those great things on your chest all day.

He had the sudden childhood feeling of being called in from the waiting room to see the dentist, gripping his mother's hand as if the demons were going to rip her from his grasp before they got stuck into him with their instruments of torment.

Without knocking or any other to-do, Miss Barquist opened the panelled door behind her desk and stepped half into the room beyond. Holding the door open and standing to one side, she announced into the room, 'Here's the artist, Sir Malcolm.' She put her hand to Pat's shoulder and urged him forward. 'Go on in, Mr Donlon. Sir Malcolm doesn't bite at this time of day.'

Pat stepped into the room. The door closed behind him with a snick of the latch. It wasn't a weasel who came forward to meet him but another big Scot, like Edith's brothers, over six feet tall with a great round head like a bullock set squarely on broad shoulders above the solid carriage of a deep chest. Pat was the weasel himself. Sir Malcolm's hair was dark with grey at the edges and parted flat down the left side, slicked neatly into place with a dab of cream just the way Pat usually wore his own hair, just a light sheen to it. His eyes were dark brown and sharply focused, as if he were aiming a weapon, or was looking for something he wasn't sure of, something he hoped or expected to see but feared he might not recognise when he saw it. He was not exactly frowning, but was straining after this something, an interrogation in his carriage and his features. A big question in the whole set of the man. He was not handsome but was a physically strong-looking man, upright and sound, a year or two beyond his fiftieth birthday. He was dressed in a dark three-piece suit and a striped tie—no tie pin. As he extended his hand the white cuff of his shirt came out of his jacket sleeve a good four inches or more, to permit the sparkle of a gold cufflink. The back of his hand and the backs of his fingers were covered with a pelt of bristly black hairs. And if it was a smile he wore on his face it could also have been an expression less welcoming, needing only a fine adjustment to sail out into cold evasion, or even a direct rebuff. Pat could see his likeness done by Longstaff, fitting and appropriately stern-faced, framed in gilt and hanging in the reception area alongside his brothers in the money and the power of things. The chairman of the board. Someone to be taken seriously. There was no doubt about it.

Pat took his hand. 'How do you do, sir.' The hand was large and cool and dry, the grip firm and encompassing, and those dark brown eyes looking out from under the shrubbery of his heavy brows, probing for that something he was afraid might elude him, the little extra thing that would slip past him if he didn't remain alert. The telephone rang. Sir Malcolm withdrew his hand and excused himself. He stepped to his desk and picked up the telephone. His manner to his caller was calm and courteous but it was clear he was not pleased.

Pat placed his bundle and his hat on the floor beside a chair and looked around the room. It was panelled in the same manner as the reception area. Through the window behind Sir Malcolm's vast desk, over beyond the railway yards, the white tower of Government House thrust up through the green canopy of elms in the park on the other side of the river, the Governor's imperial yellow ensign stretching out in the breeze—look at me! Look at me!

Pat turned back to the room. Not one of the half-dozen paintings on the walls was as large or as imposing as the one in the foyer downstairs, but like that painting these too were examples of the work of British and European modernists. There was something familiar about each of them, but Pat could not have named the artists with any confidence. He hoped he was not going to be tested. The great European modernists and the less than great. It made his stomach ache to see them. A geometric group of shapes occupying multiple overlapping perspectives at the centre of one canvas might have been a Braque. He could take a punt on that one, but his judgment had no certainty in it and the painting could as easily have been the work of a follower—someone like himself, trying to catch up. He had seen the work of none of these painters in real life and had acquired no eye for what might be authentic among them. In their presence he was aware of his provincialism and the vastness of his ignorance.

On a low coffee table by the chair, where he had put down his bundle and hat, recent copies of *Apollo* and the *Burlington Magazine* and one or two other expensive art journals whose titles were not familiar to him were neatly displayed. No doubt artfully arranged by the hands of Miss Agatha Barquist. A woman you might easily underestimate.

He was in a place where an interest in art was supported by a great deal of money. He made a new decision. It was a simple enough decision, and not so different from the audacity of the original one made on an impulse as he rode his bicycle to Mr Creedy's butcher's shop yesterday morning (was it only yesterday morning?). It was a decision that had a less audacious feel to it now that he stood in the heart of the citadel. Sir Malcolm, after all, talking on the telephone a few feet from him and looking out calmly towards the river and the tower with the flag waving from its pole, was just like any other man, and at worst could decline a modest call on his bounty from an aspiring young Australian artist. Sorry, son, there's nothing I can do for you. Followed by a smile and handshake of farewell. There was nothing to be lost here.

Sir Malcolm was off the phone. He waved at the chairs that stood on either side of the coffee table and came around his desk. They sat facing each other across *Apollo* and the *Burlington Magazine*, the newspaper tycoon in his suit and the would-be artist in his mock rags. Neither spoke. Pat looked at the picture of a pale Chinese celadon vase on the cover of *Apollo*. He raised his eyes and met Sir Malcolm's steady scrutiny. Pat cleared his throat. Was Sir Malcolm waiting for him to get to the point? No doubt the chairman was used to men who knew their own minds and spoke their minds freely.

Pat said, 'I came to see you, sir, to ask you to grant me one of your bursaries.' There, it was done. Not so difficult. Simple really. Just out with it. What was the problem with that? Would anyone else have had the cheek to do it? The unimaginable hurdle cleared at a single bound. Pat smiled. Sir Malcolm's expression did not change. There was no inner response to Pat's smile. A little flutter arose in Pat's stomach and he would have liked to light a cigarette. He noticed that a fly had got into the office and was buzzing around the back of Sir Malcolm's head. He watched it settle on the shiny nap of Sir Malcolm's hair. Sir Malcolm moved his head and the fly took off, then landed on the shoulder of his suit and began cleaning its legs.

Oblivious to the fly busying itself on his shoulder, Sir Malcolm regarded Pat steadily from under the dense hedgerow of his eyebrows, like a sniper gazing out from the concealment of his hide. He had only to pull the trigger and this irritating young man would be blown away. Pat began to doubt the wisdom of having come so abruptly to the point. Might not this hurry to talk about money have seemed to the great man to be a display of bad manners? Wasn't he accustomed to evasion and delicacy and even to charm, flattery and diplomacy from the numerous mendicants who came to call on him? Maybe Sir Malcolm even felt that his dignity and intelligence were belittled by this crude frontal attack, reducing a meeting whose potential pleasures might have involved a discussion of the higher values of art to the question of a small amount of cash. Pat was wishing he had waited, had left the issue of a bursary to find its own way into the conversation.

'So you're an admirer of Wyndham Lewis?' Sir Malcolm said. 'That makes you a rare bird in these parts.' Sir Malcolm crossed his legs. He glanced down at his crossed legs, as if the manoeuvre had taken him by surprise, his legs having assumed the initiative without consulting him. Although his observation to Pat had been delivered in the tone of a question, Sir Malcolm went on speaking. 'He's the best of the British modernists. If it was up to me and Guy, Wyndham Lewis and his mates would be hanging in that bloody great mausoleum up the road they call the National Gallery, instead of that brown muck those bloody tonalists call art.' He regarded Pat with narrowed eyes. Something had stirred his emotions. 'The place is being run by fools. Do you and your fellow students know that, Mr Donlon?' He shut his mouth firmly on this question and waited to hear from Pat.

'Many of us do,' Pat said. 'Yes.' This was not a lie. Didn't he despise the values taught at the Gallery School? And hadn't he rejected them, just as his hero, Rimbaud, would have done?

It was sad to think of it all now. That episode of empty bravado. But it was all he had to draw on. Instead of telling Sir Malcolm this he said, 'We have to do our own art. We can't just follow the British and the Europeans.'

'And is that what you're doing? Your own art?' The question was bluntly put, Sir Malcolm's cold rebuff waiting in the wings for its cue. 'Can you artists ignore the great art of Europe and Britain without paying the price of provincialism and condemning yourselves to obscurity? Hmm? Eh?' He drew in a rapid gasp of air. 'So where have you seen Wyndham Lewis before today?'

'In reproductions only, sir,' Pat said. He gestured at the journals on the table. 'In magazines. I didn't recognise him. You don't see the hand of the artist in those glossy little pictures. You get no idea of the grandeur of their work. There was definitely something familiar about it. It stopped me dead when I came through the front door. But I couldn't have told you who the artist was. Not an Australian, for sure. I could see that.'

'Why not an Australian, Mr Donlon? Why so sure not an Australian? Miss Barquist told me you recognised it as Lewis's work at once. Aren't we as good as them? Can't Australians do it, Mr Donlon? Is that your opinion?'

'She was mistaken, sir. It's not her fault. I was impressed with it. I didn't recognise it. More impressed than I can tell you, but I didn't know who'd painted it. There aren't any Australians doing work as confident as that.'

'You do know he gave up painting abstract pictures twenty years ago? He's been doing very fine figurative work since then. That's one of his early ones. A pre-war work. I was lucky to get it. It wasn't for sale. Guy Cowper winkled it out of a private collection in London and we made them an offer. It's only been hanging here a month. Guy's a wonderful man. A great man. There's no one else like him in Australia. You and your mates would have to know his critical writings in my paper?'

'Yes, of course, everyone reads Guy Cowper's reviews.' Pat laughed. 'The teachers at the Gallery School are scared of him.'

'Do you think so? That's not my impression. What a bunch of blundering idiots. You think he's got them scared? Are they bright enough to know when they should be scared? And you and your fellows, do you agree with what Guy has to say? He's the only man for that job. He's lived in Paris and London. He knows everyone over there. If a picture comes into the market he knows exactly where it's from and who owned it last and if it's any good or a dud. He speaks three European languages. All fluently. If it were up to Guy and me, we'd have Georges Braque and Picasso and Lewis and his mates all over the walls up there at that tomb. I've been elected to the board, did you know that? We're going to make a few changes up there.'

'I heard something, I think, along those lines, sir.' Pat wished he had kept in touch with things and hadn't despised the idea of involvement.

'You're not familiar with the politics of art, Mr Donlon, I can see that.'

'I just try to do my work, sir.'

'If your business is going to be art, Mr Donlon, then my advice to you is to get involved in the politics of your business. And the sooner you do that the better for you. It's in board-rooms, not in studios, where decisions about the reputations of fellows like yourself are made. You're going to need a few mates on the right committees if your work is to be brought to the notice of the right people. Ignore the politics of your business, and the politics of your business will ignore you.' He motioned briskly to the untidy bundle on the floor by Pat's chair. 'Is that your work?'

'I brought along a few drawings.'

'The mackintosh is a novel idea,' Sir Malcolm said drily. 'Miss Barquist said you were carrying a folio.' He sighed heavily and stood up. Was he getting bored? 'Put them on the desk. Let's have a look at them.' He stood back, watching Pat struggling to release his drawings from the clinging embrace of Edith's damp old mac. Pat didn't mind the smell of it. He was reminded of rainy days at home in St Kilda.

Pat said, 'I didn't intend to be so blunt just now, sir. About the money, I mean. The bursary. But I need to get to Europe.' He thought he'd have more chance of success if he mentioned the word Europe. The small black fly settled on the back of his hand then flew off towards the window, deciding it had had enough of the place. Pat freed one arm from his struggle with the mackintosh and waved at the pictures around the walls. 'I need to see these first-hand. I need to find out what the rest of the world is doing before I can know what it is I have to do myself. To know where the gaps are, if you see what I mean.'

'The gaps?' Sir Malcolm said sharply, as if he questioned himself about cracks in the wall that needed attending to, or suspected a criticism of his collection. 'What gaps are we talking about?'

The drawings did not want to roll out flat but curled back on themselves—terrified of being exposed to the gaze of this great man with the eyebrows and the money. Pat was sorry he had mentioned the word *money* again. And *gaps* had been a mistake. Mentioning money a second time had doubled the clumsiness of mentioning it the first time. But how else, if he didn't speak about it, was he supposed to get Sir Malcolm to speak about it?

Sir Malcolm stepped up to the desk and held down two corners of the curling paper with the tips of his fingers. Big hands. Pat noticed his fingernails were pink and carefully manicured. They seemed too delicate to belong to his hairy fingers.

'Thank you,' Pat said. He held down the other two corners of the sheets himself, his shoulder touching Sir Malcolm's shoulder then easing away. The two of them restraining a weakened patient on the operating table, ready to begin their dissection. A modern *Anatomy Lesson.* 'The things that no one else is doing, I mean,' Pat said, trying to explain his use of the word *gaps.* They stood looking down at the flowing bosom and oddly displaced swirl of hips of Mr Creedy's buxom daughter. Pat could smell her sweet clear skin, intriguingly tainted with the sawdust and blood of the shop. He looked up at Sir Malcolm.

But Sir Malcolm was not thinking of art. 'I think you'll generally find, Mr Donlon,' he said, adopting the magisterial tone of an elder of the tribe, 'that the things other people are not doing are things that are not worth doing. And that is why they are not doing them. Contrary to what you say, we must do the things that other people *are* doing. And we must take careful note of *how* they are doing them. Then we must strive to do them better.' He drew breath and paused to scan each drawing before folding back the sheet and delivering it into Pat's care, his head first on this side then on the other, repeating a small sound in his throat, keeping his lips closed and giving a bit of a nod of his head. The sound in his throat underwent a number of minor variations with each drawing, as if he were trying out a new flute, a slight modulation of tone or decrease of intensity, tuning his reactions. Pat paid close attention to these sounds, but if they implied an expression of interest, that expression did not reach a level where it might have been taken by him for enthusiasm. When Sir Malcolm had got to the last drawing, the one of Mr Creedy's daughter's buttocks, he paused a little longer, reading the poem. 'So you're a poet too, Mr Donlon,' he said. And only then did he look directly at Pat. 'Are you sure art's your vocation?'

'I'm either an artist or I'm nothing,' Pat said. He realised how hopeless about it all he had sounded. And wasn't there also a note of impatience and anger in there too? If serious men such as Sir Malcolm were to have any confidence in him he would have to find a way of concealing the rawness of his emotions and tempering his private truths. He was not very good at playing this game. He was aware, suddenly, that the interview was over. He had failed Sir Malcolm McFarlane's inquisition. For that was what it had been. A final mistake had been to include his poem, which had only provided Sir Malcolm with a distraction from art on which to close their meeting.

'Well, young man,' Sir Malcolm said, freeing his hands from the butcher's paper and stepping away from the desk, leaving control of the drawings to Pat and lightly dusting off his fingers. 'You'd better stop by Guy Cowper's office on your way out and show these to him. I leave judgments about bursaries in his capable hands. He's the finest this country has.' He summoned a cold smile to his eyes and held out his hand. 'Miss Barquist will show you where Mr Cowper has his office.' Sir Malcolm moved to the door and held it open for him.

Pat shook his hand and thanked him for his kindness in seeing him, then he tucked his untidy bundle of drawings under his arm, gripped the brim of his hat between two fingers and went out the door, which closed behind him with that curt little click he had noticed before, the brass lock evidently well aligned, his father would have been pleased to know, and sweetly oiled, thanks to a man doing the rounds with his long-nosed oilcan and a wad of cotton waste whipped from the back pocket of his green dungarees, making his periodic appearances in the executive suite after the boss and his bosomy pal had gone home. The invisible maintenance of things so dear to his dad's heart. Was it where he was always going to belong himself? Pat wondered. Although he loved and respected his mother and father, and wished to retain their love and respect for himself and his way of life, he had a cold horror of becoming trapped in their class. Of being like them. As he left Sir Malcolm McFarlane's office that day the piston in Pat's head was thumping and he was longing for a smoke.

•

When Pat stopped talking the only sound penetrating through the thick glass and stone of the building into the foyer was the squeal of a tram going past along Flinders Street.

'What do you do with yourself all day here?' He was looking over Helen Carlyon's head at the agitated blue and grey field of the great Wyndham Lewis on the wall behind her. The painting now seemed to him forlorn and stripped of its power, displaced and not belonging here, pillaged from its rightful home on the other side of the world by Sir Malcolm's foraging critic, the much-feared Guy Cowper. It came to Pat then that a work of art can only retain its full power in its own place. Looking at the picture he knew in himself a kinship of exile with it, a sense that each of them had been subjected to the same wilful coercion, the same peculiar cultural violence, of the men in command of things. Those who could command the pillaging. Displayed here in this silent foyer, Wyndham Lewis's masterpiece had become a trophy merely of wealth and power, a rare and expensive object, like the Chinese celadon vase on the cover of *Apollo*, with which to augment the prestige of its owner, the great chairman of the board. Pat's voice broke across the empty spaces of the foyer. 'I'd go bloody starkers sitting here all day with that looking over my shoulder.'

'I thought you liked it,' Helen said gently. 'And there's no need to swear, Pat. You're upset. Go on with what you were telling me. I've got plenty to do. Don't you worry. The foyer is my kingdom.' She giggled at this. 'Go on! Tell me what the great Mr Guy Cowper said to you.'

Pat looked down at her upturned face, her red lips parted just sufficiently to reveal her two front teeth, like a tiny new pair of glistening ballet shoes presented to him for his inspection. He could lean down and kiss them. He was confident he was the most interesting event in Helen Carlyon's day, possibly in her entire week.

'He was sitting at that big fancy French desk writing something,' he said. 'An article for Sir Malcolm's newspaper, I suppose. Thinking up how he was going to rubbish some poor bugger's paintings. He didn't even look up when your mate Agatha showed me into his office. He just sat there with his head down and went on writing as if nothing had happened.

I waited half a minute for him to say something. I was thinking what a rude bugger he was. I should have turned around and walked out of there, but I was still hoping he might like my drawings. So I said, Sir Malcolm said I was to see you, Mr Cowper. Well, he sort of paused and frowned at this, as if the sound of my voice irritated a sensitive nerve in his head. He laid down his pen, carefully lining it up with the edge of his blotter. You would have thought it was costing him a pound to do it. Then he took his time blotting the page, pressing it down evenly all over. When he'd done fussing around with this performance he stood up and came around his desk. He was still not acknowledging my presence in any way at all, no hello or how do you do or even a little smile of welcome. Not a thing. My drawings might have arrived on his desk by magic. Hello! I should have said. I'm here too, you know! He flicked through my drawings with a sneer on his face, a dreadfully distasteful chore for him, obviously, to be interrupted in the middle of his important work with this—his lips were twisting around as if he had his nose in a stinkpipe.'

'His lips are too wide for his mouth,' Helen said. 'They're all over the place. And did you notice how still his eyes are? They're uncanny. The way he looks through you gives me the creeps. I feel like turning around to see if I'm standing behind myself.'

'It took the mongrel about thirty seconds to make up his mind,' Pat said. 'You would have thought I'd insulted his mother. You've got no respect for art, Mr Doolan, he said. It's Donlon, I told him. He went straight back and sat at his desk and picked up his pen and he examined it as if he thought it might have got contaminated and then he started writing again. Is that it then? I said, raising my voice. I was getting angry.'

'I'll bet you were.'

'He did look up at me then. I know what you mean about his eyes making you feel like he's looking at someone standing behind you. He barked back at me like a sergeant major, Learn to draw! Learn some respect for the craft! You're untrained! I replied that I intended to do my own training. Then do it with your own money, he said. Not on Sir Malcolm's charity. Now get out of here and take that rubbish with you. You're a charlatan.'

Helen put a hand to her mouth. 'Did he really call you that? A charlatan? You're not a charlatan, Pat. You're definitely not that.'

'I had to hold myself back from going around the desk and belting him one over the ear.' But Cowper was right. Pat knew he was a charlatan. The man was right. The trained critic in him had seen it at once. It hadn't taken Cowper more than a few seconds to sniff it out. He was only stating what Pat already knew about himself.

'I'd have paid good money to have seen that,' Helen said. 'Someone needs to punch him. Which reminds me.' She ducked down and opened the cupboard under the drawer in her desk and took out her handbag. She ferreted around among the numerous treasures in her bag and drew out a little blue leather purse with a gold butterfly clip. She clicked the purse open. 'I owe you five bob.'

'You don't owe me anything at all,' he said.

'I pay my debts, Pat.'

He looked at the two half-crowns in her palm. She was offering them up to him. 'I won't take your money,' he said. It wasn't his dad's moral authority that was stopping him from taking her money. His dad would have said it was a fair bet with Helen and needed to be settled. It was his mother who was Pat's guide in matters such as this, a woman for whom honesty was not degrees and opinions but was something as simple and clear as washing day. Pat was with her when she found a bag of banknotes on the footpath. He was twelve. She handed him the bag and told him to take it around to the police station. Which he did, with a weight of great reluctance on his soul that he could still feel a trace of lingering there now. He knew his mother had two shillings in her own purse for the shopping that day. 'I'll not take your money, Helen. You can hold it up as long as you like. I'm not taking it from you. It wasn't a real bet.' Why didn't he tell her Cowper was right about him?

'My word's my word, Pat, joking or not.' She looked him steadily in the eye with her own green-flecked eyes. 'Take it!'

Pat smiled. 'You remind me of my mum.' Wasn't Helen just like what his mother was like when his dad first met her? In Luna Park, it was. His dad had told them the story a hundred times. It was his regular song after coming home from drinking with his mates. Your mother and me first met one summer evening in Luna Park, didn't we, darling? Clawing his way back into her good books after doing the housekeeping on the gee-gees and the beer. Pat loved his dad, he loved him passionately and was proud of him for all sorts of reasons. But he wasn't going to be like him. He felt a sudden rush of fear that he might lose the honesty of his own eye, whatever that was to be, and he didn't know yet the form it was to take, but knew it was the most precious thing he had. He knew too that if he were to hang around currying favour with the likes of Sir Malcolm and that slimy bastard Cowper he would be certain to lose any chance of his own way of seeing. And it wasn't some romantic innocence he was talking about either. When he got his eye in, if he ever did, it would be something real as hell. He was sure of that much. An eye like the flaming tongue of Rimbaud. He could have wept for himself.

'You're away with the fairies there, Pat!' Helen touched the sleeve of his jacket. She was holding up a business card to him. 'He cares about artists like yourself. He cares more about art than anything. He stood here telling me all about himself after he came out of a terrible meeting with Mr Cowper. He and Mr Cowper had fierce words. I could hear them shouting at each other in the lift. I've never forgotten him. He was a man my father would have called a gentleman. I would have been happy to run away with him if he'd asked me to. He wasn't at all like Mr Cowper, always wanting to be the centre of attention and haughty with everyone, letting me and Agatha know we're only Sir Malcolm's servants. Which makes me want to vomit over his shiny shoes. And he's only working for Sir Malcolm himself. This man wasn't at all like that. You'll like him. I promise you. Here, take it. It's the only help I can offer you. He was trying his best not to look like a lawyer, but I had him pegged for a lawyer the minute he walked through that door.'

'You're a bright girl, Helen.' He took the card from her.

'Don't you patronise me now, Mr Pat Donlon.'

'I'm sorry.'

'It's all right. I'm the forgiving kind.'

'Do you have a boyfriend?'

'I do. And I suppose you have a wife?'

'I do.'

'Well, that's that then, isn't it? Good luck, Pat. Let me know how you get on.'

'I will,' he said. He put the card in his breast pocket and leaned down, intending to kiss her goodbye on her rose-scented hair, but she presented her cheek to his lips at the last minute. He straightened and put his hat on his head. 'You're a lovely girl, Helen.'

'I'm a woman, Pat, not a girl any longer. It was nice meeting you. I hope you get what you want from life.'

'Is your boyfriend good to you?'

'Yes, he is. He's a kind man. We're going to be married.'

He stood there, knowing he should leave, but reluctant to go.

'There's no chance of anything between us, Pat, if that's what you're hanging about for. You know that. Be off with you now. I'll bet anything your wife's a lovely woman.'

'You'd win that one.'

'I know I would. I have an instinct for people.'

'You have.' He smiled. 'I don't know why I'm standing here.'

'Neither do I,' she said. 'Life's a funny business, isn't it?'

'It is that.'

8

Arthur

THE DOOR AT THE TOP OF THE SHORT FLIGHT OF WOODEN STAIRS was half open, a pale light filtering across the landing, dust flecks dreaming in a thin pall of aromatic cigarette smoke. The muffled sounds of the street outside. Pat looked again at the card Helen had given him: *Arthur C. Laing—Laing, Carter & Playord, Barristers & Solicitors*. He went up to the door and tapped with his fingernail on the frosted glass. There was no response. He put his head around the corner of the door. A man was sitting at a desk in the corner of a small cluttered office. He had his feet on the desk and was reading a book. In his free hand he held a cigarette close to his lips. He was taking little puffs from the cigarette, as if he was sipping a drink, his lips forming a fish mouth from which one perfect smoke ring followed another. A faint smile of deep interior pleasure enlivened the man's handsome features. At his back a tall uncurtained window, its numerous panes of glass streaked with vertical deposits of grime, looked onto a nest of tram wires and the elaborate brick facade of a mock Gothic building on the far side of the street.

Pat took his hat off and stepped into the doorway. A board groaned under his weight.

The man looked up. 'Ah, you're here,' he said. 'I'm so sorry.' He took his feet off the desk. 'I didn't hear you. Do come in, please!' With a deeply perplexed look at the page he had been reading the man closed the book and set it aside. He stubbed out his cigarette in an ashtray that was already the mass grave of a dozen or so crushed butts. He brushed at his tie and shirt front then looked up. His dark hair was long and uncombed, falling about his ears in glossy waves. He was wearing a bright carmine and canary-yellow tie over a pale blue shirt. His jacket was silvery grey, an expensive sheen to the material—the gleam of a sylvan glade in moonlight. He pushed the hair back from his face. 'Do forgive me.'

Pat stood across the desk from him. 'There's nothing to forgive,' he said. 'You weren't expecting me. Unless Helen phoned you and said I was coming? My name's Pat Donlon.'

The man leaned across the desk, offering his hand. 'Arthur Laing.' He smiled quickly. 'Do excuse the mess in here. How can I help you? Sit down, won't you. It's a bit cramped there. Put that stuff on the floor. Can you fit yourself in?'

The smell was a mixture of the dust peculiar to old books and ledgers that have not been opened for decades—not since Pat's mother was a young woman like Helen Carlyon, no doubt—and the smell of the foreign cigarettes. There was something else that Pat could not identify. 'Helen Carlyon gave me your card, Mr Laing.'

'Helen?'

'At the *Herald* offices in Flinders Street. She's at the desk in the foyer.' Pat made a wide sweep with his free arm, as if he would summon before them an image of Helen sitting at her desk in the tomblike silence of her kingdom, overlooked by Wyndham Lewis's exiled masterpiece, her white teeth on point.

'Ah, yes, Helen. Of course. I'm sorry, I thought you were referring to a client. I have a client whose name is Helen Carpentier. Or *had*, I should say. A distant cousin, so she told me, of the great French boxer Georges Carpentier. You don't have an appointment, you say? That's fine. I'm not busy, as you see. I was about to leave the office when this came.' He tapped the book. 'I couldn't resist taking a peek.' He looked up. 'You're in luck. I've missed my train.'

'Helen said you're supposed to be interested in art.'

'Supposed to indeed, Mr Donlon. And are you an artist yourself?' Arthur Laing sat down again. His gaze drifted over Pat's rags and settled on the bundle under his arm.

Arthur Laing's dandyish appearance didn't appeal to Pat at all. He decided the man was too full of himself to be of any use to him. He was tired and fed up with being dismissed by these superior types. A bolt of resentment flared through him at the lazy tone of Laing's question, and a determination to reclaim his self-respect made his face flush. Helen had obviously been sucked in by this bloke's grand manner and his smart looks. 'Whatever you or anyone else might think of me, Mr Laing,' Pat said, his tone belligerent, challenging the other man to contradict him if he would, 'I believe that's what I am. An artist. Okay?'

'Well, bravo, Mr Donlon,' Arthur Laing said cheerfully. 'And aren't we defensive about it.' He put his hand over his mouth and gave a soft laugh of amusement. 'Please do sit down. I beg you. The world is full of misunderstood geniuses, Mr Donlon. I have met a great many of them. I do hope you're not a member of that unhappy tribe. Won't you please sit down? If you can fit yourself in there. Tell me, what is it you hope I can do for you?'

An upright chair stood in the cramped space between the wall and the desk. There was a pile of files on it. Pat placed his bundle of drawings on the desk in front of him, shifted the papers onto the floor and sat down. He was glad to set the drawings aside.

Arthur Laing picked up the book he had been reading and turned it, holding it up for Pat and waiting for him to read the title, which was embossed in gilt on the spine.

Pat read, *The Modern Movement in Art*, R.H. Wilenski.

Arthur Laing had a pixieish smile in his gentle grey eyes. 'My credentials, Mr Donlon. Interested, that's the word for what I am.' He put the book down flat on the desk, leaving his hand on it, as if he was about to swear a solemn oath by the virtues of modernity. 'Can I ask what you were doing at the *Herald* offices, apart from chatting to our friend Helen?'

'I was seeing Sir Malcolm and his art critic mate, Guy Cowper.'

'You had an interview with these men?' Arthur Laing's tone remained carefully without inflection but his eyebrows betrayed interest, and some incredulity. He picked up a blue packet of cigarettes and offered it across the table. 'Not everyone likes these. But I'm an addict, I'm afraid. Nothing else tastes quite like a real cigarette once you've become accustomed to the bite of these little devils.'

Pat reached over and gripped a cigarette between his thumb and forefinger, and slid it from the soft embrace of its packet, on which was displayed a blue *dolce far niente* of a gowned woman in an attitude of dreamlike dance among curling smoke. 'I was asking them for money.'

Arthur Laing laughed. 'And how did Cowper respond to that? I'll lay you odds Sir Malcolm wasn't privy to that discussion?'

'He threw me out of his office.'

Arthur Laing grew serious. 'Ah, yes. Guy Cowper is a difficult man to warm to. And is that why you've come to see me? To ask me for money?'

Pat lit the cigarette and drew the smoke into his lungs, the sharp clutch of the darkly aromatic tobacco on the back of his throat making him catch his breath. He said huskily, 'I thought you might buy these.' He spread his fingers over Edith's mac. 'Fifty quid. It's all I'll need to get myself over to England and the Continent.'

'All indeed. Fifty pounds is a lot of money, Mr Donlon. Did Miss Carlyon tell you I would fund your dreams?'

'She said you were interested in art and artists.' Pat stood up. 'I shouldn't have bothered you.'

Arthur Laing held up his hands. 'You're not bothering me, Mr Donlon. Please, sit down!' He waved at the clutter that surrounded him, a momentary anxiety clouding his features. 'You are an unusual visitor. Do you mind me saying so? I loathe this ghastly business. It's got the better of me. The law, you know? I really do hate it. I've hardly anything left to do here. I meet miserable people intent on making difficulties for other miserable people. It's not a way of life I'd recommend.'

Pat sat down again. He didn't feel well.

'What sort of an artist are you? Perhaps I'd better have a look at those.'

'I don't know yet what sort of artist I am.'

'My wife says an artist doesn't need to know what he wants to paint until the inspiration to paint comes to them. At which point necessity takes over. Or should do. What do you think? Is she right? Is that the way you do it?'

The strong cigarette was making Pat dizzy. He hadn't eaten anything substantial since breakfast. He belched softly, tasting Sir Malcolm's Dundee shortbreads. He watched Arthur Laing get up and come around the desk and begin fumbling with the belt buckle of Edith's mac. He was reminded of their old sportsmaster at school, smelling of pee and nervously fumbling at the buttons of a boy's shorts before letting loose with the strap. 'Let me do that,' he said. He took the belt from Arthur Laing's hands, their fingers touching as he did so. Arthur Laing looked down at him, his lips forming into a delicate smile, as if the touch of their hands confirmed for him a sensitive perception about his visitor; the beginning, perhaps, of a guarded respect for Pat's guileless request for help.

Arthur Laing, with his hair and his yellow tie and his silver suit, leafing through Mr Creedy's daughter. Pat's fictions of the girl, that is, of the naked young woman, whom Pat had never seen without her clothes. Laing, his head on one side then the other, murmuring, 'Yes! Interesting,' or even, 'Very interesting.' And once, 'Unusual, Mr Donlon.' Striving to make sense of what he was seeing. Eager to respond. In fact responding. Delighted to have been distracted from Wilenski. His lips moved as he read the poem under the last drawing. When he had finished reading the poem, Arthur Laing returned to his seat and, with great care, lit a fresh cigarette.

He did not blow smoke rings this time, but formed a small circular opening with his soft pink lips and exhaled the smoke in a narrow thread, as if he wished to imitate the exhaust of an idling motor car on a frosty morning. He sat without speaking for a while, gently making his smoke trail and evidently absorbed in his thoughts, or perhaps listening to the clang of tram bells outside and the sound of footsteps—was it a man or a woman?—hurrying down the stairs. Then someone passed along the corridor whistling. It was a perfectly keyed version of 'Dance a Cachucha' from Gilbert and Sullivan's *The Gondoliers*.

Arthur Laing said, 'He can do an interesting realisation of a Chopin nocturne for you if you ask him to. Perhaps it's this that keeps him happy. He's a lawyer too, but received from his gods not only the charming ability to whistle sublimely, but also the even rarer gift of a reposeful soul. He is a man blessed with the wisdom of contentment.' He looked at Pat, feigning astonishment. 'I envy him.' He sat gazing at Pat for a long half-minute, the receding whistler eventually silenced by the closing of a distant door. 'I shan't pay you fifty pounds for your drawings, Mr Donlon. But how about coming to dinner with us this evening? What do you say? There are extravagant aspects to my wife's character, but her cooking is renowned. And reliable.'

PART
two

9

September 1991

EIGHT MONTHS OF THIS YEAR HAVE GONE ALREADY. I'M LUCKY TO still be here. After my night in the loft I came down with a chill which developed into bronchitis. It wouldn't shift off my chest for weeks and I was losing weight that I could not afford to lose. Andrew diagnosed mild pneumonia and ordered me to stay in bed and rest. 'Or you won't see the year out.' I've never known him in such a bossy mood. He told me to never, never smoke ever again and to give up writing my memoirs. 'This whole business has unsettled you.' Unsettled?

Between wheezing and coughing my lungs up I managed to tell him, 'You're trying to bully me, Andrew, and it won't work.' But I was too exhausted to put up a serious fight. He stood beside my bed glowering at me, Adeli at his side wringing her chubby hands over her paunch as if she was an old-fashioned lady's maid—some Americans, and I've noticed this before, are oddly unsuited to our century. No doubt she was afraid she was about to lose her subject. What then, Adeli? Without me, who is my biographer? Andrew didn't shout at me. Like Arthur, Andrew is far too well mannered ever to shout. But he was seriously alarmed by my midnight visit to the coach house. 'If you're going to persist with writing this thing of yours and smoking cigarettes, there's nothing I can do for you. You won't last till the spring.' Well, Andrew, it's the first day of spring and I'm still here.

Not smoking doesn't suit the idea of myself I've been conjuring with this year—the indestructible old harridan, lone survivor from a bygone era of greatness, the standard-bearer of truth from her own time. *That* woman smokes and writes and possesses a furious energy for it all. But my night in the loft nearly did for me and I've been forced to temper my belief in my powers of resistance. The truth is, I have been humbled. Even as I write this I am trembling. The tremor has never quite left me since it started in the loft—like the precursor of a truly grand earthquake that will shatter the familiar landscape of my being for good. The night in the loft cost me more than my strength. Is it a penitent I am to become? Repenting my life? Not all of it, surely? I don't know that true repentance is possible for the intelligent unbeliever, is it?

During those long sleepless nights these past weeks, struggling to get my breath, the last of my flesh melting from my bones, I might have given up and let the angels take me. But I persisted with the struggle. I want to get this job done before I am done for myself. It was my sighting of Edith in the street that day that gave me the impulse to begin this, but it is my own stubbornness that compels me to go on with it. I will not willingly go over to the other side until I have given an account of myself on this side.

So I obeyed Andrew and laid off writing and cigarettes until this morning. Andrew thought I might also have had a mild stroke but I refused to go to hospital for the scans. 'You know very well,' I told him, 'if I go into hospital at my age I'm never coming out again.' I think he did know. He didn't argue. But he refused to let me stay on my own in the house. So I find that I am no longer the independent woman I once was, but am returned to the dependencies of childhood. If I do not agree to his terms and conditions my doctor has the power to send me to await my death in purgatory with the other creepy inmates with their dead-fish eyes and walking frames. I am powerless to oppose his will. Was he even threatening me with a return of the multiple orgasmer? This possibility inspired me to say, 'Adeli will look after me.' She smiled and leaned over to take my hand in both her own, her plump cheeks trembling. 'Of course I shall look after you, Mrs Laing. It will be an honour.' Yes, it will be an honour, I thought, but it will be an honour on my terms, young lady. As it has turned out, the terms are not quite my own. She has been feeding me my antibiotics twice a day with the quiet determination of a French farmer force-feeding his geese for the season of foie gras.

Today is the first day she has let me out of my bed. I would have defied her and been up before this but I haven't had the conviction in my legs or my head to manage it on my own. Yesterday was the last official day of winter. It was one of those days of fine purity and promise, when the world seems graced by a primal innocence and the most abject among us rejoice to be alive. Even the freeway was subdued, as if in homage to what is left to us of nature's wonder. Adeli opened the French doors for me so that I could hear the magpies and smell the wattle blossom. After she'd fed me my pills I said, 'You've got to let me up for the first day of spring, darling, or I promise you I shall die in my bed. You won't have the free run of this place when I'm gone, I can tell you that. Your dining-room hoard will be closed to you. The trustees will have you out of here like a shot.' As you can imagine, the *darling* was bestowed on her by me in a tone of gritty irony. I asked her to bring me Barnaby's stout blackthorn shillelagh. She brought it and helped me up. I held her arm and wielded Barnaby's stick in my other hand, the knob fitting perfectly to my palm. We're not in love exactly, but I am confident we understand the terms of our arrangement. If I am prepared to deal in the currency of small compromise, then I doubt if Adeli will give me any serious trouble.

She has refused to give me my cigarettes. She burst into tears when I shouted at her that she was a selfish bitch. I was overwrought and regressed for a moment to my old hysterical ways. I think I frightened her. But she did not yield. Through her trembling little sobs, her size fifties shuddering alarmingly, she said, 'I'd rather see you die than be the one to give you those terrible things.' It was very affecting. I calmed her with an apology and a fond pat to her enormous thigh and told her we had smoked day and night when I was young. But she is a woman of her time and was not to be convinced. I shall find a way to get cigarettes when I need them badly enough. It will be more fun to trick her than to threaten her. After all, I need her as much as she needs me. I can't afford to lose her. Without her I would soon be drifting about in a home for the waiting dead. Imagine the smell! And no smoking there, you can be sure of that. No fun for anyone. I can always get Stony to smuggle in cigarettes among the cabbages—all prisoners find the means for evading the rules of their jailers, and I am now a prisoner of my old age. My once-silky legs may be withered and frail, the sensual curves of my thighs reduced to wasted sacks of wrinkled skin, but my mind remains as sharp and clear as winter moonlight in the desert—and I have been loved in the desert and seen the silver of the moon laid across the trembling stalks of young wheat, and I have cried out to my lover with the breath of my passion. I am not a stranger to the desert.

•

I'm sitting at the small table on the veranda with a blanket around my shoulders and, as you can see, I am writing. Yes, I have re-entered my little world. What a joy it is. Andrew will not be pleased. In this final year of my life—surely there cannot be another?—I have discovered the joy of dwelling in a world of my own uncontested memory. Adeli has had Edith's picture cleaned and framed for me. It is hanging on the wall in my bedroom beside the French doors. From my bed when I wake in the morning I now have a view of their white cottage and the embroidered field at Ocean Grove, where Pat slaughtered Gerner's horse for dog meat more than half a century ago and received ten shillings in payment, with which he paid his fare to Melbourne and changed our lives forever.

Edith's picture no longer represents the despised work of the enemy for me, but is a window to my memory. If Arthur saw it here he would be pleased. Arthur adored me, poor man, and was terrified of losing me. I saved him from his mother and from his own uncertainties. He kept alive a hope that one day

I would find within myself the grace of a gentleness akin to his own. I'm afraid I never did. But even so, was there a need for me to be quite so fierce with her?

To be fair—and I wish to be fair to myself—I was no less intolerant with Pat. Once he was with us—once, so to speak, I had snared him in my net of love and ambition—I insisted he make up his mind whether he was to be a writer or a painter. 'You can't be both,' I told him. As if I knew. Which of course I did not. But he was no use to me as a poet. The thought of him dithering about with his verses angered me. My rejection of his poetry was selfish. I was impatient for him and me to get on with the business of deciding what sort of painter he was to be. It was not only his adoration but the collaboration in art I wanted from him. Not long after we met it was this that came to represent my sense of my own way forward. To be with him in art, *our* art. I let him know he could not have me if he was going to be a poet. I feared at first that I had overplayed my hand and he would choose poetry (no doubt a true poet would have done just that). He claimed to feel more at home with writers than with artists. 'And Freddy here,' I said, 'feels more at home with women than with men, but that doesn't make Freddy a woman.' It was easy to get a laugh at Pat's expense in those early days, especially if we'd all had a few drinks. He looked on at us and said nothing, as if he was not of our time. He unsettled our certainties (as Andrew would no doubt have said).

And he was right. He was ever a loner and was never at home even with his own kind. He was a refugee from his parents' modest home and their restricted life in St Kilda. He was, though he scarcely knew it himself at that time, in search of a home for his imagination. A grand, strange, far-off place it would have to be if it were to satisfy his needs, unfamiliar and subject to legends and dreams. In his thirties he found such a place in the soft English countryside and never did return to live in the hard land of his birth. A reverse migrant, Pat became. A bird of passage visiting us whenever the season of his soul required it of him. Many of our friends decided he was a faithless deserter for abandoning Australia, but I understood him and knew it was not desertion or abandonment that drew him away. Pat took Australia with him. To find kinship among strangers was a quest he'd had in him since his boyhood. His only home had ever been in his own head. In that strange shifting landscape of his imagination, a place he never shared with anyone.

And this may explain why despite the volumes of critical attention his paintings have received, there remains even today an untouched silence in them. Something essential about them that evaded the critics, and perhaps evaded him. Something at the centre of his art that remained undisclosed. And was it not wilful, this keeping of a sacred enclosure beyond our reach, beyond his own reach. It was the entire creative endeavour of Pat's life, to reach into that heart of his imagination and expose it. But he found in the end that it eluded him. As perhaps it always must. For the silence at the heart of art is surely art's singular precondition. The estranging silence and absence we feel when contemplating his pictures are precisely what draws us back to them. Always in us after we leave them a sense of unresolved anxiety about their meaning.

He was never able to share his innermost struggles with anyone, nor did he leave in his poetry any mention of the demons that tormented him. I often thought him a man in search of a key with which to unlock access to his own inner world. I believe he did not have a choice to be other than this. It was not acquired habit with him to be so solitary, or a vain pretension, but was in him. His boyhood love for the Icelandic sagas, his dreams of one day meeting in a gipsy his own true brother of the spirit, or finding in Ireland something bathed in the strangeness of himself, these were all for him youthful expressions of the impulse of that inner solitariness, that sense of disconnect that he never mastered in himself.

He would have scoffed if you had called him a romantic. But it would have been the outer man doing the scoffing. Inside, deep inside, where Pat inhabited his creative life, he was like a great sad bird roosting in the fastness of some bleak mountain range, exposed relentlessly to the fierce elements of his own doubts and fancies. Pat was a man on his own. To me his solitariness was immediately attractive. I sensed it in him at once. On the outside he could be hard and unforgiving, but for a brief period with me he was without such defences. Our life together was to become a tangle beyond our unravelling and would cost us and others great suffering. But I would not forfeit it for something less. In my own solitary way (and I too have my solitariness, as do we all), it was the very point and meaning of my life. Love and art combined in Pat and me to make us each greater than either of us had ever been or would ever be again. And neither he nor I understood it. We lived it. Briefly it flamed in us then died. And we both grieved for it ever after. When Anne Collins telephoned from England to tell me he had died with my name on his lips I was moved and I wept, but I was not surprised. I understood.

Freddy was the first to detect the danger Pat's arrival posed for our little group of intimates, the artists, poets and thinkers of our circle, the group that ever since our arrival at Old Farm had supported in Arthur and me a sense of meaning and purpose in our lives that went beyond the daily facts of living. It was late one wet and wintry Saturday afternoon. Arthur and I and Freddy and Barnaby, and one or two of the others, Anne Collins and Louis de Vries if I remember, were still at the kitchen table, drinking and arguing about art and life. We were reluctant to bring to an end the fellowship of the afternoon, which had begun with us meeting for lunch. That afternoon we had no doubt rearranged the priorities of the Australian art world. Pat was not with us. He returned late from an excursion into the city to visit his mother and to buy the paint he favoured. He had walked from the railway station and came up the back step onto the veranda and through the kitchen door, banging the flywire and bringing a blast of cold air and the bleakness of the day into the warm kitchen with him. His arrival among us seemed violent and sudden. His manner was aggressive, an impatience in him with our endless talk about art. He was fond of saying, 'Artists paint, they don't talk about it.' He was a workman and wanted to clear them all out of the place so that he could lay his stuff out on the kitchen table and get on with his work.

When he came banging through the back door into the kitchen we fell silent and looked at him. It had been raining and his cap and the shoulders of his jacket were dark with the rain. He was lugging a bag and was red in the face with the effort of his walk up the hill. He dumped the bag on the end of the draining board. His clothes clung to him and you could sense the heat and the impatience in him, something so physical and intense about him and his bag that none of us was willing to be the one to break the silence. It was Freddy who spoke.

There was the sound of Freddy striking a match to light his cigarette, then he said, in his soft and lightly teasing voice, glancing at me with a smile in his eyes, 'Do you know what we've been arranging here this afternoon, Pat?'

Pat was at the draining board struggling to release two dead chooks from the bag. He didn't turn around. 'No, Freddy, I don't.' From his tone it was clear he meant, 'and I don't bloody care either'.

Freddy smiled and smoked his cigarette and let the silence go on a while, then he said, 'We've decided to form a new group. We're calling it the new art society.' Freddy waited again but Pat went on gutting the first of the chooks. Freddy said, 'We'd like you to join us.'

'I don't join groups,' Pat said.

And so Freddy and the rest of us and our grand idea of a new art society were dismissed by Pat as of no consequence. I laughed and told them all it was time for them to go home.

Freddy was not a dandy, but he liked to dress well. That day he was wearing a lovely Donegal tweed suit which he'd had made for him when he was in Dublin the previous year. I loved Freddy. We entertained each other. There was never anything sexual between us but we teased each other and pretended to flirt. I don't know how much he'd had to drink that afternoon, it was impossible to tell with Freddy, but quite a bit I'm sure. He got up and went over to the sink and he put his arm around Pat's shoulders and kissed him firmly on the cheek. Freddy was not homosexual but knew Pat to be intensely sensitive to any suggestion of homosexuality. Pat was caught off guard and reeled away from Freddy, wiping at his cheek with the back of his hand and looking so fierce I thought he was going to strike Freddy. Freddy stood his ground within striking distance and smiled and puffed on his cigarette, as if he were inviting Pat to strike him if he dared, or perhaps to return the kiss. But Pat just swore and laughed unhappily. 'You're a fucking idiot, Freddy.'

When Freddy left that afternoon it seemed to all of us that he had won a point over Pat. A physical, manly point. Something to do with good manners, not courage. And we all valued good manners more than we valued courage. I got up from the table and took Freddy's arm and walked him to the front door. Neither of us mentioned Pat. As he was leaving, Freddy turned to me and said, 'The first meeting of our new art society ended rather well, don't you think?' He got in his car and waved to me and drove off. The far-side rear wheel of his car rode up over the bricks with which Stony had edged the circle of roses in the centre of the drive. The bricks are still wonky there and I still feel a pang of sympathy for Freddy's tortured loneliness when I think of that day. Freddy was not a solitary man, but he was a very lonely one. I stood at the door and watched him turn into the road, the rain falling steadily, the light fading rapidly. Our road was quiet in those days. Today it is often a drag-racing strip for the hoons in their yellow and red Holdens. In those days we had a few neighbours who still made the fortnightly trip into Melbourne along our road in their horse and buggy.

As I stood at the front door in the pleasant chill of the wet evening, the road empty, the sound of Freddy's motor car a distant murmur, I was troubled by the unrealistic demands Pat was starting to make on me. I knew myself to be at the beginning of something that was going to leave us all changed forever. Whichever way it went, for good or for ill.

I thought of myself standing at the rails of the *Cooee* at Port Melbourne with my mother when we were setting off to visit her relatives in England and to tour Europe together. It was 1925 and I was nineteen. On the boat to England I began a period of aggressive and exaggerated sexual behaviour that was to cost me dearly. My first lover was a steward not much older than myself. We made love in his cabin. I imagined I was a free woman. The thrill of concealing our dangerous liaison from my mother was delicious and terrifying. I thought myself launched on a new life. I believed our escapade was a perfect secret between my lover and myself, but it was probably known to the entire crew, and must have been at least guessed at by some of the passengers. Apart from my mother and me there were only twelve other passengers. My father's pastoral company owned a controlling interest in the *Cooee*, which carried a regular cargo of wheat and wool to England. He had given the captain strict instructions to see that we were provided with the highest level of care and attention on the voyage.

In England, and during our tour of the continent, I had many other lovers. I was indiscriminate and wild and so emotionally distracted by the hectic frenzy of my imagination that my mother took me to a psychiatrist while we were in Rome. I fell pregnant to him on my second visit. He procured an abortion for me. I have never been sure if my mother knew of it or not. It was never mentioned between us. And she didn't press me for an explanation of the mysterious ailment which kept me in bed for a few days. She and I lived like enemies together in strange pensions and hotels, I seeking out new lovers everywhere we went, the pair of us tormented by the frantic hysteria of our extraordinary uncertainty. If we touched each other by accident one or other of us would flare into an outburst of violent anger and unfounded accusations. The slightest irritation was a cause for murderous eruptions of emotion. I accused her and my father of driving Uncle Mathew to his death. He had killed himself only a year earlier and my grief was still keen. Mathew had been the only one among my family ever to have shown me any understanding. I did not think of it at the time, but perhaps my sexual revolt was a response to my regret that I had denied Mathew that last time in the garden at Elsinore when I was seventeen (I nearly wrote, in the garden of Eden).

Without the sustaining presence of my father's authority or the familiarity of home, neither my mother nor I was emotionally mature enough or sufficiently sophisticated to impose order on our wandering lives. We were in a state of nervous panic most of the time and too aimless and too ignorant and uncaring of Europe's treasures to recognise their interest for us. The tour was a disaster. There were times when we might have died on the streets of some strange city and never been heard of again. Whenever my mother tried to talk to me I sought escape from her in hysterical outbursts. In Venice I threatened to throw myself from the window of our apartment into the green waters of the canal beneath our windows. I was serious. I longed to enter the green tide below our windows and find oblivion there. If my mother had not wrestled me to the floor, the pair of us shrieking and struggling, I might have ended my life that day. My mother was frightened of me. I was frightened of myself. We were both bewildered and slightly insane. On the boat home I became depressed and refused to leave my cabin. I was bewildered and confused. I had become a stranger to my mother and to myself.

It was less than a year after we got home to Melbourne that I met Arthur. I recognised in him at once a safe place in which to shelter from myself. My mother was relieved beyond words to be rid of the burden of me and agreed to the marriage at once. I was unwell after our marriage and eventually a specialist in Collins Street discovered I had undiagnosed gonorrhoea. Arthur, a virgin when we met, was shaken by this, but he was heroic and didn't falter in his support of me. I had to have a hysterectomy. Facing up to the fact that we would never be able to have a family of our own was a terrible blow to us both, but it also drew us closer together. We shared a sense of refuge with each other from our detested families and our misfortunes. I'm sure that being unable to have children was partly the reason why, soon after my operation, we began to rely for a sense of structure in our lives on a salon of creative friends.

With these friends I was at last beginning to use the ability Uncle Mathew had recognised in me; an ability to acknowledge the gifts of others. More important than my cherished 'gift', I was a good cook and Arthur a generous judge of wine. So our little band of friends could always be confident of a good feed and something decent to drink whenever they came to see us, or stayed with us when they were short of funds. When I left home I vowed never to have a cook or a maid in our house but to do it all myself. I even went to cooking classes. My mother's total ineptitude around the house and especially in the kitchen appalled me. I learned nothing useful from her and was determined not to be like her. Arthur and I cared for our inner circle of creative friends as we would have cared for our family. Our chosen few had only to swear to a passion for defining modernism and upholding its principles for us to make them welcome and feed them. Arthur and I wished to be a source of influence among young artists and to counter the forces of an unsympathetic conservatism which was represented for us not only by the art of the establishment but by the values of the families we had each rejected, I with a greater vehemence than Arthur.

I had not forgotten the child of the Italian psychiatrist. If that child had lived—and it lives still in my imagination—it would be sixty-five. It remains my only child. What sort of a mother would I have been to it? What sort of a mother *was* I to it? The price I paid for my wild sexual liberty as a young woman was the heaviest a woman can pay. Motherhood. I swore when I married Arthur I would never be unfaithful to him. And until Pat I had kept my word.

After Freddy left that day, I stood at the front door for a long time, watching the rain falling and listening to the sounds of our familiar silence. I was terrified by my feelings for Pat Donlon. Arthur and I had been married almost twelve years by then. That I might be unfaithful to him was inconceivable to me. And yet I feared it would be inevitable with Pat. I had believed I was safe from myself with Arthur. Safe forever. Why had I become obsessed with this narrow-shouldered Irish workman? There were frightening moments when it made no sense to me and seemed to threaten me with a return to the madness of my European tour with my mother. I felt threatened that day as I stood at the front door after Freddy had gone. I stepped out into the rain and lifted my face to the heavy grey clouds and closed my eyes and let the lovely chill drops run down my hot cheeks. And I prayed to Him in whom I most devoutly do not believe to help me find my way through the chaos of emotions that were destroying my peace of mind.

My prayers of unbelief amused Freddy and, I think, interested him also. He said to me once, 'You live as if there is a God, though you know there is none.' I called him my Hebraic sage. He was my closest confidant and best friend for many years. I could and did tell him everything. Things I could not comfortably tell Arthur I freely confided to Freddy. There was no sense of betrayal in these confidences. They were the exchanges of friendship, Arthur understood the quality of that friendship and was never jealous of Freddy. Freddy loved gossip, but I knew my confidences were kept by him in sacred trust. My poor dear Freddy. How wonderful it would be if only he were here with me now; how we would make light of all this together. Or would the burdens of old age have soured his humour? Men fail at old age more readily than we do. His suicide was quite unlike Barnaby's. Freddy's suicide was a deeply self-conscious act of courage in the face of his total physical breakdown. Barnaby, the silly man, had no such reason to kill himself. Suicide with Barnaby was selfish and unnecessary. He just couldn't be bothered with the tedium of going on living and getting older. His death made suicide something ordinary, like shopping for the necessities. A few bobs' worth of nothing remarkable from the supermarket. Since the age of eighteen I had thought of Uncle Mathew killing himself in that village in Ireland, alone and lost, and his death had seemed to me something deeply sad and romantic. Barnaby made suicide banal. But perhaps Mathew's death, too, had been merely sordid. At eighty-five (or whatever I am), human behaviour is no longer a source of romantic illusions.

•

Adeli encourages me to write this memoir, if memoir it is. Which is hardly surprising. After all, she's not exactly a disinterested observer of the outcome of my defiance of Andrew. I haven't let her see any of it. But I dare say she is confident of having the opportunity to study every word of it after I am gone. Providing the trustees accept her bona fides, she will be in charge of my record when I am dead. I've no doubt she'll shove most of this into her book, and much of it without acknowledgment or editing. There is something ruthless about her kindly caring, slightly soppy manner that I find intriguing and a little repulsive. She is not simply the eager fat sook from California I took her for when she first came here. She is still from California, of course, and she is still fat, but these facts no longer carry quite the same imperative for me to bully her they once carried. I've not asked to read anything she has written about me, and she has not offered to show it to me. I don't want to see it. I have no wish to authorise her project with my approval. Historians know the official biography is worthless. Let her struggle for her own truths. I won't influence her with mine. Our truths are written in our hearts and are not a currency of exchange.

She has set herself up very comfortably in the guest bedroom, which is conveniently next door to the dining room, where the elaborate sources for her scholarship are piled on the big dining table, and under the table and on the long sideboard. And even on the mantelpiece. And there are cartons stuffed full of papers in the corners of the room. If she lives to be ninety she will never get through our archive. Sooner or later she will need research assistants. I've not been into the dining room to check on her progress in case she mistakes it for interest. And anyway, there was always something discouraging about that room and there is no reason why that discouragement should not still be there. Perhaps it is that the furniture reminds me of my mother's dining room. The furniture came, in fact, from Arthur's father's gloomy old mansion in Tasmania (that land of melancholy and despair, haunted by the ghosts of human suffering and cruelty. I visited it once and never returned. I shivered all the while I was there).

The east side of the house has become Adeli's end (why did I nearly write Edith's end?). Unfortunately she and I have to share the only bathroom. She always seems to be in there, the door bolted, just when I need to pee. I stand outside and bang on the door with Barnaby's shillelagh and yell at her, but she does not reply. Silence. An hour later I will be sitting at the table in the kitchen, my bladder on fire, when I hear the cistern flush. By the time I've hobbled along the passage to the bathroom she is back in the dining room. She sprays the air in the bathroom with some kind of chemical deodorant that makes me sneeze. I tell her I would rather smell her animal stink than this stuff, but she goes on spraying it freely. I might as well tell Sherry not to spray. I like to sit on the pan and smoke a quiet cigarette. Beside the sink there is a little old four-paned window with a view of Idaho, Arthur's favourite species rose. It has climbed into the topmost branches of the red gum, where it flowers, its face turned to the sun. Such blooms among the gum leaves.

Adeli looks after me without complaint. But then looking after me is taking care of her own welfare, isn't it? She is a good cook and the three of us eat well and the house no longer stinks of cabbages and my farts. I have insisted, however, that we maintain our order for cabbages with Stony. 'It was Stony,' I reminded Adeli when she objected to keeping our order in, 'who saved my life. You should be grateful to him.' Adeli does something with the cabbages but I have not enquired what it is. They arrive then disappear. So long as Stony gets paid for them I don't care what the fate of the cabbages is.

A week ago Adeli found Pat's drawings among her treasured rubbish in the dining room. She carried them in to me triumphantly. I was in bed, lying on my back gazing at Edith's painting, daydreaming about the two of them down there in that isolated cottage at Ocean Grove with hardly enough money to get by on. But happy, young, in love and full of hopes—just before he stepped into our picture and brought their brief happiness to an end.

Adeli came into the bedroom carrying the bundle, her round cheeks glowing with a sheen of sweat (as usual). 'I've found them!' she announced, as if she had found the lost treasure of the Sierra Madre. They were no longer in a roll. She set them down on my bed covers and leaned over to spread them, her great melons diving about like bloated water bombs. Sherry came into my room behind Adeli and sat on the Anatolian kilim Arthur gave me for my fiftieth birthday. He watched Adeli adoringly. When I was first confined to bed after the loft escapade Adeli cancelled my regular monthly order with Stony for the hundredweight bag of cat biscuits and began buying fine cuts of meat from the local butcher. Sherry was now eating from a blue and white Spode bowl such exotic combinations as devilled calf's liver with chopped smoked bacon, or smoked salmon and sardines. I stared hard at Sherry over the side of the bed, but he would not meet my eyes.

'Unfaithful swine!' I said. He drew himself up disdainfully and closed his beautiful green eyes. He was looking five years younger, his long fur glossy, his tail curled regally around him like an ermine cape. His colouring was perfectly set off by the rose madder and fig green of the rug. He was no longer my friend. The one betrayed is always hurt. Age is no defence against the pain of betrayal.

I looked up at Adeli. 'Well done,' I said, hoping she heard the sarcasm in my tone. 'They had to be somewhere.' She stood looking down at me, a hard gleam in her eyes. I realised with a little shock that she believed she had bested me in some way.

'They are drawings of my anatomy, Mrs Laing,' she said, scarcely emphasising the *my*. But it was there.

Perhaps I was feeling oversensitive after Sherry's betrayal, but it seemed to me that what Adeli really said was, 'They are not drawings of *your* anatomy, you skinny wraith.' As if she had seen in these hurried early sketches of his the expression of Pat's ideal of the feminine form. Indeed her own form. Did she believe she had discovered a shared bond with him that he and I had not shared? The possibility affronted and angered me. What nonsense. Pat *had* no ideal of the feminine form. She has understood nothing.

So, has the biographer begun to compete with her subject for ownership of her subject's story? Is she to read her own destiny in mine, displacing me little by little and inserting herself where I rightfully belong? I nearly lost my life searching for those drawings, but once they were found they held no interest for me. Adeli insisted on helping me to sit up so that I could look at them. She was right, those vast thighs and swirling buttocks were her own. I did not need to see her without her clothes to know this, any more than Pat had needed to see Mr Creedy's daughter without her clothes to see in the eye of his imagination those trembling balloons of naked flesh.

I said, 'I could do with some of that fat myself.' But my irony was of no use to me. The fact is his drawings mean more to her than they do to me. The realisation drained me. I lay down and told her to take them away. 'You're interrupting me.'

'I'm sorry,' she said. 'But I knew you'd want to see them.'

She waited but I said nothing. I felt as if it was all slipping away from me and I feared I might not have the power to hold it in place any longer. *This*, I mean. Everything. The hillside breaking from its ancient hold and easing down into the valley of its dissolution. Unstoppable. I felt the panic rising in my chest.

Adeli said, 'I thought you were just resting.'

'I am *thinking*,' I cried out. 'Do you know what that is?'

She collected the drawings and left, unabashed by my outburst. The last of those drawings, with the poem, the one that betrayed Pat to Sir Malcolm as neither quite artist nor quite poet, was not among them. I told her to close my door on her way out.

When she had gone I lay there for some time looking at Edith's painting, seeing Pat down there in that little white cottage doing those drawings that evening, caught up in the energy of his big idea, putting together what he blithely called his folio to impress Sir Malcolm. His trek the following day culminating in the discouraging discovery of the Wyndham Lewis, painted well before he was even born, and finally his humiliating rejection by the critic Guy Cowper; 'You are a charlatan.' By the time he arrived at Arthur's office Pat had run out of options, and his confidence in himself was shaken. He was, after all, a young man who had accomplished very little at that time. And even self-confidence as vaunting as his must have had its limits. When I met him later that evening I believe he was at his lowest point ever and was close to abandoning his hopes of becoming an artist. For the first time in his life, Pat knew himself to be without a way forward. He had set out that morning to take the citadel of the enemy by storm and by the end of the day had done little more than make a fool of himself. By the time I saw him he was demoralised, afraid that what lay ahead of him were the ties of fatherhood and a job at the tramway depot alongside his dad. It had been a long way down for him that day and I detected the fear and aggression in him when he walked into the library with Arthur.

In the first few minutes of meeting Pat I thought Arthur had made a dreadful mistake inviting such a person to our home. Old Farm was our haven. It was the temple of our beliefs and the base for our chosen group of like-minded artists and thinkers. Pat Donlon did not seem to me when I first saw him that evening to be the sort of person who would fit in with our friends or our aims, or who would even possess the grace to respect our hospitality. I was right about this, but not quite in the way I had imagined. My initial reaction was to be annoyed with Arthur. For when we are in doubt we blame our spouses.

We all know that. It wasn't until Pat vomited helplessly in the kitchen later that I saw how truly vulnerable he was and felt some sympathy for him, and even a desire to take care of him. Or at least to help him out for that moment. He was like a boy trying to be a man and I saw that he needed my help, not my disdain. And so my response, you will say, was to mother him. My unrewarded instinct. Which is probably all true.

Arthur had telephoned me twice that evening, the first time to tell me he had missed his train and the second to warn me he was bringing someone home for dinner. 'I've met this interesting bloke. I think you might like him.' Arthur's brief description of 'this interesting bloke' had not prepared me for Pat. Expecting an interesting man to come home with Arthur I had gone to some trouble with dinner and had made one of my famous rabbit pies, with crème caramel to follow. In those days my pastry was the envy of every woman who ever had the good fortune to taste it, and those few of our men friends who were not in love with me were, without exception, in love with my pastry. Rabbit or apple pie, gooseberry tart or peach flan, they were my triumphs. We didn't have the gas on up here in those days and I loved cooking on my wood stove and had become expert at it. Unlike modern stoves, which are clones of each other, wood stoves each had their own personality and could be moody if not treated with deference. My dependable Rayburn and I were a team.

My Rayburn has been the heart of this home since the day it was delivered from Scotland in its wooden crate and installed by Stony. It is keeping the kitchen cosy with Stony's reliable wood this afternoon as I sit out here on the veranda writing this. Adeli has no idea how to deal with wood stoves.

She needs an on/off switch for things or she is lost. I'll go in soon and draw a chair up to the firebox and rattle the stove into life. I'll select one or two pieces of red gum from the wood box and will not close the door of the firebox at once after I've put the wood in but will sit looking into the orange glow of the embers, the new wood catching with blue and yellow flames, and I shall enjoy the heat on my face and the smell of the wood smoke. I will allow a curl or two of the fragrant smoke to escape into the kitchen—I wish it would penetrate as far as the bathroom and defeat the chemical stench of Adeli's pressure pack. And, if I have enough energy left, as I sit there looking into the firebox I shall daydream of being young again. If Adeli is not about I'll smoke a cigarette and probably have a little cry. I don't like her to see me shedding tears. My sense of the situation with Adeli is that she is not really a support but undermines me. I must remain strong with her or she will not be satisfied with having established herself in her end of the house but will invade me utterly and take over. She is a fat cat—and remember, I have known cats all my life. Confined at first to a basket in the wash house and forbidden to enter the house, they are not satisfied until they are sleeping on the pillow next to one's head. True, Sherry never made it that far with me, which is just as well. Adeli will have everything if she can get it. But she will never be mistress of my Rayburn. My comforter. All those years ago—how many is it?—when Pat first came to see us, the Rayburn was my pride and joy. I was never content to be merely a bluestocking but had worked hard to become expert in all the branches of the art of housekeeping. I was proud of being unlike my mother. She scarcely knew how to flick a duster, let alone prepare a fine dinner on a wood stove.

I was ready for Arthur and his interesting bloke that evening, my rabbit pie in the oven and the crème caramels cooling on the stone shelf in the pantry. I'd had time to have a bath and change, and had put on just the lightest touch of lipstick and a feathery pass or two of powder to my perfect cheeks—perfect they were, but even then, at thirty-two, I searched the mirror for the first signs of wrinkles, the dread that I would find my beauty flawed by the beginning of ageing, the anxious question ever in my thoughts, When is my decay to begin?

Waiting for them by the fire in the library that evening I was the cool one. I took down our copy of Rimbaud's *Une saison en enfer*, the only work of his we possessed, and sat in my favourite place on the couch to the right of the fireplace. Arthur had told me the man he was bringing to dinner was a Rimbaud enthusiast. I imagined a sophisticated European, perhaps a few years older than Arthur and me. I'd been careful to ration myself to one gin while I was preparing the dinner and was enjoying a pleasant sense of intrigue and expectation at the prospect of the evening ahead. The fire was drawing well and the room was warm. I don't remember what I thought of Rimbaud's poem. The words were no doubt just sliding past my eyes. It was years since I'd read him and I wasn't really in the mood for his youthful extremes of emotion. I was probably rather enjoying just being me; that comfortable self-satisfied state of being which Arthur and I both slid into without effort in those days, before Pat Donlon entered our lives.

10

Once, if I remember well . . .

ARTHUR CLOSED THE FRONT DOOR AND WAVED PAT FORWARD, indicating the first door on the right-hand side of the passage. Pat set his bundle of drawings down against the wall and opened the door. As he stepped through, Arthur was so close behind him that the hard toe of Arthur's brogue caught the soft heel of Pat's dilapidated plimsoll and as Pat went to step forward the sandshoe was yanked off his foot. Pat stopped abruptly and put his hand to the doorjamb to steady himself while he reached down and retrieved his plimsoll and pulled it back onto his foot. When he straightened he saw that he had entered a long high room. The walls were lined with well-filled bookshelves. The only break in the impressive ranks of books, apart from the fireplace at the far end of the room, was a deep bow window behind him, a table in front of it with a great bowl filled with pale roses.

At the far end of the room, on the mantelpiece above the fireplace, a large brightly coloured abstract painting in its unframed stretcher leaned against the wall. A woman was sitting on the couch to the right of the fireplace. She was smoking a cigarette and holding a book aside in her left hand, which rested on the couch, and was watching him with interest. His stumbling entrance had evidently surprised her.

'Sorry,' he said, and lifted a hand to her in the sign of peace. 'My sandshoe came off.' He moved to one side and Arthur came up and stood beside him.

Arthur said, 'This is Pat Donlon, darling.' He turned to Pat. 'My wife, Autumn.'

Autumn did not get up. She said coldly, 'It's good of you to call on us, Mr Donlon.'

'It's nice of you to have me.' Pat bent and adjusted his left sandshoe, which having tasted freedom once seemed intent on leaving him again. After the chill of the Pontiac's cabin on the way up from the railway station the library was cosy. The house smelled of wood smoke and cooking and had a welcoming, homey feel to it. Pat's stomach growled. He was dizzy with hunger. He had had nothing to eat since Sir Malcolm's guardian angel Miss Agatha Barquist's cup of tea and two Dundee shortbreads. His eyes met Autumn's. 'What a great collection of books,' he said.

Autumn did not respond to his remark but turned and set her book on the arm of the couch then stood up. 'I'll go and see to the vegetables, shall I, darling? I've set places for us in the dining room. Perhaps you could look in and see how the fire's going in there.' She came across the room and as she drew level with him Arthur stepped forward and leaned to kiss her. She closed her eyes and presented her cheek, her head turned away from him.

As she stepped past him to go out the door Pat said, 'It smells great, Autumn.'

Beside the tall figure of Arthur Laing, the stoop of his shoulders lending a patrician humility to his appearance, his expensive silvery suit and his long hair, Pat knew he looked more like the man who had come to collect the rubbish than the man who had come to dinner. He would like to have explained his odd getup to Autumn but she gave him no opportunity to do so. She left the room without pausing, closing the door so firmly behind her he wondered if she had meant it to seem to him that she had slammed it in his face. The whiff of violence he caught from her impressed him and he looked at Arthur.

'We'll have a drink, Pat,' Arthur said. He was looking thoughtful. 'Why don't you sit by the fire and get some warmth into you.' He handed Pat his packet of cigarettes. 'You look half frozen. I can let you have a cardigan. That jacket of yours is wet.'

'It's all right,' Pat said. 'I'm okay.' He lit one of Arthur's cigarettes and handed the packet back to him, then he went to the far end of the room and stood in front of the fire and looked at the painting. He did not recognise the artist and there was no signature. He turned from examining the painting and picked up Autumn's book from the arm of the couch and read the title. Rimbaud's *A Season in Hell*, in the original French. Surely it was a message to him? He sat on the couch in the dent in the cushion where she had been sitting. The cushion was warm through the thin material of his trousers. Arthur handed him a glass of whisky. Pat took the drink and thanked him.

Arthur said, 'Cheers,' and drank from his glass, then placed his glass and the bottle on the low table that stood between the two couches at either side of the fire. He took a black iron poker from its stand and jabbed at the fire with it, as if he were thrusting a sword at his enemy. At his first jab a panic of sparks raced up the chimney. He saw in the shower of sparks a flight of children and mothers crying out in dismay, a whole town of innocents raped and murdered. He put another piece of wood on the fire and stood with the poker in his hand, a troubled expression on his long intelligent face. In the deeply private place where he kept his feelings, at that moment Arthur Laing might have been entertaining the idea of a gentlemanly melancholy.

Pat began to read Rimbaud's poem aloud, the book held out in front of him. 'Once, if I remember well, my life was a feast where all hearts opened and all wines flowed. One evening I seated Beauty on my knees. And I found her bitter. And I cursed her.'

Arthur turned from the fire and reached for his drink. 'Don't stop. I'm so glad you read French, Pat. Please go on. You read well.' He stood looking down at Pat wonderingly. 'Go on. Please.' His entreaty was gentle and persuasive, his mood evidently affected by the poetry.

Pat considered the book. He said gloomily, 'I don't read French. I know the English translation of this pretty much off by heart.' He drank the whisky as if it was beer and made a grimace. 'Jesus!' he said. He held the empty glass at arm's length and looked at it as if it had contained acid. He had never tasted whisky before. He set the empty glass on the table and looked at the book in his hand. 'Rimbaud had the sense to give up writing before he was my age.' He seemed about to go on with his reading, but turned instead and put the book on the arm of the couch face down, where Autumn had left it. 'He changed his life and never wrote another word of poetry. It can be done.' He looked up at Arthur, who was standing above him in front of the fire, as if he hoped the older man was going to contradict him. The flames were reflected redly in the silvery sheen of Arthur's trousers, as if muscles rippled beneath the material. Arthur said nothing but sipped his drink and looked into the fire.

'We think we're going in one direction,' Pat said. 'Then we go in another.' He took a drag on the cigarette and picked up one of the magazines from the table and riffled through its pages. 'We're not really in charge. We only think we are.'

Arthur said, 'You sound just a little dispirited about things, Pat. You've no cause to be. Your drawings are interesting. I told Autumn I've not seen anything quite so fresh for a long time. She'll want to see them later.'

Fresh fish, Pat thought. The magazine in his hand was the October edition of *Cahiers d'art* from the previous year. He put it back on the table and picked up a copy of *Siecle*.

'So where do you get these?' He waved his hand over the crowded table. He was thinking of Edith at the cottage on her own and wishing he was with her. They were going to be a family. He would have to bring them both back to the city, his wife and child. She would be afraid of the dark down there on her own. The unfamiliar night noises in the cottage. The rats playing polo in the ceiling wouldn't be funny without him beside her to laugh with. He was able to make the strangeness of it all seem like fun to her, but on her own she would hate it and wouldn't be able to sleep. He could see her sitting up at the kitchen window with a blanket round her shoulders right now, watching for a sign of his bike lamp coming up the track. It would be black as hell down there tonight. He was a criminal for coming to this place instead of going home. He could have been almost there with her by now, the two of them cosying up in their bed. With him beside her she wouldn't give a rat's arse for the rats. When he'd settled them in Melbourne he'd take himself down to the tram depot and apply for a conductor's job. His dad would see him right with the supervisor. His dad would be over the bloody moon. I've never said anything, son, but I can say it now while your mother's not with us to hear me. I'm glad you've got that art business out of your system at last. The Donlons have never been artists. Your mother's people neither. The Egans were rhubarb growers in Kilkenny. That was her lot. Honest working people all of us. You wait, once you're on at the depot the super will be promoting you to inspector before me. His dad would get excited and start exaggerating things. Making stuff up to clothe his son's disaster in a story of success. He'd take him down to the Albion and shout him a beer with his mates. They'd all be yelling and carrying on at him and giving him a hard time. But privately they'd be celebrating that Jimmy Donlon's son was no different to their own boys after all. It would be a confirmation for them. We're all one here, Pat. A tribe. And you're one of us, lad. His mother, alone of all of them, would know the depth of his misery but she would say nothing. She would offer him and Edith his old bedroom until he had some money coming in for rent and the two of them could find a place of their own. He would never accept charity from Edith's people. For some reason he saw himself and Edith walking along Acland Street in search of a wardrobe. Why a wardrobe? Why Acland Street, for Christ's sake? A wardrobe was going to be the least of their worries. The stupid things we think of. Edith's brothers would have a good laugh. Australia's greatest artist! They'd never let up on him. Ting-ting! How about a ticket, Mr Conductor? It would be on with those two bastards. They'd be fucking merciless.

'My life was a feast,' Arthur said, quoting from the poem. He gave a small satisfied laugh with the warmth of the whisky and the fire in it. 'I like that. Where all hearts opened and all wines flowed. It's years since we've read him. It gets rather gloomy after that lovely opening if I remember.' He looked down at the book on the arm of the couch. 'Indeed, if I remember *well*. Yes, we've a number of subscriptions to international art journals. These are just a few of them. There are plenty more. You're very welcome to borrow whatever you like.' He leaned down and picked up the copy of *Cahiers d'art* that Pat had discarded. He opened the magazine and handed it to Pat. 'Miró. Do you know his work?'

Pat looked at the coloured illustration. A random scattering of bright shapes and lines on a hard blue background. It meant nothing to him. Did it mean anything to anybody? 'Do you like him?' he said. 'Is he one of your favourites?'

'We're a generation behind Europe,' Arthur said, telling a serious truth that troubled him. He refilled Pat's glass and topped up his own then reached for the poker and gave the new log a hard jab in the ribs. It flinched from the blow and emitted a hiss. 'I mentioned your enthusiasm for Rimbaud when I called Autumn earlier to tell her I was bringing you to dinner.'

Pat looked at the piece of wood in the fire and drank from his glass. The whisky burned its way down his throat and lay in the void of his stomach like a pool of mercury, an eye of unease. He suppressed a belch. 'Your wife doesn't like me,' he said. 'Maybe I won't stay for tea after all. I can probably still make the last train to Geelong if I get going. There's a bus to Ocean Grove.' Edith wouldn't chide him for neglecting her when he finally got home but would forgive him and fold him gratefully in her warm embrace. This wife of Arthur's on the other hand, Mrs Autumn bloody Laing, or whatever her stupid name was, was set on giving the pair of them a hard time. Autumn? They should have called her Winter. Well, fuck her anyway, he thought. We'll see who gives who the hard time if she starts anything. He sat staring into the fire, the warmth on his face. There was no way for him to make the Geelong train tonight. It would take an hour or more just to get back into Melbourne. His jacket had begun to steam. It was giving off a not-unpleasant smell rather like fresh horse shit. He wondered if Arthur could smell it. Arthur was poking at the fire again uselessly. It was beginning to look as if this man might turn out to be a fucking idiot after all.

He looked around the room. The house wasn't exactly posh, not in the way Edith's people's houses were posh, but it was obviously the house of well-to-do people, people of taste and refinement. This impressive collection of books. He would have liked to be left alone in here with the books and the fire. He envied them their books. He would not deny that he knew the meaning of the word envy. The worn coverings on the couches, plain, expensive and well worn. The abundance of roses in the bowl in the bay window, as if they were always there and always freshly cut. The casual way the painting was leaned against the wall above the fireplace and had not been framed or hung properly. It was all a confident acceptance of their position. Their affluence. Comfortable and unquestioned. Nothing showy. They could do anything they wanted to do. No need to make a point of what they had. The bulk of it kept quietly out of sight. Land and property and shares in companies, all that and more than he could think of, for sure. Substance. Deep, enduring and inherited. He thought of his mother's scruffy savings-bank book and the few pieces of china she kept dusted in the front room. He wouldn't deny it, he envied these people the quality of their lives, the depth and richness of it. But he would not wish to *be* them. He did not envy them their being. Their ease with French, if nothing else, was surely to be envied. To read Rimbaud as he had read himself. Only a fool would not envy them that. He pressed his palm into the downy softness of the cushion beside him. You could sleep off a hangover on one of these couches. And plenty of people probably had done just that after a big night of talk about art and life and drinking themselves into a stupor. No one was going to feel they had to fluff up these cushions before they left the room. And how long was it since that fireplace had been cleaned out? The ashes were a foot thick. His mother cleaned out their fireplace every morning. It was the sound he'd woken to before getting up and getting himself ready for school. Her scraping about in the grate with her brush and pan and singing to herself. Something suddenly occurred to him. He said, 'That painting's not another Wyndham Lewis, is it?'

Arthur gave up blowing smoke rings. 'No,' he said and laughed. 'No. If only it were we'd all be rich and I could stop work tomorrow. It's by a friend of ours. He's living in France these days. Splendid, isn't it? I'm not sure that I understand it, but it has something to do with his theory of colour scales and their relation to musical scales. Synchronism, he calls it. Now don't ask me what that means. If you want an explanation you'll have to ask Autumn. Autumn's the one for theory in this house. I'm afraid I'm not much chop at it. But it's a strong painting, isn't it?' He stepped away until the backs of his knees were pressing against the edge of the low table, holding his head on one side then the other, as if he was trying to form a new judgment of the picture. He gave up and stepped to the fire again. 'There's a blindness about too much familiarity, isn't there? We usually move our pictures around. This one's probably been sitting here looking at us rather too long. There's a dozen good pictures in the hallway with their faces to the wall for that reason. It's our resting paddock.' He looked down at Pat. 'Roy's our most important abstract artist. By a long way.'

Pat looked up at the picture. He had no feelings for it. Or perhaps he hated it. It was obviously competent and professional. Clever even. Was he being measly-minded thinking like this? Wouldn't he have wanted to have painted it himself? Not to be that painter, but to be his own self with that much confidence. *Australia's most important abstract artist.* Wouldn't he want them saying that about him? The stretcher and the oil paint would have cost the bloke a heap. 'Yes, it's strong,' he said. The word had no meaning for him. Everything was strong, wasn't it? Water. Fire. Hate. Envy. All of it. Love. The smell of shit. He knew he was being boring but he didn't have the energy to think of anything worth saying. What was there to say, anyway? He was going to be a tram conductor like his dad. He stared into the fire. The split piece of wood had joined in now and was going for it, rejoicing in a wild release of fiery energy, crackling and spitting and popping. He wondered if the day would ever come when he would murder someone. The thought came into his head unbidden like a silent dream, closing the door softly behind it. Standing looking at him. It sent a shiver through him. It could happen, couldn't it? An impulse to murder someone sweeping through you, beyond your will to control it. You would be taken by it and thrown against a life. Edith's face staring at him, as white as the full moon over the Great Southern Ocean, howling her despair over her lost hopes for him and for herself. He would leave her nothing. Emptiness. He hugged himself. His head was going places on him. He stood up, then abruptly sat down again. *I contrived to purge my mind of all human hope.* Rimbaud's poem was on the loose in him.

Arthur said, 'Are you all right?'

Pat waved a reassuring hand at Arthur. It was those terrible cigarettes and the whisky on his empty stomach. And the warmth of this bloody great wood fire, which had blazed up and was beginning to cook him since the madman had left off poking at it. He struggled out of his jacket and tossed it on the couch beside him. If he had a heart attack now it would be days before Edith heard the news of his death. He felt deeply lonely and sad suddenly. At the bottom of a hole on his own with his misery. The pump in his head had started up a while ago. He reached for his glass and drank some more whisky to steady himself. 'Synchronism,' he said, perhaps a little too loudly, and wasn't sure why he said it, except to demonstrate to himself that despite the whisky and the heat and the impending fatal heart attack he could pronounce the word clearly. Arthur was looking at him.

Pat gazed around the walls. 'It would take a lifetime to read all these books,' he said. 'Have you read them all, Arthur? Has your wife read them?' He belched explosively. 'Sorry. I think I might be going to be sick.'

Arthur was frowning at the fire again, as if he was considering a fresh assault on it. 'There won't be any need for you to catch trains tonight. Women, you know? We always have to have done something wrong to start off with. It's the way they go about these things. I never expect to get in from the office of an evening innocent of all wrongdoing.' He looked down at Pat and smiled. He had a genuinely warm and friendly smile. He was a man who seemed untouched by bitterness or thwarted ambition. 'You've not been married a year yet, isn't that right? It's too early for these games.'

Pat looked at his hands. 'We're going to have a baby,' he said. Was it true? Of course it was true. Someone was soon going to be calling him daddy. Maybe it would be a boy. The real future artist. His dad a tram conductor too. His glass was empty again. He watched Arthur refill it.

'How wonderful. We must drink to it.' Arthur lifted his glass. 'Congratulations, Pat. It's great news.'

'Thanks,' Pat said gloomily.

'Are you not pleased?'

'She'll be sitting at home on her own worrying.' Was it really only this morning he had left Edith? It felt like a lifetime ago. Another world. Sitting up in their warm bed with her cold cup of tea and her book. The cold tea seemed particularly melancholy to him now. *Une vie*, a woman's life. He couldn't remember the author. What sort of a woman's life was it? He could hear Edith's lovely soft voice reading the French to him, his head on her shoulder, breathing the smell of her skin. She blew him that last kiss as he turned at the door dressed in this stupid disguise. What a waste he had made of the day. A waste of all of it. His life. And just as the screen door banged behind him he heard her call to him, 'I love you, darling.' Was that the last time she was to see him alive? The last image she was to retain of him? He regretted not calling his love back to her. He put his hand to his heart. He could feel nothing. He placed two fingers on the side of his neck. He had no pulse. The pump had fallen silent. Here it comes then! 'My mum and dad will be pleased,' he said, surprised by the naturalness of his tone. The last words of a dying man. The thickness gathering in his diaphragm, beginning to stifle him. He would drop his drink and slip sideways on the hot couch, his face red, his eyes popping from his skull.

'Your mother and father don't know yet?'

'She only told me this morning herself.'

Arthur was silent a while. 'Autumn would have loved to have a child.' His voice was dense with feeling.

'So why don't you have one?'

Arthur took a sip of whisky from his glass, then another, pressing the rim of the glass firmly against his lower lip and looking down into the flames. 'Couldn't have them, I'm afraid,' he said tightly. 'Not possible.' He brightened and turned to look at Pat. 'We're content. We have friends. Very good friends. Hardly any of our friends have children. It's odd that, isn't it? But it's true. I suppose it seems unnatural to you?'

Pat shrugged. 'I feel a bit sick.'

'Perhaps you should get some fresh air.'

Pat closed his eyes then quickly opened them again. He stood up.

Arthur took his arm. 'Come on, we'll stand you out on the back veranda in the fresh air. That fire's getting to you. I shouldn't have stoked it up so much.'

Pat did not resist. He thought of shouting, Fuck the rich! But held onto the impulse. It wouldn't do any good. Why hadn't he gone straight to the railway station after leaving this bloke's office and caught the train to Geelong? The bus would have had him in Ocean Grove an hour ago.

They were going through the kitchen, Arthur guiding him by the arm, Autumn at the Rayburn taking a pot from the hotplate, a cloth protecting her hand, a blue and white cross-stitched apron over her dress making her look domestic and feminine. She paused and turned from her task to watch them, when Pat suddenly vomited.

Autumn set the pot back on the hotplate and stepped across to them. She pushed Arthur aside. 'You idiot!' She laughed. 'You've filled him up with your whisky. Go and get the things from the dining room. We'll have it in here.' She supported Pat, holding him firmly under the arm, and helped him out through the door onto the veranda. She was laughing softly to herself. She stood and watched him bent over, one hand to the veranda post, leaning out into the night. He retched twice emptily and groaned. In a stricken voice he said, 'I'm sorry.'

Autumn took her cigarettes out of her apron pocket and lit one. She took a deep drag on the cigarette and blew the smoke into the fresh night air. She stood with one arm tucked under the other looking at him, the cigarette smoking between her fingers. 'You're not the first one to vomit in my kitchen.'

She went back inside and brought him a glass of water. 'Rinse your mouth.'

He did as he was told.

'Gargle it,' she said. She was enjoying herself now, finding the situation amusing. She handed him a tea towel. 'Here, wipe yourself.' She had liked the feeling of holding him under the arm. Touch was always crossing a bridge to the other side of something with people. A one-way bridge. You could never not have touched them afterwards. There was always that to be drawn on, like a small preliminary deposit in a private account. She noticed the white blue of his eyes, the strangeness of them, the way he squinted at her as if he wanted to hide his feelings from her. She was interested now and wanted to see his drawings. He was a peculiar boy in need of something strong and definite.

He wiped the drops of water from his lips. 'I'll clean it up,' he said.

'Arthur's done it. Come in when you're ready,' she said. 'We'll eat in the kitchen.' But she didn't leave, just stood there smoking her cigarette.

'Give me a minute,' he said. 'I'll be right in a minute.' He was uncomfortable with her standing there silently staring at him. He looked at her and she met his eyes. She's not for me, he thought. Too tall and skinny. He could see how people, women as well as men, would think she was beautiful. She was impressive, to be sure, he would say that, but not beautiful. Not sexy. Edith was sexy. Edith had lovely voluptuous curves. He could see this woman's hip bones poking through her apron. Edith was not as voluptuous as the butcher's daughter. He wondered what it would be like to fuck the butcher's daughter.

He was not himself tonight. Or maybe he was really himself. These people had upset him.

Autumn said, 'You've lost a sandshoe.'

The flywire screeched and Arthur came out and handed the sandshoe to Pat.

Pat thanked him and squatted and put it on.

Autumn flicked her cigarette out into the night and gave Arthur a look, then she turned and went back into the kitchen.

•

The three of them were sitting at the kitchen table among the uncleared remains of their meal. A symmetry of three cats, a long-haired ginger and two sleek oyster-coloured aristocrats from Asia, were delicately eating scraps of baked rabbit on the floor by Autumn's chair. Autumn drank from her wine glass then drew deeply on her cigarette, held the smoke in her lungs, and reached and tapped the ash onto the edge of her dinner plate.

'You might not do anything at all,' she said, lifting her chin to billow the held smoke towards the light. She looked at Pat. 'We don't know, do we? What you will do. You may have a spoiled youth and a treacherous old age.' She laughed. 'There is never a shortage of that sort. We can know nothing of what you will accomplish. But one thing we do know, if you give up now you will be deciding to be a failure. And that is no way to live.' She squinted at him through the smoke, as if she were thinking of sketching his likeness. 'Give up now and it will torture you for the rest of your days.' She paused, then said with sudden vehemence, as if she wished to be believed, 'I forbid you to give up. Not now, not ever.'

Pat would have objected but she held up her hand for silence.

'Weaklings give up. Serious people persist.' She sat there loosely in her dress, as if his fate was to be decided by her at this table tonight.

'Why should you care?' he said, incredulous and impressed at the same time that she should speak to him in this way.

'You're being churlish now.'

He shrugged.

'I am a trained artist myself,' she said. 'But to care for artists is more my vocation than to make art.'

'I'm not an artist.'

'It's too late for that nonsense,' she said with impatience. 'You sensed your gift and you made your choice. There is no way back from that. Choosing failure is not an option. If you give up now, your need to be an artist will torture you until it destroys you and everyone close to you. Art will become a serpent in your breast instead of your salvation.'

He regarded her in silence and she returned his gaze, saying nothing but observing the effect of her words on him. He was tempted to hope that what she had said was a kind of wisdom and wasn't just the boldness of the wine, but he was not sure that he could trust her. And perhaps he feared to trust her.

'What have you done that makes you think you know all this?' he said.

She stubbed out her cigarette on the lip of her plate. 'You've hardly begun the struggle,' she said calmly. 'And at the first sign of difficulty you're already thinking of giving it up.'

Arthur said, 'That's hardly fair, darling.'

Pat looked at her. He said steadily, 'Fuck you. What do you know about me?'

She smiled. 'I know about myself. Why don't you go and fetch your drawings. Then I'll know something about you. You said yourself, the friends you grew up with went off to work in factories after they left school or got jobs at the tram depot where your father works. They didn't do folios of drawings, did they? They didn't go to the Gallery School, then decide they were too good for it. Arthur doesn't do folios of drawings, does he? Arthur reads books. That's enough for Arthur, to see art and to read and talk about it. Arthur and your old school friends are not troubled by the business of making art. For them there is no struggle. They are not artists and they don't think they are artists.' She reached for her wine glass, but she did not pick it up and drink from it. 'You've had a privileged beginning, Pat. You don't seem to know your luck. The struggle has only just begun for you. Go and fetch your drawings, we'll clear this off and have a look at them.'

'You think mine was a privileged beginning?' he said incredulously.

'You've had nothing to renounce,' she explained. 'Your parents didn't object to you following your dream. You bring nothing to the struggle for art except your desire for it. There's a wonderful purity in that. It's less common than you think. Edith has her grandfather's example. Most of our friends were born into art in one way or another. Your wish to make art is mysterious to you. Yes, I believe you've had a privileged beginning.' She laughed. 'We're alike. You and I. You don't have a choice. That's the thing.'

'I'm not like you,' he said. 'I have to feed my family.'

She went very still, then turned to Arthur and said sharply, as if she was accusing him of a serious offence, 'You didn't tell me Pat has a family.'

'He didn't know,' Pat said. 'My wife only told me she was pregnant this morning.' He reached for a cigarette and lit it. 'It's not important. We're having a kid, that's all. So what?'

Autumn was silent for a long moment, looking at him levelly across the table. She said with venom, 'I hate you, Patrick Donlon!'

Arthur said, 'Now then, darling!'

She knocked her wine glass over with a furious flick of her wrist, sending the red wine cascading across the table towards Pat, and she stood up. The cats scattered around her feet, the ginger one making it through the veranda door with her like an eel slipping upstream through the reeds, the other two swerving aside as the door crashed to in their faces. Arthur and Pat sat looking at the door. A moment later her wail came from the deep night, 'I hate men!'

Arthur said in a hushed voice, 'We should give her a minute to herself.'

'You're not going after her?'

'Heavens no.'

Pat said nervously, 'Should I leave?' Her cry had sounded weird and lonely to him, as if he had inflicted on her an unbearable pain. He was a little frightened of her. Of what she might be capable of. Of her strange vulnerability and the way she had involved herself in his situation. He wondered if she was entirely sane.

'No, no, no. There's no need for that,' Arthur said. He kept his voice down, nevertheless, as if he feared she might overhear him. 'Perhaps if you and I clear some of this away.' He waved his hands over the clutter of dishes. 'She'll be walking down to the river. It's not your fault. It's what she does.'

Pat stood up and began collecting their plates. He said, 'The pie was terrific.'

'Yes, Autumn's a very good pie maker,' Arthur said solemnly. He might have been giving the oration in the chapel on the dark day of Autumn's funeral. *My wife's pastry was a wonder to us all. Let us pray.*

•

They had cleared away the dishes and were sitting at the bare kitchen table in silence smoking cigarettes when they heard Autumn returning. They both stood up as she came through the door, the ginger cat sliding in behind her. The oyster cats had not returned from hiding. Autumn's hair was shining and her eyes were bright and startled, as if the night had held some power over her. She said absently, 'Where's my glass of wine? I was enjoying it.'

Arthur said, 'I'll get us all a fresh one.'

She stood looking at Pat. She held his gaze. 'I hate you the way you hate our friend Roy de Maistre.'

'I don't hate him,' he said.

'And Wyndham Lewis. That is the way I hate you. The way you hate them.'

'I don't hate either of them.'

'Yes you do. You are lying to yourself and to me to deny it. It is our envy that makes us hate.' She took the glass of wine from Arthur.

He said, 'Why don't we go and sit in the library? I've kept the fire going.'

Autumn went ahead of them down the passage. At the library door she paused and indicated the bundle of drawings lying against the wall. 'Bring them in.'

They spread the drawings out on the table in front of the fire and Autumn began to look at them. She said to Pat, 'Sit here,' and pressed her hand on the cushion beside her. Arthur stood in front of the fire and watched. Every now and then he turned and looked at the fire as if he was wondering whether to take to it with the poker. Autumn said nothing until she reached the last drawing, then she read the poem silently to herself, her lips moving. She turned to Pat. 'To dwell secretly in the solitude of my convictions?' she quoted. 'What a state? What an achievement?'

Pat said uneasily, 'It was how I felt at the time I wrote it.'

'Are you a poet as well as an artist?'

'I don't know.'

'You'd better find out, hadn't you? You can't be both.'

'Why can't I be both?'

'I don't know. But I do know you can't be fully an artist and fully a poet. We can only give ourselves fully to one thing. Art demands everything. Art is a woman, Pat. She is not kind to those who only give her a part of themselves. She wants everything or nothing. She sees everything else as betrayal. The artist and the poet both reinvent reality. They extend it. It takes time for them to learn to do this. A lifetime. That reinvention of reality is their way to their private truth.'

He couldn't hold her gaze, it was too intense. He didn't

know what she wanted. Or what she meant. He looked down at his drawing of Mr Creedy's daughter's buttocks.

Autumn rested back against the couch and closed her eyes. 'I wanted a family of my own more than anything.'

Arthur and Pat were silent.

She opened her eyes and looked up at Arthur. 'We both did, didn't we, darling?'

Arthur reached down and took the hand she held up to him. 'Yes, darling, we did. More than anything.'

Autumn turned to Pat. 'But we weren't given a choice.'

He waited for her to go on.

'So what are you, Pat? Poet or artist?'

He said, 'I think you know what I am.'

She surprised him by leaning over and kissing his cheek. 'Yes, I know what you are.' There were tears in her eyes.

Arthur said, 'Bedtime, you two, I think?'

'You go on in, darling. Pat and I have things to talk about.'

11

November 1991

WE USED TO CALL IT ARMISTICE DAY, TODAY IT IS REMEMBRANCE that is asked of us. But there is too much to remember now. The eleventh hour of the eleventh month and so on . . . Let us forget. And *was* I entirely sane? I'm sure he was right to fear for my sanity even then. Am I sane now? How are we to know? In 1938, when he and I first met, the greatest insanity of all was about to break upon a trembling Europe. The great European civilisation we had all known and loved was about to be destroyed.

I have often wondered since if I should have made a job of it that night and thrown the wine glass at Pat's head while I had the strength to do it, instead of meekly tipping its contents in his direction. There is never any satisfaction to be had from half measures. At that moment I did hate him. And have hated him and loved him many times since, but for other causes than envy of his child. Not deeper causes, but other. There is no deeper motive in us than envy—not even a deeper motive for the insanity that causes men to make war on each other.

The season of storms began early this year and has persisted throughout the spring. The ground is sodden and Arthur's sacred Algerian oak has developed a dangerous lean—sacred to him and me. It was not the wind. The ground is sodden. The night was still, the freeway strangely silent. I woke to the shuddering of the earth and lay in my bed wondering what had happened. Had the sky fallen in? Was it a message from the gods?—at *last*! Adeli came into my room with the iron poker clutched in her fat paw, ready to slay the ogre at my throat. The dog next door was howling. Adeli barefoot in her thin nightdress, Sherry attendant, the pair of them standing at my French doors gazing out at the moonlit garden, Adeli's enormous body in silhouette. I was fascinated.

'What was it?' she asked, puzzled by the deep stillness of the night.

'A tree has fallen somewhere,' I said. 'Hopefully it has fallen onto the roof next door and has killed the lycra woman and her ugly infant in their beds.'

She said sorrowfully, 'That is a cruel thing to wish for, Mrs Laing.'

'Are you a Christian then?'

'You know I am.'

I hadn't known she was a God-fearing woman but I might have guessed it. For I did know that God in his infinite wisdom has not bestowed on Christians a sense of irony. It is as if they receive at birth only one ear with which to hear plainly the straight talk of this world. My biographer, alas, is not a poet either. It is the plain truth only, I'm afraid, that Adeli looks for in her research, and not the poetry of a life. If there were such a thing as a biographer of sympathy for my life, I think I should be quite content if they were to title their book, *The Poetry of a Life*. But historians, as Goethe famously said, are without imagination. So there's not much hope of that ever happening.

When Stony told me later it was the red gum, a tree beloved of Arthur and me, I knew the force of this omen in my belly and was shaken by it. Absurd, but there it is. The power of omens is known to us. It's lucky I was still using Barnaby's shillelagh for balance—the walking frame of the gods—or I too would have fallen. Stony stood with one foot on the veranda step to address me, knowing the solemnity of the news he brought me. He looked up, his cap in his hands—he is a short, stocky man of a great age and refuses to use machines—and said, 'The red gum's come down, Mrs Laing.' We were ever Arthur and Mrs Laing for Stony. His stout arm raised, cap dangling from his fingers, pointing behind him down the slope of the garden towards the coach house and shaking his head. 'It's beyond me to deal with her.' I had not realised before this that for Stony trees are female. I sucked in air and trembled and I bore down on Barnaby. 'I'll have someone see to it,' I said, my voice weaker than my knees, and I turned and stumbled back into the kitchen. The red gum was probably five hundred years old.

I stood by the stove and wept. It was as if Arthur had returned to tell me he was leaving me for good and I would not hear from him ever again. The spirit of Old Farm had withdrawn in fear of me. This was his last word. What power had taken him? What deathly insight was his? The renewal of his absence was a shock, massive and not deniable, as cavernous and empty as his vastly echoing death had been. I will do nothing about the fallen tree. It can lie where it has fallen until it returns into the earth from which it rose. I think now of Mahler's line, I come from God and I will return to God. I wonder how long it will take for a five-hundred-year-old red gum to return into the earth? Five hundred years?

When I run my hand along the knobbly shank of Barnaby's shillelagh—as I am doing now, it is an idle thing to do—it gives me the pleasantest creepy feeling in my bowels, just sufficiently reminiscent of the rush of sex to be bearable. If I am not deluded. The stick has a fine balance to it and would be a deadly weapon swung in the right hands. Not mine. I'm past killing. I didn't say I am past wanting to kill. I will never be past that, I hope. And a little strength is slowly returning to my legs. Andrew insists it is Adeli's improvements to my diet that's doing it, but I believe it is more due to my own improved will to see this to the finish. The two of them confer in low voices in the hall, like junior politicians at their shenanigans in the back passages of power, and have become great mates. Good luck to them. Perhaps he is astonished by the volumes of her flesh. Who can know another's tastes?

I stood on the veranda the other night looking out over the dark garden, Adeli snoring in her room—she has the grand snore of an Irish navvy on her—the ball of the stick cupped snugly in my palm, and I wondered if I might yet find the strength to get to the river one last time. I will not ask Adeli's help for that excursion. She knows nothing of my desires, nor shall she. At the river I shall be alone under the moon. Put that in your biography! I am not past dreaming. The more of this I get done the more the nightmares leave me in peace. Why is that?

What did Pat and I talk about that night after Arthur left us and went to bed? I told him his drawings were interesting to me not because they were art, for I didn't believe they were, but because he had executed them with the intention to make art. It was his desire for art, I said, that interested me. I'm sure I talked a lot and probably bored him with my views on the politics of the art world. I had been excited to find out earlier that he not only lacked the commonplace drawing skills of our Gallery School graduates but that he had refused to sully what he called the purity of his eye with the conventional training. The rest of our little gang of artists had assiduously acquired those skills in abundance, Anne Collins to an almost genius degree—but not quite. It is surprising how many brilliant students excel at drawing but are not artists. Anne became a curator in Melbourne then in Sydney and finally made a career as a curator of colonial art at the Tate in London—from where she called me to tell me of Pat's last words at the moment of his passing. Most become teachers. Pat would have starved rather than teach art. His response when asked about it was, 'I don't know what I'm doing myself so how can I teach someone else what to do?' Freddy wanted to know from him why, at the beginning, when he was a boy, he had thought himself an artist. 'For what reason did you think you were an artist, Pat? Did you know anyone else who was an artist?' But Pat would never discuss such questions. He shrugged and said something evasive like, 'Why is anyone anything, Freddy? You tell me. You're the psychiatrist. You should know.' Freddy realised he would need a more oblique approach if his enquiries were to get him anywhere with Pat. Pat liked to work and remained a workman at heart all his life, even at the height of his international fame. Nothing shifted him from that. He didn't care why things were as they were. He was not an intellectual but was intuitive and unquestioning in the exercise of his vocation. The source of his inspiration and his desire to paint were a mystery to him and he was happy to leave it at that.

After he located the subject of his own material, he became clearer about what it was that he valued in others. He reserved his mature admiration for a select few of the naive artists and thought of himself as one of them. 'The untutored eye' remained his favourite and most often repeated phrase. And when he heard the work of the naive painters criticised for its lack of sophistication he would say, 'It's their craft not their vision that's naive.' It was one of the few perceptions about art I ever heard him articulate. He gave art no thought. It was there for him. And he didn't think his opinions should matter to other people, but only his art. The depth of such deceptive simplicities was often missed by more tutored minds. But Pat had no desire to understand, he just wanted to do. When he was working he was happy and was impatient with questions of motive and theory. He and Freddy were wary of each other and never became friends. Freddy treated him, in many ways, as an interesting case study, and naturally Pat was sensitive to the implied condescension of this.

Like Pat, Freddy was born in Australia, but in everything else he was Pat's opposite. Freddy came from a cultured and very wealthy family. His father, a mining engineer, died in Paraguay when Freddy was seven. His mother, a strikingly beautiful woman, was a fine pianist and became, as Vera Henning, a much-sought-after accompanist on the international concert circuit. She had inherited a fortune of her own from her father, a Geelong wool merchant. Freddy moved with his mother freely around the world in society from the time he was a young boy until he went to school in England. His ideas about art were inseparable from his ideas about politics. Europe was his source for both. He would say in his quietly insistent voice to anyone who disagreed with him, 'You can't espouse the conservative in art in our time without espousing fascism.' He met with no counter-arguments to this from the members of our little group, for whom to be a modernist in art was to be radically left wing in politics. In this we were perfect conformists. Pat was the exception. He didn't know what Freddy was talking about and couldn't have cared less. Pat used to say, 'Freddy talks. I paint.' For a time Freddy was a card-carrying member of the Communist Party of Australia. A visit to Moscow in 1957 cured him.

What interested Freddy most deeply and most persistently throughout his life was understanding human motivation and the processes by which that understanding might be acquired. He was analysed in London by Wilhelm Stekel, a pupil of Freud's who'd had a falling-out with the master. Freddy believed that one day science would acquire the means to prove that the basic theoretical assumptions of psychoanalysis were correct. The highest post he held during his career in Australia was Medical Superintendent of the Sandy Heights Mental Facility, at the time Melbourne's largest mental hospital. On his appointment to the post he was charged by the state government with bringing about cultural change in the area of mental illness. Freddy quickly discovered that his masters, being politicians with their eyes fixed on the next election, wanted results within months. He told them two generations and a great deal of money would be needed for the kind of cultural change they envisaged. It was a famous public row and dragged on unhappily for a number of years before Freddy tired of it and resigned. After Sandy Heights he worked as a private consultant. He was always living in hope of meeting interesting patients, but was usually disappointed.

And yet for all his frequent boasts that his was a professional and a scientific approach to the understanding of human behaviour, for Freddy, in a deeply private way, our lives remained poetic, the web of our motives a kind of shifting of clouds forming and re-forming, vague shadowy dawns and romantic sunsets, the tragedy of storms and the merciless in our souls. He was in awe of the wonder of it all and strove rigorously to make systematic sense of it. But he could never quite hold his faith in any system and always referred to himself as a failure. Indeed he was in thrall to a morbid fascination with failure and believed himself fated never to escape the traps set for him by this particular demon. Stekel, his analyst, set the pattern and committed suicide in 1940.

A contradiction to himself, Freddy was as much a poet as a scientist and I loved him for it and for the richly layered ambiguities of his infinitely complicated nature. He never wrote verse but the poetry of his understanding was in his soul. He spoke German fluently and not long after we first met, which was several years before Pat came into our lives, he recited Rilke's 'Herbsttag' to me flawlessly. We had not been at Old Farm long and several of us were gathered in the library. It was late, the fire had burned down and there was a heavy and contented silence between us. Suddenly, out of that silence, Freddy's voice. After he had finished his recitation he turned to me and smiled. 'That was for you,' he said. I thanked him and told him that even though I had no German I had found it moving and very beautiful, as one might find a piece of music beautiful and affecting without being able to say why. He then recited the poem in English. 'It is called "Autumn Day",' he said.

> 'Lord: it is time. The huge summer has gone by.
> Now overlap the sundials with your shadows,
> and on the meadows let the wind go free.
>
> Command the fruits to swell on tree and vine;
> grant them a few more warm transparent days,
> urge them on to fulfilment then, and press
> the final sweetness into the heavy wine.
>
> Whoever has no house now, will never have one.
> Whoever is alone will stay alone,
> will sit, read, write long letters through the evening,
> and wander on the boulevards, up and down,
> restlessly, while the dry leaves are blowing.'

Freddy was not religious himself but found the quality of Rilke's religious faith deeply interesting. He once told me Rilke's faith gave him a hope that he dared not hold for himself. I was not sure what he meant by this. Which was often the case with Freddy. That he spoke as if he was his own most enthralling mystery was part of his charm.

He was beset periodically by debilitating sieges of depression, during which he lacked the will to stir from his bed. He lived in a large apartment on the top floor of one of Melbourne's oldest hotels in the centre of the city. His mother's Imperial Bösendorfer had pride of place in his sitting room, which overlooked Collins Street a few doors down the hill from the building in which Arthur's firm had their offices. Both the hotel and the building which housed Arthur's offices were demolished in the eighties to make way for the towering headquarters of a bank. (Who will ever know the geographies of our town or the intimacies of our days if I do not memorialise them here?) While Freddy was enduring his depressions I was the only visitor he would admit to his flat. In company and in public he played the difficult piano works of Leoš Janáček and Béla Bartók, composers whose music was rarely heard in Melbourne in those days. Privately he reserved his first love for the dreamy realms of Chopin's nocturnes. That was Freddy. If there was such a creature as a romantic modernist it was Freddy Henning. His sense of duty and of what was right called him to the project of modernism, but his heart called him to the melancholy works of the romantics. He was ever divided against himself and was more jealous of my feelings for Pat than was Arthur. As I said, Freddy foresaw the danger of our affair long before I or anyone else saw it.

'Your Pat has the narrow morality of the working class,' Freddy said to me the day after I introduced the pair of them. 'It will mean disaster for the three of you.' He advised me to send Pat back to his wife.

I told him it was too late for that and accused him of hypocrisy. 'You say you are all for the people, Freddy, but most of the people are working class, just like Pat.'

'I'm telling you what I see of the man,' he said. 'He isn't capable of the kind of sophistication you're asking of him with this three-hander of yours.'

'Pat's a quick learner.'

'His morality is that of a literalist. He will require symmetry in his affair with you. For him you are either Arthur's woman or you are his woman. That is the way he will see it. He has left his wife, or from what you've told me is going to leave her, or she has left him, and he will expect you to leave Arthur. Anything else will seem to him unjust and a betrayal.'

'You know I'll never leave Arthur,' I said. I was shocked by the suggestion. Without Arthur I would be naked in the world and prey to my own instability.'

'*I* know it, Aught. But does Pat know it?'

I didn't want to hear Freddy's warning and I dismissed it. 'You're jealous,' I said. 'And sometimes you can be a snob.' This last was unfair. Freddy possessed too much empathy to be a snob. The other person's situation always interested him. Pat interested him.

He shrugged. 'Yes, that too, of course. Only a fool wouldn't be jealous of sharing you with other men.' He poured himself another glass of Arthur's whisky and lit a cigarette. He went and stood at the bow window and looked out into the front garden, where Stony and I had not long since planted a new bed of roses. 'You have your first bloom,' Freddy said. He sounded a little sad.

I went and stood with him and took his arm in mine. The rose was the deep and richly scented red of Mr Lincoln. 'Arthur's not jealous of *you*,' I said gently.

'Oh, for heaven's sake, Aught. I'm not jealous of Arthur either. This man will destroy you, and he will destroy Arthur with you. He will take everything from you and give you nothing in return.'

'What nonsense,' I said. 'Now you're being silly.' I was annoyed.

'I felt his enmity, Aught. You have a generous spirit. You believe that your inherited position and your education oblige you to help those less fortunate than yourself. You feel a need to give something back to the society that has given you so much. It's not just the responsibility of your caste with you; your heart *feels* the debt. It's in your sense of belonging as an Australian. You love this country in a way I never can. My attachments to Europe and my love for Australia are far too conflicted for me to ever have anything like your uncomplicated love of country. I envy you that. Something important about yourself that can never be settled for me is settled for you by that certainty. You are grounded by it.'

Freddy loved to talk in this way. To me the word *grounded* made it sound as if I had concrete boots. But I loved to listen to him. I didn't believe everything he said, of course, and often thought him wrong in his estimation of people. But I wanted to believe he was right about this. I said nothing to it. It had pleased me to hear him say it. My hopes had always been with Australia. Unlike most of our friends in those days, I'd never considered the possibility of living anywhere else. My travels with my mother had probably cured me of any uncertainty I might have had—if I ever had any. I don't remember that I had.

'In order to fulfil yourself, you have to give,' Freddy said. 'That's the sort of person you are. You won't defeat that in yourself. This man has no such needs.'

I squeezed his arm. 'Please call him Pat, Freddy. It's awful to hear you calling him *this man*. As if he is not our friend.'

'He is hungry to take whatever he can get hold of,' Freddy said. He was sounding a little surly, which was not like him. 'And when he has taken all that he can carry away with him, then he will abandon you. And if you have given him every-thing, you will have nothing left. To see you making cow eyes at this man makes me weep, Aught.'

'You're being unfair.' I was unhappy with our disagreement. 'And you called him *this man* again.' I was very cross with Freddy.

We were both silent after this, standing at the window arm in arm, looking out into the front garden at my single rose, neither of us sufficiently at ease with the other to be the first to break the silence. I was probably waiting for Freddy to apologise. Sooner or later it was usually Freddy who was the one to offer an apology and end our difficulties. This time he remained silent. It was not like him.

I can't remember how that day ended for us, but for some time after there was an uncertainty between Freddy and me that I found painful. Arthur asked me the cause of it but I denied it and told him he was imagining things. Arthur never pressed me when I was evasive with him but took my evasion as his answer. For a while I was frightened I had lost my precious freedom to confess my secrets to Freddy. I could not disclose to either Pat or Arthur the full gory truth about myself the way I could with Freddy. Without Freddy's trust I was alone with myself and I didn't like it. It frightened me. But Freddy was not a man who could sulk for long or hold in himself a sense of having been wronged, and it was no more than one very long month before we had regained our old trust and had securely reinstated the wonderful intimacy of our friendship. I never had such a friendship with a woman. Freddy could see into the hearts of women with as much clarity as he saw into the hearts of men. His perfect empathy with the conditions of others was his gift and his burden. He disliked Pat but was fascinated by him.

I didn't wish to hear Freddy's analysis of Pat and dismissed it. We don't want to have our futures disclosed to us. We don't wish to know that our hopes are to come to nothing and our passions are to wane and turn to disgust. I have never understood why people are eager to listen to fortune-tellers, or why our newspapers are full of expert opinions about the disasters that lie ahead of us. But there has been an eager market for prognostications since antique times, and probably before then if we only had a record of the caveman's sense of doubt about himself, and I suppose there will be no stopping those who like to fossick among the entrails of slaughtered beasts, even though what they purport to see there is generally mistaken. We forget nothing more readily than an incorrect forecast. It is the next forecast we are listening out for. And there is always someone ready to give it to us with confidence. As a species we have no wish to accept that the future, where our death lies in wait, is closed to us aside from that one grim fact.

Freddy told me that day, though in a rather more elaborate and mannered style of delivery, what Uncle Mathew had told me simply the last time I had seen him when I was seventeen and had asked him, What is my gift? To give, they might both have said. But of course they never met. Both suicides. Both dearly beloved men in my life. Both grieved for and cherished in my heart to this day. I was never sure what Freddy made of my confession to him of my childhood sexual carryings-on with Uncle Mathew under the peppercorn tree in the garden of Elsinore. I think I wanted Freddy to reassure me that the experience had been normal. Or perhaps I'd hoped that, despite my view of myself as a modern liberated woman, he would put it into some kind of bourgeois place of conventional feminine safety for me. At eleven years of age Mathew's kiss had touched in me something of the fierce uncaring wildness of sex, that source of our helpless moaning, the pulse we would all willingly ride to our deaths, and I think I had always feared a little that he had shaken loose in me at that tender age some force that was not quite normal or healthy—whatever we are to mean by such contented terms as these in our bewildered world of fearsome insanities.

The first time I kissed Pat under the silver wattle trees in the moonlight on the river bank, when my lips met his I was aware of how much older than him I was, and it was the gentle touch of Mathew's lips on mine when I was a girl that came into my memory. That touch such that a butterfly might have landed on my skin, so thrilling my body bloomed for him with a pang I have not forgotten. For the first time since then it was there again with Pat. Who but the coldest among us can resist that song of the blood? Gone now, all that. I am reduced and am no longer a woman, but I have memory—and the knobbly shank of Barnaby's shillelagh to press into the lines of my palm. Arthur and I were lovers, but of another, calmer, more sequestered order altogether than were Pat and I. With Arthur I never risked my story of Uncle Mathew under the peppercorn. I did not wish him to know it. I did not wish it to be misunderstood by him. It was sacred to me then and has remained sacred to me. My golden amulet when I lie in my tomb—so to speak. I shall, of course, be ashes, and will have no tomb. Scattered here at Old Farm by Adeli the penguin. Or not, as she sees fit.

When Freddy's own real analyst, Wilhelm Stekel, committed suicide in 1940, Freddy told me that in a note Stekel asked his wife, with extraordinary grace, to kindly apologise to his patients for him. It was the sort of perverse sense of responsibility that greatly appealed to Freddy. He described for me the scene of Stekel's wife turning up at her husband's rooms on Monday morning and sitting in his customary place at his desk. Solemnly waiting until each patient in turn appeared for their usual appointment and made themselves comfortable on the couch, before asking them if they would please accept her husband's apology for being absent. Not a cold in the head or the funeral of a favourite aunt but absence excuse Number One. He ate a bucket of aspirins on Friday night and has died. He says to tell you he is sorry. Freddy was subject to the same wrenching contradictions in himself as his analyst had been. When Freddy killed himself, however, he did not ask anyone to apologise to his patients for him but wrote me the note which ended with those terrible words, *I have a rat in the wainscot to dispose of.*

It frightens me when I realise that this, my memorial to our times—as it seems to have become, whatever it was when I began it or will become in the hands of others after I am gone—is all I have left to believe in. 'Others'. I should say the robust Adeli Heartstone. What would Freddy have made of her? Despite her flab she has something of Pat's steeliness, something of his hunger to eat up the whole cake for herself then run away with it, leaving only the smell of her departure in the air behind her—her little pressure pack of synthetic floral air cleanser with which to sweeten the stink of her leavings. If I were to kick her out Andrew would pack me off to the house of the dead immediately. I am as bound to the penguin as I was to Pat. And wasn't she right when she flattered herself with a connection between the two of them? As contemptuous as I was in my dismissal of her suggestion that she and the naked Mr Creedy's daughter were sisters of the idealised womanly form in Pat Donlon's imagination. There is a cruel symmetry in this. My life the skipping rope swung by these two thieves at either end, keeping me dancing to their tune in the middle. If thievery is not too disheartening a term for their performances. The meaning sucked out of things. His drawings no longer a source of my dreaming but her dreaming now. How did she manage that? What biographical sleight of hand was it that enabled her to do it, as if she was bringing me something precious while stealing it from me? I need time to see when I've been tricked. I'm still too innocent. Can I say that at eighty-four? Or whatever I am. I look at her with new respect. She is no longer to be dismissed by me as the dullard bollard. Harmless and silly with her belly roll pushing her twin set out of shape. Oh, no. There is far more to Adeli Heartstone than that.

How to avoid the gall of bitterness when ample cause for it has entered into our life? I would plead with Pat to try to understand the deeper causes of his misbehaviour and he would shout back at me, 'Understand what, for Christ's sake? I know what I feel.' And he would plunge onward, trampling through the debris of broken things without a backward glance to see if I was still on my feet, then urging me to admire his latest picture, as if I had had no hand in its creation.

Freddy and Arthur were not great creative figures of my time as Pat was soon to become, but were of another, more contented and gracious world than his. Without them the disarray of life with Pat would have been impossible for me to endure for long. They not only admired but liked and understood each other. When Freddy talked with enthusiasm of the novelist Martin Boyd's latest book—for Freddy, Boyd was our finest living novelist—Arthur understood it was Boyd's troubling uncertainty about whether he was an Australian or a European with which Freddy was identifying, and not Boyd's conservative politics or his loose meandering style—though I think in his contrary heart Freddy admired both these qualities in Boyd. Arthur also had the grace to understand that my flirting with Freddy was a quality of our friendship and had nothing to do with infidelity. Freddy was much better looking than Pat. But it was Pat, with his agitated view of our realities, who stirred in me the unease and restlessness that had disabled me during my travels in Europe with my mother when I was a young woman of nineteen. I feared and longed for that experience again and often despaired that I was never to know it. The helplessness of it. The inability to bring it to an end or to contain it. The knowledge that I could do nothing to keep myself from it once it was ignited. And my pressing intuition that it would end badly for me. Sex.

Safe sex had quite another meaning for me and Arthur than the meaning it has today for young people (anyone under sixty). It wasn't a question of condoms with Arthur and me. We never used those things. With Arthur beside me in bed I felt safe. From myself more than from external dangers. What was there for me to fear in the external world, after all? I had always been intrigued by the dark, and the attentions of strange men delighted me. Arthur and I enjoyed each other's bodies, but never frenziedly. He always wore his pyjamas to bed and I wore my nightgown (cotton). Even in the early days of our marriage, after my operation, most nights we read ourselves to sleep.

It was a relief for me to be with Arthur after being the tormented lost girl of my family. With him I knew myself cherished. The only unsettling moment before sleep was if one of us interrupted the other's reading to insist on reading out something amusing. 'Goodnight, darling,' was our regular refrain. There was not a lot of moaning or ecstatic howling in our nights. None at all in fact. A fond kiss before lights out usually settled any doubts we had about how the night was to develop between us. Or, once we were lying there in the dark, he felt for my hand and we made love, simply and in silence, almost as if we made love to ourselves. Afterwards we lay side by side and he held my hand a while, as if he thought I needed comforting, which I didn't, but I was glad of his hand in mine all the same. When I wanted an orgasm I gave one to myself.

Here, Autumn, one for you! A series of gasps, a moan or two, but no howls to give pause to the neighbours or alarm their dogs. Wasn't that what every mature woman did? Dreamed of her demon lover? In my case the Roman psychiatrist looked into my eyes and I was nineteen again.

I have never found it easy to go to sleep, and while Arthur snored and twitched beside me I would lie in the dark listening to the night noises beyond the house, away in my private fantasy world. It was my favourite moment of the day. The two oyster cats were hunters and I kept them confined at night to a cat run attached to the laundry. To be at peace with myself I needed to know they and the birds were safe in their nests for the night. The ginger tom (Sheridan's spiritual ancestor) was only interested in other cats so I let him have his freedom. I'd hear them yowling dismally to each other across the river, the feral cats in those days in the old forest.

Safe sex. That was our life. When Arthur and I were first married I was ambitious to become a fine housekeeper and to make Old Farm a haven for ourselves and our friends. I began work on transforming the surroundings of the house into a beautiful garden the first week we were here and with Stony's help was soon growing our own vegetables. We bought a cow for the fresh milk and hens for their eggs. In those first months I saw myself at the centre of my own little kingdom. That is how it was for me then. I was fired by a fierce determination to build my own place and to shake off my family's emotional parsimony and my mother's barren legacy. Stony was happy to see the house occupied again and became my steady ally. While Arthur was at his office all day, Stony and I remade this place.

In our second year Arthur and I began to publish a new art journal (it lasted for two years and ten issues, which we counted a success). With our journal and our support of young artists we imagined ourselves established at the centre of an influential third force in Melbourne's narrowly partisan art world. We believed ourselves to be revolutionary, but in fact we subsisted in a state of self-congratulation, comfortably unaware of the narrowness of our own partisanship. We were young, we had money, and the world was ours to refashion as we chose. What else but to commit the great follies is youth for?

•

My walk across the night paddock to the river the evening of Pat's first visit to us calmed me. The ginger cat kept me company. Stony brought him to us in a shoe box as a kitten, saying, 'He's a tom.' Arthur plucked the golden ball of fluff out of the box and cuddled him. 'Welcome to your new home, Tom,' he said. I reached for him. 'Let me hold him.' I remember the rush of desire that possessed me, to have the little kitten in my arms and for him to know it was me who was his first and only true friend. A misty rain was falling as Tom and I stood among the wattles and watched the glint of the water over the rocks and listened to the night sounds—he to his, I to mine. I was upset and I wept for the psychiatrist's child, my poor discarded baby. No vixen barked.

When I returned to the house and went into the kitchen and saw the nervous way both men stood and waited for me to speak, I could have laughed aloud. I had regained my ground and for the rest of the night I was in charge of the tone between us. Which was the way I liked things to be. I was aware of myself as the intellectual superior to most men of my acquaintance. Freddy, when he came into our lives, was the first man I was able to accept as my equal. My respect for his mind was the foundation of our elaborate friendship. In this he never disappointed me. Not even in the manner of his death.

After Arthur had gone to bed to read his new book, Pat stayed on the couch beside me and we looked through his drawings for a second time. He smoked one after another of Arthur's cigarettes and said very little. I felt more motherly than mistressly towards him that night. He was exhausted and I have a vivid recollection of him sleeping on the couch beside me, his upper body slipped sideways, his head pillowed on his arm. I was regretting my aggressive insistence that he could not be both poet and artist. Asleep he looked more like a boy than ever, his lips slightly parted, his pale hair falling across his face, his features unmarked and unremarkable. I fetched one of my Turkish shawls and spread it over him and I kissed him on his cheek again—as chaste a kiss as it is possible for a woman to give a man, I swear. His feet were crossed at the ankles, his battered sandshoes a pathetic token of his poverty. I did not know at the time that Pat's habit was to dress as neatly as the tramway inspector he feared he was to become. I left him, looking back at him from the doorway before I turned off the light and went in to join Arthur.

Arthur was sitting up in bed reading Wilenski.

I said, 'We should do something for Pat. You were right to bring him home.' I wondered at myself for speaking as if I thought our home might become the home of this scruffy young stranger. Even then I discounted the existence of Edith and her inconvenient child.

Arthur said absently, 'Yes, of course we will, darling,' and went on reading contentedly, travelling the familiar path of our comfortable bedroom silence.

How self-satisfied we were. How right we thought ourselves. I lay beside Arthur that night and thought of Pat curled up asleep on the couch in the library. It seemed to me he was under our care, almost as a son might have been to us, a slightly wayward son who had returned home discouraged and in need of our support. Australia's most influential art critic had told Pat he was a charlatan and had thrown him and his drawings out of his office. Pat's confidence in himself as an aspiring artist had been badly undermined by his experiences that day, and by the time he came to us he was almost ready to abandon his dreams. The critic's job is to deepen our understanding, and no critic has a right to be as severe as Cowper was with Pat. I tried to cheer Pat up by reminding him of the German poet Rilke's answer to the young poet who asked for his opinion of his verses; *There is nothing*, Rilke wrote back, *that manages to influence a work of art less than critical words*. But I don't think Pat was listening to me by then. He was too tired and too drunk on Arthur's whisky. I was confident I had the means to help him get over Guy Cowper's bullying dismissal of him and his work. I loathed that man. I'd often watched him displaying his erudition, as if he were the only man in the room ever to have read a book or looked at a picture. In conversation Guy Cowper did not address himself to his companion but to an imaginary absent equal—the greatly admired shadow of himself, no doubt. In public he was in performance. Needless to say he was contemptuous of women and their opinions, unless they were a wealthy patron of the arts.

Pat had strayed into the den of his natural enemy, announcing himself a mendicant, and been mauled. Until I fell asleep that night I let my fancies play with my plans for providing sustenance to Pat's depleted confidence in himself as an artist. I was, had I been aware of it, already beginning a private project in which the advancement of Pat Donlon's career was to be the principal theme of the story. My motives, however, were complicated. Arthur and I and our group were opposed to the influence of Sir Malcolm and Guy Cowper. And I was probably setting out not only to promote Pat but to show these powerful men how mistaken they were to have dismissed him. Who now remembers either of them? It is the name of Patrick Donlon that today still has the power to excite a crowd in the fine-art auction rooms of Europe, America and Australia (but mainly Australia, I have to admit).

At breakfast the next morning, before Arthur and he went off to catch the train to the city, I told Pat we would motor down in the Pontiac and visit him at Ocean Grove one weekend soon.

Arthur loved an excuse for a long drive and was keen on the idea. 'We'll bring a picnic,' he said.

Pat said, 'We should have it on the beach if it's a fine day.'

Perhaps it was for my sake that neither of them mentioned Edith.

I walked around to the coach house with them and stood and waved as Arthur drove out onto the road. The morning was cold and it was raining. I was happy. After they had gone I stood in the grey drift of rain, looking down the slope of our paddock towards the river, excited to know in myself that

I had so much to give, and moved by the beauty of our home and its glorious setting. My own rather grand self-regard had the better of me that morning. I felt Pat had been given into my care to form and to shape into the great artist he dreamed of becoming.

In that moment of euphoria I could not have imagined that I was not to be the one in charge, but that in Pat Donlon I had encountered not a boy but a man who would prove more than my match at controlling the tone of our relations. The strange flatness of his style, his plainness quite beyond my experience of artists, his unaffected attitude to the work of the painter, and his astonishing rejection of the conventional training, which he feared would limit his ability to see with a fresh eye, had all impressed me. The idea that he might become a tramway inspector and devote himself to the narrow life of supporting a growing family of children in some dreary hovel in a St Kilda back street appalled me. I was determined not to let that become his fate. I would save him from it. And Arthur would help me save him.

I couldn't wait to tell Barnaby all about it. I went back into the kitchen and set the kettle to boil on the Rayburn. When Barnaby arrived he was so full of the news that his friend, Harry Croft, a Central Queensland policeman, was coming down to stay with him for six weeks during Christmas and the New Year that I could scarcely get a word in. Barnaby's limp, which he made the most of, was from a riding accident when he was a boy mustering cattle on his father's station. Scrub bashing, he called it, and made it sound both thrilling and hazardous to man and horse. He posed for me in the kitchen doorway that morning, leaning on his shillelagh and smoking a cigarette, gazing out at the garden and the paddock beyond as if he viewed the broad landscape of his childhood adventures, telling me the story of his days as a boy in the wild outback of Queensland's hinterland and how he met there the son of the local sergeant of police. His first lover, and still, twenty years on, his most deeply cherished friendship. When he was drunk and it was late at night, with just a few trusted friends, Barnaby often said, 'Harry is my darling wife.' And if he was asked if he was married he would always answer with an emphatic, 'Yes, I am very married.' Harry died the year before Barnaby committed suicide. He returned to Sofia Station at least twice a year for a month or two to see his friend and, as he put it, 'To refresh my poetic soul.'

In the end I didn't tell Barnaby the story of Pat Donlon that day. He was in one of his large self-absorbed moods and I let him have his head. My story was too good to waste. Barnaby could have it when the rest of them got it. He had missed his chance at an exclusive. It annoyed him greatly whenever I reminded him of this later.

Pat was different to the others. That much I had seen. But despite my confident assumptions about him I had not seen just how very different he was any more than had Sir Malcolm or Guy Cowper. Pat was not to be easily understood. He kept his truths to himself and eluded us all. But at that time I believed implicitly in the gift Uncle Mathew had told me was mine when I was seventeen. And I still think Uncle Mathew was right. But he was only partly right. And a partial truth that is held sacred by us can be more corrupting of our behaviour than a lie. When I took on Pat Donlon I saw myself as a kind of Mother Courage, feeding and caring for the spirits and aspirations of my little tribe of artists. Pat was to be the principal among them. But I misjudged him. And I misjudged our situation. There is a perversity in us, however, that knows no limit. And thinking of our day at Ocean Grove as I write this my heart even now beats a little faster and I would change none of it.

But I must stop this and go in and see to the Rayburn. The air is suddenly cold out here. I put my weight on Barnaby's stick and rest my free hand on the table top but I can't rise. I sit back and rest and try again. I don't want to go on about old age. It bores me to do so. But the plain fact is that after sitting still for some time I have scarcely enough strength in my legs to get myself upright. As if she senses my call, Adeli comes out onto the veranda and says in her best coaxing Californian, 'It's time we went in, Mrs Laing. We can't have you catching your death out here.'

We? My death.

How bitterly I resent my dependence on her. How I would love to swing Barnaby's great lump of a stick at her big soft gut and watch her go bouncing down the slope of my abandoned garden. Is there a magic word that will summon my youth back to me?

12

Picnic at Ocean Grove

A LARGE OLD-FASHIONED MIXING BOWL STOOD ON A WOODEN crate beside Edith's bed. A lamp without a shade, a book and a tin cup half filled with water beside the bowl. The green cloth cover of the book damp-stained in the shape of Italy, the title in gold, *Une vie*, partly obscured by the toe of the boot. The bowl was made of yellow glazed stoneware with a raised pattern of acanthus leaves around its belly. Autumn could not resist peeking into its sallow interior. An inch of opalescent bile, green, translucent and still—a lens drawn up from a mysterious ocean deep. The air in the room was sour and smelled of stale bed warmth. A solitary fly dragged its heavy body slowly up the grimy windowpane towards a spider web already damaged and hung about with the embalmed corpses of various luckless insects.

Autumn was sitting on the side of the bed. She was holding Edith's hand in hers. Edith's eyes were closed, her hand cool and slightly damp resting slackly in Autumn's. The two women had fallen silent, the sound of the men's voices from the kitchen and the steady drip of rainwater striking the galvanised top of the tank below the window. Autumn watched the fly climbing the window glass towards its doom. Edith's hair was spread around her skull on the pillow, her forehead pallid and gleaming with an unhealthy perspiration. The top two buttons of her nightdress were undone, her chest rising and falling unevenly. Her lips, which were dry and cracked, were apart and after every few breaths she gave a little gasp, or a sigh.

The fly encountered the web and panicked, becoming at once hopelessly entangled. Autumn watched but no spider appeared to embrace its captive prey. It seemed to her the web was so old and dusty and so in need of repair the spider must have died or gone elsewhere long ago, leaving its deadly trap behind—like a sin committed in the past. She would have liked to have got hold of a broom and swept the whole thing away and given the window a good wash and the room a thorough airing. The fly was frenzied, its legs and wings more securely entangled in the sticky skeins every second. The sound of its frenzy was of a remote aeroplane high up somewhere in a clear summer sky.

Autumn saw that Edith's eyes were open. She realised, with an uncomfortable feeling of having exposed her private thoughts to the other woman, that Edith had been watching her.

Edith said, 'Please go in and join them, Autumn. He's been talking about nothing else ever since he met you both. He can't wait to spend some time with you. I'm feeling much better. Honestly. I might sleep for a while.'

Autumn bent and touched her lips to Edith's sweating forehead. She closed her eyes and held her lips against the cool skin for a long moment, then slowly straightened, a faint taste of salt and something of animal decay on her mouth.

The two women held each other's gaze. Neither spoke.

A faint imprint of Autumn's lipstick on Edith's forehead reminded Autumn of the pinkish export stamp on New Zealand legs of lamb. She said, 'Well,' with the sense that everything between them was inconclusive. She took her hand from Edith's and pressed her freed palm on the sheet where the bed had been roughly turned back at Edith's side. She looked at her hand pressing into the used and rumpled bedding, and she thought of Pat's boyish body lying there naked. 'I'll come in and see you again a bit later,' she said, and patted the bed and stood up. 'Is there anything I can get you?' The drone of the trapped fly ceased suddenly, as if it listened, expecting imminent rescue or death.

'If you wouldn't mind closing the door when you go out,' Edith said.

Autumn gave Edith's hand a little pat then she turned and went out of the bedroom and closed the door. She stood with her back to the closed door and gathered her thoughts. She could not help feeling pleased that Edith was too unwell to join them. She wiped her lips with her handkerchief and walked down the passage to the studio, the drone of the fly's death struggle in her head, the dark of the sickroom behind her, the sourness of Edith's skin persisting on her mouth. Her throat was dry. She needed a drink.

In the studio the two men were leaning together over Pat's work table. There was no sun but the room was bright and filled with signs of life and work, paintings and drawings piled against the far wall and pinned to the plaster. Both men looked at her as she came into the studio. A bottle of champagne and an empty glass stood on the work table. Arthur poured champagne into the empty glass and handed it to Autumn. 'How's Edith?'

Autumn looked at Pat. 'She's going to sleep for a while.' She drank the champagne.

Arthur refilled Pat's glass then his own. Pat drained his glass in one go and set it down on the table. He watched Autumn examining his painting.

She put down her glass beside his and picked up the square of cardboard and held it to the light from the window. It was Pat's boot polish and house paint abstract of what might have been a squashed chocolate layer cake, or perhaps a mood of despair.

Pat said, 'It's no good.' He laughed. 'It's nothing.' There was something of nervousness and aggression in him.

'I can't say whether it's good or not,' Autumn said coolly. 'But everything you do is disconcerting.' She looked at him. He shrugged and looked away. She put the painting down on the table. She didn't like it. 'I've no idea what to think of it. Except that it's utterly different from anything else I've seen.' She turned to Arthur. 'We should put it in the show and see what the public have to say about it.'

Pat said, 'They'll hate it. What show?'

She sipped her champagne. The wine had lost its chill and tasted bitter. She set the glass down again. 'You sound as if you *hope* people will hate your work.'

'Maybe I do. Maybe they should.' He was noticing things about her.

'We are hoping to put together a show of modernist work for the winter. There is a new space in Flinders Lane. The freehold is available. Arthur is looking into the possibility of acquiring it. It would become the centre for the new young artists whose work we favour. Our winter show is sure to create a lot of interest.'

Pat said, 'I'm not putting that thing into a show.' He had lost his confidence in his ability to make decisions about his work. The energy had gone out of him for it. He was afraid of where his life was going. He felt sure he and his work would never belong with the people these two favoured. It was all a joke. He was sick of the whole thing. Her dress was blue and smooth and had slipped over her body like a skin. There was no shape to her. Her legs were too long and her feet were bony. She had nervous eyes. Slightly mad. Some painters would paint her. Some painters would fuck her. He didn't like her. He didn't trust her. She was bony all over. What did she really want with him? Why was she bothering? He was sorry now that he had left his drawings of Creedy's daughter at their place. Leaving his drawings there might have made it seem as if he had pledged himself to her in some way. He had just forgotten to take them when he left in the morning. That was all it was. They should have brought them with them and given them back today. What were these two doing here anyway, carrying on about acquiring galleries and putting his stuff in a show? It would have made more sense if they'd brought beer with them instead of this French piss. He reached for the champagne bottle and filled his glass and drank it off and grimaced and set his glass down.

'I don't think that decision is completely up to you,' she said, watching him. 'What an artist makes is his own private affair, but what he shows to the public is a decision he must share with others. Preferably a decision he must delegate to others whom he trusts to have his best interests at heart. Artists themselves are not to be trusted as judges of their own work. What else have you got for us to look at?'

'There's heaps of stuff. None of it's any good.' He met her eyes directly for the first time. He rejected what she had just said as a load of crap, but found the thought interesting that others would decide about his work. He was trying to remember this tall self-possessed woman who seemed to imagine she had some authority over him in her apron at the stove in the kitchen of Old Farm. An image he had of her a second or two before he vomited at her feet. The one moment when she had seemed to him to be a real woman. He could still feel the strong grip of her hand on his arm as she led him out the back door. She looked frail but she was strong. He must remember that. Just because people were rich, it didn't mean they were weak or stupid. Did it? His dad would not have agreed with that idea. The rich were all dogs for his father and his mates. In his heart, despite his reasoning, and despite his love for Edith, he believed as his father believed. He had always known he would have to betray his origins if he was to get on in life. And it worried him. It always had worried him. Maybe it had even held him back. Right now he wanted to ask a simple straightforward question of this woman in front of him and get a simple straightforward answer back from her. But what was the question? He didn't know and it angered him. *They* angered him. It would not be a bad thing to see them damaged. He would like to try something with this lanky bitch to see just how good she really was. Nothing came to his mind at this moment but he would think of something. A test. Courage might have something to do with it. Physical courage. He'd see how she performed then. It was always the real test. Front the bastards with fear and see how they did. Who the fuck did she think she was anyway? He realised he was breathing heavily. He cleared his throat and stepped away from the table and said, 'I don't know what I'm doing yet. I may not go on with art.' This was not what he had intended to say. 'I haven't decided. I haven't done anything much for a while. I've been working for old Gerner next door trying to get a bit of money together.'

She looked at him and he looked back at her. What was it these two hoped for from each other?

'You have all the right ideas,' she said. 'But you don't have a subject. That's all it is. You have to find your subject.'

'Is that all it is?' he said sarcastically and laughed.

'Your material, I mean,' she said and frowned. 'Do you take that seriously?'

She made it sound simple. As if all he needed was a bit of common sense in order to become the artist he had dreamed of becoming. But he knew there was something stale and unhealthy about that old dream. It wasn't his any more. He knew he was never going to return to it. If he ever did make art seriously again he would make it for some other reason. He didn't know what that reason would be. He knew only that it would not be the old reason. The reason that had betrayed him. Or by which he had betrayed himself. He would share these thoughts with no one. Not even with Edith. She would look at him strangely and be puzzled and would wish to understand. But he did not understand himself. He had appealed to the rich bastards for help and they had humiliated him.

'You must meet people, Pat.'

He shrugged. 'I met a couple the other day.' He didn't know the questions. And he didn't know the answers. And although he knew it was unreasonable of him, he could not help blaming these people in some way for his ignorance and his bewilderment.

'Being down here on your own isn't good for you.'

'I'm not on my own.'

'I meant living here isolates you from what is being done.' Her tone was just a little impatient now.

'We can't afford to live in town.'

'Oh, well,' she said lightly. 'You're obviously determined not to listen to anything I have to say.' She went over and stood looking out of the window at the rain. The dark pines behind the house, broken limbs torn savagely from the great black trunks as if artillery had been fired at them, the beautiful wild sky rushing along overhead, black and grey and vivid white. So much power. So much purpose. The gods they all longed to believe in. What a shame the excitement of her expectations during the drive down this morning had slipped away from her quite so quickly now that they were here. Why is reality always so disappointing? she asked herself.

'What a pity it's raining,' she said aloud. 'I was so looking forward to seeing the ocean today.' As if it was for the ocean that she had left Old Farm so early this morning and driven all that way with Arthur.

Pat said, 'It's not a problem. I'll give you a dink on the bike.'

She turned from the window. 'On the crossbar, you mean?'

He stood looking at her.

'But we'll get wet.'

'Then we'll get dry again,' he said. 'The stove's going. Come on!' He walked across to her and took her hand. Now she would feel *his* strength. 'I'm kidnapping your missus, Arthur.'

•

Arthur went out and stood at the kitchen window and watched them. Pat cooeeing wildly and pedalling furiously down the steep hill towards the sharp turn at the bottom where the laneway met the road, gravel spitting from the rear tyre. Autumn's shriek of terror and delight, was it? The skirt of her pale blue dress flying up like a cloud of smoke, as they neared the turn. 'Idiots,' Arthur said quietly.

The Pontiac sat smugly just outside the lopsided gate, its roof and bonnet gleaming in the rain. The sight of his motor car reassured Arthur. He turned away from the window and looked into the hamper that sat on the kitchen table. He took out a bottle of red wine, uncorked it and poured wine into a clean glass. He took a bread roll from the hamper and spread it liberally with the duck pâté and took a bite. He stood by the table alternately taking bites out of the roll and swigs from the glass of wine. When he had finished the roll he took the bottle and the glass with him and went back to the studio.

He sat in the vacant chair near Edith's easel and looked at her painting of the house and the embroidered field, the bottle of claret within easy reach beside his chair. He lit a cigarette and sat smoking, blowing his little smoke rings, and looking at the painting. After a minute he said, 'Yes, it's lovely. A piece of music. A little nocturne.' He drank the wine and puffed the cigarette, being his Uncle Harold being a steam train. The house was quiet. The sound of his own voice made the room familiar and private. The rain pattered steadily on the tin roof and every now and then a cockatoo screeched in the pines. Arthur was pleased with the quiet and the company of the painting. He refilled his glass. Despite his grandmother's assertions, the claret was far more satisfying to his palate than the warm champagne. Autumn had been excited and had talked non-stop on the way down and he was glad to have this moment alone with his thoughts. He was enjoying the interior effect of the wine, a mist of encouraging claret dreams sitting behind his eyes in the bed of his skull.

He was undecided about Pat Donlon. It was a little disappointing. Pat didn't seem to be quite the man he had met in his office but seemed less, rather average in fact, here in his own home. Pat was Autumn's project, however. She believed him to be gifted. Her favourite word; *We all have a gift.* Well, maybe. Arthur wasn't so sure about this. What, for example, was his own gift? Contentment? Was contentment a gift? Tolerance? Steadiness perhaps. Were these things gifts? He had not seen any obvious evidence of Pat's giftedness here in the studio. But he would support her nevertheless. Autumn had rarely been mistaken in her choice of people. He could not now recall what it was that had prompted him to invite Pat to dinner that night. But he supposed he must have detected something about the man that he had thought would interest Autumn. Pat had seemed to him that evening to be someone who might be worth taking up. But from memory it had not been because of his drawings of the large naked girl, which Arthur had thought slapdash, but had been more due to his unorthodox attitude to the artist's conventional training and his rejection by Cowper. An energy in him that was unusual and which had aroused his curiosity. Any enemy of Cowper's naturally drew upon his sympathies. He had also been reading Wilenski, whose description of Gauguin's unorthodox beginnings had fired his imagination with thoughts of the great number of notable artists who were self-taught. Then here was this young man in his office with his bundle of drawings and his determination to be a painter. The moment had been right, he supposed. But was that all it was? Or had there been something else? Autumn had thought him right. He wondered how she would feel towards Pat after today.

He had enjoyed the drive down from Melbourne this morning. Now he was enjoying Edith's painting and his cigarette and the claret. By the time they'd arrived at Ocean Grove their own ice had melted and it was a pity Pat and Edith had had no ice here for the champagne. Autumn preferred champagne to claret and they had brought several bottles. His grandmother had maintained that warm champagne was good for the digestion. She had died content at the age of one hundred and one. But these facts had never been sufficient to convince Autumn that she might enjoy champagne when it was not perfectly chilled.

Arthur sat there in the studio on his own that rainy afternoon thinking about these inconsequential things, and was soon lost to remembrances of his family and his childhood. He enquired of himself for the thousandth time what it might have been that had convinced his mother to be so implacable about the law for him. His father and uncles were farmers. He lit another cigarette and puffed some more rings and had no answers for his queries. He was still looking at the picture, but he was no longer seeing it. He suddenly became aware of someone standing beside the easel.

Edith said, 'I'm sorry. I didn't mean to startle you. I thought everyone had gone out. I was on my way to get a cup of water when I heard a voice in here.' She was wearing a green velour dressing-gown and had grey slippers on her feet. She held the dressing-gown closed at her neck with both hands. Her hair was dark and uncombed and hung about her face as if she had been out in wild weather.

Arthur stood up. She looked like his idea of Hardy's Tess. Not what he had expected for the wife of the little Irishman. This girl was a country lass. Pat was all city. A little sad, perhaps? Certainly in hope of better things to come. She didn't look particularly ill.

'I'm Edith,' she said, pressing her palm to her chest. 'I shan't disturb you. I suppose you must be Arthur?'

'Pat's taken Autumn down to see the ocean on his bike.' He reached for the back of the chair to steady himself. 'I was probably talking to myself.' He stepped forward. 'Here, let me get you the water.' He took the cup from her hand. 'I've been admiring your painting.'

'I'm afraid it's rather old-fashioned,' she said.

'I'm a little old-fashioned myself.'

Their eyes met briefly and they both laughed.

'It's a lovely painting,' he said firmly. He took her hand and led her to the chair. 'I'll be back in a second.' She did not protest but seemed content to sit down and wait for him, crossing her legs and pulling the skirts of her green dressing-gown over her knees. He went into the kitchen and filled the cup with cool water, then came back into the studio and handed the cup to her. She took a sip. He said, 'Your grandfather would have been proud of you.'

It was what Pat had said to her. 'Did you know his work?' she asked.

'Everyone in our house knew Thomas Anderson. I met him once when I was a boy. I suppose it was during the holidays and I was home from school. I remember his moustache and his kindly smile. But that's all. My mother has several of his Tasmanian landscapes. And there is a portrait of my grandfather that she is especially fond of. Your palette is lighter than his. I much prefer it.' Her painting made him feel comfortably at home with her. He knew himself to be a familiar of the values and the social situation in which both she and her picture had their origins.

They both looked at the painting on the easel.

Arthur said, 'Do you have a title for it?'

'I call it the embroidered hillside.'

They were both silent again for quite a long time. The silence was not a difficult one, but seemed to Arthur to be a natural extension of the larger silence of the house, which was made apparent by the proprietorial screeching of the solitary cockatoo in the pines. Arthur wondered if someone in the house had kept the cockatoo as a pet. He was aware of sharing something of value with Edith and liked her.

She said easily, without apparent self-deprecation, 'There's no future for my kind of painting. None at all. But it's what I love to do.'

Arthur considered complimenting her again on her skill, which she must certainly have been aware of, but said nothing. Might she not reveal something unexpected to him if he kept his silence? And surely she would close up and say nothing more if he were to say too much. They were naturally in tune, the two of them, he was sure of it, but they were also both modest people who would readily defer to a companion, and for whom an awkward word at this delicate moment might destroy the small area of trust they had discovered with each other. He hadn't meant to speak, therefore, when a moment later he heard himself ask her, 'Are you feeling better then?' It was his habit of good manners, to show care of others, to offer a sense of his concern, that prompted him to break the interesting silence between himself and this young woman. He was annoyed with himself.

But Edith did not respond to his question. 'It's Pat who'll be charting the future of our art,' she said. 'Not people like me.' She looked up at Arthur and held his gaze steadily for a considerable moment. 'I don't have any illusions about that. I suppose if I tried I could make a living from painting. But Pat's work is too strange for people. No one will venture to buy it until it has been acknowledged. People will need to be emboldened before they can have confidence in it. No one knows what to make of it.'

He granted her a larger readiness for reality than he and decided she was an admirable person. 'What do you make of Pat's work yourself?' He hoped to hear something from her that might persuade him to believe in Patrick Donlon's genius.

'Oh, I can't say,' she said simply. 'Pat doesn't ask himself what is to be *made* of his work. What *can* be made of it? It has already been made. This is not a question with him. The work is just there. He is impatient with talk about art and why we do it and what it means and all that. He has no time for any of it. When people ask him such questions he asks them what they mean and they can never say what it is they mean because there really isn't anything *to* mean. The work is either there or it isn't and when it is there what can be said that will add anything to it? If you ask me what I make of my own pictures, what can I say? That one is there and you say you admire it.'

'I do admire it. It is very skilled. It is a picture that lets me dream a little.' He stood looking down at her, waiting for her to say something more, but she sipped her water and looked at the picture on the easel and added nothing. 'You believe in Pat,' he said. 'And that's enough, is it?'

'Pat will do something new and important one day. I'm sure of it. I've always known it. Since the first time I saw him at the Gallery School. When I saw him I knew at once he was not like the others.' She laughed. 'He has never offered anything for sale in case no one wanted to buy it. So I suppose we don't really know yet if some peculiar person might have the courage to buy something just on their own feeling for it. But it's hard to imagine anyone doing that.'

Arthur said, 'Pat offered me his drawings of the nude young woman for fifty pounds.'

She looked up at him. Evidently surprised. 'Well, I would say you missed a bargain.'

'It wouldn't be the first. He must be very grateful to you for your faith in him.'

'It's not gratitude Pat feels for me. Did he tell you we're having a baby?' She smiled at the thought of the child and passed a hand across her belly.

'It's great news for you both.' He felt he should say something more encouraging but he was thinking of Autumn and hoping the subject of babies could be avoided. He could not see how he might share his private thoughts with this young woman, no matter how responsive to her trust he hoped to be. In taking on Pat Donlon, it had begun to seem fairly clear to him that Autumn would be not simply supporting the career of a difficult young artist but taking on the welfare of a family. He wondered how much thought she had given to this, if any, in her enthusiasm. It was his first sense that there might be trouble ahead for Autumn in her guardianship of what she had begun to refer to as Pat's genius, a relationship she had set her heart on elaborating. He said, 'How will the three of you live?'

'We're both resourceful people.'

'You're not afraid of poverty?'

'Not nearly as afraid of it as I was before I experienced it.'

Arthur was self-conscious about the tendency of his cherished good manners to render his responses to people merely conventional and platitudinous. How to be real with people had always been a puzzle for him. Even at school he had struggled with this dilemma. And as an adult he had never quite given up trying to resolve it and often found himself wanting to be more spontaneously responsive and open with attractive strangers, men as well as women, than he was able to be with a convincing naturalness. The problem, as he saw it, was how to have good manners but not conceal himself behind them. His sense of the absurd was in fact quite well developed but almost never received the grace of expression, except when he was on his own; in his office, in the bath or on the toilet, and sometimes on the train, when it was not unheard of for him to laugh aloud at some inner observation of a fellow passenger. At such times he could be quite witty and was often able to scan a wide field of irony in the lives of the people around him, clients and fellow passengers especially. The moment he was socially engaged with another, however, the shutters went up, as his mother had once put it. All he could think of then was to be perfectly gracious and polite. He had always found it easy to be kind, and sometimes wondered if kindness with him hadn't become merely a substitute for something more real, something deeper that was really him. People usually appreciated kindness, however, and he liked the feeling of being appreciated. Whereas Freddy and Barnaby were prepared to be misunderstood and thought cruel in their observations. You avoided one field only to flounder about in the neighbouring field. Life, he supposed. Wasn't it? How to exist in the confident zone of behaviour where others seemed to sit without effort? It was unimaginable to him that he would have been capable of doing as Pat had done just now, walking up to Autumn and taking her hand like that, and going off with her in that harum-scarum way down the hill on the bike, as if she was a young girl. Had it been merely his habit of kindness, he wondered now, that had prompted him to invite that hungry and rather forlorn young man to dinner that night? Today a young man neither hungry nor forlorn. What might he have set in motion with that invitation? Whatever it was, he was aware that the consequences of his kindly act, whatever they were to be, had passed out of his control. He sighed and lit another cigarette and looked down at Pat's wife. How was she managing? She looked up at him and smiled. He decided to risk a confession.

'I've never been without sufficient funds to do the things I've wanted to do,' he said. This wasn't quite the confession he had intended, but it would suffice. 'It is only a lack of ambition and imagination, not a lack of opportunity, that have prevented me from attempting something first rate.' He smiled, wondering how she was taking this. He saw no reason to hold back. 'Unlike you and Pat, and unlike Autumn too, I've never been troubled by a desire to excel at anything.' He shrugged. 'Not really. That's the truth.' He frowned. It *was* the truth. He decided something needed to be added to this and tried rounding it off with, 'I can't imagine how dreadful it must be to be poor.'

She said easily, 'Poverty's something our families dread more than anything else. The idea of it haunts them and they give us an unreasonable fear of it. But it's something they have no experience of. Pat's family is poor. But they never give their lack of money a thought. I discovered with Pat that the poor don't fear poverty as we have been taught to. If it is mentioned at all it is to laugh at it. Unless his dad has spent the rent money on the horses. Then his mother gets seriously upset. It's a matter of honour with her to have the rent money ready on the right day and to never have to ask for a postponement. Our artists are wrong when they show working people as unhappy and oppressed. Pat's mother's always singing. They are happier than we are. If we are with the person we love, poverty isn't frightening. And anyway, it won't last for me and Pat. It will be a precious period of our lives. It will be our period of struggle together. The time when we prove ourselves. And I've been offered illustrating work with the *Age*. It pays quite well.' She said, 'I'd like you to have my painting, Arthur.'

He must have looked uncertain, or a little startled.

'It is a present from me,' she explained.

'I can't possibly accept it, Edith.' It was the first time he had used her name. The colour had returned to her cheeks and he thought her very lovely. He almost said so but restrained himself, recognising the urging of the champagne and the claret just in time. 'It's very generous of you, but you must keep it and show it one day.'

'You and Autumn have given so much support to Pat just when he needed it. No one else has done that. The others have scoffed at him and ridiculed him. He appreciates your kindness more than anything. So do I. I think you can accept my picture and not be troubled by my generosity, Arthur.' She reached and put her hand on his arm. 'It is from me to you. It's not a repayment of a debt or anything like that. I've decided to give it to you, so there.'

Arthur put his hand on hers. He said nothing. A life with her could be imagined: the two of them seated by the fire reading, their child (children?) safely asleep in bed after he had read the little boy (it was a boy) a story. How he had wanted children! A man was not supposed to care so much. This was the confession he had wished to make to her but for which he had failed to find the words. The shutters of his mind. Would his law practice have meant something real to him if he and a woman like Edith had had children together? Would that missing thing in his life, the thing that other people seemed to possess and which he did not possess, the thing that made them care deeply and want to do something excellent, the thing that made them behave as if they were real, would it have been satisfied in him if he'd had a son? It saddened him to think that he would never know the answer to this question. To have been a boy's father. He closed his eyes. The image that came before him was not that of a child, but was his mother's anxious features relaxing into a smile. Grandmother.

'Please, Arthur!' She shook his sleeve. 'I just know it should be yours.'

Arthur turned and took the painting from the easel and held it. As he took the picture in his hands his throat tightened and he might have wept.

'I love Pat,' Edith was saying. 'But I'm not like him. He and I are opposites. We complete each other. It has always been like this between us. Isn't it like that with you and Autumn? Forgive me, but I think you and she are opposites too, aren't you? Pat is boiling inside with an enormous need and energy to make something new with his art. I believe he will succeed in doing it. And I want to be there with him and to support him until one day, whenever it is to be, his hopes for his work become a reality.'

Arthur did not hear what she was saying. He was holding her picture and looking into its tranquil meadow embroidered with the golden stars of the oxalis. He cleared his throat carefully and said, 'Thank you, Edith. I shall treasure it.' He turned and leaned down to kiss her cheek. He felt himself blushing.

'There is also a need in us for tranquillity,' he said. 'That is what you have achieved here. The mind is invited to rest in your picture. The new is always a little frenzied. A little afraid of itself. The new is driven by chance, by risk and by uncertainty. In seeking to establish itself, the new seeks to disestablish the old order. The new is apocalyptic and is forever exulting in its courage to court failure, as if there is virtue in that.' He drew breath and turned to her. 'I'm sorry,' he said. 'I'm going on rather.'

'No,' she said, 'you're right. That is Pat you are speaking of. It is why he needs me.'

•

Autumn was running along the sand, the seas of the Great Southern Ocean making their landfall in an explosion of spume to her right, riding themselves in against the slant of the rain. She could see she wasn't going to catch him. She wanted to call out to him to stop but she was out of breath and her voice would be lost against the thunder of the seas. They had left their shoes with the bike on the black rocks at the bottom of the ramp behind them. She kept going, her legs tiring, her lungs unable to take in enough air. He was dancing from one foot to the other, daring the waves. A big sea rushed up the slope of sand and knocked him down. He went over and rolled and the following crest burst against him. He regained his feet and stood a moment, arms flailing, one leg coming free of the turmoil as if he mocked the waves, then the back tow took him off his feet.

She stopped running, standing on her toes at the edge of the tide, a hand to her eyes, the roaring of the great waves terrifying now. She began to run again, calling his name, her voice whipped from her mouth and lost. Before she reached the place where she had seen him taken into the sea she saw him rise up and wave a hand, then he was in a dip of the water and was gone again, like a little boat. She thought she heard him call but it could have been the cry of the speckled skewer riding the green and white hills of the thundering water. Then there he was again, further out now, his head the size of a floating coconut, an arm coming out of the green undercrest. No one could swim in such a turmoil of water. She was sick in her stomach and stood staring out to catch glimpses of him until he was to be glimpsed no more but was gone forever into the boiling ocean.

The windbroken crests of the roaring waves were higher than her head and she could not see into the troughs. Then suddenly he was coming towards her, body surfing a wave almost to her feet. He stood and ran to her and picked her up, then turned around and ran into the sea with her. She screamed and beat him about the head and he laughed and stood in the foam a moment before retreating and carrying her back up the beach out of the reach of the waves.

He set her on her feet and stood with his hands on his hips laughing at her.

She hit him in the mouth with her closed fist and screamed at him.

He ducked away, stung by the blow, his hand going to his mouth. He looked at the blood on his fingers. 'Jesus Christ!' he said. 'I've a good mind to chuck you in the fucking sea, you bitch.' He stepped up to her and she backed away, raising an arm to shield herself. He pinioned her arms to her sides and kissed her hard on the mouth. He drew away then he kissed her again, leaving his blood on her white teeth.

She cried out desperately and he released her arms suddenly and she fell backwards onto the sand. As he came towards her she scrambled away from him. He stood over her and held out a hand to her. She crawled backwards away from him up the sand then got to her feet, pulling her dress down and beating at it with her hands. He didn't follow her but stood watching, fingering his split lip. He examined his fingers. The wound was sore, the salt firing it up.

They stood looking at each other, the rain coming down. She turned and began walking back along the beach towards the ramp. He watched her a moment then followed her. He caught up with her and walked alongside her. The sky was heavy and grey out over the ocean, the great seas colliding furiously with the land.

After they had gone a little way she stopped and turned to him. 'Is your lip all right?'

'No, it's not. It's bloody sore.'

'You shouldn't have kissed me.'

'You looked ready for it.'

'Don't talk like that. It's cheap. I'm Arthur's wife. I love him. I want you to understand that.'

He narrowed his eyes and examined her. He couldn't help smiling.

'What are you smiling at?'

The rain streaming down her face, her blue dress soaked and covered in sand. 'You,' he said. 'I'm laughing at you. You're a sight.'

'This is not funny.'

'I think it is.'

They stood on the deserted sands of the long beach in the rain.

'Well?' he said. 'Is it funny or isn't it funny?'

She said, 'You're quite mad.'

'You're crazier than I am,' he said. 'This is better than being stuck up there in the house, isn't it? Admit it.'

She said, 'What are we going to tell them?'

'About what?'

'How you hurt your lip, for one thing.'

'I'll tell Arthur you smacked me in the mouth for kissing you.'

'You wouldn't.' She looked worried.

'Why not?'

'Please don't do that.'

He shrugged. 'It's the truth.' He was glad to see her looking worried. 'We have to tell the truth. No? We can't start off with a lie.'

'Start off? What do you mean? I'm getting cold.'

'Let's run.'

'I couldn't.'

'Okay. Let's walk then.'

He took her arm and they set off along the wide sand, two figures, the man holding the woman by the arm. The woman the taller of the two. From a half-kilometre distant they might have been a mother and son.

13

November 1991

THE FIRST OF THE SUMMER HEAT STRUCK US TODAY. A BLOW IN THE face when I went outside this morning. Our nameless north wind from the desert. It wasn't predicted on the radio. Then this afternoon it rained. Everything is damp to the touch. A smell of mouldering already in the closet warmth of these rooms. The page of my exercise book sticks to the side of my hand as I lift it. *John Waters, Grade 3, Albert Park Primary.* My shift hangs on me as heavy as armour. And there's a rash under both my arms. I'll be red raw by tonight. If it weren't for Adeli I'd go about the house naked in this weather but I have no wish to disgust her. I saw her naked a few days ago. Neither she nor I have spoken about it. If she doesn't mention it soon then I shall. It is too delicious to leave in the silence.

I thought she had gone out and I decided to take a peek into the dining room to see how she was progressing with the papers. I had a sneaking desire to view her ordered piles of neatly catalogued materials. Thinking she wasn't there I didn't make a particular effort to be quiet and stumped along the passage gripping Barnaby's knob as I usually do. I eased the dining room door open a crack and was astonished to see her posing completely naked in the middle of Arthur's father's dining table. Spread in a circle around her on the table were Pat's drawings of Mr Creedy's daughter. Adeli was smiling coyly and turning this way and that the better to view her reflection in the large mirror that is screwed to the wall above the fireplace. She was enormous. Far larger than I had imagined. And she was beautiful. Yes, it was her beauty that astonished me. Her skin was of a light creamy tone, silken and shading, in certain parts of her anatomy, to a delicate pink of exceptional gloss and smoothness. Adeli is a perfect Max Factor. So there! The only blemish, if it can be called a blemish, was a beauty spot below her left breast. Her belly was not gross but shapely. She was jiggling it, the way some African women jiggle their backsides, rhythmically. Only this was her frontside. I gazed at her in wonderment. Sherry was on the table with her, looking up adoringly, as mesmerised as I was—Sherry worshipping at the feet of his deity. I have no hope of ever winning his allegiance back again.

Adeli's extraordinarily refined beauty was a revelation. Are all fat women like her under their tents? I have always worshipped the tall and the slim, in honour of myself I suppose. Though it occurred to our ancestors, particularly to Rubens, it had never occurred to me to imagine that these hidden acres of beauty were real presences nearby—indeed herds of them in the supermarket. The fatter the better. It is a competition, surely, to see who can be fattest.

She saw me and went still, her stomach appearing to deflate and lap over her crotch, rather like the distended crop of a

New Guinea bird of paradise when it has completed its mating dance. We stared into each other's eyes for a timeless moment before I eased the door to and crept away, shamefaced for my intrusion, but strangely elated.

As I tiptoed down the passage back to the kitchen, I was reminded, with a sudden sharp revelation of memory, of my feelings on the way home with Arthur the night after our visit to Pat and Edith at Ocean Grove. An echo of that particular mix of shamefaced guilt and private elation sparking across the years to touch the old scene into life.

The more I write about my past the more detailed my memories of it become. Vivid prompts of my imagination, such as this one—more usually making their entrance during the night or when Andrew is prodding about with an enema up my backside—carry me down into deep layers of memory I had believed lost forever. But there they are! Bright treasures of perception, as good as new, standing before me as if no time had elapsed since they were experienced, ready to be clicked into my present reality like Lego blocks, each with its predetermined place in this dream of a purposeful life that I am spinning with my pen. Is that what I am doing? Am I to title it *A Purposeful Life*? When I first wrote in this (let us call it an exploratory memoir) of Edith's painting, I could not then recall how it had got into the loft. I hadn't even remembered it was in the loft or that we still had it here or that we had ever had it here. Now that I have recovered the whole of the story of that picture it is as if I had never forgotten it.

•

When Pat and I got back to the house, Edith had returned to her bed and Arthur was drinking on his own in the kitchen. As we walked Pat's bicycle up the gravel laneway to the gate I saw Arthur's face at the rain-streaked window watching us.

I have seen peasants in Spain walking through rain in the mountains without coat or head covering, a look of unconcern on their faces and in their unhurried manner. Something of that same unconcern was in Pat's earlier observation to me when I objected that we would get wet if we went down to see the ocean, 'And then we will get dry again.' And it is true, there was something of the gipsy in Pat, and one day he would go looking for confirmation of this intuition in Ireland. Did he find it? Did he meet his brother-in-the-spirit? I don't know. He was lost to me long before that.

Arthur was very quiet on the way home that night. He drove as if he was not my beloved husband but my chauffeur, a responsible and rather grimly humourless man with a job to do and a surly determination to do it well, whatever the cost to his peace of mind. He was not the Arthur I knew and loved. It was dark and still raining heavily, water cascading across the road. I prayed we would not become marooned along the way, caught between rising streams, and forced to sit side by side in the cold silence of the hours. I was wearing one of Edith's frocks and her cardigan. The frock was far too short for me. I was uncomfortable and chilled. My wet clothes were in the back. I had not thought to put in a rug when we set off from Old Farm that morning.

Beside me Arthur drove within a bell of silence which inhibited conversation. I was feeling sorry for myself and feared I was coming down with something. I was longing to be in my own bed in my right and customary frame of mind. It was an emotion close to homesickness, this, a desire to reaffirm a deeply familiar reality. And a grief for something already lost perhaps. Fear of the reality which was to replace it. Arthur hadn't told me why Edith's painting was on the back seat with my wet clothes and I didn't trust myself to ask him to explain its presence there. The resistance between us bewildered me and I knew I didn't have the ability to deal with it peaceably. Perhaps I also lacked the nerve to make the attempt. There was, of course—of course there was—my strident ambivalence about the whole business. Of my life, I mean. My secret shamefaced guilt and elation.

So the silence between us persisted. Edith's star-spangled painting on the back seat waiting for a word to set off the explosion.

We drove on for hour after hour, through the black rain, along deserted roads. And we seemed to make no progress. I could distinguish nothing familiar in the thick darkness outside the car. It was all the same. Just blackness. It was as if by some awful twist of ill fortune we had blundered into a foreign country where we were not known and were unwelcome. As if we had taken a wrong turning and might never find our way back to our own familiar world. I was sure nothing would ever again reassure me. About myself, I mean.

As the drive went on it began to assume for me the trapped feeling of a nightmare; the darkness darker, the rain heavier, the roads more lonely, the terrain more threateningly unfamiliar. Before I would wake, surely I must arrive at some terrible end? I crouched miserably in my seat, hugging Edith's inadequate cardigan around me, my gaze fixed on the trembling beams of our lights skidding over the glistening macadam. Now, as I write this, I seem to recall a fugitive music accompanied me that night. I know this sound of music is not a recollection of fact (how could it be?) but is the addition of fiction seeking to soften the moral contours of the unfolding events in which I felt myself to be trapped. The intractable forces, I mean, of character and destiny. Just as Edith's painting waited on the back seat for a word from one of us, so this situation had waited its time, nestled sweetly in my unconscious. I knew myself to be helpless against it. I was still the crazy girl on the boat going to Europe with my mother.

How was it, I asked myself that Arthur and I had set out from home that morning in a mood of optimism, Arthur delighted with the prospect of a long drive in his beloved car, I looking forward to an interesting encounter with Pat and his art, and now here we were returning like defeated people through an unknown landscape towards a destination that would not know us or make us welcome? The premonition that something precious had come to an end haunted me, in its various guises, throughout that terrible drive. And I was right. Although we survived—our marriage did, I mean—Arthur and I were never again quite as we had been before the excursion to Ocean Grove. The period of our untrammelled optimism together had lasted for twelve years. Now it had come to an end. And it was I who had brought it to an end. My long-forsworn capacity for a wildness of the spirit. This sleeping child of my past had been revived at the touch of Pat's bloodied lips. It sounds very melodramatic, but it's true.

When Arthur spoke I jumped at the sound of his voice.

'What's that ticking?' he demanded.

'What ticking?'

'Listen!'

His tone was so stern and so angry I thought he might have gone mad. 'I can hear nothing,' I said carefully. 'It is just the sound of the road.'

'There! Listen!'

We ran on behind the beams of the headlights, the rain lashing the windscreens. I could hear nothing that sounded anything like ticking. Did he think there was a bomb in the car? I looked at him. The brim of his hat shaded his eyes, the lower part of his features faintly lit by the back glow of the headlights, his mouth set in a hard line. I sat hugging myself, waiting for whatever was going to happen. But Arthur lapsed once again into deep silence and I did not have the courage to break it with the sound of my own voice.

We were grinding our way slowly up into the hills in first gear and I had at last begun to recognise the landscape when Arthur said, in that same tight angry voice he had used when speaking of the ticking in the car, 'If you take on Pat Donlon you'll be taking on responsibility for a family. You've considered that, I suppose?'

I stared at him. I was scarcely able to believe what I had heard, or the accusing tone of his voice. So he was accusing *me*! I felt myself assaulted by a powerful surge of self-righteous fury. 'What did you say?'

'I think you heard me.'

He was busy negotiating the final tight bends in the road that led to the entrance to Old Farm.

'Repeat what you just said!' I shouted at him. I was so angry I lost control and without considering what I was doing

I grabbed his arm. The car dived to the left. Arthur had very good reflexes and stamped on the brake before the car went off the road. To have gone off at that point would have meant a plunge down the hill for us and almost certain death or serious injury.

We both sat very still. Then Arthur engaged reverse and eased us back onto the middle of the road. I was trembling as we turned into our gate and drove down into the coach house. I didn't trust myself to speak.

Sitting with his hands on the steering wheel, still in the driving position, the engine silenced, staring ahead at the back wall of the coach house and no doubt still watching the road unfold before his eyes, Arthur said in that tight and very deliberate voice that he had found for the occasion (I had never heard it before), 'I said, if you take on Pat you'll be taking on the care of a family.' He turned to me, his eyes looking into mine as if he were the judge and knew the whole case and had made his judgment. 'Have you thought of that?'

It is not possible to recount exactly what happened then, but I can still hear my voice screaming accusations at him, utterly incoherent and unreasonable, something to do with him having always denied me the important things in life. He fought off my blows, gripping my wrists and restraining me without too much difficulty, for he was quicker, more controlled and far stronger than I. When he released me and stepped out of the car I stumbled out on my side hardly able to see where I was going. It was blind impulse then that made me reach into the back and pull out the square canvas of Edith's painting. With a howl of fury I threw it with all my force. If I'd been aiming for the loft I would probably have missed. When it didn't come down again I was mystified as to where it could have gone. As we know, it remained in the loft for more than fifty years, like a forgotten bale of hay. Tossed.

Once I would have said Edith's painting was forgotten by us. Now I would say we had no wish to remember it. The mind is capable of deep silences on subjects we have no desire to deal with. The loft swallowed it and the problem of Edith's painting conveniently disappeared from our sight for half a century. We didn't ask any questions. It was enough that it was gone, *like the rainbow's lovely form evanishing amid the storm*. And so on.

We didn't sleep together that night. Arthur and I had had rows before this. He was usually controlled and severe at such times (being his mother) but I'd had several richly florid outbursts in our early days when the influence of my own mother and my family was still a raw wound with me. But this was the first time Arthur and I had not made up and gone to bed together, friends again. He slept in the guest room, if he slept at all. And I slept in our bed. I locked the door. I could not have faced his gentle fumbling attempt at a reconciliation that night.

I undressed and climbed into bed and lay down. My emotions were in turmoil. But I must have been exhausted because I fell asleep at once. I woke, suddenly, into the night; the metallic taste of Pat's blood when I slid my tongue over my teeth after he kissed me was vivid and compelling in my mouth. I slid my tongue over my teeth again there in my bed, my eyes closed, testing the recollection of his blood. I was appalled. By all of it. The thunder of the waves. Lying there in the dark, strangely awake in the warm intimacy of my bed, it seemed to me that I had danced with Pat Donlon in the eye of life and death; as one might dance in the eye of a storm for an instant before being tossed helplessly to one's death. A *totentanz* of the liberated spirit. I knew I could not give it up. *It?* Yes, it. The edge. Freedom. The thing between us that compelled me. I had no name for it then and have none for it now. It is no good calling it love. I loved Arthur, my life's companion.

I had feared it would come out sooner or later. My emotions were fragile and exaggerated. I felt superstitious, and as if I carried a taint of evil. The wonder was, it seemed to me that night, that Arthur and I had managed to enjoy so many years of peace and contentment together. The thought that I would risk it now, that I would risk losing him, terrified me. In our early twenties we had been each other's saviour. Nothing could replace that bond between us. Ever. We had saved each other. We had made sense of each other's life. That could not be undone. I knew this then and I know it now. Its truth was never a question for either of us. We belonged. That is love. That deep belonging.

Words. Language is useful for a few restricted realities. But for the rest, for the life of the gods, language has nothing to say. One can only know such things as experience in the heat of one's blood, not as descriptive possibilities. Even Milton and Dante, with their headlock on language, couldn't do it. Our blood, not our words, carries the message that compels us to submit, just as an invading army of superior force compels the submission into barbarism of gentle civilisations. Is that too much? Well, we shall see.

Arthur and I never spoke to each other of Edith's embroidered field. And on the single occasion Edith stayed with us at Old Farm she did not mention it. Her picture (and soon she) dropped out of our lives into a well of silence from which they have only now finally re-emerged. It is surely as if they have had to find their way to me along that same haunted route on which Arthur and I travelled together that night; to live with each other thereafter at the still centre of our own private labyrinth, where calm was never more than a temporary illusion and the menace of the ocean deeps was ever with us. Ah well. From that day on we knew our love to be fragile, tested, beleaguered, damaged, marked indelibly, and often so sad it made us weep, but somehow, yes, enduring.

At the time it seemed to us both that to attempt to deal with the charged enigma of Edith's painting would be to risk touching off an explosion of unreason that would finish us. Eventually distance and time, the loss of friends, ill health, and finally a kind of forgetting eroded our interest, until at last we were alone again with each other, she and her picture no longer a feature of our horizon. A buried city of the plain whose ramparts I have begun to unearth.

The morning after our return from Ocean Grove I woke to the sun streaming through the French doors and the sound of Arthur singing in the kitchen. I lay listening, disbelieving, seeing the pale green leaves of the Algerian oak he had planted out in the middle of the lawn. A blackbird stood on the oak's topmost branch challenging all comers. Tom was flattened in the grass, staring up at him with evil in his eyes. Arthur didn't bring me a cup of tea. Perhaps he had tried my door in the night and knew it to be locked. I got up and looked at myself in my dressing-table mirror. My eyes were red and had little lines in their corners. I put on my dressing-gown and went into the kitchen.

He was at the Rayburn. There was the comforting smell of toast and coffee and the kitchen was bright with the lovely day. He turned to me and smiled and said good morning, not as if *nothing* had happened, but as if he was determined to demonstrate to me that we could proceed *as if* nothing had happened. So in a way nothing *had* happened. But all was changed. I had become a liar and a hypocrite.

'I can do you a couple of boiled eggs?'

He was not over-cheerful. In fact he did it very well. Almost as if he were a practised hypocrite himself. I thanked him and lit a cigarette and stood in the doorway looking out at my garden. Stony was among the tomatoes, pruning and tying them up. There were birds busy everywhere, going for it after the rain. I suppose the leaves and weeds were alive with insects. The sun was already warm. Arthur came to my elbow and handed me a cup of coffee and kissed my neck. I turned and kissed him on the cheek. He fetched his coffee and stood beside me. I prayed to my godless god that he would not mention last night. The smell of the country was in the morning. It was why we had come here, this smell of our reality, this peace, this beauty.

It was a Sunday so he was home for the day. After breakfast we walked down to the river together and sat on our log and watched the water. Owing to the heavy rain the night before the river was up and had a lovely strong energy to it. Arthur pointed. 'There!' he whispered. A tawny water rat slipped along the bank into the churning water. Arthur took my hand in his.

When he came home from the office on Monday he looked tired and worried. I had cooked a beef pie, which was his favourite meal, and had opened one of his better clarets. We sat at the table in the kitchen eating our dinner. I just wanted life to go on. He looked up at me in a way that made me realise he was about to say something important. His fork was halfway to his mouth. I waited, cold creeping into my stomach.

'Something seems to be coming apart in the Ponty,' he said. He kept looking at me as if he was expecting a strong response from me, possibly an explanation, even a convincing reassurance from me that all was well with his precious car.

I said, 'You mean that noise you think you heard?' I hated having to speak of anything to do with Saturday night. But he was forcing me to it. I wondered where the conversation would lead and was terrified he would bring it around to Pat and to Edith's painting and, well, to the whole sordid mess of my exhausted emotions. I did not think the ticking he had complained of was something that could be worth talking about on its own.

'*Thought* I heard?' he said.

'That you *heard*, then,' I said with care.

He forked the paused food into his mouth and chewed. 'It was there again on the way to the station this morning and when I drove home this evening.' He reached for his glass and took a good swig of claret.

Did he murmur, *Thought I heard*? Or did I only imagine it?

I waited, but he said no more. The evening was charged with nasty possibilities. I had lost my appetite and pushed my plate away and lit a cigarette. He looked at me, his eyebrows raised. 'Smoking already? Not hungry, darling? Are you feeling okay?'

'I had a late lunch with Barnaby,' I said.

'The pie's terrific. How's Barnaby?'

I knew we were not done with the ticking in the car, but the initiative was not mine and there was nothing I could do to hurry things to a conclusion. I drank some claret and smoked my cigarette. 'He's going up to Sofia Station on Wednesday. Harry can't come down. He wanted me to go with him. He complains that he knows our home and our lives in every detail and we only know most of his life thinly and from hearsay.'

'Will you go?'

'I'm thinking about it. Would you mind?' I was certain I wasn't going to Sofia Station with Barnaby, then or ever. Eventually, but not on this occasion, I was to change my mind. The results of my change of mind could not have been foreseen and were momentous. The biggest thing, in fact, to happen to me and to Australian art during my lifetime.

Arthur ate more pie and drank more claret and frowned and sniffed a couple of times. 'I would a bit,' he said. He looked up at me, obviously unsure of what he was letting himself in for. It hadn't been easy for him to say this. 'But if you'd really like to go . . .' He didn't finish what he was about to say but voiced a new idea. 'Perhaps I should take a couple of weeks off and we could both go?'

I knew he didn't mean it any more than I had meant that I might go with Barnaby. 'There's too much to do here,' I said. Would Pat arrive at the door one day and demand to become part of our lives? Or demand that I run away with him? In this last fear (or was it a hope?) I wasn't so far off predicting what eventually happened. I said, 'Will you take the car into Martin and King and have them look at it?' I knew that for Arthur the suggestion there might be something amiss with the bodywork of the Ponty was about as acceptable to him as sacrilege to a nun—there was a moral dimension to his faith in that car.

His frown deepened. 'Oh, I doubt if it's in the body,' he said, dismissing the idea as a form of idiocy. How dare I suggest such a thing? What did I know of the bodywork of the masters? If it came down to it, what did women know of anything much? For his time Arthur wasn't particularly sexist, but I knew he could reach for the popular male view of women whenever he was feeling insecure about himself. Arthur's sexism was, as it usually is, a form of self-defence against a sense of his own inadequacy to meet a particular challenge. His implied belittling of my opinion on this occasion was a useful means for diverting his anger away from himself and its real cause. I don't know that he ever understood things in this way, but it is how I understood them.

We left it at that for the time being. Was he thinking of having been done out of children by my condition? This often worried me. My barren condition was itself the result of my youthful search for a kind of wild mythical freedom that does not exist, mistaking at seventeen the idea of free sex for something far more substantial and elusive. Particularly, I knew, Arthur regretted not being able to have a son. I can't say how I knew he was thinking of this at the time, I just knew it. And knowing it froze something in me. There was no obvious sign, and of course he didn't say anything about it. If we had not concealed our true feelings from each other that evening, we might have had our big row and got it over and done with. Or is this too simple? I fear it may be. The big row, after all, was as dangerous for him as it was for me. We never had it. Its potential, like nuclear weapons, was useful as a deterrent. To have resorted to it would have left the survivor with little to celebrate. Was it our mistake to have secret lives? I know I should believe this, but I can't make myself regret what we did. The open and the concealed. The concealed leaking dangerously into the open, like a levee bank beginning to give way and threatening to drown the entire town when the pressure of the flood outside becomes too great.

Arthur drove the Ponty into Melbourne the following Friday. The people at Martin and King took him for a drive around Albert Park Lake. One mechanic (were they mechanics or something else?) stuck his head under the dashboard and the other drove at over a hundred miles an hour. When they were unable to detect the rattle, as Arthur was now calling it, they drove the car at various speeds and changed drivers and listened again. They said that whatever it was, it must have righted itself. Their joint conclusion (and it annoyed Arthur that they stuck together on this) was that something, a piece of wire or a twig, had probably lodged in the chassis during the drive home from Ocean Grove in all that rain and that it had been dislodged during the high-speed circuit of the lake.

On Arthur's way home it began again; ticker-ticker-ticker.

He was sitting up in bed beside me (we only spent the one night sleeping apart) trying to read his Wilenski, which he was making rather a labour of. He said, evidently speaking out of a conversation he had been having with himself, 'It's quite clear.' He was being comically earnest and I was glad I was able to shield my expression from him with my book. He turned to me. 'Will you come for a drive with me in the morning and tell me what you make of it?'

I said, 'If it would help, darling, of course.'

'I don't think they believed me,' he said miserably. He was like a little boy and was hating the difference that had arisen between himself and the craftsmen he so admired at Martin and King. I believe he had managed to convince himself that this was the principal cause of his unhappiness at that time. He was determined to resolve it. He respected them and wanted to know that they respected him in turn. Otherwise it wasn't fair. And Arthur liked things to be fair. Despite his loathing of the daily practice of the law, justice in all things was Arthur's guiding principle throughout his life. Justice and decency. Arthur was a good man.

'Their explanation sounded reasonable to me,' I said, as lightly as I was able. I would have much preferred to have read my book but was determined to be helpful. 'Perhaps another stick has got caught up in the same place,' I suggested. 'Maybe you should take it in to the dealers and have them check the chassis and the motor?' I was not so dumb as not to know the difference between bodywork and chassis and motor, was I? So there.

The dealers were unable to find anything amiss and a week or two after they had looked at it Arthur declared that the ticker-ticker-ticker had deepened and become a much larger jagger-jagger-jagger. 'It's impossible to ignore.' He was alienated now from the dealers and their mechanics as well as the craftsmen at Martin and King. The whole business with the car demoralised him. He had no way of stepping back from it and laughing at it and his own earnest obsession with it. It had caught him. That it was really something to do with his manhood was obvious to me. He was a man, after all. A surrogate problem, I thought it was. That it was not the real, the deeper, cause of his unhappiness only made it more impossible for him to deny its reality. He was stuck with it.

And he couldn't let go of it. Which is perhaps not surprising. Men cling to these obsessive illusions in the hope they will be saved. But they never are saved by them. The truth remains suspended beneath such surrogate problems like a gondola beneath a hot-air balloon. And sooner or later the whole thing must come down. Men probably know this and it is no doubt this knowledge that makes them cling the more strongly to the illusion that they are sailing aloft when in fact they are sinking into the depths. Pressed to a severe enough desperation, men kill (often their own loved ones) to keep their precious balloon aloft a little longer. All extremes are possible and all have been tried by them. Is there any truth, indeed, no matter how humane and sacred, that has stood in the end against a sufficiently persuasive rationalisation of men under pressure? I had no fear that Arthur would become a killer. But I did fear he might have some kind of breakdown if this thing went on indefinitely.

I soon ceased to laugh, even secretly, at his silliness. I felt sorry for him. I had been persuaded by then that it was serious. 'Take it in to them again,' I said, and I stroked his hand. 'Before something falls off.' I hardly dared to think what it might be that could fall off. It was his car's bodywork, its perfection, after all, not his own that was in danger of falling apart. Wasn't it? I had been unable to hear the first ticker-ticker sound but had not had the nerve to tell him so. There might just possibly have been something, I didn't know engine sounds well enough to be certain, so I said yes, I heard it, but that it sounded rather too slight to worry about. Now I was being told it was not slight but major. Would I listen again? I did so, reluctantly, but heard nothing to alarm me. When I said I heard something like a ticking and attempted to mimic it he responded scornfully, 'That's the bloody tappets, for Christ's sake!'

Arthur, unlike the rest of us, didn't usually swear. Not even mildly. I had never heard, or heard of, tappets before this so far as I knew, but now that I was listening seriously I was able to hear all sorts of things, and after an hour of driving around I became quite confused by the medley of peculiar noises coming from the car. I might have pointed to any one of them. Apparently expert mechanics can 'see' inside the engine of a car by listening to the sounds it makes when it is running. The engine of the Ponty, indeed the entire organism of the car, spoke a language of its own. Cars like whales in the ocean depths, clicking and whining and howling to each other across the vastness. I've never been very convincing in my attempts at anthropomorphism. It is all just meaningless noise, I think.

But was I hearing *his* sound or not, Arthur wanted to know. His tone by now was edged with anger and frustration. Was I deaf, or daft, or what? Why couldn't I say something useful? *Bloody women!* Indeed.

I leaned closer to the dashboard. What was I hearing? There were bound to be other things than tappets that I had no knowledge of. I said I wasn't sure. He very nearly drove off the mountain in his desperation to get me to identify his big jagger-jagger sound. Of course we both knew it was a lost cause, but we were prevented from telling each other this in a nice friendly mild way by the hidden lives we had begun to live, which depended for their conviction on being kept hidden. They could be managed no other way.

The tension between us was hideous. I could hardly stand it and was on the point of insisting he stop the car and let me out when a lorry drove up close behind us and began tooting repeatedly. Arthur pulled over to the side of the road and as the lorry went past the driver screamed a string of obscenities at us. Arthur sat leaning on the wheel with his head in his hands. I massaged his neck, which was hard as wood, and almost said to him, It's all right, darling, you can relax now. I'm not in love with Pat Donlon.

But I didn't say that, did I? We don't, do we? Even if it were true, and I didn't know if it were true or not, I couldn't have said it. No one had said I *was* in love with Pat Donlon. So what would I have been doing denying it? No, for the double life there is always a double bind that requires our silence. Until the great break-out, that is, until the day the prisoners of silence have had enough and set fire to their prison. The night it all burns down and the next morning there is nothing left but smoking ashes. We've seen that. We know what that is. The conflagration of the secret life.

Some great man once said everything is either symbol or parable. Maybe it was Paul Claudel who said it. How good is my memory! I stroked Arthur's hand and suggested he see Dr Hopman (it was before the days of Andrew) about getting some sleeping pills. He said he might. We lay down together and had a cuddle, my cotton nightgown and his fleecy pyjamas between us. And it was no more than a cuddle. Though I'm sure he would have been happy if I'd encouraged him a little further. He was asleep before me.

I dreamed something that night that impressed me for weeks. I even wrote it down somewhere, but I can't remember what it was now or where I wrote it. Adeli will find it on a slip of paper one of these days. Unless I wrote it in one of my burned diaries. Why is it I can remember something Paul Claudel said and I can't remember my grand dreams of old? I shan't be around much longer, thank God, to trouble myself with this kind of question.

It was a problem for me at the time that Arthur never mentioned the Ponty noise when any of the others was around. I confided in Freddy, but he said unless Arthur spoke to him directly he couldn't very well bring up the subject. There was nothing much wrong with hearing noises, he said. 'It's when you're hearing voices telling you to do things you would not normally want to do that it's time to get concerned.' He thought Arthur was looking well and said there was nothing seriously the matter with him. 'My patients are really sick people. Arthur is just a bit confused. He'll get over it.'

I was not so sure. I said to Freddy, 'I don't think I've ever seriously thought I would lose Arthur, but I fear it more than anything. I know I wouldn't be able to manage without him.' Freddy listened. He was good at listening and playing the piano. 'I called Edith's painting muck,' I said. 'When we first arrived at their place in Ocean Grove, before I went in to sit with Edith. Arthur had started praising it extravagantly to Pat. Brown muck, I said, to be exact. The brown muck of the dead school of painters. Arthur was offended. Pat thought it was amusing.' I was silent a minute, Freddy watching me and smiling a little. 'I'm sure Arthur could find someone much nicer than me if he decided to look.'

Freddy agreed that it wouldn't be a difficult thing for Arthur to do. We were sitting by the river. Not on the log, but next to it on the couch grass under the wattles. On hot summer days it was ten degrees cooler there by the water than it was in the house. I swam naked with Freddy looking on. I loved the delicious feel of the sweet water over my skin and Freddy's admiring gaze on my body. I'd heard nothing from Pat and I hadn't tried to contact him. More than a month had gone by since our visit. But I thought of him at some point every day.

•

Nothing had come of our plans to buy the gallery space in Flinders Lane. None of Arthur's business contacts thought the idea interesting enough to back it. But I wanted to give Arthur something to occupy his energies that would hopefully displace his obsession with the Pontiac, and I convinced him we should sponsor an exhibition of the works of a wide circle of Melbourne modernists in another gallery space that was to let in Collins Street. We would not need to buy this place but could rent it for a season. It was a more manageable plan and the others were keen on it. When I suggested I might contribute some of my early watercolours I was met with the usual resistance from the men. They were happy for me to do the organising and for Arthur and I to meet the expense of the whole thing, but they feared they would invoke the taint of amateurism if they were to show their work alongside that of a woman. I knew they were thinking something along the lines of, Why can't Autumn be satisfied just to manage the show and leave the art to us? They wanted to be the creative stars, and for me to be their impresario. It was an attitude that was eventually to wear me down and leave me feeling ungenerous towards them. Most of them eventually made their way to Paris or to the Slade in London or found their vocations in something other than art.

Anne Collins was exempt from the charge of amateurism. She was such a brilliant draftswoman it placed her works beyond conventional criticism. She was also well connected socially, and her pen-and-wash drawings of notable people and places were universally admired, in Sydney as well as Melbourne. She was the only one of us to remain untouched by the rivalry between Sydney and Melbourne, whereby if your work was acclaimed in Sydney, then Melbourne scorned to comment on it, and vice versa. Anne's work was highly skilled and clever but her drawings did not interest me. They challenged nothing of our ideas of what art might become for us but reaffirmed, with uncanny accuracy, what it already was. They did not make us uncomfortable or puzzle us, but simply made us all feel good about ourselves. She put me in mind of an obedient and gifted senior student who has set out to delight and gratify her awed professors. Anne always had an agenda to be served in whatever she did. Nothing with her was ever intuitive. She wasn't beautiful but men were attracted to her. They were drawn to her. They listened to her with respect. I saw her a number of times in her one-piece black swimsuit (Italian, I suppose, then), her white legs bony and unlovely, her back pimpled. I could not understand the fascination she held for serious and intelligent men. Arthur thought she was the real thing. She and I were never close. I wonder why?

Distracting Arthur from his Ponty obsession wasn't my only motive for wanting to mount a show in town. It was a little more complicated than that for me. Anne Collins, Louis de Vries, Arthur and I, with Barnaby roaming around in the garden whistling opera, Freddy as our silent witness (happily suckling at the breast of his first love, his doom, his death, a melancholy smile in his beautiful eyes) and our captive Central European, Boris Karabashliev, were lunching in the garden to discuss our strategy for the show. The members of our immediate group of friends each had his or her own circle of artist friends and hangers-on and collaborators, and they in turn had their own circles beyond that. My intention was for us to draw on the widest possible array of such people, people who would have an interest in our venture and be inclined to support it. Most of them would be brought together for the first time by our show. It was a grand plan.

There was a feeling of excitement between us at the lunch table that afternoon. Louis in particular seemed to believe himself present at the birth of a new movement, of which he was to be a member of the founding nucleus. I was excited for other reasons and had no such alarmingly grandiose dreams. And of course nothing of that sort ever happened. Louis was eventually to lose himself somewhere in South America, searching for fresh inspiration—or perhaps it was drugs he was after? I can't remember. Perhaps I never knew. At the time of our lunch his work had recently enjoyed some early favourable notice and as a result he had felt encouraged to believe there would be no limit to the eventual exercise of his refined genius. Although it was a warm day, he was wearing his usual black velvet outfit with a wide-brimmed floppy hat and deep purple bow tie against his black silk shirt. Louis was fond of affirming, If you're going to be a great artist (such as himself), then you may as well dress the part. His motto was, Why be modest? What is the point of pretending to be someone you are not?

There is a photograph of us. I suppose Barnaby took it, as he is not in it. We were at our most self-congratulatory. Each of us looking anxiously at the camera, projecting our sense of the importance for posterity of the occasion, posturing. All of us now forgotten. I was sure of not meeting with any resistance when I said, as if the idea had occurred to me only that minute, 'You know, we should let Pat Donlon in on this show. His work startles and puzzles everyone who sees it.' My throat thickened when I said Pat's name and I feared I had betrayed myself. Freddy allowed himself a private smile.

Arthur said mildly, 'If we're going to do that, then Pat must meet everyone first. What do you say?' Louis and Anne both said they were eager to meet Pat. Freddy remained silent. As did Boris. Boris was a butterball of a man. His nickname was Mr Sheen. He rarely spoke unless he had something to say, then he was inclined to deliver a lecture to us poor benighted antipodeans. He was sure we understood nothing of the international life of art, and he was probably right.

Arthur looked at me and said easily, 'Why don't we invite them both up for a weekend, darling, and get everyone together over here on the Saturday afternoon?'

I was soon to discover that while I was a competent manager, I did not possess the instincts of a social tactician; those skills (if skills is what they are) of forming alliances and driving wedges between rivals, and so on. I lacked the ruthless calculation for it. It wasn't the way I saw things. I don't see them that way now. I had not counted on having to deal with the circling menace of sensitive male egos, last-minute withdrawals, betrayals, counter-cliques and vicious gossip. It was all part of the deal I was taking on but I didn't know it. That afternoon in the garden, drinking and talking, I wasn't thinking about tactics. I thought I had been very clever in clothing my deeper motive in such a plausible disguise. I was even momentarily able to convince myself that the show was the main idea behind all this.

So it was settled. I would get in touch with Pat and invite them both up for a weekend. 'Them,' Arthur had said. It was the only thing that marred the sweetness of my secret joy that afternoon. I had forgotten her, hadn't I. An image of Edith sitting on the veranda observing us now came into my mind; not drinking or joining in with us but watching us, being smugly pregnant and womanly, not saying anything, a helpless smile occasionally passing across her lovely features. Yes, she was lovely. She was what some men call a *real* woman. That is, she was motherly and voluptuous at one and the same time. A suitable object for the male dreaming. I was building an image of her to be detested.

I was wearing a wide straw hat that afternoon, which shaded my face. But even so I think Freddy noticed my colour was up. Drunk or sober, Freddy didn't miss a lot.

No sooner had the plan to invite Pat and Edith to Old Farm been decided than I began to feel sick with worry about it and to wonder if I was doing the right thing or was getting myself into a mess that I would never be able to get out of ever again. My worry took the form of an unpleasant combination of desire—fuelled by the phony liberties of the alcohol—considerable fear, confused expectation and utter self-loathing. I drank a great deal at that lunch and talked far more than I meant to.

I was on my own in the kitchen later when Barnaby came stumping onto the veranda from the garden, whistling something piercing from one of his operas. I said, 'Please, Barnaby!

I've got a headache.' The others were in the library getting some serious drinking done and no doubt flying with their imaginings of greatness. I told Barnaby I wasn't feeling well enough to cook dinner. He said cheerfully, 'I'll cook it for you, my darling. Go and lie down.'

I can't remember what Barnaby cooked. He was a good cook. It would have been something tasty and not too complicated and probably a little surprising. Perhaps with an Asian flavour. He had spent some years in Thailand. He loved foraging in my vegetable garden, which was partly his garden too. He knew something was up with me and wanted to get the full story over the meal. I gave him the bare bones of it. He suspected more and came back in the morning and helped me break up the irises and plant them out. Barnaby wasn't Freddy. Anything you told Barnaby in the morning was all over town by lunchtime. Anyway, what was there to tell? It was all just a confusion of the soul at that stage. I didn't know whether to hope Pat Donlon would feel as confused as me when I contacted him, or would have forgotten me by now.

•

Adeli has just come out to the kitchen. I closed my notebook and set it aside with my pen on it. She looks as hot as I feel, her apple cheeks glowing. Maybe she's been dancing again. She's been doing something, that's obvious. She asks me if I'd like a cold glass of lemon and orange. She calls it lolly water, a phrase she's picked up. It sounds like *lally wadder* when she says it and I wonder for an instant what she is suggesting. I tell her that would be lovely and to please put some gin in it. She asks where the gin is and I tell her it's in the refrigerator.

I watch her making the drinks. She puts gin in mine but not in her own. I can see the perfect tone of her skin through the fine white linen dress she's wearing. Open sandals on her small and rather shapely feet, and nicely tanned. I don't know in which direction her tastes lie. There has never been any mention of a special friend either way. She brings my drink over and sets it down next to me on the table. When I see that she's about to take her own drink back to the dining room I say, 'Stay and have it here with me.' She looks at me and I give her my nicest smile. She hesitates then pulls out a chair and sits. She takes a sip of her drink and looks at me again, not smiling, her look having more purpose in it now. She's got something on her mind.

She says, 'I suppose you want to talk about my naked fandango?'

'Is that what it was?' I say pleasantly, trying not to smile.

She sips her drink and looks into it and doesn't say anything for a while. I let her think in the silence. That is what Freddy used to do. He allowed big silences in a conversation when the conversation was between two people. He invited confidences from his companion into the silence he offered them. Even though I knew what Freddy was doing I fell for it every time. When he was in a group he would take his share of the talking space and use it strongly. In this situation that I am in with Adeli he would sit saying nothing, not moving around or jiggling a foot or tapping a finger or giving out any sign of nervous waiting, like sipping his drink more than once in a while. I'm watching Adeli as if we both agree that it's her turn to speak. To expand on the word *fandango*. The Americans, I'm assuming, call anything a fandango. For me she was not doing a Spanish dance on Arthur's father's dining table. But I let it be. Fandango will do for now if that is what she wants to call it.

She looks directly at me, just a touch of aggression in her big amber eyes, holding her glass tightly so that the skin under her nails has gone pale, and she says, keeping her mouth tight and holding her shoulders in, 'I suppose you think I'm trying to take him over?'

I let a couple of seconds pass, then I say carefully, still being Freddy, 'Do you want to take him over?' I'm not sure that I know what she means by *take him over*. Pat's been dead some while now and taking him over may not be an option for anyone, let alone this big girl. When I first saw her that day, coming around the back and surprising me on the veranda with my nightdress up around my waist, I thought she had nasty eyes. Today the amber of her eyes has a strange clarity, as if some fine perfection of thought or feeling has drawn all calculation from her soul and left her intentions pure. I can, it seems to me for an instant of insanity, see into her depths. And I am fascinated. The gin has not yet kicked in.

She says seriously, her Californian accent suddenly more pronounced, 'I've formed a deep spiritual connection with his work.'

So much for the pure intentions of her soul. I'm still enough of an idiot to beguile myself into thinking such things. And there's no time left now for me to learn better. Once again I give her a long silence. A flock of white cockatoos is going over, reclaiming country with their banshee screeching. I find it hard work not to mock this stuff she's coming out with. 'That's good,' I say. What else can be said to such nonsense?

She looks at me; an innocent little-girl look that I haven't seen before, her shoulders relaxed and her fingers releasing the glass. I wonder if she has been to acting school and all this body language is a studied effect to impress me with the veracity (not simply the truth) of what she's getting at.

She says, 'You don't mind, Mrs Laing?'

'Does it matter if I mind?'

'But do you?' she persists.

'Do you care if I mind?' I'm determined to keep her offering up what's in her mind while keeping my own thoughts to myself.

'Yes, I do.'

A big silence now. I could have taken a nap if I'd known how long it was going to go on for. As it is I have to suppress a yawn. She notices.

'I'm sorry,' she says. 'I'm tiring you.'

'I was already tired,' I say. 'At eighty-four or -five or whatever I am there isn't a lot of energy left by four in the afternoon. Please go on.' I have a feeling I've spooked her with my interest and she won't pick up the thread of this thing again. I resist prompting her and am half expecting her to get up and leave.

She says with solemnity, her hands coming together, the one clasping the other, like two plump pink crabs joined in the ecstasy of mating, 'I have found my spiritual guide in Patrick Donlon.'

I can't deal with this and decide there is nothing to be hoped for from her. And who ever called him Patrick? I forget to be Freddy and tell her, 'Well, you'd better watch where he takes you.' I'd rather have Arthur's Ponty rattle than this shit. Poor old Arthur. God save his soul. I can say that if I like. What*ever* it means. We stayed together till the end. I nursed him for his last two years here in this house. His last night I was with him holding his hand in the Austin Hospital. He was looking into my eyes, trying to stay focused on me, when he went. I saw him leave. It was three in the morning. Then he was gone and I was suddenly alone. I had no idea what the word *grief* meant till the moment he left me. An iron band tightening around my body and my mind and crushing me . . . I see Adeli is looking at me as if she feels sorry for me. I realise she's seeing some poor lame old biddy not long for the bonfire. I am surprised and a little proud to hear myself say firmly, 'I think it's time for you to pack your bags and go, Adeli. You can take one of his drawings with you. But that's it. I've had enough.'

She says calmly, 'You've been working too hard at your writing today.' She fingers a corner of my exercise book—what was the child's name?

I snatch the book away. 'Haven't you got enough of me in the dining room? You'll have to wait for this for a day or two yet.'

'I'll make you some scrambled eggs and toast,' she says. It is no effort for her to remain composed. 'Would you like a fried tomato with that?'

'I need a pee,' I say bitterly, and I grab the table and try to stand.

She comes around the table and helps me get onto my feet. She steadies me and hands me Barnaby's stick. I snatch it out of her hand and slam its bronze tip down on the floor. She takes my free arm and comes with me to the bathroom door. 'Will you be all right?' I shut the bathroom door violently on her and feel my way around the wall to the pan. I pee then let out a satisfying fart. I sit for a minute, then yell, 'Give me a hand in here!' I know she's still out there. I have no strength. I can do nothing without her.

14

The flies

LUNCH WAS DONE WITH LONG AGO. IT WAS NOW LATE IN THE afternoon. A lovely autumn afternoon it was, the sky clear, the air warm, bees among the flowers, birds in the trees, other birds flying over in small flocks, going home to roost or maybe to their favourite watering places, crying to each other for passion and comfort as they went. The human company had scattered a bit since lunch. Two friends down the hill in the garden, concealed from the house by the coppice of elders, planted by Arthur on a fancy for homemade wine of the old country. The young man lying on his back in the rich smell of the grass, she reading Yeats to him, searching in the little book for poems to fit their moment, so that he will laugh and reach up and hold her to his chest and kiss her lips. 'Never give all the heart,' she read, 'for love will hardly seem worth thinking of to passionate women if it seems certain . . .' Her young voice in the autumn afternoon, full of hope and charm and dreams. He watching her lips forming the words. They were nice lips but the wine and the food was making him wish for sleep more than for love. Voices and laughter drifting to him from the river, where some of the party had gone to swim. He closed his eyes, imagining the swimmers' golden bodies glistening in the lantern sun of late afternoon, hearing Yeats's words in the young woman's voice. He was not in love with her enough to have anxiety about it, his situation pleasant rather than passionate. What was his name? Who was he? She was Alice Meadows and had once been a model in the life class at the Gallery School (Pat called it the lifeless class). She had become a painter herself and was one of our group of young artists at the time.

After the lunch was done with, a core of guests had not moved but had stayed to drink and talk earnestly about art and other matters. In the kitchen Pat was sitting at the table with his back to the screen door and the veranda. With his right hand he was holding onto a glass of beer, as if he thought it might wander away from him if he did not restrain it, and in his left hand he was touching a cigarette to his lips, his eyes narrowed, squinting at Louis de Vries through the smoke.

Louis de Vries was sitting across from Pat and was waiting for a response to some proposition he had taken care to compose, directing his words to Pat but talking for the sake of the company, confident his friends were favouring his arguments over the arguments of this barbarian of Autumn's, if the barbarian had any arguments of his own. He was yet to hear anything half sensible from the man. A couplet of Eliot's was in his mind to deliver to Autumn later: *The heathen are come into thine inheritance, And thy temple have they defiled.*

A bottle of beer was on the table in front of Pat, several empties and numerous wine bottles down the length of the table, glinting nervously at each other among the disarray of dirty crockery and the scatter of leftovers.

Pat took a long drag on his cigarette, his gaze not leaving Louis's face. He might have been considering a purchase. Unusually, for he preferred to dress neatly, Pat was wearing a stained singlet that had once been white (when his mother was caring for his laundry) and a pair of old khaki shorts. His feet bare, crossed under the table, the toes of his left foot anxiously gripping the toes of his right foot. His narrow shoulders were bony and freckled with sunburn, his arms firm and strong enough to wield an axe all day, his chest without a sign of hair. His hands, too, despite the work he undertook for Mr Gerner, were fine. They were strong sensitive hands, you could see that, and had a suggestion of intelligence about them. What an ungenerous soul might have called native cunning. Nothing, at any rate, in Louis's opinion, that could have been attributed to refinements due either to upbringing or education.

A woman's sudden shout of laughter came from the garden.

Pat said, 'Someone's having fun.' He skolled the beer and reached for the bottle. Turning his glass on its edge, he watched it fill, bringing it upright as the beer approached the top, then setting the glass and the bottle down on the table in front of him. Delicate bubbles of condensation, the bottle sweating.

At the laugh from the garden Autumn turned from where she was standing at the sink. She could see Edith's head and shoulders above the tall staked dahlia blooms. Edith on Barnaby's arm, Barnaby waving his stick over his head, acting out a story for her of his youth in the wild outback. Edith leaning back against his arm and laughing. She was without a hat and her dark hair was catching lights from the low sun. Autumn turned back into the room. She had been following the conversation between Louis and Pat and was interested to hear where it would go.

George Lane was gloomily watching Louis and Pat from the far end of the table, his head lowered, his eyes dark and brooding. Lovely Alice Meadows had gone off with a friend, going at a run to hide in the garden with him, to read love poems to him. And George was getting drunk. His intention was to get a lot drunker before the day was done. It was quite likely he would want to fight someone. Just at this moment he had a tight smile in his eyes, visualising a series of Alice in gipsy dresses with bloodstained fangs, her thighs gaping, revealing some kind of dark evisceration. The gross images of delicate Alice swam satisfyingly in his mind against a deep green and black background, in which were shifting lights. Fairy lights, were they? Was it a fairground in hell? He would like to know. He would find out. It would come to him, he was sure of that. He might get up and go looking for those two. Yes, he might. He glowered down the table at Pat and Louis, as if he couldn't make out whether they were human or animal. Isn't it all the same? He laughed. A black laugh with no sun in it.

Arthur looked at him and smiled, ready to hear something from him, as if his laugh had been a preparation for speech.

But George had gone back to contemplating his hellish images. They came to him. He didn't invent anything. It was all there waiting to be painted. Tormenting and delighting him. And when it wasn't there he despaired of it ever returning and drank. Blankness for ever. He would kill himself (he never did, but was one among them who proposed it more than once. He became successful instead). He shifted on his chair and reached for his beer glass, missed it, steadied himself, and grasped it firmly in his fist. He emptied the contents down his throat, belched, and reached for the bottle.

Louis was wearing his black velvet suit with black silk shirt and deep purple bow tie as usual. His hat was on the floor beside his chair, his hair a springy mop of darkly bouncing curls. He applied a wash to lend it raven highlights. Strangers at parties remarked on his remarkable hair. Anne Collins was sitting to his right. She was sober and was watching Pat with close interest.

Watching Anne watching Pat, Autumn asked herself, Is she measuring him for a suit of clothes? Freddy was sitting at the end of the table on Pat's side and Arthur at the end opposite the Rayburn. Boris was drawing in the square pad he always carried with him. Arthur was lolling back in his chair, his right hand reaching down beside him, his fingers playing with Tom's ears. The two oyster aristocrats from Asia had eaten well at the table and were asleep in one another's arms in Tom's basket. Tom purred loudly.

Louis said, 'You've rejected the conventional training of the artist not from some high disciplined principle, as you seem to claim . . .'

Pat muttered, 'I don't have principles.'

Louis continued, '. . . but from the commonplace need of youth to effect some kind of revolt against the elders. What you are doing is utterly traditional. That is what it is. That is all your wonderful revolt is, Patrick. It's commonplace. You know? Ordinary. You have nothing with which to replace what you've rejected. If you had, then what you say might be interesting. Either you'll soon see the error of your ways and re-enrol at the Gallery School, or you'll stop doing art altogether.' Louis straightened his shoulders and brushed at something on his shirt front. 'Full stop! Your ideas, if I may say so, amount to very little. It takes enormous skill and heroic persistence to make something new in art. Either we follow Europe in this, or we Australians will fall by the wayside and remain a pointless backwater forever.'

Freddy said composedly, 'Forever. That is a very long time, Louis.'

Louis frowned.

Barnaby came into the kitchen. He was without Edith. He waved his wonderful black stick. 'She's gone for a walk down to the river.' He gave the timber wall a loud whack with the ferrule and made everyone jump. 'Your wife, Pat, is a lovely woman. You are a very lucky boy. You don't deserve her.' He reached and poked Pat playfully in the small of the back with his stick. 'Do you hear me? That girl's too good for you.'

Louis was annoyed. Drink didn't suit him. His thoughtful formulation had gone unanswered and was drifting away into the emptiness of a conversation going nowhere. He leaned forward. 'So, what's your response, Patrick?' He saw that Pat was not paying attention and looked about him distractedly for cigarettes.

Arthur reached forward, offering his blue packet with the dancing lady on it.

Louis said gratefully, 'Thanks, Arthur. Thank you.' He slid one of the cigarettes out of the packet. He didn't see why he should give in. He wasn't going to. He lit the cigarette with his Ronson and drew in a lungful of the fragrant smoke. That was better. He looked about for a drink. He couldn't remember which was his glass. All the glasses were dirty.

Pat was watching him. Observing a specimen. Little Lord Fauntleroy, wasn't it? Where did that come from? Lord Fauntleroy. He smiled at Anne Collins and when she didn't smile back he lifted his glass to her. 'Cheers, darling.'

Anne Collins did smile then. 'You're an idiot,' she said, mildly amused by him.

'True.'

'And you're drunk.'

'And you're sober.'

Freddy noticed that Pat had nice teeth. They were even and white. Had his parents taken him to the dentist regularly, which seemed unlikely, or was he just lucky?

Pat said, as if it was neither here nor there to him, 'Making it new is Europe's problem, Louis. That's what they're doing. It's not our problem.' He smiled at Anne again. 'What do you reckon, Anne?'

'So tell us,' Louis said. 'What *is* our problem, Patrick? We are all dying to know. Here we are, living in the dark ages without you. Please Patrick, do tell us what we are doing wrong, won't you?'

Barnaby stood in the doorway to the passage. He looked around the kitchen, waiting for silence, then drawing breath, his arms out wide, his stick hanging from his right hand, he began to sing, 'Ah! Godiamo, la tazza, la tazza e il cantico, le notte abbella e il riso; in questo paradiso ne scopra il nuovo di.' He bowed and turned and walked down the passage, his fine tenor voice trailing away with great effect, 'Quando non s'ami ancora.' A moment later the library door slammed shut and the singing was silenced, as if the lid had been put on Barnaby's tin. A faint murmur remained. If one listened keenly.

Pat smiled at Louis and took a drag on his cigarette. He refilled his glass and held it up, like a barman checking the head, or maybe he was just watching the bubbles rising, catching the light in a reflection of the doorway behind him.

'Well?' Louis said. 'Your wisdom, Patrick. We are waiting to hear it.' He chuckled. 'You don't have an answer, do you?'

Pat went on examining the beer.

Barnaby came back and stood quietly in the doorway. He was carrying a book he had promised to lend to Edith. It was not his book, but he assumed neither Autumn nor Arthur would object. Pat's wife, after all, seemed a pretty safe bet.

'Our problem is to make it Australian, Louis,' Pat said, as if he was stating the obvious. He was preoccupied with the beer bubbles and might have been talking to himself.

'And just how are we going to do that?'

Pat looked up at him. 'You're a persistent bugger, Louis. I'll say that for you. If I knew the answer to that one I'd be doing it, wouldn't I? Instead of sitting here listening to your shit.'

There was a silence.

Arthur sat up straight. His chair back creaked and Tom stepped out of the way. Autumn looked across at Arthur.

'Beer bubbles,' Pat said. He laughed uncertainly and raised his glass to Louis. 'Here's to you, mate. Long life and happiness, my dad always says.' He looked around the room, possibly aware of having given offence. 'Here's to all of us.'

George said, 'You rude bastard, Donlon!' He made to get up but stumbled and had to put a hand to the table to stop himself toppling with his chair. 'You scabrous little bastard!'

Pat laughed. 'You're pissed, George.'

'Apologise!' George shouted.

'Or what?' Pat said quietly. He turned to Louis and said lightly, 'My sincere apologies, Louis.' He looked at George. 'And to you too, George.'

George scowled at him. 'Fuck you,' he said.

Pat said, 'Other things offend me, George. This bloke's sarcasm's one of those things.' He drank some beer. He appeared, suddenly, to be downcast and sat looking into his beer, an expression of sadness on his face.

Barnaby waved his stick dangerously close above George's head, the book clasped in his other hand, an evangelist on a street corner. He shouted, 'Bravo! Let us all stand and drink to Pat's singular truth.' He tucked the book under his shillelagh arm and reached over George's shoulder for George's glass of beer. He raised the glass. 'Come on, boys and girls, a toast to Pat Donlon!'

But something had come to an end. The energy had gone out of the room.

'For God's sake!' Barnaby cried. 'We don't have to admire his bloody singlet, but we'd do well to have the modesty to acknowledge the truth of what this savage little bugger has just said to us.' He took a sip from George's beer, grimaced and set the glass down again. He laid a hand heavily on George's shoulder. 'I don't know how you can drink that muck.' He looked around the room. But he saw it was no good, they weren't to be driven.

Freddy said, 'I'll give you a lift home, George.'

Barnaby turned away. 'Damn you all!' Then he turned back. 'You're all hoping to be in Paris or at the Slade by this time next year. And when you're there, you will not forget what you've just heard here at Autumn and Arthur's lunch table. The truth of it will eat into your confidence that there is any good reason for you to be in Europe and not here at home making it Australian.' He raised his stick in Pat's direction. 'Good on you, Patrick.'

'And I suppose your poetry's not going to be referring to European precedents any more, Barney,' Louis said, 'now that you've converted to Saint Patrick's philosophy? Is that what we are to expect from you?'

'Louis, I'm like you. I'm doing it the old way. The provincial way. I want to get to Europe as badly as you do. Europe is the home of the life of my mind, just as it is yours. I am as Australian as you are, old mate, but making my art Australian, whatever that may mean, is not something I can take on. The only training any of us have ever had has been in the European tradition. We know nothing else. So I'm not pretending to take on something I know nothing about. Modernism's already an old-fashioned idea. It's dead. We know that. They've dealt with that one. We're a generation behind them. All we can do now is to follow them and hope for the best.'

Boris roused himself and gave a bit of a shake of his shoulders. He was like a big golden house dog, moon-faced and moon-bodied. He tucked his little square sketchbook into the inside pocket of his corduroy jacket. When he was silent people often forgot he was among them. But when he spoke they listened. He carried the authority of the old world with him.

They looked at him before he spoke, expecting to hear from him. He said, 'There is no Australian art. It is like Canadian art. Or South African art. Or white Kenyan art. What are they like? Have any of you enquired? You Australians have no musical or artistic or literary traditions of your own. And what is worse, you have no folk art with which to sustain and renew yourselves. So unless you interbreed with the Aboriginal people and adopt their cultural forms of expression, you will have to either continue to be Europeans in Australia or improvise something entirely new of your own. That is your opportunity. But will you grasp it? Improvisation is a great freedom. We are all scattered about the world now. The African was enslaved and scattered and he came up with jazz. It was the greatest stroke of genius, and everyone has been influenced by it.' He surveyed the room like a schoolmaster checking to see that his poor little ones were paying attention. 'Your feast days, your cuisine, the songs you sing on such occasions. Your surroundings engender melancholy and regret that you are not at home where those things are at home. The great opportunity for you is not to follow Europe but to improvise as the Africans did in America. Perhaps you can do something like that? Do you think you might? What can it be? Any ideas, any of you?' He dragged himself to his feet. 'Is someone going to give me a lift to the station, or am I going to have to walk?'

Barnaby said, 'I'll be content in beautiful Paris or lovely London, Boris. Don't you worry. Dreaming of being a true cosmopolitan while I worship at the feet of the great ones and lament the sad history of my own country in their words. Pound's and Eliot's and Yeats's, and the rest of them. To be a provincial at the courts of the kings, that's my fate. Fortunately

I'm content to embrace it. Go to London, Barnaby, my mother always urges me. Go to Paris. You will hear what the great world has to say to you. My mother is too sensible to say, And the great world will hear what you have to say to it. She knows the great world cares no more for me than I care for some poet in the wilds of British Columbia. When it comes to her son's gifts my mother is a realist, not a dreamer.'

Pat scraped his chair back and stood up. They watched him leave. He went out past Autumn onto the veranda, gave a wild yell and jumped into the garden, clearing the fish pond and its sharp bricks at a bound.

No one said anything. The atmosphere in the kitchen was suddenly flat without him. There was to be no further contest.

Arthur said into the silence, 'Never mind about Paris and the Slade. We'll be at war with Hitler this time next year.' He looked around the table at them all, as if they had already vanished. 'Khaki,' he said. 'That's going to be our colour.'

•

Autumn stood at the front door waving Freddy off. George was slumped beside him in the passenger seat. When Freddy had gone she did not return through the house to the others but walked round the southern side of the garden through the rhododendrons. She eventually found Pat sitting on Stony's rustic bench behind the deep holly hedge that sheltered the vegetable garden from the north wind. He was smoking a cigarette and leaning forward with his elbows on his knees, apparently contemplating the grey-green spikes of the artichokes. He looked up as she came through the rose arch—Félicité et Perpetué, a delicate white-pink climber, faintly perfuming the air.

Pat pointed. 'Look.'

She leaned down to see. A praying mantis swayed on an artichoke leaf, its colour perfectly matching the green of the leaf. 'Stony will spray it with something,' she said.

'What is it?'

'You really don't know?'

He shrugged. 'Am I supposed to know?'

'It's a praying mantis,' she said. 'Of course you're not supposed to know. I didn't mean that.'

'Yes you did. You thought, What an ignorant bastard this bloke really is.'

'All right, I did think that.' She sat on the bench beside him. 'I thought everyone knew what a praying mantis was.'

'I'm kidding you,' he said. 'Of course I knew what it was.'

'I don't know whether to believe you or not.'

He laughed. 'Neither do I.'

She sat puzzling at him. 'You mustn't be too hard on them.' She reached and took his hand and laid it in her lap and examined it. She was drunk.

He watched her looking at his hand, as if his hand no longer belonged to him. 'You just do that?' he said. His hand resting against her thigh, the astonishing warmth of her skin through the thin material of her dress. His throat thickened. 'You turn things on their head. You know that?' His voice was a little husky.

She said nothing to this but smiled.

'The first time we met, you told me I'd had a privileged upbringing. Now you say I'm being hard on your friends. It all seems the other way around to me.'

'They say the soul is in the eyes.' She considered his hand, holding it in both her own in her lap, then looked up at him. 'Your soul is in your hands, Pat.' She passed her fingers gently over the ripple of veins on the back of his hand.

He drew his hand away.

'I'm sorry,' she said.

'No, it's fine. It tickles.' He rubbed his hand.

'Have you got another cigarette?'

He handed her the cigarette he was smoking.

She took the half-smoked cigarette from him and put it between her lips. She closed her eyes and rested against the bench and drew the fragrant smoke into her lungs.

He watched her, the sun on her face, her long hair in disarray, the high dome of her pale forehead. The strands of her hair were fine and light, her scalp visible where the fall of the hair parted. It was the opposite of Edith's hair, which was strong and dark and thick. Impossible to see Edith's scalp. Even in bright sunlight. He was tempted to lean forward and sniff Autumn's scalp, just to see. But he didn't. He could not be as free with her as she was with him. She was different from every woman he had ever known. He was not sure what it was that made this difference an issue for him. He did not feel at home with her, but felt rather as if he was in a foreign place, another country than his own. Not his Australia. Her language was not his language. He did not know what to expect from her, or what it was she expected from him. He was unsure of the signals here between these people, what this or that sign or this or that look or word might mean. He caught only the surface texture of their conversation. He struggled to find his sense of humour with them and resorted to the coarse in place of the comic. He was aware of all this. Something in him was dampened down by them. Were they aware of it? Or only of his coarseness? Was this woman aware of it? That he was only half here, the subtle, the eloquent, the emotional half of him held in abeyance? Edith was one of their caste but she was immediate and present to him. Edith was his familiar. He knew what Edith meant. He knew himself to be understood by Edith in the way he understood himself. And yet Edith was at ease with these people. He decided it could not be their caste that estranged him, but something else.

She opened her eyes and handed the cigarette back to him. 'Thanks. I needed that. You don't think much of them, do you?'

'They're okay,' he said. He examined what was left of the cigarette. 'They're just people. I can only take so much of that crap. Art's what you make, not what you talk about.'

'It's both,' she said. 'Art is many things. You mustn't try to say what art is or you'll be required to say what it's not. And that will be impossible for you.' She was silent a moment. 'Wilde said it's more difficult to talk about a thing than to do it.'

'Well, Wilde, whoever he was, was wrong.'

'He was a praying mantis,' she said. 'And I'm sure you know him. He was a satirist who meant everything he ever said. And I quite liked what you had to say in there just now. Only I don't think it's that simple. Louis is a very fine artist. It would be a mistake for you to dismiss Louis. He paints wonderful semi-abstracts. Like all good artists he renders the familiar strange to us. He has done a brilliant series of Luna

Park. Luna Park is your own backyard. It is the Luna Park we know and yet it is somewhere else, somewhere we wonder if we might have been in another life, a richer and more poetic life than this one. And a more tragic life. Louis is good. Make no mistake. He will be a success in London, I'm sure of it. His manner is too showy for you but he's disciplined with his work. You would admire it if you knew it. He's got an exhibition on at the Basement. It's been getting good reviews. I'll take you.'

There was shouting and laughter from the outer garden. The swimmers were returning.

Pat slapped her cheek suddenly, not hard but with a quick dart of his hand.

She flinched and put a hand to her face.

'Mozzie,' he said. He held out his hand for her to see the squashed insect in his palm. 'One little bloodsucker less.'

The offence of the mild blow to her cheek had shocked her. She said with feeling, 'I hate being struck.'

He saw that she was upset. 'I'm sorry. I'll let the buggers eat you next time.' She did not respond. 'I keep having to apologise here, don't I?' he said. 'I made a mess of it in there. Why did you invite us?'

'Oh, you didn't make a mess of it at all. Don't be silly.' She was impatient with this.

'George and Louis thought I did.'

'And Barnaby loves you. So what? We argue and fight endlessly here. No one ever agrees with anyone else. Ever. That was mild. I invited you because I believe in you. They'll be your friends next time you see them. They are all people of courage and integrity.'

'And are you and I friends?' he asked.

She drew back, the better to see him. 'I don't know,' she said. 'Friends? Is that our word? Say it often enough and we empty it of meaning. I don't know if you and I are friends or not, Pat. But I know we are something.'

He took her face in his hands and kissed her on the lips.

'Don't!' She pulled away. 'Please don't do that.' But she had permitted the kiss for a moment before she recoiled, just as she had permitted it at the edge of the ocean.

'A kiss between friends,' he said. He was not sure if he had reached for the coarse response once again. Or had it been something more than that? The repeat of this impulse to kiss her lips? It angered him that he was not able to know himself with her.

She stood up and flattened her skirt with her hands. She looked down at him. 'I don't know what I am to make of you.'

'Make of me whatever you like, then.'

'Let's go in to the others and have a drink,' she said. 'Freddy and George have gone. I need to be among people.'

'You're afraid of me,' he said.

'That's stupid. No. Of course I'm not afraid of you. If I'm afraid of anyone, Pat, it's myself.'

'Well, I'm a bit afraid of you,' he said.

'Are you?'

'Just a bit. Don't get carried away.'

'Come on!' She reached for his hand.

He got up from the bench but he did not take her hand. 'I'm going to look for Edith.'

They stood a little apart, uncertain. Neither quite able to decide to end this nor quite wishing to prolong it any further, but held by their uncertainty about what 'this' was exactly, or was to become, if it was to become anything.

'Yes,' she said. 'You'd better go and find her. Barnaby said she went down to the river.'

But still they stood, not leaving.

'What?' he said.

'I believe in you.' She said this strongly, needing a response to it from him. It was important for her to say it.

'Thank you.'

'Does my belief mean anything to you?'

'It helps,' he said. 'I don't know why it helps, but it does. It's why I came.'

'I'm glad you came.'

'I probably am too.'

They both smiled. And each of them wondered why they felt there was something sad in this. Their smiles an admission, it seemed to them, of something a little hot, of something to be regretted. Was that it? An expectation, or a fear, of some undisclosed element of this they would rather not have encountered?

He went down towards the river to look for Edith.

Autumn walked back to the house on her own.

The moment he was away from her Pat thought of things he might have said to Autumn and he determined to say them to her the next time they were alone. The taste of her was on his lips, her mouth, her breath, tainted with tobacco and wine, and something that was her alone. He rubbed his lips with his fingers and spat. Going to find Edith he struggled with the guilt of his betrayal and hoped she would not see it in his eyes. Edith always looked deeply into his eyes. Would he be able to deceive her?

He found her sitting on a log by the water, her back to him. She was alone. The most intensely familiar figure in his life. He would have known the back of her head from a hundred miles away. A thousand. She was Edith and could be no one else. He could have wept for her and for himself and for their child. He was overcome with dismay.

She turned around and smiled at him. 'I knew you'd come to find me.' She held out her hands to him. 'Isn't it beautiful here? I just saw a yellow robin. We're so lucky.'

He took her hands in his and lifted her up and held her in his arms.

'You're crying!' she said, astonished.

'I'm sorry.'

'What is it? Tell me, darling.' She leaned away, anxious to see him. 'You must tell me.'

'I don't know,' he said. He wiped his eyes with the back of his hand. 'Nothing. Everything.'

'You're so silly.' She pulled his head onto her shoulder. 'There. Cry if you want. You gave me such a fright.' She held him close against her. 'Sometimes I want to be your mother. Do you mind me feeling like that?' She stroked his hair and looked beyond him across the river to the forest of gum trees where she had seen the yellow robin a moment before he came to find her. 'You are such a silly,' she said again, and she smiled to think of his distress and that it was she who comforted him.

•

The four of them were in the library. It was after one in the morning. Barnaby, the last of the others, had left a few minutes before, hallooing and sounding his horn as he drove out the gate. Arthur was standing with his back to the dead hearth. He was looking at Edith. He turned to the mantelpiece and picked up his glass of whisky and took a drink, then placed the glass back on the mantelpiece. Edith was asleep on the couch to the left of the fireplace, her legs tucked under her, her head resting on the arm of the couch where Pat had slept with Autumn's shawl over his shoulders. It was a warm night and the windows were open. Purple shadows rimmed Arthur's eyes. He looked middle-aged and tired. His cheeks were dark with the day's stubble. He was saying something that no one was listening to. He gave a soft belch, for which he murmured an apology. He would have liked to bring up the matter of Edith's painting but he knew he would never mention it. He was daydreaming how simple it would be to go and retrieve it from the loft and put it on the mantelpiece in place of Roy's abstract. When she woke she would see it there and he would witness the pleasure in her lovely eyes. He was very fond of Edith. He was not sure if he could detect a sign of her pregnancy or not. She had a much healthier colour than when they'd seen her at Ocean Grove. He had noticed that she had been happy all day. Her happiness had reassured him and made him feel less guilty about her painting. It was nice that she had become friends with Barnaby. Barnaby was one of the people Arthur liked best in the world. A truly trusted friend. He realised he had said something aloud and he looked at Autumn as if expecting a response.

Autumn was sitting beside Pat on the couch across from Edith. She had been selecting passages from Wilde's *The Critic as Artist* and reading them to him. The book lay face down in her lap. She looked up at Arthur when he spoke and said, 'I'm going to take Pat down to the river to see the moon.'

Arthur reached for his drink and waved his hand in a generalised gesture at the room. A slop of whisky lipped his glass and landed on the skirt of Autumn's dress. His gaze fixed on the small stain. 'Go on,' he urged them. And, as if Pat was not present with them in the room, he added, 'He should see the river by moonlight. It's a painting. A David Davies nocturne. *The Yarra by Moonlight*. Or it ought to be if it's not. Go on, if you're going. I'll finish this and turn in.' He looked down at Edith. 'I shan't wake her. She's sleeping the sleep of the just.'

Edith sat up slowly and looked at them. 'I'm sorry,' she said. 'I think I went to sleep.' She looked across at Pat. 'I'll have to go to bed, darling.'

Pat said, 'Autumn's just suggested we go and have a look at the river by moonlight. Why don't you come with us? The fresh air will wake you up.'

'Can't you do that in the morning?' Edith realised what she had said and laughed. She struggled to her feet. 'Sorry. I think I'm still asleep.' She stepped around the low table between the couches.

Pat stood up and she put a hand to his arm and kissed his cheek, reclaiming him from the doubts of her solitary sleep. She said something to him then turned to the others. 'Goodnight. Thank you both. It was a lovely day. I saw a yellow robin by the river. Did Pat tell you? I'll see you in the morning.' She went to the door, turned and raised her hand and smiled at them, and went out.

A moment later they heard the door of the guest room close.

Pat was still standing beside the couch.

Arthur spoke into the silence, his voice tempered to the rhythm of the poem, 'Where has Maid Quiet gone to, nodding her russet hood? The winds that awakened the stars are blowing through my blood.' He looked at Autumn.

Autumn said, 'And the rest?'

Arthur made an impatient gesture. 'It's gone from me for the moment.'

She kept her gaze on him until he looked at her again.

'Has it?' she said when their eyes met.

'Yes, darling, it has. Now why don't you take Pat to see the moon on the river if that's your intention.' His tone was just a little severe, just a little reprimanding or impatient. He lit a cigarette and frowned. He looked up and realised they had gone. Perhaps she had spoken to him on the way out.

He reached for his drink and sat on the couch where Edith had been sleeping. His gaze rested on the bottle on the table. He would climb up into the loft in the morning and get her painting and speak to her about it. He drank some whisky. He should go to bed. He sat staring at the bottle. He was not sure if everything was all right or not. It was just as well no one had wanted to finance the Flinders Lane gallery idea. They hadn't really worked out what it was they wanted to do. They would have been left with it. Autumn's idea of a one-off show was a much better way to make a start. He realised his eyes had closed and he opened them wide and breathed deeply. There were sounds out in the bush. Little howls and yelps and the whip of a bird woken by the brightness of the moon. Perhaps their cock would crow. What had she meant when she screamed at him that he had always denied her the important things in life? Had he? He recalled fending off her blows with a feeling of sickness in his stomach. They couldn't talk about it. Something stirred in the garden beyond the window and he turned to look. The moon was big and cold and distant and alone and very beautiful. A possum.

•

Autumn was lying on her side on the grass on the low flat bank of the river, her dress under her. She was naked, her body shining with the river water. Pat stood above her, his own nakedness dappled by the moonshadow through the silver wattles.

She said, 'Lie with me for a little while longer.'

'And suppose Arthur decides to come down after all?' he said.

'He won't.' She held her arms up to him. 'Please, don't just leave me like this. I feel empty. I need you to hold me.' I am pleading with him, she thought. He will despise me.

Pat looked up the hill towards the house. He reached for his underpants and pulled them on.

She sat up on her elbow, her dress rumpled under her where she had laid it out for them. 'You're not attractive when you're afraid.'

'I'm just being sensible.' He dragged his shorts on over his damp underpants.

'You weren't being sensible just now.'

He said, 'Get dressed!'

'No. Give me a cigarette.'

'Not until you get dressed.'

'I'll get dressed if you give me a cigarette.'

'It's all very well for you,' he said. 'Arthur probably doesn't mind. But this would finish Edith if she knew about it. It would destroy her.'

'Then why did you do it? You're a swine, Pat Donlon. It would kill my Arthur to know of this.'

A vixen barked across the river. Pat stood transfixed, staring in the direction of the deranged cry. 'Christ! What the fuck was that?'

'A girl fox. You are so panicky. I don't like it. You are spoiling everything. This is a sacred grove for me.'

'Who else have you brought here?'

'I loathe and detest you! You are the only man I have ever *brought* here.'

He lit a cigarette, drew on it, then handed it to her.

She took the cigarette from him and smoked, leaning on her elbow like an odalisque, her body polished marble. 'And how many women have you had since you married Edith?'

'You're the first.'

'Why don't I believe you?' She thought of him with another woman as he had been with her a moment ago and knew she would kill them both.

'Because you're a fool.' He couldn't see his singlet anywhere and wondered what he had done with it. He sat on the log and looked at her. He was astonished by the refinement of her beauty in the moonlight. He couldn't believe he had just made love to her. 'You're beautiful,' he said. 'I didn't realise.' A twig snapped among the wattles behind him and he whirled around. The moon shone clear and white among the polished trunks of the spindly trees. A moth flew into the light, fluttering like a white ghost across the open space, then suddenly disappeared into the darkness. He was afraid Arthur or Edith had heard Autumn crying out at the height of it. He had never heard a woman make such a racket. Was it anguish or pleasure she had been feeling?

'You're a scaredy-cat,' she said. She lay there, languid, deeply relaxed, the warm night air on her skin. She caressed her flank. She was still drunk and too relaxed to care about anything. 'I'm surprised you're so fearful,' she said. 'I'd imagined you being fearless.'

'Men being fearless is bullshit.'

'I like to believe good men are fearless in defence of what they cherish.'

'Yeah, that's what they'd like you to believe. Only they're not. Look around you. See what men do. Anyway, I'm not a good man. And you're not a good woman.' His brain was infested with small black figures leaping and running about in the eerie darkness, climbing over each other. An insane directionless panic of small black flies with grey markings on their backs. His head was thumping. The pump had started up. He supposed he would soon die and it would be over for him. Poor Edith, walking the streets of St Kilda with their little child. What would she tell the child about its father? . . . Sitting on the log looking at this goddess in the moonlight, he knew he would not be able to refuse her. The only way for him and Edith to survive this would be for them to go away without telling anyone where they were going. To England. And if they couldn't raise the money for England, then to New Zealand. Somewhere deep in the South Island among the Maori. Out of Autumn's reach. Eventually he would forget her. She was watching him. He knew he would never forget her.

His admiration made her feel young and reckless. 'I want you again,' she said.

He stood up. 'Jesus! I'm going up to the house.'

She sat up. 'Don't be an idiot,' she pleaded.

'I'm going.'

'No!' she shouted.

He turned on her. 'Be quiet, for Christ's sake!' He was beginning to fear that she wanted them to be caught. 'You're mad,' he said. 'You like to make a scene.'

'Yes, like you.'

'No, you're dangerous. I'm going back.'

She jumped to her feet and caught him in a stride and held his arm, her nails digging into his flesh. 'Wait, or I'll scream and everyone will know.'

'Yeah, I can believe you would do that.' Even as he looked at her, knowing he would not be able to resist her, his stomach was churning with fear and remorse and the desire to be innocently with Edith again. 'Okay,' he said, his voice unsteady, missing a beat as if someone had jogged the gramophone needle. It was true, he was a scaredy-cat. 'I'll wait while you get dressed.'

'No one,' she said, holding his arm, 'has ever made love to me like that.' But she was thinking of the Roman psychiatrist. It was him she had thought of when Pat was making love to her just now. He had been forty and married and she was barely nineteen. Surely it had been like this with him? The fear and the excitement, the knowledge that they would make love no matter what the consequences, no matter what the cost to them. Life itself. She couldn't remember his name. She remembered his child. Her lost child. The child would have been sixteen this year. She longed suddenly to sit quietly by the river with Pat now and tell him everything that had ever meant anything to her, so that he would know her and understand her and no longer be a stranger to her.

'This was a one-off,' Pat said. His tone was harsh. 'I shouldn't have given in to you.'

'You bastard! It was you who seduced me.'

'You insisted on swimming naked in front of me. What was that supposed to be?'

She said helplessly, 'Oh, I hate you.' She kissed him on the mouth, pressing herself against him, thinking of him holding her to him in the river. He began to caress her and she pulled away from him and laughed. 'You'll have to wait.' She went over to where her dress was lying on the grass and put on her pants and bra. She held up her stained and crumpled dress. She put it on over her head and dragged it down. 'Arthur will know at once.' She looked at Pat. 'What are we going to do?'

'Can't you say you fell in? Or you swam in your clothes?'

She said, 'Look,' and pointed through the tall gum trees on the far bank of the river behind him. 'It's starting to get light.'

She looked like a girl standing there in the faint dawnlight, her hair in wet braids, her feet bare, her dress like the dress of a gipsy or a peasant.

'You look innocent,' he said. 'Like a girl.'

•

Edith opened her eyes. Moonlight, she supposed it to be, was showing in a strip around the curtains. She thought she was at home in their bed in Ocean Grove. Then she remembered. Something had woken her. Had someone called to her? Then she heard it again. A man's laughter followed by talking. She realised Pat was not beside her. She switched on the bedside light and looked at her watch. It was a quarter past four. She got up and put on her dressing-gown and slippers and went out along the passage to the library. She stood outside the door. A man's voice. It was Arthur. She opened the door and went in. Arthur was standing with his back to her in front of the fireplace and seemed to be addressing the large abstract painting that was leaning against the wall on the mantelpiece. His jacket was off and his braces hung over his trousers. 'Well, dear boy, that's how things stand here.'

Edith coughed.

Arthur fell silent and turned around.

She said, 'Where's Pat?'

'Well, dear girl,' he said, 'I thought you would have been well and truly in the land of nod by now. Would you like a drink?'

'Where's Pat?'

He looked around the room, as if he thought he might see Pat and cry out, Ah, there he is! 'Won't you come in properly and sit down?' he said. 'I can make us a cup of tea if you'd prefer.'

'I think I'll go and look for them,' Edith said.

'Oh, they'll be all right. I shouldn't worry.'

'But the moon must have gone down ages ago.'

'The moon?' he said slowly, as if this were a piece of a puzzle he had been looking for and it had just been handed to him. Now to fit it into its proper place. One problem solved, another confronts us. 'Look, Edith. Talking. You know.' He was talking with his hands. 'I dare say. About life and art. That's it, isn't it?' He grinned at her, but she did not respond. 'Life and art. You must know what it's like yourself. Time gets away when we're talking. We have all our lives. What about that cup of tea? I'll come with you, if you like, and we'll look for them together when we've had a cup of tea. What do you say to that? Do we have a bargain? I don't think Autumn will be wildly pleased to find us skulking about in the dark spying on her, but if it will put your mind at rest. Well, no doubt it will be worth it. Aren't you tired? I am frankly exhausted. No work tomorrow, thank God. God, I hate that place.' He stood looking at her as if he had only just realised who she was. 'I have all the courage in the world in theory. In theory I tell my mother I am through with the law and I resign from the firm. It's simple. Then I visit my mother and she asks me about one of her dear friends who has business with our firm and she wants me to do something to hurry things along. I can do very little. Nothing really. Believe me, it is not humanly possible to hurry the law. This woman, or man, and sometimes it has been a man since my father passed away, is unknown to me except by name. Their affairs are a mystery so far as I am concerned. And, what's more important, they are not my client but the client of one of the senior partners. So I promise Mother I'll see what I can do, because I know she has told her friend that her son, the prince—you know what I mean?—has influence at court, if you'll allow the pun, and is able to fix these things. So it is my mother's standing with her friend that is at stake. It is this she places in my care. Her standing with her friends. So what can I do if I am not to seem to betray her, but eat my cake and drink my tea and kiss her cheek and give her my worthless word and sneak off like a hyena who has just pinched someone's lunch? If that makes sense. I'm sure you know what I mean. I am a hypocrite. What would you do?'

Edith said, 'You look very tired, Arthur.'

'Yes. Yes. It's kind of you to notice. My car has been misbehaving. But look here. I'm boring you. You don't want to hear any of this. My troubles are nothing, are they? When you compare them to the troubles of some people. The thing is, I don't have the pleasure of driving any more. It was one of my very few private pleasures. I don't think Autumn quite realises. But I mustn't criticise Autumn. It is Autumn who has made sense of my pointless life for me.' He knew he was rabbiting on in case, if he permitted a silence, Edith asked him about her picture. Why couldn't he just tell her about her picture? Why not sit her down and explain the whole thing to this intelligent young woman? Like a physician explaining the disease you have contracted through no fault of your own. A good bedside manner required for that. And if the patient weeps, you comfort them. Simple really. Surely she would understand? You see, my dear, it's like this: Autumn and I had a nasty row. Autumn can be terrible when she is aroused. She hit me several times. Or would have hit me if I hadn't held her wrists and prevented her from hitting me. Don't ask me what the row was about. I can't remember what it was about. Everything and nothing, I suppose. The usual thing. It was the night we drove home from our picnic with you at Ocean Grove. Not that it was much of a picnic, was it? It was that same night that my car began to rattle. Troubles never come singly, do they? Troubles band together, my father used to say. I had the purest trust in my car till then. Now it is not possible for me to have confidence in it. It is like a dear cherished friend who has betrayed me. I dread getting behind the wheel and driving out the gate. I know the rattle will begin as soon as we are on the road. It is so unfair.

But no, he could not revert to memories of that night drive or their so-called picnic. That could not be done. Why are our lives, he wondered with a sense of futility, these forts in the wilderness, each palisaded with spikes to defend its silly little secrets and repel the larger truth of the wilderness? Why can't we be open? He decided to get rid of the 'forts in the wilderness' idea. Why can't we just tell each other the truth, in other words, and be done with it? And if the truth upsets us then we can have a cuddle afterwards and confess our stupidities? He might write something about this dilemma; the general dilemma, that is, of truth and its difficulty. Not the specific one of why he couldn't tell Edith the truth about how her picture came to be up in the loft of the coach house . . .

Edith said, 'I think I can hear them coming. Or someone.' She couldn't hear them or anyone else coming but she said she could because the sound of Arthur's voice was like someone sawing her head in half.

They went out to the kitchen and he rattled the Rayburn and put some sticks in the firebox, not noticing there was no fire, and he set a full kettle of water on the cold hotplate. He was surprised by how heavy the kettle was. His admiration for Autumn knew no limits. She was astonishing. She ran the house like a machine. No, like a friend. A dear close good friend whom she loved and who loved her in turn. The things she did! He did not know the half of them. He went over and stood beside Edith. He hoped his presence was a comfort to her. Poor girl.

Edith was standing at the back door looking down the slope of the garden. A thin band of grey and yellow light peered back at her through the forest beyond the river—the evil squint of a yellow-eyed cat.

'There, that's done,' Arthur said. 'She'll be boiling in no time and we can sit down and have a nice cup of tea.' He wanted another whisky but felt the moment was not quite right for it. He had noticed that Edith did not drink and he didn't want to risk disappointing her. She would have no confidence in him if she got the idea he was a drunk. Any more sudden rattles starting up in his life might be the last straw. He took a deep breath and blew it out. Everything was going to be all right. Wasn't it? Of course it was. Things always work out. Surprises, that's all. Life with Autumn was full of surprises. He put his arm across Edith's shoulders and gave her a small squeeze. He felt her stiffen and realised he had given her the wrong impression. She had large breasts. Well shaped and firm. Generous breasts. European. Was that it? Lovely. Autumn's chest was like the country beyond the Grampians, flat as a tack. But she had very good nipples. He went, 'Hmm,' and removed his arm from across Edith's shoulders.

Edith eased away a little. She didn't mind his arm but his breath was sour. The garden was so still and so silent in the grey dawnlight. It was eerie and it repelled her, as if there was no one out there and had never been anyone out there. And why were there no birds at this time of the morning? She had liked Barnaby, but this place seemed evil to her. Yes, evil. As if a spell had been cast over it, and the people who

gathered here were trapped in an invisible web of disdain for
the rest of humankind, bewitched by their own way of talking
and their vain egotism. Unaware of the trap that held them.
Their supercilious contempt for artists like her grandfather
had embarrassed her, but she had said nothing. What was the
point of arguing with such people? They held their own narrow
hateful view of art and life and excluded everything else from
their field of vision. How would her arguments change them
or make them reconsider their views? They were like the flies
with their legs caught in the sticky paper that Mrs Kemp
hung from the light flex above the big table in the kitchen at
the farm. They were stuck and that was that. No fly had ever
escaped Mrs Kemp's sticky paper. Just as these people had no
hope of escaping the evil spell of their prejudices. Wasn't the aim
of art to be free of prejudice? Such had been her grandfather's
view. The cosmopolitan man and woman, he said, are liberated
from prejudice. In reality the opposite was true. But he had
made the world of art seem large and generous and warm,
embracing all the strong and good feelings of what it is to be
human. These people engendered an atmosphere of a kind of
yellow sickness. When George's drunken gaze had settled on
her breasts a shiver had passed through her. It was as if he had
touched her insides. His eyes frightened her.

She had been terrified all day, in fact, that Arthur was
going to bring out her painting and show it to them, or that
he was going to announce to them that she too was an artist.
She was grateful to him that he'd had the grace to do neither
of these things, and also had not hung her picture somewhere
in a prominent position where they would have all seen it and
felt compelled to rubbish it in their sophisticated way, while

making it sound as if they were praising it. If he had shown her painting to them she didn't know how she would have managed the situation without telling them the truth of what she thought of them. She knew she would have had the courage for that if she had been pressed. But Arthur was not quite as they were. He wanted to be more human and more relaxed and was not out to make a big impression on everyone. He was like one of the flies she had watched in horrified fascination as a child, he was still struggling a bit. His weak struggling made his life seem futile to her, and he seemed to know this futility in himself and to acknowledge it with her in a silent way that they both knew they would not be able to talk about openly—mainly because to have done so would have been to betray Autumn. Edith had sensed this already at Ocean Grove when they had had their talk while Autumn and Pat were at the beach. Arthur was trapped too, but he was still trying to attract the sympathies of outsiders like herself, as if he thought there might be a chance of being rescued. She knew she was right about this. For the others, art and life were the conditions of a kind of war that preoccupied them to the exclusion of everything else (including the real war that would soon be upon them). This meeting in the house was not really a gathering of friends, with all the strangeness and surprise that friendships have, but was a meeting of a clan with its own secret signs and codes. She was glad she had not been present in the kitchen when Pat had his disagreement with them. She enacted in her mind now how she would have stood behind his chair and put her hands on his shoulders and looked her defiance at them boldly. Pat was worth more than all of them put together.

She wished they had never come here. And she could not wait to be gone. The moment they were alone she would take his hands in hers and tell him, We must never come back here, ever again. It will change you if you go on knowing these people. You will become like them. Their influence will hold you. Would she use the metaphor of Mrs Kemp's fly paper in the service of her argument? Perhaps not. We can do this on our own, would be a better thing to say. Thankfully Pat had recovered from his obsession with the solitary ideals of Rimbaud, but he still liked to think they could do things on their own and without the charity of others. She felt suddenly dizzy and reached for the doorjamb to steady herself.

Arthur said with concern, 'Are you all right, my dear?' His hand tentatively extended towards her shoulder, but he did not quite touch her. He felt she had asked him not to touch her. She had rebuked him. He liked her and felt sad for her and for himself and he did not know why he should feel this sadness. Perhaps he was just exhausted. The long night had drained his spirits.

'I'll have to go and lie down,' she said. She thought she was going to be sick. She turned and walked away from the door and the night and the garden of death. Once she was in the bedroom she could no longer hold back her tears. She climbed into the bed and pulled the covers up close around her and closed her eyes. When she stopped crying she said a prayer to the old god of her childhood, murmuring it aloud as she had done then, 'Please God, make everything be all right.' Just as if she was a little girl again in her bed at home on the farm or at her mother's house in Brighton when something was going wrong, when there had been no rain and the grazing had failed, or when her mother and father had an argument. And she thought of her dear grandfather and saw herself pressed against his coat in the library at Brighton, his smell of Erinmore tobacco, his hand guiding her hand safely across the Great Southern Ocean to the shores of Australia. There we are, the two of us. See us? I can. 'Dear God, please make everything all right.'

She must have gone to sleep. She opened her eyes. The door was opening slowly. She watched through slitted lids. Pat crept in and turned and closed the door, holding the knob with one hand and easing the door to with the other. He wasn't wearing his singlet. The room was filled with a grey light and she could see his features contorted with the effort to be silent. When he turned towards her she closed her eyes. She heard him taking off his shorts, the soft hush of material against his flesh. The next minute he was easing himself into the bed beside her. Now she smelled the sour river water on him and knew it must be her she smelled.

He lay still beside her. She waited, hardly daring to breathe. If he went to sleep she would wake him and ask him. She could not hear his breathing and thought he must be breathing with his mouth open. She could smell his fear. The sourness of his body. She waited. Slowly the room grew lighter. She heard a shout and something being banged or struck a number of times in another part of the house. Then silence. She was sweating. She waited. She felt Pat ease his limbs.

She said, 'Did you make love to her?'

His silence screamed in her head like her brothers at the bench-saw, cutting wood for the winter fires. She waited, her heart pounding. She felt her baby stir. She waited for Pat to deny it. It was light now. Pat said nothing.

She pushed the bedclothes off her and felt for her slippers. She stood up and went over to the door.

He said, 'Where are you going?'

'To call Dad.' She went out and closed the door. In the passage she picked up the telephone and dialled their Brighton number. Her brother Phillip answered immediately. 'Dad's up at the farm,' he said. 'I'll come and pick you up, Sis. Did he hit you?'

She said she would get a lift to the railway station and he should meet her there. She put the phone down and turned and saw Arthur silhouetted against the morning sky at the far end of the passage. She asked him to take her to the station. 'I'll wait there for my brother.'

She went back into the bedroom and put her clothes on and packed her few things in her bag. Pat lay watching her. He did not ask her to forgive him. She knew he had been weeping. She did not say goodbye when she went out the door with her bag and she did not look around.

At the station she sat on a bench under the awning and waited for Phillip's green and red International to come around the corner at the top of the incline. When they were reading Grote's *History of Greece* in her senior years at school she had begun to address her letters to him as Phillip of Macedon. 'You are my hero,' she wrote, 'oh noble son of Amyntas.' And such like. It was a game. But it was a true game. She knew Phillip would come and rescue her if she was ever in trouble. He was ten years older than her. There was a photograph in the sitting room at the Brighton house of him holding her in his arms when she was newly born, a look of pride and exquisite delight on his face, his joy and responsibility to have a little sister to champion.

Arthur had tried to insist on waiting with her until Phillip arrived, but she told him to leave. 'It will be better if my brother doesn't meet you.' She was sorry to see that Arthur seemed to take this as a personal rebuff, which it was not. She felt sorry for him. He seemed like a very sad man to her. She could not think of what had happened. She knew she was crushed. Something was holding her together. People would call it courage.

She waited, watching the people coming and going across the station forecourt. Frowning mothers with prams, their older children at their heels or holding the pram handle. Fathers striding ahead, gripping a boy or girl's hand, and calling to their families to hurry up or they would miss the train. Old people who could hardly move faster than a snail, their legs caught in the sticky paper of life's end. She watched them and she didn't watch them. She saw them and she did not see them. She had been buried alive beneath the cold earth. Her womb was still. Her baby dared not move for fear it would bring about the end. She did not weep. She no longer prayed. She waited. She had lost him. It was the end.

PART
three

15

Retribution

PAT WALKED UP THE LAST PINCH OF THE GRAVEL TRACK CARRYING his bag. Gerner was on the hill above him with his dogs. The old man was calling and waving, his hands going about wildly in the air, the dogs howling and straining at their leashes. Stuck up there in his wheelchair, Pat thought. He raised his hand in a greeting to the old man and kept going. Lonely old bugger, he was always wanting something. The yellow oxalis was flowering again. Wasn't it flowering all the time? Or did it have a season? He had taken no notice. If Helen Carlyon had not given him Arthur's card that day and he had not gone to Arthur's office as a last resort but had caught the train to Geelong, none of this would have happened. If he'd spent the rest of his ten bob at the pub that day he would have been better off. You made the right choice and finished up in the shit. You made the wrong choice and came out smelling sweet. You could never tell which way it was going to go. Planning was not enough to determine destiny.

He saw them before they saw him and stopped on the track. He said, 'Shit!' He knew who they were. There was a pile of stuff burning in the front garden, the spade still sticking in the ground beside the fire, more or less where he'd left it last spring. Their truck was parked on the sidling to the right of the gate. A flat top. One of them was tying something onto the tray body of the truck, throwing the rope over and going around to tie it off at the cleats on the other side. Pat watched him. It was the younger one, Euan. A weird name for a weird bloke. The nasty sod. Pat's stomach knotted with fear. The other one, Phillip—the older one, Edith's favourite—would be in the house for sure. He realised Gerner had been trying to warn him. He could turn around now and walk back down the track and no one would be any the wiser. He would not even need to make a run for it. Just walk away. He wondered how bad it was going to be. It's my house, he thought, resenting them. The bastards are in my house. He knew she wasn't there. She would be at the farm in Bairnsdale with her mother by now. He could feel her up there in that big cool house with the veranda looking out over the valley, the river glinting here and there in the distance through the trees, that range of hills, cattle all facing in the same direction in the paddocks, heads down, feeding forward as if they had been trained to it. He could see Edith sitting on the veranda with her mother, having a cup of tea and telling the story of being betrayed by the little Irish bastard they had all warned her against.

He went on towards the gate. His legs were weak and shivery. He drew in a couple of breaths. The brother at the truck was out of sight now. Pat went on through the gate. It was a pity he couldn't close the gate properly and tie it shut.

It would have given him that extra bit of time. Phillip was the one he might be able to talk some sense into. This other one was not a talker. He went over to the fire and looked at what they were burning. His pictures and books and some bedding and clothes. His best trousers. He could smell the kerosene they'd doused it with. Father Brennan's book of the sagas was face up, burning. He thought of Njál's house burning around him, his wife refusing at the last minute to plait him a new string for his bow. He felt sick to see the book go. There was no use trying to rake it out with the spade.

Pat stood looking at the smoking ruin of his book and wished he had the wild courage of the Viking warriors. It was lucky, he supposed, that he had left his drawings of Creedy's daughter at the Laings' place. A small piece of luck that, sitting in this disaster like a word of encouragement from a friend. Which friend would that be, then? He laughed despite everything. He was deeply sorry to lose Father Brennan's book. There would be no replacing it.

He heard the brother coming up behind him. He didn't turn around but started walking away towards the house.

The man behind him called, 'The conductor's here to look at our tickets, Phil!' And laughed. 'You fucking little mongrel!'

Pat sensed him closing in and dropped his bag and sprinted the last yards, taking the steps in a flying jump and going in through the kitchen door. The older brother, Phillip, was coming towards him along the passage from the studio. He was carrying the square table Pat used as his painting table. He was even bigger than Pat remembered. A country footballer. Pat stepped to one side of the door and got his back to the wall. There was nothing handy to smash at the bastards with.

He was going to have to think of something pretty smartly. 'Get out of my house!' he said, leaning at the older one as if his intention was to go for him. The older one was calm. He set the table down and looked at the doorway. The younger one came through the doorway with the spade in his hand. The older one said, 'There's no need for that, Eu. We don't want to kill this piece of shit. He's not worth going to jail for.'

But Euan didn't always heed his brother's advice. He swung the blade of the spade at Pat's head.

Pat was too quick for him. He ducked the blow and snatched the spade out of his hand and ran at them both with it, screaming and swinging wildly. 'You're fucking dead now, you maggots!'

The brothers collided with each other then pushed off, collecting themselves, the older one going to the left and the younger going to the right. Pat did not hesitate but swung the spade at the legs of the younger one. The older one hit him hard with his body and brought him down in a tackle. Euan piled on and smashed Pat's face with his closed fist. He kept smashing until Phillip hauled him off. 'He's done,' he said. 'He's done, for Christ's sake.' Both men were panting heavily, the older holding his younger brother to his chest with both arms around him. They stood looking down at Pat.

He was unmoving. His face covered in blood. One eye was half open, the pupil unseeing. His teeth gleaming behind his bloodied lips.

Phillip said, 'Jesus, Eu! We've fucking killed him.' He got down on his knees and put his ear to Pat's mouth. 'He's not breathing.' He looked up at his brother. 'We've killed the fucker.' He got up and stood with his brother. 'What are we going to do?'

Pat coughed then sucked back on the air. He looked up at them. 'Did you hit me with that spade?'

Euan said, 'He's going to live.'

'Let's get out of here.' Phillip stepped to the door.

'We should burn the place.' Euan stood above Pat, looking down at him as if he was thinking of kicking him in the head with his boot. He spat on him and turned to the door. He wanted to do more damage, something final and satisfying, but his threat to burn the house had no strong intention in it. He followed his brother out to the truck. On his way across the garden he picked up Pat's bag and tossed it onto the fire.

Pat wiped the spittle from his shoulder and raised himself on his elbow. He watched them back the truck then turn and head down the gravel track. He hadn't felt a thing. He should have gone lower and caught that sod in the ankle with the spade then swung it up hard into the other's groin as he came for him. Well, it was over for now. It was no good theorising about how he might have got the better of those two. He would probably have had to kill them to stop them. He lay back on the floor, his arm across his eyes. The pain was coming to a peak now. He would like to get another chance at them, one at a time. The younger one first. Catch him off his guard and knock his teeth out with an axe handle. He hadn't got a punch in that he could remember. It was over before it had really got going. It was very disappointing to him that he had not marked one of them. Well, this was not the end of the story. He would go up to Bairnsdale and demand to see her. They couldn't refuse to let a husband see his wife.

He lay there for some time, dealing with the pain and waiting for his thoughts to settle. Then he got up and went over to the sink and washed the blood off. His shirt was torn and there was blood on it and on his pants. He turned out his pockets. He had seven shillings. At least the buggers hadn't robbed him. He went into the studio. Everything was smashed. There was nothing worth picking up. They must have taken her stuff out first. Had she been with them when they arrived? Driving down separately with her father to supervise the removal of her own belongings, then leaving them to get on with the act of retribution once she had made clear to them what they should take? Surely she could not have known they intended to destroy his stuff then beat the shit out of him? Surely she didn't hate him? But perhaps she did. It occurred to him then for the first time that the pair of them might not be going to get through this. Maybe the damage he had done to her trust in him was too great for her and she wasn't coming back. Too humiliating. She would *want* to go on loving him, he was sure of that, but would she be able to? Would she be able to overcome her repugnance after what he had done?

He went back to the kitchen and drank some water and stood at the sink, looking out at the fire burning in the garden, considering his life without Edith and their child. Dan Brennan's book burning on the fire. He had destroyed everything good in his life. There was nothing left. He was a bad man and a fool. Could there be a less worthy combination? His mother would be ashamed of him. Had he injured Edith for life? Would she carry this with her for the rest of her days? She and the child? He leaned his elbows on the sink and put his head in his hands. He didn't know what to think.

•

Arthur said, 'Well, of course, Pat. It will have to be just for a few days, though. Autumn is not herself at the moment.' He had thought it was over and had doubted they would see Pat Donlon again. He'd had only one appointment before lunch, with an old and very deaf client. He had been deeply lost in his book when Pat walked in. He could hardly have turned him away. Autumn would not have thanked him for that. Of course he did not have to tell her that Pat had come to see him. But the thought of deceiving Autumn was deeply repugnant to him. Deceiving Autumn would be deceiving himself. No, it was not an issue. He knew he was going to tell her.

Pat was seated in the clients' chair across the desk from Arthur. He was smoking one of Arthur's cigarettes. Sitting where he had sat that fateful evening when he turned up out of nowhere with his bundle of drawings. If Wilenski's book had not arrived in the post that day and he, Arthur, had not stayed back late reading it, he would not have been in his office and Pat Donlon would have gone away and they would never have met and none of this would have happened.

'You don't have to,' Pat said. 'I'd go home to my mum and dad's place, but they'd have a fit if they saw me looking like this. My dad would get a bunch of his mates together and go after those two. There'd be no end to the trouble. I'm not going to put her through that. It's not her fault.'

'No, of course not. I understand you perfectly.' Arthur was aware that his manner must seem to Pat to be a little tight and that he was being less than wholeheartedly welcoming, and he was sorry for this, but was not able to do anything to relieve this impression. He *was* tight. Pat made him feel tight. Having Pat sitting there asking for sanctuary (that was how Arthur thought of it) had put him horribly on edge. Pat had taken him completely by surprise. He had looked up from his book and been dismayed to see Pat standing there in the doorway, grinning at him like an apparition from a battlefield. Arthur was shocked. But he had no wish to be unkind and had done his best to make Pat feel at ease. Pat, he soon realised, was more at ease than he was himself. Arthur's impulse was ever to be generous. And indeed what was to be gained by making things difficult for everyone? He sat looking at Pat unhappily, his book set aside, the calm of his day and his peace of mind shattered.

He looked across the desk at Pat. Pat's eyes were swollen and richly discoloured, and his jaw bulged out on one side, the tight skin brightly inflamed. It made Arthur's knees feel funny to look at it. Wounds had always made Arthur's knees feel funny. Animal wounds on the farm as a boy in Tasmania no less than human ones. Autumn was able to deal with such things without blenching, but not he. He looked away from Pat's jaw and wondered if Pat had eaten lunch, or would be able to.

Arthur examined something in his bookcase and said, 'Did you lose any teeth? You would have been better off, you know, if you'd walked away from those fellows.' He reached and took down a tome, the title of which he did not bother to notice. The book had been on the shelf unopened since before his own time in the office. He sneezed and put the book down and took out his handkerchief and blew his nose.

Pat smiled. 'Thanks for the advice, Arthur. You're right. A sensible person would have turned around when he saw those boys and walked back down the hill. But they were in my house burning my things. I don't know what you would have done, but I found it hard to walk away from that.'

The picture in Arthur's mind of these two enormous men, as Pat described them, burning his belongings then beating him insensible, was so without precedent in his private experience that he found it frightening to think of it. No such thing had ever happened to anyone he had ever known or to anyone his friends had known. George could be belligerent on occasion, and the others might get drunk and shout at each other, but burning and beating belonged to the world of criminal violence. That Pat did not seem particularly depressed or shocked by these events was a worry to him. Did this sort of thing happen often in Pat's life? Was it an experience he was accustomed to dealing with? Was he inured, as Arthur could never be, to this kind of deranged criminal behaviour? The idea that Pat's father would take it upon himself to gather a band of associates together and go in search of Edith's brothers to exact his vengeance on them was utterly foreign to him. It made his mouth go dry to think that he himself, as a friend of Pat's, might be called on to join such a party of vengeful miscreants. In inviting Pat back into their home now, might he not also be inviting this kind of extreme behaviour into their lives? The thought frightened him. Who was it who had invited the arsonists into his home out of pity, only to have his home burned down by them?

Pat said, 'It's all gone. Even my trousers and my only clean shirt. My toothbrush too.' He laughed. But it was not a happy laugh. Privately he was grieving for the loss of Father Brennan's book, and for his Rimbaud poems. He might be able to find another book of Rimbaud's poems, but he would never again have Dan Brennan's book. With the loss of that book, one of the few precious and beautiful things in his life had gone for good. He was not grieving for the loss of his paintings and his drawings. He had already moved beyond them and the phase of life they represented. He was now located in a kind of void of art. An open nothingness. Indeed, he might have burned them himself if Edith's brothers had not done the job for him. He had done nothing worth preserving. Nothing at all. He no longer saw himself as the young Rimbaud. That illusion of youthful genius was done with. He would always cherish the boy poet's work but he would not mistake himself again for that kind of person. He did not have that dangerous wildness. It was not his. He did not regret the loss of the illusion. Its loss had brought him closer to who he really was. One day, soon or not so soon, when her wounds had had time to heal, surely he and Edith would get back together? If he were a poet he would write poems about all this. But he had no desire to write poems. He stubbed out his cigarette in the ashtray and looked up at Arthur. 'I've got nothing to show for my twenty-two years, Arthur. Except those drawings I left up at your place.'

Arthur said it *was* very little, he could only agree. He picked up the telephone and dialled the Old Farm number.

Autumn picked up the phone and said a cautious hello.

'Hello, darling. Pat's here with me.' He was looking across his desk at Pat, wondering how best to describe his facial injuries without alarming her. 'He's had a bit of a fight, I suppose you'd call it, with Edith's brothers.'

Pat could hear the squeaks and squawks of Autumn's excited voice but was not able to make out anything of what she was saying. He feared she might be telling Arthur she never wanted to see him again.

Arthur said, 'No. Not seriously.' He listened. 'I thought you might say that.' He hung up. 'Autumn said I should bring you home until you're recovered. I have to tell you, Pat, I was glad I did not have to make that suggestion to her myself.'

Pat said, 'It's very kind of you both. I'll make sure I'm no trouble to you.'

The phrase rang in Arthur's head: *I'll make sure I'm no trouble to you.* He shied away from thoughts of Autumn's night of the moon and the river with this young man. He trusted her. Of course he did. Their trust was inviolable. It was sacred to them both. In new company she took his arm and held him close to her side and repeated their private formula—their truth, they called it: 'We made sense of each other's life.' It would be their epitaph, carved in gilded letters on their joint tombstone. *We made sense of each other's life.* To doubt her would be a betrayal in itself. And anyway, she had assured him that nothing improper had taken place between herself and Pat that night. Arthur's rational mind could accept Autumn's assurance; unfortunately his viscera could not.

He said to Pat, 'Would you like to get something to eat before we go? Can you eat with that jaw of yours? It looks very tender. We have time before the train. There's a buffet at the station. It's licensed.'

Pat said he would like that very much.

Arthur said, 'Give me a minute and I'll close the shop.'

16

5 December 1991

WHOEVER HAS NO HOUSE NOW, WILL NEVER HAVE ONE. WHOEVER *is alone will stay alone.* These lines from Rilke's portentous 'Autumn Day', once recited to me by my confessor, Freddy, had been repeating themselves in my head all morning. It is my birthday. But it wasn't until after lunch that I realised it *is* Autumn's Day, and that my unconscious was singing me a birthday message. Freddy, I should say, strongly disapproved of my affair with Pat.

I didn't see Edith again until I thought I saw her in the street outside the chemist's shop late last year. And what a shock that was. Flinging open the offending archive of my memory and bad conscience. I've sided with her, haven't I? I mean, that's what this is. I've dived back into things and resurrected her and I've taken her side. She's the one I've made us feel sorry for. I have made myself seem hateful. In this story I'm the evil fairy and she is the good fairy. Isn't it the ever-solitary good fairy who wins out in the end after enduring injustices heaped upon her by the evil fairy? I don't see how that can come about. I seem to have agreed, in principle at least, that Edith was right about life and art and we were wrong. My friends who suicided; my darling Uncle Mathew, then Freddy, my confessor, and finally dear old Barnaby, the last of my true friends. Surely no further proof is needed than these deaths that empty choices were made by us? Choices that did not result in happy lives. *She* didn't kill herself, did she? She had her child to live for. Was it all really as simple as that? A happy life? Surely that is not the point of this, is it? To live a happy life. Contentment, happiness, satisfaction? I'm afraid I am not to be convinced. Surely we engaged with the struggle, risked everything in the cause of a creative life? Wasn't that it? Didn't we, in our youthful fervour, put the idea of happy families a poor last on our list of choices? Didn't we seek some higher and more noble end than mere personal happiness?

I'm not at the kitchen table writing this. I'm sitting up in my bed looking at her picture of the embroidered field, her clever solution with the yellow oxalis. Pat wondered if oxalis had a season of flowering. Of course it does. Everything has its season of flowering. And this late flowering may be mine. And speaking of flowering, I'm seeing her painting for what it was then, not what it is now. Now it is a period piece, a fine tonal study in the conservative manner (if I am permitted a pun) of the long-forgotten Max Manner and his followers. Then it was that young woman's modest hopes spread out on this piece of linen canvas. I'm weeping for her. Not sobbing, but weeping silently, inside. Perhaps for myself too. For all of us. I did not weep for her then. Pat wept for her then, and for himself. Now that it is too late to make amends I seek to make amends and I weep. Isn't that life, after all? The inescapable irony of survival. That it is always too late to make amends.

I've had a fall. An elegant slow-motion sweeping fall from the veranda to the bricks that edge the fish pond (still no fish). The house bricks Stony edged the pool with yonks ago have waited for me. They are hard and have sharp edges. Punishing. The same bricks on which Adeli placed her foot when she first arrived here, standing like Cortes surveying the empire it was her fate to conquer. I've broken my right wrist and torn something in my knee. A ligament, Andrew says it is. But he is not sure. I fell with infinite grace through the warm summer air, passing butterflies and bees. I felt no internal panic as I fell, but a kind of sleep of the senses.

Lying there helplessly in a crumpled heap in the hot sun beside the fish pond, half on the bricks and half on the grass, was no fun. I was in pain and unable to get up. It was humiliating. Being in pain is nothing new, it is being unable to help oneself that is humiliating. I have learned to endure pain by submitting to it and taking painkillers. If one doesn't work, the other usually does. I called for Adeli but she didn't come to my aid. When I want that woman she is not available to me. Stony came. Good, solid, ever-reliable Stony of the hands stained with the earth. I have not done him justice here. Yet it is a kind of justice to him if I keep him in the shadows. For that is where Stony prefers to be. He does not hanker after his own spotlight. He did not ask me how I came to be lying there but picked me up without a word—I might have been a broken bird—and carried me into the house. He laid me gently on my bed then fetched Adeli from the dining room. I didn't ask him if she had been dancing naked before the mirror and he didn't say. He came back a minute or two later with Barnaby's shillelagh and set it against the bed end. Stony is older than I am. He too is a survivor. I wonder what ironies inhabit his dreams? Or is he innocent of irony? I do not know him deeply enough to guess his inner life with any assurance. Andrew has given me painkillers, but they don't seem to be working so I shall have to practise submission. Luckily it was my right wrist. I am left-handed and can still scribble this.

Andrew carried on with his usual patter. Attempting to reassure me, while he was strapping up my ankle and plastering my arm, that I'd soon be up and about again. I told him, 'Everyone knows at my age, Andrew, that a fall is *the* Fall. So do please stop talking nonsense. I might be old but I am not stupid. My next stop,' I said to him, 'on this little journey of ours is the crematorium. We all know that. It's where you will be going too one of these days.' He snorted at this and asked me to keep my arm still. 'Time's bitter flood will rise, Andrew,' I quoted at him. 'Your beauty perish and be lost.' He asked me where this was from. I told him I had forgotten. What is the good of telling people such things who will never read poetry but will only ever look at the television? The one serious possession remaining to me is my mind, the great container of my memory. When it goes, I shall go with it. There are tablets at the back of the drawer in my bedside table. I hope I shall have enough judgment to know when the time has come for me to swallow them. What I didn't tell him (he would have had me in for scans and tests) was that something deeper than knee ligaments and wrist bones seems to have been jolted out of position by the fall. I don't feel right standing up. And I don't mean perching on one leg like the stork I am. But being upright at all. My body does not like it. Something has ended. I am not panic-stricken. Let it end when it will.

•

The first night with Pat and Arthur sitting up at the table across from each other eating their rabbit pie was easier than I'd thought it was going to be. I'd patched him up earlier. I enjoyed doing it. Being a mother to my boy. So there had been closeness and touch between us, and his breath on my face when I bent to stick the bandaid above the worst eye, the left one. That and catching the look in his eyes, of course, that too. And I'd seen it was all still there with us. And Arthur sitting at the table nursing his whisky and watching. We might have been a little family after all, the three of us. I had put Pat's clothes in the wash for the morning and he was wearing one of Arthur's old dressing-gowns. A grey one I'd always liked. Silk. He had very nice feet. I told him he could have been a dancer. He pointed a foot and looked at it, as if he had never thought to look at his feet before this.

I had noticed he did not greatly prize his natural gifts, but was inclined to dwell on his poor education and his family's lack of money, believing himself deprived of life's good things. I saw him differently, seeing in him a man endowed with certain beauties and a cast of mind and temperament that would assure him of some achievement one day. He seemed to me far more naturally an artist than the rest of our friends. His confident rejection of the training they had embraced, and on which they relied for their confidence, convinced me of this. Pat possessed a rare sense of personal belief that referred to nothing outside itself, no community or school or circle of like-minded friends. It stood alone. Where did it come from? Not, apparently, from his family. Not from some inheritance of a sense of worth. It came from within himself. That he might misplace it from time to time was nothing. We all know absence and despair, and know not why we know these things, or why it is we wake the next morning, our confidence restored to us. I saw the good things that had come to him at his birth, and which he did not see. And I pointed them out to him. There was the beauty of his hands. To look at Pat Donlon's hands you knew he was not a man who was meant to do nothing with his life. He was always surprised to hear these things from me. I think no one had ever said them to him before. Not even Edith. It is impossible for me not to notice a man's hands. Stony's I could draw exactly as a study from my memory. And Arthur's. All of them. They were all known to me by their hands. And by much else besides. A man's hands tell a whole story, whereas a woman's hands conceal more than they reveal. We are misled if we read a woman's soul in her hands.

I was already, even that first night, dreading the day Pat would leave us (the day he would leave *me*). The day Edith would come and reclaim him. Or the day he would return to her. Surely that day would be when their child was born. I knew how precious this little eye of the storm was to us, the three of us quietly tucked away together up here at Old Farm, the world roaring outside. My men with me. There was surely something of fate in this, if there was ever fate in anything. I wanted to believe it, but have always struggled to quite put my belief in fate. Pat could turn a key and I would be young again. This I did know. Touch my hand, my cheek, the instep of my foot and I was a schoolgirl ready to faint. A feeling more dear to me almost than my life, for the life it signified (if that makes sense). That I was more alive with him than with anyone. More dangerously stirred to acts of folly and excess. Pat restored my youth to me.

But that first night there was no urgency in it for us. No anxiety. We were three, not two and one, that night. We all felt it. Arthur and Pat had enjoyed a drink together at the station buffet before they caught the train and it seemed they had talked all the way home. Apparently Arthur had told Pat the story of his life and had laughed (of all things) when he told him the story of his mother moving to Melbourne to be close to him after his father passed away and the farm went to his brother. His brother, Don, pulling down the old family home and building a new yellow-brick one on the high bank overlooking the river, giving his father's collection of books and the dining room furniture to Arthur. Ridding himself of his parents. I had never heard Arthur laugh at this story. It was always a gloomy old Tasmanian relic, damp and green and heavy, whenever he brought it out for my sympathy. So it appeared Pat and Arthur had become mates on the train journey. It's wonderful what a glass or two of beer with a mate does for a man at the end of a long day at the office. Ah well.

Arthur went to work in the morning in great spirits. There had been no sign of Pat at breakfast, so once I had seen Arthur off I took Pat in a cup of tea. He was sitting up in bed reading.

'I found this,' he said, and held up a book for me to see. 'Is it all right if I borrow it?' He was like a bruised schoolboy. It was Ludwig Leichhardt's *Journal*. I had never read it. I scarcely knew we had it. I don't think Arthur had read it either. It had belonged to his father. A heavy old tome with a cracked spine.

I set his tea on the bedside table and stood looking down at him. His face resembled the backside of a mandrill. Purple, blue, yellow and red, his lips, eyes and jaw swollen, twisting his features out of shape. He might have been a Francis Bacon portrait of one of that peculiar artist's friends, but of course we didn't have Bacon's skewed view of ourselves until the 40s. His face was the right colours but was too distorted for a Van Gogh.

'Of course you can borrow it,' I told him. 'They're all there in the library, the journals of the explorers. Arthur's father collected them. Arthur will be delighted if you read them.' They were books that no one else had ever given any thought to since Don pushed them Arthur's way. Books from the past, they had occupied a dead area in the library and in our thoughts. Was it just chance, and his eager curiosity for things, that had led Pat to them? His hunger for knowledge was great. He felt he had missed out. I think he would have read the entire library if he had had the time to do it.

I should have left his room as soon as I put his tea down and exchanged these harmless pleasantries about the explorers' journals with him. But instead of leaving I continued to stand there looking at him. He looking up at me. I became aware of the silence of the house, the sound of the train in the distance. My blood surged through me, delicious and intoxicating. Stony was in the garden waiting for me to come out to help stake the tomato plants. Pat set the book aside and drew back the covers. He was naked. I took off my clothes and got into bed with him and we made love. He put his hand over my mouth when I howled. I opened my eyes and saw that he was laughing.

I was afraid Stony had heard me. We muffled our laughter, like children playing a forbidden game in terror of being overheard by alert parents in the next room. If to be old or to be young is but a state of mind, then I had been old all my years with Arthur and now was young again.

Pat came out onto the veranda later and watched me and Stony working in the garden. He did not return my wave and didn't offer to help but stood smoking one of Arthur's cigarettes as if he was alone in his thoughts and it was his own house. When I looked up again he was gone. That we could be so intimate one moment and in different worlds the next confused me. It made his presence elusive and I dreaded to lose him at any moment without explanation or reason. This feeling kept me in a state of nervous suspense. When I had set our lunch in the kitchen later I went in search of him. I found him in the library reading.

He did not greet me but held up his hand and said, 'Listen to this.' He beckoned me to his side. He was sitting on the couch reading Leichhardt's *Journal*. 'It's poetry,' he said, his voice filled with enthusiasm. He was in the dream of his reading. I went up and stood beside him and he took my hand in his (his hands were soft) and he read to me from the book in a voice of rapt interior attention, 'Charley also, whilst bringing in the horses on the morning of the 22nd, passed a numerous camp, who quietly rose and gazed at him, but did not utter a single word.' He looked up at me, his bruised eyes alight with the wonder of it. 'Isn't it beautiful? Don't you feel it? Out there a thousand miles from another white man and these people seeing Charley coming along. Never having seen anything like him before. Standing up and gazing at him. Can't you just feel the silence of that moment? The whole of Australia is in that silence.' He looked down at the book in his lap. 'What a great thing that is. That silence. It calls to you, doesn't it?'

But I had never heard the call of the silence as he had heard it. I loved him for being sensitive to such feelings, and I envied him, and I feared for myself.

He looked at me. 'I'll read to you whenever you like.'

'That would be lovely,' I said. He was still holding my hand. He had not mentioned Edith, but she stood in my mind day and night. Surely she must come to reclaim him soon? Melancholy is to know the beauty of life, and to know it must end.

He read to me often. And we made love all over the house and down by the river. Wherever we made love, those places became my sacred sites, each one of them a daily signal to me as I passed it. But never in the bedroom where Arthur and I slept. Pat made making love seem natural and nothing to be feared. And while we were together I felt as he did and was free of guilt and uncertainty. But as soon as I was no longer with him my fear that I was to lose Arthur because of what I had discovered with Pat returned to torment me. Arthur and I still made love every once in a while in the old silent way. It was a torture for me. I gritted my teeth and prayed for it to be over each time. That last gasp and sigh as Arthur finished and withdrew. Even as I write this I believe that no one should have to speak of such things as these. But it is the place to which I have led myself in this search for my truth, and from here there can be no turning back to more innocent themes if I am to persist in that search.

Pat spent his days in the library. I could always find him there. And when the three of us sat in there together after dinner in the evening he did not join our conversation but read and smoked, lost in the world of the Australian explorers and oblivious to our presence. I soon came to understand that Pat possessed no sense of social obligation. He felt no need to make a contribution. To anything. To the budget of our household or to the conversation (the two chooks he brought home that time Freddy kissed him he told us he had won in a pub raffle, and hadn't known what to do with them so had brought them home). He never washed the dishes or made his bed or offered to help in the garden. Not once. And he didn't even suggest that he might find a job and pay his own way. He seemed not to notice these things. They were not important to him. They *yielded* nothing. He lived with us as a child might, unaware of his dependence on us for his every need. I envied him his freedom and knew I should never be able to fake such a detachment from any situation. For me, as for Arthur and our caste, all situations possessed their social dimension. Obligation attached to everything in our lives. There was no place where we felt ourselves to be free from the need to contribute. It had been bred in us. Pat was the first person I had known intimately who was without this sense of obligation. I wondered if it was just him, or if it was common to all people of his class. But Stony was a working man and he was rich in a sense of responsibility to his fellow human beings. So it wasn't just a working-class thing. But of course Stony was not strictly an Australian either. Though he was uneducated, Stony was like Boris, essentially an outsider who would always be an outsider. The deeper connections of the native born would never be forged for them. They were not there and could not be brought into being. Neither Stony nor Boris, as much as we loved them, would ever be mistaken for an Australian. They carried something with them that we lacked; the marker of their cultures and their histories. The old world of Central Europe was in them. We knew nothing of them first-hand, as it were. To think of Stony did not help me to understand Pat. I saw it was a dead end and abandoned that line of thought. Pat could not have been mistaken for anything but an Australian.

The art journals Arthur and I kept on the low table between the two sofas (it was a Chinese cherry wood table given to us by Louis) were now covered with numerous old volumes of the journals of the explorers. Pat kept all the old books out and had scraps of newspaper sticking out of them marking places he wanted to find his way back to. He would dart from one volume to another to check some fact, or to relive a scene that had appealed to him, or to make some comparison. On these occasions his lips moved while he leaned forward to read, an eagerness in him. When he was reading Charles Sturt's two-volume journal of his South Australian expedition, he would look up and exclaim from time to time, 'Not a patch on Leichhardt.' He did not address this remark to Arthur or to me but to the vacant air around him. The absent tone of his voice made me want to look for the other person among us to whom he was addressing his remark. He read all the journals. Leichhardt remained his favourite, Major Mitchell his least favourite.

One weekday, when Arthur was at his office and Barnaby was with us for afternoon tea in the kitchen, Pat suddenly said, speaking his private preoccupation aloud and breaking into our conversation, 'It would be such a great thing to do.'

'What would be a great thing to do?' Barnaby asked. He was interested in Pat. 'Autumn and I were just filling in the tedious hours in the hope you would share your thoughts with us.'

Pat said, 'To follow Leichhardt's trail. To see that country. To go where he went.'

'Is that all? It might be boring, Pat. There are a lot of flies and it is very hot.'

'I'm serious,' Pat said.

'I can see that.'

'It would all be changed,' Pat said, disengaging from Barnaby. 'It wouldn't be the way it was in his day.'

Barnaby said, 'On the contrary. Most of that country hasn't changed at all since he went through. The Aborigines are gone, of course, pretty much, but little else has changed. You should come up home with me one of these days. I'll show you that country. Nothing simpler. Leichhardt went through just to the east of us. The Expedition Range is named after him.'

Pat's eyes, which were fully healed and recovered by then, filled with a look of boyish wonder—it was the look English public schoolboys once wore on the illustrated covers of stories about adventures among the savages of the South Seas. He said, 'Would that really be possible, Barney? I mean seriously?'

Barnaby laughed at him. They had got on well together ever since the day Barnaby took his part against the others at lunch. Barnaby said airily, 'Nothing simpler, old mate. You'd love it. You city boys are full of romantic notions about the bush.' He turned and kissed me on the cheek. 'Thanks for the leeks. I must be going.'

When Barnaby had gone Pat wanted to make love, so we went to his room. It was wonderful as usual and I was lost to everything. Before I was really quite finished, Pat withdrew abruptly and said, 'Was he just saying that, do you think?'

'Who saying what?' I said, my mind reeling as if I had run into a door.

'Would it really be possible for me to go up there with Barney?'

'You're a bastard,' I said. I rolled away from him and got off the bed and put my clothes on (I was still throbbing). A bright little flame of hatred was flaring inside me. I hoped I would be able to contain it.

'What's up? What have I said?' Pat seemed genuinely perplexed. What could possibly have annoyed me? The flame of my anger burned brighter.

'You might have waited a minute,' I said.

'Sorry.'

While I was in my delirium, imagining us to be at one, he had apparently been thinking about Barnaby and the bush.

'Sorry,' he said again. But he was quite cheerful about it and not the least bit contrite. He lay there with his arms behind his head and his nakedness presented to me. 'Do you think he really would take me up there, though?'

I tottered, trying to put my sandals on, and had to sit on the edge of the bed. I didn't want to be touched. Pat sat up and put his arm around me and kissed my cheek.

I said, 'You never know what Barnaby will do and what he won't do.' I stood up and moved to the mirror and combed my hair out with my fingers.

Pat said, 'So what's the big hurry? What's all this about? Don't tell me you're jealous of Barney? Jesus! What a thought.'

He laughed and reached for his trousers and felt around for his cigarettes.

'*My* hurry?' I said icily. 'I have to put in my orders for the week, Pat. If I don't phone before lunch there will be nothing for your dinner tomorrow night. But you wouldn't know anything about that, would you?'

Was this our first disagreement? It is the first I recall. It left a distracting stain on the way things were between us. For a few minutes I had been capable of hating him. When we made love after that I was wondering if he was as deeply lost with me as I was with him, or if he was thinking about something else. It defeated things a bit. We both noticed it, but neither of us was able to be honest with the other one about it, so it stayed with us and I began to fear it each time we were together.

•

When Barnaby was in Melbourne he had a flat above a pub in Swanston Street, and when he was up the river near us he rented an old cottage overlooking a tight elbow of the Yarra. Barnaby was in and out and about the place all the time. You never knew when he was going to turn up, or with whom. He had nothing to say about me and Pat. It was all part of life in the theatre, as he called it, the daily dance and drama of things. Barnaby was not burdened with uncertainties or longings about family life. He loved his parents but adored his liberty and enjoyed it without a bad conscience.

It was not long after this that Barnaby started taking Pat into the city with him and introducing him to his friends in the wine bars. I hated this. When I asked Pat what they did and who they met on these excursions he said, Not much at all, just having a drink and a laugh with some of the fellers. He said I could go with them if I wanted to. But I knew he didn't mean it, and anyway I loathed those places, the basements along Swanston Street and in back alleys (Barnaby said he remembered seeing Pat and Edith in the Swanston Family Hotel but Pat did not recall ever seeing him there). To me those so-called bohemian dives were sleazy and depressing places patronised by make-believe people who would never accomplish anything, rings of despair in their drunken laughter, the comfort of helplessness in each other's company. Barnaby loved all that stuff. He was not its victim but liked to observe it. George was a regular at one of the bars and was more a victim of the cult of drink and noise and the seduction of young girls. George was oppressed by the white man's Christian preoccupation with good and evil and couldn't really enjoy the freedoms he required from life. His was a bitter struggle against the dark. He became very successful and his paintings are still greatly valued. It was the urban landscape, never the bush, that fascinated George's eye. The glitter and fascination of decadence. He lived it deeply and knew first-hand what grossness was. His work carried the stamp of authenticity.

Pat and Barnaby were always very late getting back from these expeditions. Barnaby would drop Pat off here in the early hours of the morning. Most often Pat was drunk and noisy getting in. Arthur and I would lie awake listening to him bumping around before he finally fell into bed and settled. Our home was no longer the private haven of our dreams it had once been.

When Pat was in town with Barnaby, and Arthur and I were having our dinner alone, I was hardly able to speak a word or swallow a mouthful of food for the sickening anxiety and jealousy that engulfed me.

Arthur said to me cheerily (cheerily!) at the table one evening, 'It's like old times, darling. Just the two of us.' It was impossible for me even to pretend to agree with this. Old times were gone and were never coming back. And this was not like them. He had never asked me outright if Pat and I were lovers. But I knew he knew. How could he not have known? Nothing was said. It was unsayable. To have said it would have destroyed us. Like the surprise of the Aborigines when they saw Charley coming through their country with a mob of horses. There are many ways in which life can be unspeakable. It can't all be reduced to words. And the best of the poets have always known this. It is the legions of lesser poets who think otherwise. I was grateful to Arthur for his silence, but his silence was not enough.

The worst of it was, I had stopped being able to talk to Freddy. He was no longer my confessor. There was no one to whom I could tell my private joys and terrors. He did not approve and did not want to hear what I wanted to tell him. Whenever he came to see me, which was less and less often, he and I sat and drank and smoked and looked out the window or leafed through a magazine together, or we walked arm in arm down to the river as we used to. But it was as it used to be only in appearance. While we walked I was thinking of Pat, and Freddy was feeling me thinking of Pat. He did not like what we were doing and saw disaster in it for me and Arthur, his friends. He soon made some excuse and left. It was horrible. He kissed my cheek at the door and got into his car and saluted me sadly and drove away, and I went to my room and wept for the friendship that was no more. The day would come when Freddy and I would regain our trust, but by then we were different people and the source of our joy was soured and buckled out of its former shape and had become something else. We would never have the original thing again. By then he was suffering from his alcoholism and I had become a survivor who believed herself to have been betrayed. Though I did not know we were to regain our friendship, I was not mistaken to mourn what I had lost with Freddy.

I asked Pat if he was staying out of Freddy's way on purpose. He said he wasn't, but I knew he was. 'Freddy likes to talk to you on your own and I'm happy reading,' he said. None of it seemed to trouble Pat. He sailed in clearer airs than I. And there were times when I hated him for this and was alienated from him because of it. Times when I could have torn the book out of his hands and ripped it apart and thrown the pieces in his face and screamed at him, Why must you read all the time! Don't you ever notice other people's pain? I think he would have laughed at me if I had done this. Laughed, then made love to me. And I would not have resisted him but would have wept with helpless fury.

I went to the library to look for him one morning, determined to distract him from his reading. The day was pure and light and still, cleansed of its sins after days of darkness and rain, the roar of the river was the welcome sound of a new beginning. I was going to suggest he join me in the garden and help me pick the peas for dinner. It was an innocent thought. Something simple and good that he and I might do together. Pat did not see the beauty of Old Farm as I saw it. I wanted him to know it at its best, in its clearest light, in its strongest mood. It was always the river that determined the strength of this place. When the river was in drought the bush became quiet and still and refused to grow and just waited. I longed to share with Pat my enthusiasm and love for my home. Which was foolish and wrong-headed. My home was Arthur's and mine. It could never belong to Pat in the way it belonged to us. Pat did not want to see it as I saw it. But I ignored all that.

He was in the library day after day and night after night, breathing his own stale cigarette smoke, his nose buried in those old books of last century that had belonged to Arthur's father. He did no drawing. He never painted. He never spoke about art or his ambition to make it. I knew it was still with him. Down there simmering quietly in the stones of his being, and that he was in there with it, the door firmly closed. He never once came out into the garden and asked me what I was doing, or stood and looked in wonder at the day. He showed no interest in anything except Arthur's father's old books. He ate, he made love, he slept. And he read. And when Barnaby asked him if he would like to go into town he went with him, and drank and played up, I suppose.

I had begun to feel that I was being used. I resisted this feeling and hated it. But it persisted and there grew in me an unexpressed fury that I needed to do something about. I needed to find for myself a patch of the clear air in which Pat sailed. But I couldn't. My life was not like his. My life would never be like his. I refused to see it. I would not accept these things. I mistook my defiance, my obstinacy, for intelligence and determination. Why must I be responsible for everything and he responsible for nothing? We never mentioned Edith.

Autumn Laing

When I went into the library Pat did not look up from his book to see who had come into the room but went on reading, his lips quivering, murmuring his approval. I thought of a dog following a scent through the bush, going this way then that, turning back on itself, then darting forward again, deaf to the whistles and shouts of its master. I stood watching him a while and was about to leave when I decided instead to sit on the sofa across from him and see how long it would be before he acknowledged my presence.

I sat down and folded my arms and watched him. I may as well have waited for the moon to speak to me. His silence and the way he had of turning the pages of his book began to infuriate me. As he drew near the end of a page his right hand slowly rose to his mouth, as if it were acting independently of his conscious mind, and touched the tips of forefinger and thumb to his tongue, which emerged pinkly from between his lips (the pronounced veins on the backs of his hands always reminded me of his penis). Then, with an equally mechanical deliberation, his tongue withdrew and his hand descended slowly to the book, where forefinger and thumb gripped the top corner of the new page and rubbed it between them. It was not necessary to do this. The pages of the explorers' journals had been cut by Arthur's father and the blunt paper knife had given their edges a deckled effect, which made it easy to know you were turning only one page at a time.

I wanted to scream at him to stop. I wanted to force him to look up and speak to me, to ask me to share my thoughts with him. I laughed aloud with haughty derision, but he still did not react. Why was he torturing me? Fuelling my fury, I imagined him to be telling me that I should be in the kitchen preparing his next meal, or in the garden growing the vegetables he loved to eat, or washing his filthy smelly clothes. In the end I could stand his silence and his cruelty no longer and I shouted at him the one question neither of us ever mentioned, but which lay like a cold stone in my heart every day: 'Have you heard from Edith?'

The sound of my voice was very loud in the quiet room.

He started and looked up from his book and glared at me.

For a moment he said nothing. Then he looked down at his book and closed it on his finger. 'Yes,' he said. 'I have.' He was very calm and might have been waiting for me to ask him just this question—and even been puzzled as to why I had not asked it of him long before this. His calm made me feel that I was in the wrong and had overreacted clumsily.

I waited until he looked at me again. 'So did you get a letter? Did it come here?'

He regarded me with a peculiar expression, and might have been seeing me for the first time and wondering if I was worth bothering with. He said, 'No. We met in the city.'

I was chilled by the tone of his voice, by his detachment, the immense distance that lay between us. Were we really lovers, this man and I? Did I know every part of his body in the most intimate ways possible? Had we given ourselves to each other and shared our most intimate delights freely and with joy? It seemed impossible that we had. My throat was dry and when I spoke there was a catch in my voice. 'And what does she say?' I said. I was furious with him for not telling me before this and was determined to force an apology from him. Why did I feel as if it was me who was in the wrong? 'So, are you going back to her? Is she coming back to you? Are her brothers bringing her here to pick you up—or to thrash you again? What is it to be, Pat?'

He said quietly, 'Fuck you, Autumn.'

'Thank you,' I said. 'And fuck you too.' I was not in perfect control of my emotions as he was. I hated him. I wanted him to make love to me. To lose himself in a wild torment of passion for me. I was afraid he had decided that I was too old for him.

His expression did not change. 'I had a meeting with her in town. It was in a cafe in one of the arcades. I forget which one. Her dad was with her. Her brother Phillip waited outside the cafe and watched us.' He laughed softly to himself. 'What did they think I was going to do to her? They wanted to offer me something. They were afraid I was going to have them charged with assault. I told them not to worry about it. Her father wouldn't let me see her on my own. I could see how painful it was for her to be sitting there and not be able to say anything real to me.' He was silent a while, still looking at me in that odd way. 'She's not coming back,' he said. 'I've lost her.'

'When was this meeting?' I asked. I needed to know how long he had been keeping it to himself.

'Last week.' He looked down at the closed book and rubbed its binding with his free hand. Then he looked up at me.

I saw there were tears in his eyes and I suddenly realised how much he was suffering. How greatly he missed her. It occurred to me only then that burying himself in the books had been his way of smothering his pain. His way of keeping from his thoughts the fact that he and Edith were done for. That their lives together were finished. Was he regretting becoming my lover? I watched him sitting there like a lost boy, rubbing the back of the book. He looked very alone. I longed to take him in my arms and comfort him.

After a silence that felt as if it was never going to end, he looked up and said, 'She's going to divorce me.'

I was unable to say anything, but a little flame of joy leapt in my heart.

'I'll admit I'm the guilty one,' he said. 'I won't give them any problems. They don't trust me. They don't believe I'm going to make it easy on them. I don't blame them. I wouldn't trust me either if I were them.' He laughed suddenly. 'You and me, eh!'

'What about us?' My voice was small and afraid.

'It's a bit different, isn't it? You and Arthur. Me and Edith. Then you and me. We're a pair.'

'A pair?'

He set the book aside on the sofa and got up and came over to sit beside me.

I did not know what to expect from him.

He looked into my face, his gaze going over me, giving me a thorough looking over, as if he was trying to make up his mind about something. 'I don't know you,' he said. 'You know that? I don't know who you are.' His gaze focused on my eyes and he gripped my chin so that I flinched. 'Meeting you has changed my life. Completely. I knew Edith.'

I reached out and held his wrist. He was squeezing my chin painfully.

'Is this love that we have? You and me? Or what is it?' He laughed again, an unpleasant laugh. 'That's not a question.' He took his hand away and lay back on the sofa beside me, his hip pressing into mine. 'I don't know what we are, you and me. But we're two of a kind. We're the destroyers, aren't we? But are we also the creators?' He was silent for a little while. Then he said 'I miss her. I miss the life Edith and I had together. The life we promised each other. The life we are not going to have now. Our struggle. Our plan for the future. Just the two of us against the world. I miss all of that. And I miss her. She understood me. And I hate not being able to talk about her. I've wept for it and for her lost trust. For that more than for anything. Edith trusted me. And for the sound of her voice when she read to me in French. And I've wept for my lost child. I've wept for what I have done to her. The pain I have given her, which she did nothing to deserve.' He sat up abruptly, as if he had remembered something, and searched in his pocket for his cigarettes. He offered me one then lit both cigarettes from the same match. 'It's not your fault,' he said. 'I don't blame you.'

There was a dread in me that he was working his way around to telling me he and I were finished. That it was over. That he would be leaving Old Farm. Tomorrow, or the next day. Or maybe today. I imagined him asking if he could take Leichhardt with him. I was too afraid to say anything.

He rested back against the cushions beside me, smoking in silence for a long time, gazing at the bookshelves on the wall opposite. He gently took my cigarette from me and he kissed me on the mouth. His kiss was not bruising and searching as our kisses often were, but was gentle, almost an apology.

We had never made love in this way before. It was as if we approached intimacy as children might have, or strangers, feeling our way with caution, interested, caring, finding each other a little at a time, curious, looking for something in the other we had not yet found. Exploring our mysterious suffering even more than our passion. He did not cover my mouth at the high moment but joined his voice with mine, a terrible drawn-out sob from his throat that made my heart contract. I had not known how great his suffering was, his remorse for what he had done to Edith. He had expressed his pain in me. He had expressed it inside me. I felt the strange responsibility of it and I held him to me as a mother would hold a forsaken son to her breast. He was right. He and I were of a kind. No one would pity us or have any sympathy or understanding for what we had done. I knew, suddenly, that I could not see the end of us and that I did not know what that end would be or who would be caught up in the tragedy of our love before it was over. I held him tightly to me and he lay in my arms and wept.

•

The sound of the Pontiac coming down the drive and the slam of its door in the coach house entered my dream and woke me.

When I made to get up and gather my clothes Pat held me to him. I struggled to my feet. He said, 'We've got to tell him. Or we'll have nowhere to go with this.'

I wrenched myself away from him and collected my scattered things. 'For God's sake, pull your trousers up, Pat. He'll be in for his whisky in two seconds.' I pulled my dress down over my head and ran my fingers through my hair. Pat's cheek was red where I had been lying against him. I grabbed his arm and dragged him off the sofa. 'Get up! Get up!' My heart was pounding.

He got to his feet and buttoned his fly. 'We should live together,' he said. 'You can get a divorce too. We'll find somewhere of our own. We can't just keep going as we are here.'

I was terrified Arthur was about to walk in on us and heard myself say, 'That will never be possible! Never! Do you hear me? I shall never leave Arthur. This is my home. Please, tuck your shirt in!' I was suddenly fully ten years older than him and I was not going to put up with any of his nonsense. I might have been his headmistress at that moment.

Arthur came in. 'Hello,' he said. 'All huddled in here on a magical day like this?'

He came straight up to me and kissed me. 'I've got some good news. And no rattle in the Ponty.' He went over to the cabinet and poured himself a whisky. 'She's decided to behave herself. Touch wood.' He turned and looked at us. 'You won't have one?'

Neither Pat nor I drank whisky.

I was in agony waiting for Pat to tell Arthur everything. I almost heard him saying the words. Pat lit a cigarette as Arthur came over and sat on the sofa across from him.

'What's your news then?' Pat said. 'Apart from the no rattle.'

Arthur made space among the books on the table for his glass.

I was incapable of sitting down. I stood to one side, my body trembling, waiting for my life at Old Farm with Arthur to fall apart.

Arthur looked at me and smiled. 'You okay? They've agreed to let us have the gallery for six weeks. How's that?'

I said in a hollow voice, 'That's wonderful.'

Arthur looked into his glass and picked a hair or a scrap of something from the top of his whisky then took a sip. 'The terms are very reasonable. The only catch is we'll need to have the show in before March, which gives us less than six weeks at the outside to get everything organised. It's going to be pretty tight. Most of the pieces will need framing, and there's the lead times on advertising. Do you think you'll manage it? Anne will help you and I'll do what I can.' He looked across at Pat. 'Of course you can put in whatever you like, Pat. We'd love you to have something in the show.'

Pat examined the end of his cigarette. 'I might have a glass of that after all, if you don't mind.'

Arthur said, 'Please, Pat. Do help yourself.'

Pat got up off the sofa and went over to the cabinet and half filled a glass with whisky. He turned around. 'I won't be putting anything in your group show, Arthur.' He stood looking across at Arthur. He raised his glass to me and drained the whisky then turned and set the glass back on the cabinet and wiped his mouth with the back of his hand. I noticed he had missed a button on his fly. It gaped slightly with the shocked expression of a fish's mouth. 'Good luck with it,' he said. He did not look at me again but walked out of the library and closed the door.

●

Pat didn't join us for dinner. I went to his room but he was not there. Arthur was sitting at the kitchen table reading the newspaper. He said, 'If you're looking for Pat, he said he was going to walk to the station and catch a train into the city.'

'Why didn't you tell me?' I said.

Arthur turned his paper inside out and reached for his glass. 'What's for dinner?'

I wondered for a brief moment of complete insanity if Arthur was really worth it. Was I making a terrible mistake by clinging to him and the security he offered me? Was I forfeiting my last chance for a life of real engagement with a passionate man who loved me and with whom I would know the dangers and follies of the creative life? Was I merely hanging on to safety and comfort here with Arthur, unable to let go of the commonplace illusion of security, like any other suburban housewife? Were Arthur and I—I asked myself as I stood there looking at him reading his newspaper and drinking his whisky, waiting for me to serve him his dinner—were we cowering with each other in the shelter of our own timidity and weakness? I walked out of the kitchen and went down to the river, leaving Arthur to serve himself his dinner. I didn't return until late.

He had done the washing-up and was in bed reading. He greeted me as if nothing out of the ordinary had passed between us. I understood why intimates sometimes murder each other.

I said, 'Did he come home yet?'

'Hmm?' Arthur was not to be distracted. 'Who, darling?'

How much did he know? How little did he care? How sure was he I would stick with him? There was no way for me to discover the answers to any of my questions without confessing everything to him. Should I do that? Should I just tell him and be done with it? I hated him for so smugly seeming to have achieved the upper hand without doing anything, while all my lies and scheming and clever stratagems had left me alone and vulnerable and angry and without the certainty of anything.

I didn't sleep at all that night but lay awake waiting for the sound of Pat returning. I didn't know what I was going to do. I felt as if Pat had left me with an ultimatum. Was it even too late to decide to leave Arthur? Arthur slept beside me without once stirring. When I went to Pat's room in the morning after Arthur had gone to work Pat wasn't there. I knew he hadn't come home, but I looked in every room of the house all the same, pretending to a hope that I was mistaken and he had somehow returned without me noticing. I went back and looked in the library several times. I could *see* him in there reading, turning the pages of Arthur's father's books with that infuriating mannerism of his. But no matter how often I went in and no matter how hard I stared, the library remained empty. I felt taunted by his absence, the untidy scatter of books on the table where he had left them, the derisive tongues of torn newspaper sticking out from between the pages where he had marked them.

I walked down to the river and stood by the log and called his name. The sound of my voice made the river a desolate place.

As I was returning up the hill, the house and the garden had the air of an abandoned place. Abandoned long ago. When the plague came. Or when the war took everyone. When the unnameable disaster passed over the house with its biblical finality. The stillness was eerie. There were to be no explanations. God does not explain the horrors he casts on us. There are no reasons for our misery. There are no excuses. To complain is pointless. To ask for help is futile. To confess is to confess to the silence. I walked up the hill through the damp green grass and saw my home in flames. Rilke's words ringing in my head, *Whoever has no house now, will never have one. Whoever is alone will stay alone.*

I looked for Stony but had forgotten it wasn't one of Stony's days. And for the first time I knew myself to be alone and vulnerable and helpless here, and I asked myself if I really had found my true home at Old Farm or had I been beguiled by a false turn in life and arrived at the wrong place? Had I really been waiting all these years for Pat? When was the moment of my error? Or was my error to believe in Pat? Was that it? Was it for the exercise of my gift I was being punished? And I did believe in him. I still believed Pat would make great art one day. My belief was a stubborn unreasoned thing that sat in me blind and dumb and refused to negotiate its position, a toad that buries itself in the clay and waits for rain, and when the first drops of rain strike the dry ground it shifts and opens its eyes and gives voice; at last emerging into the air and standing proudly for everyone to admire, the beautiful manly prince. All foolishness was mine that day.

I sat in the kitchen looking out at the garden for hours, unable to find the conviction to set my mind or my hands to any of the tasks that waited for me. I did no washing, but left it sitting in its smelly pile in the laundry basket; I ordered nothing from the butcher or the baker or the grocer; I did not bother to brush my hair or put on my makeup or cut fresh flowers for the library and the kitchen. It was as if the hitherto benign spirit of my home had withdrawn from me. I knew, as we know in dreams, that I would never find my way back to my innocent days here with Arthur. The silence sang in my ears and nothing moved. The sun stood still in the sky and no wind touched the leaves or set the ripening summer grasses to weaving their familiar patterns. I talked to myself and went again and again into Pat's room and stood in the doorway and looked helplessly at his rumpled bed, his clothes lying about on the floor, the books he had borrowed open face down, their pages turned under, carelessly discarded, cigarette butts stuffed into a tumbler, and I searched in my heart for the true reason for my despair. I could smell him. I was sure I was never going to see him again. I longed to be making love with him. Just the two of us lost to the world and our passion. And I was sure that would never happen again.

How long had he been with us? Six months, was it? Eight months? Forever? The day dragged on, empty, lonely, waiting helplessly, minute on minute, hour on hour. When I looked at the clock in the kitchen again I saw it was only five to ten in the morning. It felt like three in the afternoon.

Pat did not come back that night either. There was no dinner ready for Arthur when he got home from the office. I was sitting at the kitchen table smoking the last of a packet of cigarettes and halfway through my second bottle of claret. He came in and stood looking at me. I was exhausted and drunk and had decided to tell him everything. To throw myself on his mercy, was how I thought of it.

Without any sign of anxiety in his voice, he said, indeed with an edge of sarcasm, 'You're looking a bit peaky. Is everything all right?'

I was stung and I laughed and my resolve to confess my sins vanished. It was not I who was the sinner.

I said, 'God, I wish Freddy would come and see me.'

'Why don't you call him, darling?'

I could not accuse Arthur of cruelty. I could do nothing. I put my head on the table and howled. He did not come near me or touch me or seek to comfort me but left me to suffer on my own. I was sure my good world had ended and only the bad world would now have me.

At around eleven the following morning I was still in my nightgown, lying on my bed, when I heard the screen door out the back bang shut and the sound of footsteps crossing the boards of the kitchen. I jumped up and went to the door of my room as Pat came along the passage.

He said, 'So how's it going here, then?' He glanced into the bedroom and brushed past me and went on to his own room. I followed him.

I said, 'Why are you doing this to me?'

He dragged his bag out from under the bed and opened it and began putting his things in it.

'So you're leaving me?' I said.

He stopped and turned to look at me. 'No, Autumn. I am not leaving you. You are staying here with Arthur. Remember? Because this is your home and you will never leave it or your husband to start a new life with me.'

I went up to him and took his arm. 'Can't we talk? Please, Pat?'

'Have you told him?' He waited. 'No. I thought not. Okay. I'm going up to Sofia Station with Barnaby. I might come back here afterwards and I might not. It's up to you. If you want to change your mind, we can front Arthur tonight and get it over with. We can do it together. It's the only honest thing to do. This must be killing him. The choice is yours.' He looked me up and down, as if he was wondering how much more trouble

I was worth. 'You've lost weight,' he said. 'It doesn't suit you. You were already skinny enough.'

'I haven't slept,' I said. I began to cry. He went on putting his things into his bag and took no notice of me.

I never did put that weight back on.

After Pat had gone I telephoned Barnaby and told him I was coming to Sofia Station with them. He did not sound surprised. 'You've always said I should.'

He laughed. 'True, Autumn. Does Arthur know yet?'

Arthur came home from the office later than usual. The lemon chicken I had prepared was spoiled. I was wondering what he would do for his meals while I was away and had been trying to think of someone who could come and cook for him. It occurred to me that if he told his mother he was alone she would come here or he would go to her. The thought of either solution disgusted me. I served the dried-out chicken and we sat across from each other as usual in the kitchen. I said, 'I'm going to Sofia Station with Barnaby for a visit. He's always wanted me to.'

Arthur stopped eating. 'What about the show? Who's going to manage that?'

'Get Anne Collins to curate it,' I said. 'Curating is what she's good at.' I looked up at him. He looked into my eyes and I felt sick with guilt. I was astonished at my ability to dissemble at such a depth. 'You know Anne. She'll be delighted to be put in charge.'

Arthur didn't say, What about the others? They are relying on us. And he didn't say, What about me? Who's going to look after me while you're gadding about in Queensland with Barnaby and Pat Donlon? He let it pass. He refused to go the way of the grand domestic row. Would it have made any difference to us if he had not avoided a confrontation? Arthur had always laboured quietly at maintaining the status quo with friends and with his family, no matter what. If Arthur had been a sheriff in the wild west he would never have drawn his gun. Did Arthur even *have* a gun to draw? Was that why he was so perfect at keeping the peace? Was he afraid he would not be able to stand up to a fight? Had he ever had a fight in his entire life? He was silent until we had finished our meal and were standing at the sink doing the washing-up together, me washing and he drying, our usual arrangement. This had often been the best moment in our day, the moment when we shared unconsidered thoughts, when we looked out the window together and admired how well his oak tree was growing, or shared our enthusiasm for our plans, or gossiped about our ideas and the friends we kept close to us. It was the moment in our day when he and I came together and were best friends and companions, undistracted by the presence of other people or by the pressures of our affairs.

He put his hand on my shoulder.

I was startled. It was a gesture of peace. I understood that. I stopped scrubbing the pan in which I had sautéed the chicken breasts. But I did not turn to him and acknowledge his request for a reconciliation. I stood there looking steadfastly out the window at my own reflection in the dark garden, and I waited for him to speak.

He said, 'Please don't go to Queensland with them.'

I resumed scrubbing at the base of the pan.

His hand lingered on my shoulder a moment, then he took it away.

'Why not?' I asked, bent vigorously to my task, my shoulder turned against him.

'I don't want you to go.'

'Why not?' I asked again.

'Isn't it enough that I don't want you to go, but want you here with me?'

I stopped scrubbing and straightened. I pushed my hair back off my face with my forearm and turned to him. 'You have always denied me the important things in life. And your reason has always been a selfish reason. You think only of yourself. What you want and what you don't want are all that matter to you.' I went back to the pan, which was by now very shiny. 'I'm going. You can't stop me.'

I had first accused him of denying me the important things in life on that terrible night when we returned from Ocean Grove. It was a claim I felt in my heart to be just, but I knew I would have great difficulty demonstrating the justice of it to a fair-minded jury of twelve honest citizens.

But Arthur did not ask me to justify my claim. He said quietly, 'No, I can't stop you. You had better let me have that pan before you wear it through.'

•

There are certain moments in our lives when chance and mischance conspire either to elevate us to a new state of being, or beat us down and leave us without hope of achieving our heart's desire. Such unplanned and arbitrary moments come upon us with the force of revelation and seem to us to be the unfolding and disclosure of our destiny. We look back on them for the remainder of our days and say, That is when it happened. Such moments mark the boundary, the point of departure, the demarcation of our before and after. The bend in the river. Such was our visit to Sofia Station with Barnaby. I have often asked myself whether, if I could have foreseen the outcome of that visit, I would have persisted in my determination to go with them. Or would I have attempted to thwart the unfolding of my fate and looked for some other way forward? I never know which of my two answers to this question is the right one.

•

The pain in my arm woke me half an hour ago. I was lying on my cast, pushing it into my upper arm. It is almost dark. The sky beyond the garden is white and green against the larger evening, the trees in perfect silhouette. I suppose I have been snoring and am dry in the throat, but there is no water left in my jug. My exercise book has fallen to the floor. My pen is caught in the folds of the blanket but I can't be bothered getting at it.

I call out to Adeli. My voice is hoarse and weak. The house is still and quiet and my call is absorbed and silenced. I had another nightmare. I do not wish to write about my pain and my nightmares and the thousand other afflictions of old age. I endure them. There is more dignity in endurance than in complaint. The demoralising effect of the nightmare will wear off. It will fade. I touch my face with my fingers. My glasses are still on my nose. Some things don't change while we sleep. There is a capriciousness in it. I call to Adeli again and hear her cough as she comes along the passage in her stocking feet.

She has been outside in the garden. Does she meet someone there? Does she have a friend? Do they make love among the rhododendrons? Or on the lawn, naked together in the moon shadows of Arthur's oak tree?

I am low tonight. Mean-spirited. Drained by remembering. Empty. At this moment I can't believe my energies will ever revive sufficiently for me to write the account of our visit to Sofia Station. My mind speaks to me. It says, Let it end when it will. I reply defiantly, I will end it when I am ready. But where is my conviction? I listen to the voice of my mind and I long to give in to the slide into perfect torpor; the offer of death my mother called to share with me, it surfaces and whispers to me, Let go, Autumn.

I shout Adeli's name and she bursts into the room and switches on the light.

'Where have you been?' I scream at her. 'You're never here when I want you. You'll get nothing from me! My jug's empty.' I reach out and knock the glass jug from my bedside table to the floor. 'I could die of thirst for all you care. Give me my exercise book!'

Adeli makes no comment but picks up the jug and helps me to sit up. Her hands are warm and her touch is tender as she holds me forward while she (the plump one) plumps the pillows at my back. When she has gone to fetch my water I open the exercise book at a new page and adjust my glasses on my hard white nose and I begin to fight my way forward into memory, making myself believe the energy will come for the struggle so long as I do not give in . . . If I remember well, it is Dante's great insight that illuminates my endeavour. After his return from paradise he says, *I saw things which he*

that descends from it has not the knowledge or the power to tell
again; for our intellect, drawing near to its desire, sinks so deep
that memory cannot follow it. But he follows it. He presses
forward and does not give up. Dante knows that to succeed
in his noble endeavour to recapture his vision of paradise he
must first survive failure, and that the key to surviving failure
is persistence enlivened by inspiration. Of course, Dante begins
his journey at the portals of hell, and through long endeavour
climbs slowly upward until he at last reaches the portals of
paradise, but not without help. Despite my great regard for
Dante as a poet of his time, it seems to me (lying here in pain,
helpless and dependent upon a woman I do not love) that he
got it back to front, and that the rest of us make the journey
in the other direction, descending from the gates of paradise
in our childhood years to the gates of hell in our final days.

But poets are an inspiration to us (for Barnaby they were
his consolation), and isn't inspiration the source of our energy?
Suddenly we are energised, where before was boredom and
lassitude. So while I disagree with the direction of his poetic
journey, Dante's solution to his problem will be mine all the
same and I shall persist as he persisted. Everything is shared.
The world is one. And it is my birthday. Sofia Station took
me from the gates of paradise to the gates of hell in less than
two short weeks. But what is time except the measure of
experience? There are those in whom experience settles in the
heart as a layer of dust, and those in whom it takes fire. Dante
appealed to Apollo to fire his imagination for his last labour
(his *ultimo lavoro*). In what is surely the most perfect invocation
to inspiration in the poetic world, Dante quietly pleads, 'Come
into my breast and breathe there.'

I need help too. I have never told the story of Sofia Station. I have never had the courage to relive the humiliation of its outcome. But I can't very well appeal to Apollo in the present century and expect to be understood or believed (who was Apollo? I hear you ask), but I can nevertheless hope to take fire from Dante's example. One thing is certain, we do nothing on our own. If our dust takes fire it does so only because a voice other than our own enters our breast and breathes there. Without that voice our experience is only dust.

So here goes. Suffice to say, we went to Sofia Station. The three of us, that is. Me, Barnaby and Pat. Barnaby drove us in his car to the railway station and left his car there to be picked up on our return. It was a very long journey. How far I am not sure. But all the way from Melbourne to the Central Highlands of Queensland via Sydney and Brisbane, most of it by train, except for the last few hundred miles, when we enjoyed the swift luxury of flight. A small bright red aeroplane, with the wonderful name of Beechcraft Staggerwing, took us on a bumpy ride from Rockhampton to the portals of paradise, Leichhardt's Expedition Range, where Barnaby's mother and father and a solitary stockman lived in the calm isolation of their cattle station. The portals of paradise, it turned out, were in the outback, Australia's home of heroes and legends (wasn't it?). Apollo was needed there. He would have found much work for himself turning dust to fire.

17

Paradise garden

SHE LEFT THEM STILL AT THEIR LUNCH ON THE BACK VERANDA AND
went down to the cottage and changed into her swimming
costume. She put her robe on over her costume and took a
towel and her notebook and pen and walked down the track to
the creek, where Barnaby had taken them the previous evening
after they arrived and they had stood to watch the sun setting
among the paperbarks. The water was deep and clear, the
bottom sand rippled with bars of shadow and lit by sunbeams.
Blue and purple rocks projected into the water from the bank.
She watched four silver and black fish swimming lazily around
in a slow circle below her, following the shimmer of a sunbeam.
Beside her the tree creaked in the warm drift of air.

She arranged her towel on the couch grass in the shade of the
paperbark and opened her notebook. She sat a while watching
the fish, then unscrewed the top of her pen and, resting her
journal against her thigh, she began to write in her clear,
well-rounded, slightly forward-sloping hand, her head held a

little to one side, biting her bottom lip, considering her words. The broken shadows of the paperbark moved back and forth across her page, the hum of insects in the air all about her; and in the distance, across the valley, a crow lamented its fate.

This must be a new story, for this is a new country. It is a country unpainted and unwritten. A country that waits to be celebrated. Barnaby's people belong to a modest culture. Theirs is a more measured world than the world we inhabit in Melbourne. With an ease that has astonished me they have made me feel at home among them, as if they and we are distantly related and they have known of us and heard rumours of our stories from the south, a distant place visited only by their eldest son, the poet.

Here there are no betrayals in my past. Here I have no past. These quiet people look out from their home upon their red cattle grazing the open savannah, where great ironbark trees dot the landscape, as if some powerful landowner in the past ordered them planted for their beauty. The fine grazing stretches unbroken from the garden fence of the timber homestead to the foot of the distant escarpment, the land rising abruptly from there to a height of several hundred feet, the slopes topped by grey parapets of shining stone, which resemble the walls of an antique citadel. As we stood here by the creek last night watching the sun go down, for a brief moment those cliffs of grey stone glowed with an inner light, green and orange and amber, while the silhouettes of great flocks of birds passed silently far above us, as if the birds knew the citadel and its mysterious inhabitants beyond those escarpments and went home to them, the old spirits of that place. I slept alone in my little cottage like a child for ten hours and woke this morning deeply refreshed, my new purpose clear in my mind.

There is real vulnerability and there is the more debilitating *sense* of vulnerability, about which little can be done. In the days and weeks before we left Old Farm I suffered from that sense of helpless vulnerability. It was gone when I woke this morning. It is important to me that I make the attempt to record here what has happened to me. It is simple enough, and yet it is profound, as simple things almost always are when we pause to reflect on them.

I was twisted around in my seat for more than an hour after we rose from the end of the Rockhampton runway to begin our journey westwards away from the shining Coral Sea towards these cool highlands of the hinterland. I could not take my eyes from the landforms unfolding hundreds of feet below us. The wheel suspended from the shiny red underside of the left wing trembled in the thrust of wind and I imagined how it would rip off and float and fall away and leave us up there alone in the empty sky. The seeming fragility of the wheel's attachment to us was a perfect mirror of my fragility of mind at that time. Pat had made it clear to me that he did not want me along. I could be sure of nothing. Mesmerised by the scene below me I soon forgot my fears and became lost in the unfolding revelation of my country. A country of which I had no knowledge.

Scrawled lines of green and gold and deep brown, random silver foil meanders, broken and uncertain in their courses, and white sky windows through to the world on the other side of this world. Australia was revealed to me as an elaborate multicoloured etching; the vision of an unknown artist's eye. A portrait of my country unfamiliar to me, wrinkled and crumpled, scratched and scoured, broken with abrupt shifts of tone and form, stains and inexplicable runs of colour one into the other, purple and rose madder, vast swathes of grey and fierce angry dragon spots of emerald green.

I saw in this image of the land below me an undreamed-of freedom from formal arrangement. I was thrilled. My country! My own country. Unknown to me. Its history mysterious, inscribed in the hieroglyphics and elaborate arabesques of its unrecognised landforms, waiting to be deciphered. As we shuddered and bumped our way across the uneven sky my inner voice announced to me, No one has painted this. It was a thought that carried for me the force of revelation. No one has painted it. It is uncelebrated. Untouched by my culture. And (what is more) it is undreamed in the dreams of Europe.

This last perception at once gave me new confidence in the purpose I had conceived when I first met Pat: to acknowledge and make known his gift. I was certain I had made a discovery that would prove of great importance for Pat and for his art. I had felt vulnerable and helpless and had been bewildered and in pain, but I had never lost my faith that Pat's art waited in him for the moment of its release and expression.

And so my original intention in joining them on this journey was dispelled in an instant. I had forced my presence on them because I had been desperate to bring us back into the first innocence and simplicity of our love (as if such a return could ever be possible). This was to have been my journey to reclaim him (or perhaps merely to cling to him weakly and offend him forever). Either I would succeed in this or I would fail. And if I failed I would fail for all time. So even though I knew he did not want me with him, I came. It was a decision made in a panic of helplessness and vulnerability. A decision made against all the odds. Suddenly all that changed. My fear and my uncertainty fell away and I was sure of my purpose.

So it is not a weak and selfish purpose I have now in being here, but a noble one. My Uncle Mathew would say it is my destiny. I will show Pat that his country waits for him. Here, I will say to him, is the subject and material of your art. And, somehow, though I do not know how, I will make him believe me. Somehow I will make him see his country as I see it. Or I will fail to make him see it as I see it. But if I fail, then my failure, like my purpose, will have been an honourable one. I am filled with new optimism and nervous anxiety at the thought of bringing my offer to him. On a certain level, I know he wishes to be rid of me.

She feared that he not only wished to be rid of her but that he hated her. But she could not write the word. It was too much. Hate is a greater disaster than love for those whose soul it enters into. Hate breeds its own malignant offspring; demons without the sensibilities of human morality—that otherwise universal gift which gives to each human life its unique value. A value that can never be described or understood. To love, she knew, was more important for the human soul than to understand. It is love that redeems us from the demons of hate. She feared to be hated by him, and could not write the word. It was too terrible. She would write it later, when she was old.

From her cramped seat in the shuddering red aeroplane high above the country, the ear-shattering struggle of the engine to keep the propeller spinning fast enough to drag them through the sky had seemed to be such a strain on every part of the material that was keeping them precariously aloft, she felt certain something must give way any minute. She waited for the one small falter that would send them spiralling out of the sky, to fall to their deaths locked inside their shiny red coffin. Earlier, when it had seemed to her that she had little or nothing to lose, she would not have cared if they had fallen out of the sky. Now she dreaded it and prayed (to the old god in whom she did not believe—was it Apollo? That most Greek of all the gods?) that they would reach their destination safely.

Barnaby had leaned against her and cupped his hand to her ear, pointing past the wing with his other hand towards a great dark bulk that seemed to hang on the edge of the world below, and he shouted, 'Leichhardt's Expedition Range.' The landscape was grand and fearsome. A place of great mystery and terror. A place waiting to be dreamed.

Autumn read over what she had written then closed her notebook and screwed the top on her pen. She set the book on the grass beside the towel and she took off her robe and slipped into the water. The water was cool against her skin. She ducked beneath the surface and swam down and touched the sand. The fish darted away a couple of yards, paused, then reassembled, resuming their formal sunbeam dance, their bodies curved to the circle of their desires. The sunbeams bounced from the purple rock, now a pure and dazzling light, now a shimmer of viridian green.

She surfaced and swam a steady breaststroke along the middle of the stream until she entered the sudden cool of shade. Grey limbs of a sunken tree reared from the water ahead of her. She saw in their gesture the supplicating arms of a drowning woman and felt the chill of the omen in her stomach. She turned and swam back towards the sunlit paperbark tea tree and her towel, which already seemed to be her own little camp by the creek. She would soon forget the drowning woman, only to recall her again in memory at Old Farm.

He was waiting for her. Leaning against her paperbark tree smoking a cigarette, watching her. When she reached the bank he reached down and took her hand and helped her out. She thanked him and wrapped herself in her towel.

He said, 'You look great.' The sun was in her eyes.

'Thank you.'

They sat apart, both looking at the water, smoking their cigarettes.

He touched her notebook.

She said on a sudden impulse, 'You can read it if you want to.' She had not thought of him reading what she had written. But why not? If it didn't convince him, or even interest him, then she would try another way. But she would keep her new purpose clear and simple this time. She would do as Uncle Mathew had predicted and acknowledge another's gift: encourage this man, Pat Donlon, to the vision and confidence that would help him to make a reality of his dream; an art of his country untutored by the traditions of Europe. Nothing in art is pure. It would not be pure in its newness or in its origins, but she would refuse to let him slip away and become distracted by dreams that were not his own. She watched him reading her notebook, his lips moving every now and then in that familiar way she had witnessed in the library at Old Farm, his hand holding her book open, the *relievo* pattern of his thick veins. The deep physical familiarity of him. The taste of his juices in her throat. Her body clenched to think of him.

Yet they were like strangers here by the sunlit creek. Polite and careful. She might have been visiting a distant cousin in the country, not visited since they were at school. Here the rules were not the same. Here there were no past difficulties from which to take their bearings. No Arthur. No Edith. No betrayals. No past at all. Was it possible, she permitted herself to wonder, that this could also become a new beginning? He seemed relaxed. At ease. He was not a man consumed by enmity or hate. Had he come down to the river to look for her and to apologise for his grimness on the journey, then found there was no need for an apology between them? This place had changed them. She knew him well enough, stranger though he was, not to ask him if he too had felt the change. He would recoil and refuse to speak of it, fearful that talk would break the spell and leave them with the dead silence of their understanding.

He had slept in the guest room in the house. She had preferred the offer of solitariness in the cottage. The cottage was a bare unlined fibro-cement worker's quarters, furnished with a narrow iron bed and a two-drawer chest, a table beside the bed. A naked bulb suspended from the ceiling flex, nails driven into the timber studs for hanging clothes. Barnaby's father and the stockman, Peter, had added a shower outside, loosely connected to the cottage by a piece of corrugated roofing iron and a narrow concrete pathway. The shower was a concrete slab under a shower head, the walls split slabs from a pepper gum. A red valve on the pipe in place of a tap. It was dark inside, cool and damp, green fingers of small ferns seeking entry between the timber slabs. The water fell straight from an overhead tank fed by a windmill. The windmill creaked as it turned, the regular clang and lift of its plunger, the continuous sound of running water. An area of lush kikuyu grass and boggy ground where the tank overflowed steadily onto the ground outside. She had enjoyed lying on her narrow iron bed last night listening to the water running into the tank. Already, even on that first night (perhaps more on that first night than she ever would again), she had felt that time here was not measurable in hours but was like Rilke's clock without hands. Lying in the night under the pale gauze of her mosquito net, memories of her childhood came back to her. Memories of an age before time had begun to move. Before her life had begun to accelerate along the narrow pathway of the years. A time of small desperate fears and sudden desires. The time of Uncle Mathew and the garden of Elsinore.

She woke and knew she had slept deeply for many hours. When she stepped under the shower the water chilled her and she yelped and danced around on the wet concrete. Glossy green ceramic frogs clustered like the bloated fruit of darkness against the struts of the ceiling until the cool of nightfall, when they fell, their ripe bodies slapping onto the wet concrete pad with a little self-satisfied clap of approval. In the morning they were up there, sucked in tight against the roof beams and each other again, smugly defying gravity through the heat of the day. Barnaby's mother, Margery, told her carpet snakes sometimes climbed up and devoured them. 'Don't worry, dear. The carpet snakes are not poisonous and won't bother you.'

Pat lifted her notebook and shook it. It might have been a Bible and he a preacher about to quote some judgment at her. 'Yeah, I thought this too,' he said, and he looked at her. 'Not with this clarity that you've got here. But I was interested. I didn't see it as fully as this.' He set the book on the grass beside him and looked at it. Then he looked up at her. 'You don't have to convince me.'

She waited, wondering if he would deny wanting to be rid of her. But he said nothing. He flicked his cigarette into the stream. They watched as one of the black fish rose to the butt then dived away. 'I wonder if they've got any paint here?' he said.

So there was nothing to be discussed. She should have known. No dissection. No post-mortem. There was no corpse. No one had been murdered. There was no mystery to be unravelled. He would find some paint, it seemed, and start painting. What more was there to say? Barnaby had told them the station store had everything they would ever need.

Was it the sound of the wilderness beyond the homestead's limits that imposed itself on them and made speech an effort? They sat there by the creek, a little apart, as if they were newly met, and watched the fish a while longer. She did not ask him if he had come in search of her, or had come on her by chance.

That night after dinner, Pat and Bill, Barnaby's father, together with the stockman, Peter, sat in chairs on the wide back veranda. Barnaby and his friend Harry had gone to town earlier in the day. Autumn helped Margery with the washing-up and when they were done in the kitchen the two women joined the men on the veranda, carrying out tea and biscuits to them.

They sat in the dark drinking black tea and eating Margery's Anzac biscuits, watching white lightning flicker along the crest of the citadel range. Whenever the crickets paused in their chirruping to permit a silence, there was the distant rumbling of thunder. Autumn imagined an artillery battle raging up there behind the fortress walls. Napoleon's cannon at Austerlitz, or the Somme hidden in the Expedition Range, battles at the portals of hell, never won or lost. No one spoke, and so she kept her silence too. The night and the stillness. Stars and distant lightning. Sudden white images of the serrated ridge far off, making them narrow their eyes. Bill's two dogs lying at the foot of the veranda steps, their white eyes on Bill, their ears moving when he moved. A large black cat on the top step looking down at the dogs, its feet curled under its fat body, its studied gaze superior, imperious. A caste above the dogs, who waited for the day their chance would come to shake it to death in their jaws.

In the morning she went for a walk on her own after breakfast (there was no one else to go for a walk with). She followed the track along the top of the creek bank, passing the dusty stockyards where the stockman was milking the cow, its calf penned and bawling for its mother. And she went on a mile or so until she reached a grove of vivid green lime trees she had seen in the distance and had wondered at. Something moved within the solid shade under one of the trees and she stopped, a stab of alarm going through her chest. An enormous black boar stood bandy-legged, gazing at her, a skein of slaver swinging from its swollen jaws, from which white tusks curved upward, lethal and threatening. After a half-minute of studying her, the enormous pig grunted and went back to snuffling among the spread of fallen limes. From where she stood Autumn could see a corner of the green roof of the homestead above the trees, a thin sliver of white weatherboard. She did not know where the others were. People dispersed without signs to each other and went about their business. The sound of a motor in the distance was an indication of work going on somewhere. There was nothing at Sofia that could be called conversation. The homestead sat in the middle of the wilderness, like a fat boy in the schoolyard, eager to cause no trouble and hoping not to be noticed. Fencelines dwindling to nothing in the haze, barely there at all, an accidental touch of the pencil. Cattle stood upside down in the shimmer of heat. A horseman appeared then disappeared, accounting for nothing. Was it the stockman? Trees defied gravity. The serrated ramparts of the range had closed the curtains for the day, asleep behind the wavering haze of yellow distance. The crickets were sleeping too. Or was it cicadas? They would wake in the heat of afternoon. The perfect sound of silence.

She looked at the pig again and he raised his head and looked back at her. There was a smell of something decaying. She walked back along the track. At the yards the stockman was gone and the cow had been rejoined with her calf. She was determined not to go looking for Pat. She went up the back steps. Margery was gutting and cleaning a chicken she had beheaded and plucked earlier. The radio was playing country and western music. The black cat sat by the door observing the movement of Margery's hands through narrowed eyes. Margery looked up and smiled and offered a cup of tea.

Autumn put the kettle on the stove and stood watching Margery while she waited for the water to boil. 'I saw a huge wild pig just up past the yards.'

'That's Tiny,' Margery said. 'He supplies us with sucking pigs on a regular basis. Bill wants to shoot him. But I say so long as we don't shoot him he'll keep the other old boars away. I wouldn't get too close to him. Those old fellers are unpredictable. He has lost his fear of us. They're like us, they'll eat anything.'

After they had drunk a cup of tea and smoked a cigarette, Margery put the chicken in the oven (it was to be eaten cold later with salad), and said it was time for her lie-down. Autumn took a jug of chilled lemon water with her and went to her cottage and lay down too. Had the stockman gone back to *his* bed? And Bill? Where was he? She might have written in her journal but the heat pulsed through the thin walls and the day outside was so quiet and so still it was too distracting to write. How had Leichhardt found the will to write up his journal every evening by the light of a candle?

When the breeze dropped the windmill stopped turning. Was something going to happen? She listened to the sound of the overflow dwindling to a trickle, then become a rapid series of drips. The intervals of time between the drips grew longer and longer . . . and longer. She waited for them to cease, then forgot to wait and imagined she could hear Margery's radio. But it was her imagination filling the silence. Whoosh-whoosh, whoosh-whoosh, went the insides of her ears. On a ceiling beam a pale gecko watched her with its black eyes. Thinking was difficult.

While they were sitting out on the veranda in the dark watching the lightning the night before she had broken the silence to say she could imagine living out here contentedly for the rest of her days. The silence had resumed after her comment. Was it a silence of disbelief? Then Margery said, 'Well, that's nice, dear.' As if she wanted to nip off the possibility of any discussion of the question of living *out here*. We won't be having any of that! Isolated comments such as these did not connect or rise to the level of conversation, but drifted and were forgotten, as if the intention was ideally to return all questions to the silence out of which they had unfortunately found their way. But Autumn had meant it when she said she could imagine herself living at Sofia contentedly. Now she wondered how she could have meant such a thing and wished she had not said it. Like making a claim while drunk.

Lying there on the narrow bed in the heat she was keyed up and listening. For what? The immense weight of the silence out there stifled her. The heat was bearable, it was the silence that was pressing down and stopping her from thinking. She forgot to hear the persistent shrieking of the cicadas, then realised they had stopped. It was wearing away at her. Like someone rasping the edge of a piece of tin, back and forth, back and forth. You could take it for so long then you just had to tell them to stop or you would go mad. If they kept at it too long you would have to shriek back at them, For Christ's sake, shut up! Your eardrums would surely burst if they didn't stop. Once you heard it you were forced to listen to it. She began to fear the onset of a migraine and sat up and looked through the small window.

The path to her cottage continued on through the grass to the wire enclosure where the hens lived. There was no sign of movement there. Twenty yards or so beyond the hen run the stockman's small square hut, another fibro construction like her own, stood on its short stumps out in the blazing sun. There was a lovely big shade tree no distance at all from the stockman's hut. Why hadn't they built the hut there? Was the stockman inside? Lying on his bed staring at the ceiling, hands behind his head? He was a young man. Dreaming what dreams? What was he thinking about? What did he do with himself all day here when he was not working? She was not tempted to go and ask him. His response to her had been formal and old-fashioned. When she passed him on the way to the outside toilet she said hello and he lifted his hat to her and murmured a greeting, his gaze unable to meet hers, an unbearable shyness making him hunch his shoulders and look off to one side. On horseback he was transformed into a confident man. But she was not going down there to his hut to try to search out the confident horseman inside the shy boy. Still she had to do something or her morale would plummet.

She swung her legs over the side of the bed and got up and went in search of Pat. The perfection of her plan would have to be scrapped. Keeping it simple and ideal here could easily mean the end of her. Maybe the end of everything. The dry boards of the cottage floor creaked when she put her weight on them. She realised the cicadas had fallen silent again.

There was the sound of sawing from the machinery shed and she went in. Barnaby's father, Bill, was a tall stooped man nearing sixty. He was cutting out squares with a handsaw from a large sheet of masonite. He did not look up but kept his rhythm going, the board behind him wobbling and snapping. 'We was going to line your cottage with these,' he said, and he stopped and looked up at her and grinned. 'But we never got around to it.' He resumed sawing.

Pat was over by the side of a flatbed truck, leaning over a square iron welding table painting on one of the squares of masonite that Bill had prepared for him. A dozen or so two- and four-gallon tins of various coloured paints were lined up along the back of the table. Pat's tongue was sticking out the side of his mouth and he was brushing paint onto the ply as if there was no time to be lost. She had not seen him at work before and she stood and watched him, astonished at the way he was going about it. He didn't seem to be giving what he was doing any thought. He was wearing only a pair of khaki shorts and unlaced boots. The sweat was running down his back, making streaks. Leaning against the wheels of the truck were four paintings already done and drying.

Bill stopped sawing and walked across to Pat and set down four squares of ply against a leg of the table. He did not look at what Pat was painting. 'Will this do you for now, Pat? I'll cut you some more later if you need them.'

Pat stepped back from his painting. 'That's lovely, Bill. I can cut some myself if I run out.'

Bill lifted his hat to Autumn and said good day and went on out of the shed.

She went up to the table and stood beside Pat and looked at what he was doing.

He lit a cigarette and took a drag then passed it to her, standing looking at the painted masonite, his head on one side, considering. 'What do you think?'

She took a drag on the cigarette and handed it back to him. The reserve they had felt with each other at the creek yesterday was gone. They were out in the open with each other again now. The curtains open.

'Is it dead or alive? You're the only pair of eyes I can trust here,' he said. He gave her a look. 'The only pair of eyes in the world I can trust.' He kept looking at her. 'So tell me, Mrs Autumn Laing. Do I persist or do I shoot myself in the head with Bill's gun and get it over with at once?'

'You've got green paint in your belly button,' she said.

'Is that your answer then?'

She met his gaze and said nothing for a moment. 'It's the only answer I've got for you.'

He said, 'If I was a real artist I'd do your portrait.'

'I wouldn't keep still for you.'

'I've got ways of making you keep still.'

She felt the thrill of sex between them. The current was on again. She turned her back on him and walked over to the truck and looked at the drying paintings. She could feel his gaze through the thin cotton of her dress. His pictures were all the same. A three-tiered landscape. It was the view of the citadel range from the homestead. Not observed but imagined or recalled. A reinvention of the real. Part of the landscape that lies beyond reality. It wasn't what she had been expecting. She said, 'So you're not doing the view from the aeroplane?'

He came over and stood close beside her, his bare shoulder touching her upper arm below the strap of her dress. They stood like that, neither of them breaking the contact. The cicada chorus going full bore, as if someone had placed the needle on the record and turned up the sound. He reached for her hand and her heart gave a violent thump. She turned to him and kissed him on the mouth.

They went to her cottage and made love on her narrow bed. Afterwards they stood together under the shower and yelled as the cold water fell over their hot skin, slapping at each other and shrieking like children. She pointed out the green frogs clustered against the dark beams and he stood looking up at them. 'This is a magical place,' he said.

In her room they put their clothes on without drying themselves and went back to the shed.

'We ought to prime those other pieces of board,' he said. 'What do you think?'

He went on with his painting while she primed the squares of ply with a flat white paint that Bill and Peter had used for the garden gate posts and which had lime in it and was quick-drying. She wasn't sure it was a good idea to prime the masonite with it but she was loving the two of them working together and said nothing about her doubts. Being with him was having the effect of making her feel his age, like a girl again, without responsibilities, an excitement in everything they did. The silence of the valley had ceased to trouble her. She called across to him, 'Let's go swimming in the moonlight tonight.'

'Is there a moon?' He didn't pause in his work.

'We can make one if there isn't.' She had a sudden flash of the gesturing arms of the dead tree rearing out of the water.

He painted the same three-tiered arrangement on each square of ply. A dark green sky (there was no blue paint), shading down to pale, then the hard brown and black mass of the jagged citadel range, and the deep creamy foreground of the savannah sweeping right up to the foot of the viewer. Each picture the same arrangement and more or less a copy of its predecessor. He put the paint on without hesitation in broad sweeps of the brush. It didn't take him long to do one and he was soon out of squares.

He went over to the truck and picked up the square he had finished first and tested the paint with his thumb to see if it was dry enough to work on. 'I might put in some figures. What do you think? Should they be black?'

She said, 'I saw a huge black boar up past the stockyards this morning.'

'I don't know if I can do a boar.'

'He will be *your* boar and no one else's.'

He picked up the narrow sash cutter and scooped on some of the citadel dark and made a quick drawing of something. He stepped back. 'Is it a pig? It's not sitting on the ground properly.' He leaned in and drew a quick stick figure against the green sky. 'Let them float if that's what they want to do. This one's called *The Pig Hunter.*' He gave the stick figure a gun, or maybe it was a spear. He began putting in a blazing sun. 'Is the pig a symbol of anything?'

'Swine,' she said. 'Filth and gluttony.'

'That'll do.' He bent down and worked in his black pig, stepping back to see how it was looking, then stepping in close again and adding a dab. 'Swine,' he said. 'I like that. The swine of Sofia Station. Do you think Bill and Marg would mind if we called it that?'

•

The clanging of the ploughshare called them to lunch. Barnaby and Bill were sitting at the table in the kitchen while Margery dished up plates of steaming corned beef with boiled potatoes and carrots. Bill ladled several spoons of hot English mustard onto his corned beef. There had been a suspicious death after the dance the previous night and Harry had had to stay in town to investigate it. After lunch Barnaby came down to the machinery shed to see what they were doing. He stood looking at the painted squares of board.

Pat said, 'They're not finished. This is just the start.'

Barnaby turned to Autumn. 'Your little Irishman's revved up. There's going to be no stopping him now.' They stood watching Pat putting in detail, a horseman in the sky on a red horse, an upside-down cow, dismembered limbs and other odd bits and pieces that took his fancy. A teapot with flowers on it floating by. Trees liberated from the embrace of the earth, levitating in the undulations of the air. He was enjoying himself. 'None of this has to stay in,' he said. 'I can paint it all out if I want to then put it all back in again the next day.'

Barnaby said, 'I think we're going to remember what happened in the machinery shed at Sofia Station today for some time.'

'D'you think your dad would mind if I put your mum here? The green and red lady in the flowered dress with the yellow straw hat?' He was already drawing her in with his brush.

During the rest of the week the majestic ironbarks became black and green shimmers in his pictures, vaporising in the waves of heat. Forty paintings all the same and each different from the next. A suite, Barnaby called them. Like aspects of a man (Pat himself, no doubt) at different times of his life, in different moods, with different longings and appetites. One thing and many. Busy with movement over here, still as a corpse over there. And the picture Pat most favoured was the one with the grinning corpse withered in the grass, yellow daisies growing through its shirt pockets. 'That's me,' he said. 'My first self-portrait.'

Autumn wondered if it might be a portrait of his grief for the loss of his Edith.

No narrative emerged. There was no linear story connecting one picture with the next. The bloated green carcass of a pig attracted him and he kept going back to it for days, the detail of its worm-eaten innards fascinating him. 'I see this pig when I'm nearly asleep. I'm never going to be done with some of these pictures.'

Pat was in awe of the energy the series had released in him and feared the day his energy for them would wane and desert him. He did not wish to be done with the painting. He believed in himself with an excited fear that maybe it was all wrong after all and he would wake up and realise he had done nothing.

'So what do you think?' He must have asked for their reassurance a hundred times. He slept the night with Autumn and woke early each morning and went straight across to the machinery shed to reassure himself that his pictures were still alive for him, still needing his attention in their growing towards a maturity he had not foreseen, eager to see that maturity come into being, surprised by what he did, by what he saw, as if they were strange plants and were to present him with unknown fruits and blossoms. 'This is my country,' he said to Barnaby. 'God, I feel it right here!' And he poked his chest hard with his finger.

Barnaby put an arm around his shoulder. 'You're doing it, old mate.'

'You guys believed in me. I wouldn't be doing it without you two. I'm too scared to think about it. I hate to think what I might see if I did think about it.'

On the day before they were due to go home Autumn and Pat and Barnaby stood in the machinery shed looking at the collection before packing it up. Pat said, 'So what are we going to call it?'

Autumn said, 'Well, we've been calling it *The Citadel Range*.' He said nothing and she saw he was not content with such a title. 'You don't like it?'

'*Hinterland*,' he said with certainty. 'That's what this is. Guy Cowper and his mates can make something of that. They'll see it as a metaphor for all kinds of shit. My interior life as a swine for sure.' He laughed. 'What do you reckon?'

And so the machinery-shed collection became *Hinterland*. Without the article. The last painting contained the only hint of narrative or sequence. A final addition of the brush, that was perhaps at first no more than an accident, and a corner of the homestead found its way onto the far right-hand edge of the picture. A narrow vertical of white-painted weatherboard topped by a triangle of green tin roof. A face at the only window. A woman looking out towards the citadel range. Pat turned to Autumn. 'That's you,' he said. 'You're in here too. You and me both. Your eyes will always be in these pictures. They wouldn't have come into being without you.'

Barnaby found some hairy pink twine and they tied the paintings in four bundles of ten. When Barnaby had gone back to the house Pat and Autumn went down to the creek and swam naked in the cool clear water, ducking under to meet and embrace. That night they made love for the last time on her narrow iron bed in the so-called cottage (just a few feet away from the green frogs, which she was never to forget, the frogs and the supplicating arms of the drowning woman and the old boar under the lime trees).

•

And that (except for the details of saying goodbye to Bill and Peter and Margery and getting the shiny red aeroplane back to the coast and travelling for all of two days from Rockhampton by train to Melbourne) was more or less the end of their visit to Sofia Station in the Central Highlands of Queensland. Another country, that Autumn would come to think of as a country entirely foreign to her mind and way of thinking. Pat revisited Sofia and the country around the ranges whenever he returned to Australia from England during his long and fruitful career, but Autumn never did go back there. Pat found there his source and drew on it confidently for the material of his art until his last days, painting his strange pictures of those uncelebrated landscapes, those silent people, their broken dreams and unspoken hopes, the passions that flew around their heads like imprisoned ghosts. But always really painting himself, if you knew him. Snow or shine you could have found him there in his converted barn at the back of his fine old flint and greystone house in the West Midlands, painting the Expedition Range. He had his own copy of the first edition of Leichhardt's *Journal*. Purchased from Quaritch in Golden Square for a goodly sum of English pounds.

Autumn returned to the creek and the supplicating arms of the drowning woman and to the narrow iron bed many times in her dreams, in her thwarted passion, and in her helpless nightmares. And in the persistence of memory. The citadel range haunted Autumn throughout her long life. Right to the end. Green frogs and all, the musty smell of the striped ticking mattress, the pallid gecko on the ceiling with the black eyes (like an angel in disguise, knowing everything before it had come to pass), looking down on them making love for their last time together. And the eyes of the black boar that had seen into her soul.

If there has to be a last time for everything (and how can there not be?), it is just as well we do not know it when it comes to us.

•

It was dark and raining steadily when Barnaby turned into the driveway at Old Farm and reefed on the handbrake. The brake made a loud ratcheting sound. The sharp noise and the lurching stop woke Autumn. She had been sleeping against Pat's shoulder on the back seat, his left arm around her, his right hand resting in her lap, his fingers lightly gripping her upper thigh through the thin fabric of her cotton dress. He had not been asleep. They sat up and disentangled themselves. He kissed her warm cheek gently and said, 'We're here.' (Which, of course, is where we always are.)

The porch light went on and Arthur came to the door and looked out at them, shading his eyes with his raised hand. Was he not the intrepid explorer Leichhardt himself, gazing into new country? And, no doubt, just as the real Leichhardt before him, wondering what to expect?

They all climbed out of the car and Arthur came across the gravel to meet them. They greeted each other, handshakes for Barnaby and Pat and a kiss on the cheek for Autumn. The rain was fairly coming down. Pat and Autumn stood close beside each other at the open boot, shoulders hunched against the cold rain, sheltering under Barnaby's umbrella, and watched Barnaby lift out Autumn's bag. Arthur said, 'I'll take that,' and Barnaby relinquished it to him. Arthur hurried across to the porch with the bag. Barnaby left Autumn and Pat standing on their own by the boot, the pictures stacked at the sides and on the bottom. Pat closed the boot on them.

Barnaby got into the driver's seat and lit a cigarette and started the engine.

He had left a small space of privacy to Autumn and Pat. It was a very small space as it turned out. Arthur deposited Autumn's bag on the porch and returned at once to where they stood. Pat had time only to kiss her cheek and murmur, 'Fare well, my dearest woman.'

Arthur came up and took Autumn's hand and Pat turned and walked around to the passenger side, leaving Barnaby's umbrella with the two of them, and he got into the car and closed the door. Barnaby leaned from his window and called to them, 'I'll come up and see you soon.' And with that he waved and drove around the rose bed and out the gate. Pat did not look round or wave or look back when the car turned at the gate.

The shock of Pat's sudden unexpected departure was so great Autumn did not properly begin to register it until the sound of the car was fading down the hill. Until he closed the boot on the paintings she had been expecting him to come into the

411

house and go to his old room and for everything to pick up and continue, plans for the showing of *Hinterland* racing in her head alongside her passion for this man.

Standing on the gravel with Arthur's jacket over her and listening to the fading of the car's engine, Autumn began to see what Pat had done. And to see that he had planned to do it.

•

Two weeks later she received a letter from him. There was no salutation. Barnaby had told her Pat was living with Anne Collins in Anne's flat in East Melbourne. Anne was arranging a one-man show of *Hinterland* at a gallery in Malvern.

You and I can't build our happiness on Arthur's misery. Your husband's grief can never be a foundation for our joy. That is not possible and you know it is not possible. With you and Arthur holding together there is no place at Old Farm for me to be myself. Barnaby told me you were thinking of killing yourself. I don't believe you will go through with something like that, you are far too fond of life and of yourself. But please don't go about talking as if you mean to do it, it upsets everyone and they are all beginning to hate me. I don't want to be the destroyer of another life. I don't mean yours. I mean Arthur's. By the way, you can keep those drawings I left with you.

The note was not signed. She burned it and went back to bed and cried for a long time and cursed him bitterly. Arthur took care of her until she was more settled and regained some of

her former sense of life's possibilities. Freddy came to see her
and sat on the side of her bed and held her hand and said very
little but listened with his old trust and depth of sympathy.
He was not looking well himself and she apologised to him
for being so selfish. He laughed and said he was fine. She said,
'I don't know how I would have got through this without you.'
But it was Arthur, not Freddy, who had made available to her
the safe ground she had needed. She told Freddy the story of
Barnaby taking them up to the escarpment and showing them
the intricate labyrinth of laneways between the rocks. 'We
came around a corner and there were red hand prints under
an overhang and a piece of ochre sitting in a cleft. Barnaby
said, It's been sitting there since the old blackfellow left it there.
And he reached for it. Pat grabbed his hand and said, Leave it,
Barney! If you touch it now it will only have been lying there
since you put your hand on it.' And she looked up at Freddy
and the tears rolled down her cheeks. Whenever she spoke
of Pat she was overwhelmed with the feeling of having been
abandoned and humiliated by him. She thought there could
never again be anything good in her life. 'I don't know why I
told you that,' she said, sniffing and blowing her nose on her
hankie. 'None of it makes any difference now.'

Freddy was silent a while, holding her hand in his. Then
he said, 'Let's face it, Aught. We hardly knew him.'

•

There was something missing in all this. Something flat and
not alive in her response to it. Long after she was up and about
and back in the garden spreading piles of last year's mulch

with Stony, she was still bothered by the troubling conviction that she had missed something important. She had been in shock. But that was no excuse. She was not in shock now. She stopped digging, the fork held upright in the earth, and stared off towards the wattle flat and the river. She left the fork standing in the ground and walked up to the house and dropped her gloves on the steps.

She had not written in her journal since their return. She took up the book and sat at the kitchen table and read over her Sofia entries and she saw at once what it was that had been nagging at her. It was obvious. She wrote:

I learned that for the people who live there the outback is elsewhere. Further out, that is where they say the outback is. But it is this very outback sense that weighs on them with its encompassing silence and renders them mute. When I brought up the subject while Margery and I were having a cup of tea she said, 'Oh, this is nothing, Autumn. Here is not the outback.' That is what they say. And say very little else. They deny the reality of their lives, and it is this denial that silences them. 'You should go right out,' they say. 'Then you would see the real outback.' I asked her, 'And have you been yourself?' She laughed. 'No! No, Bill and I have not been.' They know they are speaking of a place that has no location. No reality of its own. Their governing illusion is that they themselves are not the inhabitants of the outback they speak of. To go in search of the true outback would shatter this illusion and leave them defenceless before the truth. The truth that they are without imagination for their own country, silenced by their denial. They have divorced themselves from it with this lie of the land. So they speak of the outback as of something sacred, but they may not go in search of it. They know that if they were to go, their goal would be elsewhere. The outback is a mirage of itself and moves away from us as we approach it. Pat painted the truth of this in his floating animals and people, in the trees that had lost touch with the ground and melted in the haze of heat, and in the death and the daisies, the fragments of dismembered things that established no connections with the country.

I was mistaken to write that the outback is the Australian land of myths and heroes. It is this that is the governing illusion by which we deceive ourselves. The lie by which we live. I wrote it when I first arrived at Sofia and knew no better. And there is no escape for *us*, no exemption by writing of them and of us—*their* illusion, *our* enlightened state. For in truth the outback is not a place but is the Australian imagination itself. It is always elsewhere. A steady thunder of silence is imposed on the inhabitants of this island by the impossible weight of isolation in space and history. The truth is not admissible, so we deny it. Pat saw the truth, grasped it intuitively, and painted it during those few extraordinary days in the machinery shed at Sofia Station.

She screwed the cap back on her pen and blotted the page of her notebook and closed it. She got up from the table and retrieved her gloves from the back steps and went down into the garden and resumed spreading the compost from last year's bins. While she worked she knew the satisfaction of having understood something. She would talk to Barnaby and Freddy about it. Arthur would hum and agree with her and change the subject and ask what was for his dinner.

Stony staggered towards her across the dug ground pushing another barrow loaded high with the black and reeking compost. He tipped it at her feet and she dug into it with her fork, exposing dozens of tiny pink worms. Next week she and Stony would plant out the seedlings in neat rows.

18

28 December 1991

SENSING MY END, THE SCAVENGERS ARE GATHERING. ONE OF THEM threatened to do something to me she called a Lomi Lomi full-body massage. When she pulled back the bedclothes and would have lifted my nightie I shrieked at her, 'Get your hands off me, you bitch, or I'll have you charged with assault.' She was young and fled from me in tears. I was thrilled with this little surge of power. Andrew accused me of being cruel and told me he had apologised to the girl on my behalf. He brought the aged-care specialist and a nurse with him. The three of them have ganged up on me, watched over by a sad-eyed Adeli, who serves them tea and cake at my kitchen table, while they admire through the open door the spreading arches of Arthur's Algerian oak, as if my garden is no longer mine but is just there. I have served my purpose (whatever they think that might have been) and they are eager for me to be out of the way.

The aged-care specialist told me I needed to be in an aged-care facility.

'A correctional facility, you mean,' I said. 'Why don't you people ever say what you mean?'

Death is what she means. They are careful not to use the word, but it is they who are afraid of death, not I. Well, I'm not quite done yet. 'I'll go when I'm ready,' I told the aged-care facilitator. (Facilitator! I almost gagged.) 'Get out of here and leave me to the privacy of my pain. You'll get yours soon enough.'

She smiled. They have been trained to smile. To counterfeit kindliness and to bear with the irritation and helplessness of the aged without impatience. They give credence to nothing I say. They are conditioned to be unmoved by my pleas and dismiss them as the deluded ramblings of an old woman in her last days. I am to be pitied, to be sure, but *la pietà* is not a professional position, so they conceal compassion—if they ever feel it. With them nothing in our relations is permitted to be real. Andrew, however, is vulnerable to my reality. I have long had the measure of him and know his family and the private conditions of his life.

'This is my home,' I said to the aged-care bitch. (Unlike the Lomi Lomi girl, this one is large and matured in oak and is not to be trifled with.) 'I told you to get out. So would you please go?' No, she would not go. She bared her perfect teeth and stayed and measured me and weighed me and humiliated me with her instructions to lift this arm and flex that leg. I can't defend myself against her. How can I resist her? She is far stronger than me. She enters my privacy as if I deserve none and leaves the door wide open for the others to follow. I am a public thing. The respect of intimacy means nothing to them.

When she leaned over me I thought of biting her elbow, but was afraid I might crack a tooth on her pointy bones.

When she had gone Andrew reasoned with me, 'You know, Autumn, there are many residents [inmates] in the aged-care facility who are a lot worse off than you are.' It was the same old story from childhood: Think of the starving millions and eat your greens. It never made greens (cabbage?) taste better to be told there were people who did not have to eat it.

While he was cutting the plaster off my arm he gave me one of his pep talks. 'Living there could give your life a new sense of purpose,' he said brightly, as if he might take his family and go and live there himself. 'You would have a community.'

'I already have a sense of purpose, Andrew, thank you. You're pinching me! And I don't want a community. I've had one of those.'

'Many of these people suffer from advanced macular degeneration and are no longer able to read. You could read to them.'

'They have talking books for that,' I told him. 'Are you going to cut that thing off my arm or not?'

They torment me in the name of their new invention, professional ethics. Once upon a time it was enough for us to behave decently to each other if we could manage it. Now they are trained by experts in ethical behaviours.

'Adeli can't look after you on her own any longer. It's too much to expect her to do her work and look after you at the same time.'

'Did *she* tell you that?'

'You've become a full-time job, Autumn. We have to face the facts.'

'Face your own facts, Andrew. Your wife's having an affair with the postman. What are you going to do about that?'

He threatened to take my writing materials away from me. Am I to be interred in the great Australian gulag of aged care to wait for my end? I have my four little pills and will take my life in my own time and depart when I am ready. These people are bullies and tyrants acting in the name of professionalism and their precious new ethics. I can scream at them but who will defend me against their cruelties? Where are Freddy and Barnaby? Where is my dear Uncle Mathew? My friends. My champions. My men. And poor Arthur, where is he? They have all gone on ahead of me. That other one has gone too. He would not defend me. Would he even defend his own child if it distracted him from his work? His mother? Perhaps he would have defended his mother. Barnaby used to say, 'The poets are my consolation,' and would recite a long passage to me from the *Inferno* in the original medieval Italian and grin and say, 'It can't be translated.' I hear him now walking up and down the back veranda, swinging his shillelagh and declaiming in the language of true poetry, *Al tornar della mente, che si chiuse dinanzi alla pietà de' due cognati* . . . But at the end even the poets could not console him. I have begun to understand his state of mind during his last days. My dear friend Barnaby, the closer I get to my own great day, the more fondly I recall you. Friendship is my consolation.

•

After we first returned from Sofia Station I drank a great deal of wine and walked the paddock all night barefoot in my nightdress and howled Pat's name by the wattle flat in the moonlight (if there was a moon). None of it helped. He was gone. I suffered the emptiness of my despair. And when I had exhausted myself I fell ill and took to my bed. Arthur took time off work and nursed me like a mother nursing its sick child. I lay in bed all day weeping. I am ashamed to confess how low my spirits sank before I began to revive. I believe I was unspeakably cruel to Arthur—so I will not speak of it.

Anne Collins had declined Arthur's offer to curate our exhibition of the new Melbourne modernists and had begun curating for a rival gallery recently established in High Street, Malvern, and for Gallery 5 in Sydney (owned by Ginni Lamont, the flamboyant daughter of millionaire collector and racing identity Jack Lamont). Anne was known for knowing all the right people. We heard news of them from Barnaby. When her exhibition of *Hinterland* was announced Arthur and I saw the advertisement in the paper one Saturday morning. It was the illustration that caught my eye. The shock of it. The grinning corpse in the long grass in the shadow of the citadel range, daisies growing out of its shirt. It was like seeing my own flesh displayed on the page. I had to turn away.

Arthur and I did not receive an invitation to the opening. I felt physically ill for weeks dwelling on this non-invitation and decided I could never again look at those pictures that he and I had made together in our brief magical time in the machinery shed at Sofia Station.

Guy Cowper disdained either to visit or to review *Hinterland* in his column in the *Herald*. Cowper's silence was the biggest Melbourne critical reaction Pat received. And the most damning. There were others. But their murmurs of incomprehension scarcely rose above the din of Cowper's silence. I knew Pat had been hoping for puzzlement and ridicule from Cowper and that silence from his old enemy would be a great disappointment to him. I felt for Pat and longed for him to know success and to receive understanding for his work. No matter how vindictive my mood I never sank so low as to wish failure on Pat. Ever. There were times I cursed him and might have killed him if I'd had a knife in my hand. But I never hoped to see him fail.

When the exhibition had been on for nearly two weeks and it was no longer news, Rodney Armitage's review came out in the *Sydney Morning Herald* and was reprinted in the *Argus* and suddenly people were talking about *Hinterland* again. Armitage was a friend of Anne's. It had not been easy for her to convince Armitage it was worth his while coming down to Melbourne to review a show by an unknown young artist. But she had persisted and had eventually convinced him Pat was important enough for him to notice. There was more to it than this, for Armitage was Cowper's arch-rival. They despised each other and were inclined to despise whatever was going on in each other's cities. Anne argued that Cowper's silence on Pat's show was a once-in-a-lifetime opportunity for Armitage to seriously bloody Cowper's nose and reveal him to be the self-serving provincial neophyte (Armitage's words, not mine) of English artistic taste that Armitage was always claiming he was. 'Let them all know that Cowper has missed the most important art event in Melbourne during the entire period of his tenure.' Anne was good at this sort of thing. Setting dog against dog in the pit. She enjoyed the feel of it. I think in her heart she probably disliked all men in pretty equal measure but found them far too useful ever to let herself seem to be in open conflict with them. There were times, I recall, when a certain look came into her eyes at Old Farm. Impossible to describe. But bearing a lethal message. Unmasked in a moment of distraction. And if she caught you looking, her features broke into a perfect smile that managed to convince you of her perfect trust. 'I am sharing something with you, my dear,' her smile seemed to say, 'that I would share with no one else.' She possessed exactly the right character (is it?) for negotiating the labyrinth of conflicting power plays and bitchery between departments that ruled the Tate when she finally got there. She slid into that world with scarcely a ripple, an eel slipping into a muddy creek. A little flick of her tail and she had propelled herself into the centre of the action. Anne Collins was to become one of that select tribe of Australians who found themselves to be more at home in London than many Londoners ever were. I never did understand why men tried so hard to please her. It was her abiding mystery. She and Cowper and Armitage are all long gone and forgotten now, of course.

After a brief period during the seventies when interest in Pat's work slackened off and it looked as if his reputation was waning, Pat's pictures are now more widely celebrated than ever. The man is no longer with us (he hardly ever was during his lifetime anyway) but his pictures are as important to us in Australia today as they ever were. Some would say they have become more important with the passage of time. And for many their value as art is just as controversial. Such things will never be finally settled. There will always be someone coming along to build their reputation on the new things they can think of to say about old art. Whether what he did was great art or not, the fact is that Pat Donlon has become one of our immortals. And we have very few of those.

In his *Sydney Morning Herald* review of *Hinterland*, Armitage described Pat's Sofia collection as having 'a knowing simplicity that is at once new and interesting, but is perplexing to the conventionally trained eye'. (For 'conventionally trained' we all knew we must read 'Melbourne Gallery School–trained'). He compared Pat to the Douanier Rousseau. Which was stupid of him and only drew attention to his own European bias, but it did Pat no harm at all. 'There is a lack of refinement and a kind of open-faced candour in his pictures that offends commonplace expectations.' He heralded (the pun hopefully not lost on Cowper) Pat Donlon as the new in Australian art. Anne had skilfully briefed him on Pat's own views about what he (Pat) was doing. It would not have been Pat who had done the briefing. He never had much to say about his own work or anyone else's. Which happily left the way open for Anne. Talking about art was pretty much all she ever did, and she did it to great effect. Armitage employed such hackneyed phrases in his review as 'the breaking wave' and 'Australian art comes of age'. But no one demurred. 'These works are modern,' Armitage sidled along, 'but in a way seem also to be anti-modern. Most viewers will be puzzled. A few will be dazzled, as I was. Many will be repelled. And of course there will be those few benighted souls who will remain indifferent and will have nothing to say.' (Such as Guy Cowper, we all knew we were being told.)

Armitage credited Anne Collins with having 'discovered' the most important new voice (voice?) in Australian art for more than two decades. Why two decades? No one asked. The deed was done. Pat's work had become controversial. Anne had used the oldest trick in the book and it had worked. She had aroused that most provincial of all Australian antagonisms, the rivalry for first place in art and culture between Sydney and Melbourne. Sydney won this round. And red-haired Ginni Lamont invited *Hinterland* to her Sydney gallery for a four-week show in May, the best month in those days for showing in Sydney. Anne had won. But for her, Sydney was only the beginning. She was planning on taking Pat to the world, not just up the Hume Highway to Sydney. I could not have said it then, but Anne Collins was the perfect partner for Pat Donlon. I could not have done for him what Anne did for him. And he could not have done what he did without her as his champion. All art needs its champions. Without champions, art remains in the racks of the artists' studios and is unknown to us and uncelebrated in the world. And what is the point of that? The task of rehabilitating the artist whose work is not celebrated in his or her own time is never entirely successful. It is always a Lazarus affair; the pale show of life may be miraculous but is more a reminder of the death of the subject than of their current vitality.

Melbourne had had its chance with Pat and had blown it. It was not to Melbourne but to Sydney, where his work was amply celebrated, and to the Central Highlands of Queensland, where his source never failed him, that Pat returned whenever he revisited Australia. He was more at home among artists and writers in Sydney than he ever was in Melbourne, where a certain mean-spirited reluctance to acknowledge his importance can still be found among artists and their keepers to this day.

There are some events, not in themselves vastly interesting or bloated with portent, the effects of which however are never quite undone in our lives or in the cultural directions our country takes. Cowper's silence on Pat's show was one of those small events. Without Cowper's silent disdain for Pat and his art it is unlikely Armitage would have reviewed *Hinterland*, and without Armitage's review the show would almost certainly not have gone to Sydney, and without the success it was to enjoy in Sydney Anne would not have been able to convince Rodney Falk (another man keen to please her) to take the show for the spring opening of his Camden Town gallery, and if that had not happened the prestigious art journal *Apollo* would not have put one of Pat's paintings (the one with the floating teapot, his mother's) on its cover and published that long and richly illustrated piece about Pat's life and work, which drained the blood from Cowper's cheeks when he received his copy (he had to sit down) and caused such a stir here (well, a stir in the small circle of what we liked to call the art *world*, but which we might more justly have called the art island. For it caused no stir at all among workers at the port of Melbourne, nor among Collins Street financiers and the great legal minds in their chambers).

There was no mention of me or of Old Farm in the *Apollo* account of what the author of the article referred to as 'Patrick Donlon's seminal ten days at Sofia Station'. The only women mentioned in that article were Anne Collins (seven times) and his mother (once). His wife Edith and I were dropped from his history. A deep and, I am afraid to say, ineradicable scar was branded into my soul by this wounding of the truth. I shall carry that scar to the furnace with me (tomorrow or the next day).

So on we go. For we must go on in our search for truth and justice; collecting a bit of this and a bit of that, each morsel connected in some way to the invisible circuit from which the expression of our sense of ourselves and our culture is slowly (and painfully) fitted together. It is the lives of all of us, experience both as fire and dust. But is it history?

•

One morning, not long after my partial recovery, Arthur had left for the office and I was sitting at the kitchen table (not propped up in bed as I am now, writing this in my nineteenth exercise book) feeling guilty because I should have been in the garden helping Stony with the pruning. But I was helplessly in the grip of lassitude and boredom, and was too deeply detached from any sense of purpose to get up from the table and go out into the garden. Pruning roses was impossible. It could not be done. I thought of opening a bottle of wine. But an image of Freddy's sadly bloated features came into my head and I resisted. Poor dear Freddy, he was showing the signs of his alcoholism by then. Suddenly (and it was very sudden), without considering what I was doing or debating my intention, I got up from the table and went to the bathroom and had a shower and changed into my smartest suit and caught the train into town. I was on my way before I'd had time to think about it.

I sat by the window watching the suburbs sliding by and listening to the lively clatter of the wheels on the rails, knowing I looked good in my grey suit and aware of being looked at admiringly by both men in my carriage and by one of the women. I had been careful with my makeup. Pat disliked makeup that was obvious. To impress him, makeup had to be applied so delicately he would not know it was there but would mistake its effects for nature's gifts. I could see him squinting at me, the smoke from his cigarette curling from his lips, his heart contracting as mine with that pain which I knew neither of us would be able to resist if we were ever so close to each other again. I was so deeply lost in thoughts of meeting him that I continued to sit in my seat in the train after we had reached Flinders Street station and the carriage had emptied.

It wasn't a hot day so I decided to walk to Swanston Street. It was a nice change to be one of the city crowd. The young women all looked smart and busy and I was glad I had dressed up. I hardly ever came into the city these days, and almost never alone. It was Arthur who was our daily ambassador to the city. I walked along Bourke Street, perhaps in order to avoid passing his office. At Swanston Street I waited at the stop for the tram.

Standing there, calm and without anxiety, I remembered the great black boar watching me from the dark shade under the wild lime trees, and I felt a strange kindred link between us. That woman on the bank of the creek staring back at the pig was not this woman in the smart grey suit waiting for her tram, but was a woman in the imaginary life of this woman, with no future, no past and no substance, only her existence as a vivid memory, she and the pig mysterious elements of an unfinished story. I wondered if Bill had had his way yet and had shot the pig, or had Margery been successful once again in getting a stay of execution for the doomed animal?

The tram came and a man who had been waiting next to me stepped back and touched his hat, holding up the throng so that I could get on the tram first. I thanked him and as

I went up the step I half turned to him and smiled. I have never begrudged any man a smile. It was all he was after. An acknowledgment from a nice-looking woman ten years his junior. I went into the non-smoking section and found a seat facing the direction of travel, my bag on my knees. I think at that moment I was probably happy.

When I pushed open the glass door of Visions in High Street half an hour later, however, my heart was pounding and I was feeling sick with tension at the thought that I might be about to see Pat. For some reason I thought he would be there, and had imagined him watching the reactions of the people who came to look at his pictures, like a proud mother unable to take her gaze from her first child on its first day at school. But the gallery was empty. It was a long wide space, the floor of polished timber, the lighting very bright. There was no furniture, no chairs or anything else occupying the centre. Not even a rug. In an alcove at the far end a vacant upright chair stood squarely behind a polished timber desk with a glass top. A closed door, white with a shiny brass knob, was behind the desk. There was no sign of an attendant or the gallery's owner. There was nothing to distract the visitor's eye from the pictures on the walls. The message was emphatic: *We are clean and new and are not to be distracted by ornament and the trinkets of the past.* It was a space designed to harbour no shadows. No uncertainty. I found it cold and intimidating.

The forty paintings of the series, unvarnished and all on two-foot squares of masonite board, were hung on a level with the viewer's eye, twenty down the length of one wall, twenty down the length of the other. They were unframed. We were still used to seeing paintings in gilt corner frames in those days so the impression was stark. Something uniform, austere, aware of its own importance. A whole thing, not a selection or a variety of things. A large statement. It was consistency and conviction that met my eye. I had never seen works presented in this way before and realised at once the effect was due to Anne Collins' sense of design. A sign on an easel to the right of the door said, *Hinterland, Pat Donlon. Exhibition only*. The paintings were not for sale. The feeling was that whoever had done this had done it with confidence. Not in the detail of each painting—I was not registering detail—but in the bold uniformity of the series and its setting. I felt at once that I was being presented with a work of substance and that a degree of attention, and even concentration, was being demanded of me. And although there was no one in the gallery I also felt that I was being observed.

I stepped up to the picture closest to me on the left wall, just inside the entrance, and I stood in front of it and stared at it. I wasn't seeing it. My mind was searching for him like a radar searching for its target. The details of the picture slipped about in front of me, blurred and indistinct. I have no recollection of which of the pictures it was and I moved on to the next without having registered it. Even though there was no one there to see me, I pretended to be seriously examining each picture, stopping a moment, then stepping back a pace to make a more sure appraisal, then moving on to the next. I could see printed catalogues piled on the desk at the far end; the green sky and the dark bulk of the citadel range were unmistakable. I could not stop myself from shivering.

I was looking at the third or fourth painting before I began to see detail. It was clear to me at once that he had done more work on the pictures since Sofia. There was now a sense of narrative loosely uniting the pictures and giving them an order of progression, the order, indeed, in which they had been hung, progressing down the left wall front to back and then back to front along the right wall. The loose sense of order and narrative was given by the progressive inclusion of the white and green homestead. In the earliest picture it did not appear at all. In the second and subsequent pictures increasingly large sections of the homestead were visible at the lower right-hand side of each painting. By the last picture the homestead covered almost two-thirds of the painted space. The face of the woman at the window was repeated in each of them. Besides the addition of the homestead there were numerous other details that had been added since Sofia. Now there was what looked like a wild pig hunt in three of the pictures, body parts flying about in the air, a severed leg here, a severed head there, teeth flashing in the sunlight, a pair of yellow underpants with blue patches sewn on caught on the branch of a dead tree. Pat's little jokes to give his detractors something to work with. I imagined Pat working on the series, encouraged by Anne at his side in the spare room of her flat. I had never been to her flat but I could see them there together (as I can see almost anything I set my heart on seeing; I have an imagination). He without his shirt and she attending him closely. I was there in each picture, gazing out from that awful silent homestead in the wilderness. I was there but I had been disowned. Abandoned in that house. Looking at the pictures made me feel ill. I wanted to sit down and close my eyes.

I became aware of someone coming into the gallery from the back door. I half saw them sit down at the desk then get up again and start over towards me. I knew it was a woman by the tapping of her heels on the boards. She came up and stood alongside me and said, 'Hello, Autumn.'

I turned to her. 'Hello, Anne.' She seemed to be at ease with me. I hated her. I had learned hate. It is horrible. It burns you. It is hell fire. Ask Dante.

She was looking very smart and youthful, her slim figure tucked neatly into a black dress. Her black hair, cut fashionably short and curled half across one eye, was rather fetching. On her left breast she had pinned a single red bud of Mr Lincoln, the rose that was my first planting in the rose bed in the centre of our drive at Old Farm. The perfume of this rose is exquisite. It is classically the smell of a rose. If you go blind you will know its presence. I could smell it as I stood beside her. I was trembling and wondered if I was going to be able to keep my legs under me. She must have seen the state I was in. She put her hand to my arm. 'Come and sit down for a minute,' she said. 'I'll get you a cup of tea.' When I would have resisted she was firm and made me go with her. I understood that she was being kind and the thought of her kindness made me want to weep with despair.

She sat me on the straight-backed chair by the desk and went out through the back door. I don't know what made me do it, perhaps it was a panicky need to distract myself from his pictures, but I slid open the desk drawer to my left. There were probably other things in the drawer but all I saw was the hairy ball of pink twine. It was the twine we had found in the workshop at Sofia Station and had used to tie Pat's paintings in bundles. My heart missed a beat. I grabbed the ball of twine and shoved it into my bag and closed the drawer just as the door opened behind me. My heart was beating fast and I felt my face flushing, as if I had stolen a precious jewel.

Anne leaned both hands on the glass desktop and looked into my face. 'The kettle's on. It won't be a minute.'

I held her gaze, unable to disengage my eyes from hers.

She said softly, 'So what did you take from the drawer, Autumn?' She said it as if she was interested and not as if she was accusing me of stealing something.

'Nothing,' I said defensively. 'What do you mean?'

She smiled and straightened. 'Well, it doesn't matter.'

We were both silent, she standing looking down the gallery towards the front door as if she was expecting someone. I could hear the kettle whistling in the back room.

She turned to me, amused by our situation, and she said, once again in an interested tone of voice, 'Was it that ball of pink twine you took?'

I looked up at her. I remembered my mother asking me if I had stolen her perfume and I put my head in my hands and burst into tears of shame and confusion.

Anne held me against her tummy and rocked me gently back and forth. 'Life is so terrible,' she said.

I could not speak.

Hatred is as powerful a juice to the human system as love and makes us behave just as badly. I no longer hate (irritation I still know, but not hate). I have forgotten how to hate. I stopped hating Anne that day when she tried to comfort me. I have not forgotten how to love. I was never to see her again. She wrote many years later, in the eighties when his work was beginning to fetch very high prices, asking me to return Pat's drawings of the naked daughter of the Ocean Grove butcher. I wrote back to say he had given the drawings to me. She did not insist and I heard no more.

I cried all the way home on the train from the gallery that day. There was a certainty in me now that I was never going to see him again. Arthur was there with the Ponty, parked at the station, watching for me at the exit. He had guessed and had been there for hours. I was in a dreadful state by that time. He drove me home without asking me where I'd been and I didn't tell him. I never wore that grey suit again. Arthur didn't say a word about any of it. He was a confirmed devotee of the least-said-soonest-mended school. A week later I burned the grey suit in the same incinerator in which I was to eventually burn my diaries. The incinerator was new then, grey cinder blocks still surrounding the iron drum. If Pat had walked into Visions while I was there and had asked me to go to bed with him I would not have been able to resist him. I would have gone with him, hating him and loving him. His 'Fare well, dearest woman' still haunts me. His small message as we stood by the boot of the Ponty has always confirmed in me the knowledge that he wished me well, as I have wished him well. But I did not fare well. But that is another story and there is no time left to me to tell it.

•

Adeli came in earlier this afternoon to take my tray. My lunch was still on it, untouched. She stood by the door looking at me, the tray held against her ample stomach.

I said irritably, 'What is it? I wasn't hungry. Give it to the chooks.'

She said, 'There's a visitor for you.'

'I don't want to see anybody,' I said. 'I don't know anybody any more.'

Adeli stepped to one aside and Edith came into my bedroom. Adeli went out and quietly closed the door.

I probably gaped at Edith open-mouthed, the way old people do gape (you will find out why soon enough). She was smartly dressed and still attractive in her early seventies. Few women manage that. I certainly didn't. I was a scrawn by then and nearly as devastated as I am today. 'It's you,' I said stupidly.

She was confident and calm and came over to my bed and took my hand in hers. She has soft hands. 'Hello, Autumn.' Her tone just a little condescending to the bedridden old lady. She smiled and leaned down and kissed my cheek. 'Just look at us.'

My voice shook when I said, 'Your picture's up there, Edith.' I pointed to her embroidered field of golden oxalis, where it hangs beside the French doors.

She continued to hold my hand as she turned to look. 'So that's where Arthur put it. I always wondered what he had done with it. I thought I was foolish to have given it to him.'

I said, 'It has always hung there. He treasured it.' It was only partly a lie. Arthur did always treasure her picture. He just had the good sense not to insist on retrieving it from the loft before its due time.

Edith went over and looked at her picture. 'I was sorry my friendship with Arthur never matured,' she said. 'I liked him a lot.'

I felt free to elaborate the half-lie. After all, at the lie's centre I knew there to be concealed a precious truth that I might now pass on to her. 'He often spoke of you. He was very fond of you.' The shock of seeing her gave her an unreal glow in my presence, and for a brief flash of uncertainty I wondered if I was hallucinating her, my old mind at last collapsing into a dreamscape around its rotten core.

She came back and sat on the edge of my bed, which creaked with her weight. 'Your friend found me,' she said. 'I visit my daughter and her family once a year. They live nearby. On the other side of the hill. Her husband works in the medical practice with Andrew Temple.' She looked at me a moment. 'I've always known you still lived here. I wondered if I might run into you on one of my visits. We live in England. We've lived there since the war.'

'You look happy,' I said. I could see she was a happy woman. And content. Fulfilled, I suppose the word is.

'I've been lucky,' she said. 'I met a wonderful man in London. We married and had three lovely boys.' She was smiling as she said this. 'I have three beautiful grandchildren.'

'Did you continue to paint?' I said. When she was young, Edith wore her dark hair in a fringe and had a ready smile. She still wore her tinted hair in a fringe and smiled in just the same easy way, as if nothing had ever seriously troubled her and to smile was effortless. She was aged of course, but strangely unchanged. It was this that had enabled me to recognise her the day I saw her, or thought I saw her, outside the chemist's shop. The day, wasn't it, if I remember, that I was inspired (if that is the word) to write this?

'No. Oh no,' she said, and laughed. 'I haven't painted for decades. A daughter, then three boys and my husband, and now three grandchildren, have filled my life. I painted scenes for the grandchildren when they were small. There was never any room for real painting.' She looked at me. 'You never had children?'

'One,' I said, and my throat closed tightly around the word and I was not able to say more.

I am aware that I am leaving nothing behind but this memoir. Or confession. Or whatever it is. My private search for my own truth, I suppose? Is it? Does it matter what I call it?

I said, 'You were very talented.'

'There were lots like me at the Gallery School in those days,' she said. 'Hardly any of them went on to become real artists. We were skilled, I think, but not driven like he was.'

We were both silent.

She said, 'Is it all right to speak of him?'

I laughed. 'At our age everything is forgiven. Isn't it?'

'Yes. Isn't it a wonderful freedom?' For an instant she looked young. 'I don't really think I've had all that much to forgive, you know.'

'Surely you had?'

'No more than others. Life has been very good to me.'

'Did you ever see him? In England, I mean?'

'No. But I followed his career. Albert and I always went to his exhibitions when we were in London.' She was silent a while. 'I never really liked his paintings.' She frowned and looked at me. 'Is that an awful thing to say?'

'A lot of people still don't like them.'

'They seem made up to me. They don't seem to be reporting on anything real. But I'm obviously wrong.'

We talked for an hour. She said she would come and see me again. I said I would look forward to seeing her. But after she had gone and I was lying here on my own again looking at her picture, I knew, in a very quiet and calm way, that it was over for me now that I had seen her. Coming in like that she had put the full stop at the end of what I have been doing, this writing that has been keeping me alive for a year. I had not expected to see her. Ever. She has been a character in my story and no longer a real person. Have they all been that? I wonder. Would I really wish to see Barnaby walk into my bedroom here now? The real Barnaby with his stick? Arthur? Would I want to see him? Pat himself? No. No. They no longer inhabit my reality but inhabit my private fiction, a fiction that to me represents the truth of things for myself only, and only for today. My truth is for no one else. How can our truth belong to others? Edith's visit from the real world settled whatever last bits and pieces in my story had remained floating about looking for a home—like those permanently disconnected body parts and teapots and other things in his pictures that never quite attached themselves to the country.

As I lay here listening to Adeli talking loudly on the phone in her Californian I knew it was time for me to die.

I shall call Adeli in and ask her to look in the little drawer to the left of the mirror on my dressing-table. There she will find a ball of hairy pink twine that has been there for fifty years. And I shall get her to bring me all my nineteen exercise books (including this one), and will make a bundle of them with the twine. Give this to Edith, I shall tell her. It is for her and for myself. And I will thank Adeli for all that she has done for me. It is a great deal. She has been kind and uncomplaining and not an aged-care specialist but always vulnerable to my bullying and intemperance. I will make a present to her of his Ocean Grove drawings. I will sign something to say that I have given them to her so that her ownership of them will not be challenged. She will probably cry and protest, but I will be firm. These drawings are yours to dance to, I shall say.

And when that is done, I shall ask her to leave me for the night and I will reach into the back of the drawer in my bedside table and take out the envelope with the four little yellow tablets in it that a very kind doctor (who I shall not name) gave me for just this purpose. I will swallow those little yellow tablets with a mouthful of water. And then I shall lie back against my pillows and look out the French doors at the moonlight through the branches of Arthur's Algerian oak and I shall quietly leave, this place, this earth, this life. Adeli and Sherry will find me in the morning. Fancy Edith's daughter being married to one of the doctors in Andrew's practice. There is nothing we can do or say that is an adequate response to such coincidences. They lie like dormant desert plants for decades until some slight shift of conditions releases their sudden bright jolt of colour into our lives. Why do my emotions threaten me with weeping now? It is not for myself I would weep. My year of grace is done. *Adieu. L'automne déjà.*

Autumn Laing, Old Farm, 28 December 1991

Editor's note

MY BIOGRAPHY, *AUTUMN: THE NEW ARTISTS' GROUP AND THE Circle of Autumn Laing*, was published by the University of California Press to wide critical acclaim in 1998. In 2003 the biography was at last published in Australia. When my American publishers began to build a list in Australia last year they asked me to edit Autumn's memoir for publication. Its release this year is the culmination of a long-cherished dream of mine. I am not sure if Autumn would have blessed me for it.

After the important article on Patrick Donlon and his work appeared in *Apollo*, the pictures that comprised *Hinterland* were sold to a private collector and disappeared from public view for more than forty years. In the early eighties the collection was given to the Australian National Gallery in Canberra with the condition that it be kept on permanent display there. The Sofia Station pictures of the *Hinterland* series are presently housed in the Canberra gallery in their own dedicated space and are considered to be one of the great iconic series in Australian art.

ALEX MILLER

The importance of Patrick Donlon's contribution to Australian art is still a matter of some dispute among Australian scholars of art history. His work, however, is rarely mentioned today outside Australia and is no longer considered controversial.

After Autumn's death I followed her instructions and presented the nineteen exercise books in which the text of this memoir was written to Edith Taling. Edith did not even untie the knot in the twine but handed the collection back to me at once. She said it was enough for her that Autumn had wanted her to have the books, but that she had no interest in reading them or in reliving that past which, she said, had little to do with her or with the life she had led since her divorce from Pat. Edith Taling insisted I take the collection of exercise books, believing that it would be an invaluable resource to me in the writing of my biography, as indeed it proved to be.

Dr Andrew Temple signed Autumn's death certificate. He recorded the cause of death as heart failure. In her brief obituary in the *Age*, it was said Autumn died of natural causes at the age of eighty-six. Her principal claim to notability was given as her brief relationship with the artist Patrick Donlon and the circle of Old Farm.

Autumn's need to turn me into a fictional character and to distort my identity to serve her own purposes amused rather than offended me. I understood her intention as an honourable one. I do in fact have a sense of humour and I am large and robust but I am not fat. Much of what Autumn wrote was fiction, but it was fiction written in an honest search for her own truth. It was Oscar Wilde who said, 'Man is least himself when he talks in his own person. Give him a mask, and he will tell you the truth.' Autumn's fiction was the mask she wore in order to locate her truth. Her last words—*Adieu. L'automne déjà*—are taken from the final section of Rimbaud's *Une saison en enfer*.

Autumn gives the impression in her memoir that she did not cooperate with me during my researches. The truth, however, is that we spent many long hours together going through the immense collection of Laing papers in the dining room at Old Farm. I could not have had a more cooperative subject than Autumn. The burning of her diaries and day books, which she recounts at the beginning of her memoir, is also a fiction. She did not wish to consult them in the writing of the memoir, so for the sake of the memoir they had ceased to exist. It was not her past views or her daily record of her life she wished to uncover but the present truth of her reality as an old woman. I had use of all those 'burned' diaries and journals. They are held in the National Library of Australia, where they may be consulted.

Autumn had no living relatives. Stony and I accompanied her to the crematorium and scattered her ashes in the wattle grove by the river one sunny afternoon two weeks after her cremation. Old Farm is now managed by a trust. Exhibitions and events are held there regularly. Entrance is free to the public and visits may be made during normal business hours from Wednesday through Sunday. A brass plaque set into the front wall to the left of the entrance commemorates Autumn and Arthur Laing's long residence there.

Professor F. Adeli Heartstone

Chair of Pacific Cultural Studies

Vassar College, Poughkeepsie

Acknowledgments

FIRSTLY I AM INDEBTED TO RON SHARP FOR HIS EXTRAORDINARY friendship and persuasive criticism. For their support and encouragement I would like to thank my Australian publisher Annette Barlow, my editor Ali Lavau, my publisher in the United Kingdom Clare Drysdale and my publicist Renee Senogles. I am also grateful to Wenona Byrne, Siobhán Cantrill and Sam Redman.

The conversation between Sir Malcolm and his secretary, which Pat imagines taking place while he is examining himself in Edith's hand mirror, is not all mine. I read the gist of it somewhere but can't remember where and have been unable to find the source of it again. I also can't recall whether the conversation was reported as having really taken place or whether the writer imagined it taking place. Whichever the case, real or imagined, I wish to express my debt to the author, whoever they are, and to hope they won't object to me reframing their words here.

Janine Burke's biography of Sunday Reed, *The Heart Garden: Sunday Reed and Heide* (Knopf, 2004), was useful to me in the writing of this novel. Autumn Laing is my own fictional creation, but if her imaginary life touches from time to time on real historical themes in the life of Sunday Reed and Sidney Nolan, then it is in part at least due to the inspiration of this fine work of biography. My intention when I set out to write this novel was to base the story loosely on an exploration of certain tides, with which I felt some sympathy, in the life of the artist Sidney Nolan. That aim was subverted early in the project by the intrusion in my ear of Autumn's forceful voice. Autumn had other ideas about the direction this book should take and insisted on claiming her place at the centre of the story. I gratefully submitted. The book is hers, hence its title. I am very glad she had her way with me. It was a joy to be with her.